D0408179

BECKY

BECKY

The Life and Loves of
Becky Thatcher

Lenore Hart

St. Martin's Press
New York

Gift – Flock Family 10/10

standalone

This is a work of fiction. All of the characters, organizations, and events portrayed in this novel are either products of the author's imagination or are used fictitiously.

Library of Congress Cataloging-in-Publication Data

Hart, Lenore.
   Becky : the life and loves of Becky Thatcher / Lenore Hart.—1st ed.
      p. cm.
   ISBN-13: 978-0-312-37327-6
   ISBN-10: 0-312-37327-9
   1. Thatcher, Becky (Fictitious character)—Fiction.   2. Sawyer, Tom (Fictitious character)—Fiction.   3. Hannibal (Mo.)—Fiction.   I. Title.

PS3608.A786B43 2008
813'.6—dc22   2007038862

First Edition: January 2008

10 9 8 7 6 5 4 3 2 1

In memory of my father,
Patrick Mather Hart.
A hundred years later,
Florida's answer to Tom Sawyer.

Acknowledgments

The author would like to thank all those who aided in my research, fact-checking, and adjective slashing: Christine Earle, my dedicated, perceptive agent at ICM; my equally astute editor, Hilary Rubin; senior editor George Witte; production editor Elizabeth Catalano; copy editor Eliani Torres; Alyse Diamond; and everyone else at St. Martin's Press. Also due thanks are Robert Arthur; Ina Birch; Pat and Kay Hart; Robert Kelly; Lin Poyer; Sandra Scoville; Tom and Jean Wescott; the staffs of the Eastern Shore Public Library and the Northampton Free Library; and the Virginia Center for the Creative Arts at Mt. San Angelo. As always, I'm grateful for the love and support of my husband and first reader, David Poyer, and my daughter, Naia, whose patience with late meals and forgotten laundry is now legendary. Any historical or literary inaccuracies herein are mine, and probably intentional. Samuel Clemens's characterization and words are, for the most part, his own.

Tom clasped her about her neck and pleaded:

"Now, Becky, it's all done—all over but the kiss. Don't you be afraid of that—it ain't anything at all. . . . And always after this, you know, you ain't ever to love anybody but me, and you ain't to marry anybody but me, never never and forever. Will you?"

—MARK TWAIN, *The Adventures of Tom Sawyer*

1910

SAN FRANCISCO

I SEE IN THE NEWSPAPER that he's dead now, gone with Halley's Comet. Mark Twain always said he'd leave when it returned—the same comet that streaked across the skies on the day of his birth.

I knew him first as little Sammy Clemens. The barefoot thumb-sucker who followed us around the back alleys and scrub woods of Hannibal wearing a hand-me-down shirt that fell to his knees. Eyes wide, always listening, because Sam worshipped the big boys. He longed to imitate the ones who swam out to the big timber rafts to catch a ride downstream. The ones who climbed out windows at midnight to swing a dead cat in the graveyard.

Sam soon outgrew that old shirt. He turned into a stately-looking man with a mane of white hair and a baggy linen suit to match. But to me he'll always be the redheaded child who never got a story straight; the one who always had to improve on the truth. That's how he became a celebrity, traveled everywhere, and made a fortune—from writing discombobulated fantasies about his old friends. Oh yes, he changed things around. But anyone who grew up in Hannibal before the War recognized us, despite the made-up names.

The papers say he appeared on stage in all the biggest cities in the country. I wish I'd gone to see him perform, so I could lean out of the balcony and shout, "Sammy Clemens, now ain't you ashamed?"

But it's too late for that. I'll be seventy-two this year. I've outlived my parents, two husbands, and one child. This yellow-and-green house on the crookedest street in San Francisco has been my home longer than Hannibal, Missouri, ever was. Lately, though, Sam's made-up characters and my own memories seem to blend into one another. Then I have to stop and sit awhile, to think back and get it all straight again.

You might ask, after so many decades, who cares what really happened back then? Maybe only me. I knew each and every one of the folks in those books. And though Sam's stories have the *ring* of truth, it's what he left out that's important. The real Tom Sawyer was both a good boy and a hellion. A stickler for fairness, yet vengeful and stubborn. Huck was quicksilver and shadows, a startled wild thing you could never hold in one place. And Tom's cousin Sid was not the prissy-mouthed, tattletale sissy of Twain's story. He grew to be more of a man, in some ways, than Tom ever was.

And me? I was never that pale, limp, blond-curled girl-child from a sentimental chromo. I was tough as any boy, and kept my own secrets. Blame the worst things I did on envy; for I wanted to belong, to be part of Tom's wild gang, no matter the cost. Who would've imagined when I was a grown and married woman, with children of my own, that desperation would drive me to become one of them again? But after years of that so-called Civil War, we were all desperate to escape the hell on earth our state had become.

In the end, everyone feasted upon us, until they'd picked Missouri's carcass clean.

I've seen brave men die as often as foolish ones. I've seen death closer up and more often than a human being would ever wish to. I've chased after wild rascals and run from tame ones. I've loved and hated men, lost and found them, tried and failed to tempt them away from their own destruction. I've been the cause of more than one death. I've been friend and enemy and fiancée, wife and mother and widow. I've killed in a fight, and longed to do murder once or twice at home. I've taught, mothered, soldiered, mined, and even written for the newspapers. But I was never the weeping little ninny Sam Clemens made me out to be in his book.

A lady would not protest this sort of thing in public, of course. But I've never been able to act like a lady for long.

My name isn't important. Call me Becky Thatcher.

1864

HANNIBAL, MISSOURI

One

MY HUSBAND LEFT US on an otherwise pleasant morning in March. I felt the bed sag as he slid from the feather tick so slowly, it would not have waked me, had I still been asleep. When I opened my eyes and saw him across the room, packing, I watched and debated whether it would hurt or help to beg him to stay.

To be fair, he had warned me. Over dinner the night before he said he'd gone down to the federal headquarters and signed up. I'd set my fork down and almost laughed. Because it seemed like a joke to go off now, three years into the war. "Oh, Sid. Whatever for?"

"It's my duty, Becky." He frowned, cut a precise square of beef. "Sam Clemens went."

"For three weeks! And even he finally got the good sense to sit this one out."

Since Sixty-one, our war had been nothing but confusion. Who was the enemy—the secesh South, the occupying federals, or the shiftless, violent militias that sometimes preyed on the unlucky? Missouri was a slave state, true, but at the Secession Convention we'd voted to remain Union. Like many, Governor Jackson had family ties in Virginia, the Carolinas, Kentucky, and Tennessee. He longed like mad to secede. But Missourians are practical above all else. We would've been surrounded on three sides by a foreign country called the United States. The Island of Missouri, our shores lapped by the free states of Kansas, Illinois, and Wisconsin.

But when our governor told Lincoln Missouri would not provide any soldiers, the war came to us. The president sent federal troops into St. Louis to evict our state guard from Camp Jackson. We soon learned the man in charge, Captain Nathaniel Lyon, greatly enjoyed two things: to reconnoiter dressed as a woman, and to inflict hard punishments. As angry crowds in St. Louis protested, heckling the federal forces marching through their streets, a stray shot rang out. And Lyon ordered his men to fire on the crowd, killing twenty-eight unarmed civilians.

Sid had read such news aloud from the evening paper as I darned stockings or rocked the baby. We agreed it was a bad business, that we could take neither side wholeheartedly. Our friend Sam Clemens hadn't hesitated, though, when he was called up to be a riverboat pilot for the Union. While Sid sat behind a polished desk, shuffling papers and filing grievances about trespassing cows or undelivered furniture. Sid had considered going as well, even when I pointed out Sam had lasted only three weeks in uniform.

"Anyway, why go now?" I'd argued at dinner the night before. "You never went in for such nonsense. To go out seeking glory like some tin knight in a novel."

He'd looked up over his plate at me, face set hard. "No, that's true. I was never any kind of hero. Not to anybody. The job was already filled."

I knew what he meant, but was too worked up by then to have the good sense to just let it be. "And now you're acting just like him!" I slapped the dining room table, making Aunt Polly's cracked Limoges sugar bowl jump.

The wrong thing to say entirely. But Tom Sawyer was whom Sid put me in mind of just then. You never could tell his cousin Tom what to do or not do. Sid had always been the reasonable one. If you can call any man reasonable.

We went to bed mad.

Now it was morning, the light gray-dark, the spring night turning to molasses, flowing away as the sun rose to melt it. The time of day Tom Sawyer as a boy would've been slinking back into this very house, for it was Aunt Polly's place back then. But Tom was long gone, off on the Mississippi—no boy anymore but a famous river pilot. And Huck Finn no longer lurked beneath the window, calling like a stray cat. But my good, sensible Sid was creeping around in the chill dark, gathering up long johns, wool pants, a flannel shirt, a clean white collar.

Lord God, why a clean one, I wanted to say. It'll be filthy with powder-smut soon enough.

I lay still, though, eyes shut, breathing slow and even. I didn't know then that, in his famous novel, Mark Twain would portray Sidney Hopkins not as he *was*—thoughtful and kind and quietly brave—but as a smirking little sneak, a weak-chinned tattler who always envied Tom. I guess it made his hero seem misunderstood, even more romantic. But it wasn't the truth. And here Sid was going out to war at last in his thoughtful, reasoned way. Yes, that white shirt would turn black; his clothes grow dirty and stiff with blood. Someone else's, I hoped, not caring just then that it was a sin to wish calamity on others.

A board creaked, and I spoke. "Sid Hopkins. Why you stirring so early?"

He stood in the cold air hugging the white cloth to him like a modest girl. I could've laughed, except I knew where he was headed.

"Packing, that's all."

"Sid, please. You're too sensible to go fight. What a notion, so late! The Judge is ailing; he needs your help with cases and paperwork. This war foolishness can't go on much longer."

He turned back to his old calfskin valise and didn't answer.

I propped up on one elbow. "The boys and I need you here. So does Mary. We want you at home with us."

He shook his head and kept on throwing things—tobacco pouch, leather braces, hairbrush, his cased razor—into the valise.

I sat up and the covers fell away. "Oh, Sid. Why must you to do this *now*?"

"I've got to go, Bec. It may be a damn-fool war, but a fellow has to do his part. Stand up for what he believes."

"Someone's said something at you."

He paused, a lone sock clenched in pale ink-stained fingers. "That's right. And it may be foolish, but I care what folks think."

At least he didn't lie about it. I've always hated a liar most of all. "What did they say?"

He turned silently away and resumed packing.

"Well, then, come over here a minute," I said. Not giving up, but making my voice sound like it. No, I wouldn't give in until I'd tried everything I knew to keep him with me.

When he stood beside the bed I slid a hand from under the quilts. His fingers in my warm ones were so cold, it felt like mourning for him already. I held back a shiver, and pulled his hand under the covers. Slid it up under my nightgown, placed it on my warm belly.

"The baby'll wake," he whispered. "Gage, too."

"No," I said. "They sleep hard as puppies."

Then I drew him under easy as the river ought to have taken Tom, yet somehow never would. I'd always been thankful Sid was like him, yet different. A homebody. Not so brave as to be foolhardy. Dependable and kind. But bullets were even less forgiving than the Mississippi. So I made my husband stay awhile, using the only method that ever, far as I can tell, is surefire with men.

It worked for a bit, but finally he peeled my arms from around his neck. "I'll send word after I get to the camp."

"You could take Jim with you." I'd heard gentlemen were taking their servants to the war—and not just the Confederates.

"What? Oh, for . . . Becky, it's the *Union* militia. You'll need Jim here to keep things going. Besides, he's a free man, remember?"

That had been my idea. Aunt Polly had finally bought Jim, years back, from the widow Watson, since he worked so often for her anyhow. But I couldn't forget how hard Jim had once tried for freedom on that raft with Huck. After Polly died, I'd made sure Sid and Mary set him free.

Then all I could do was get up and wrap the quilt around me against the cold. I wished Aunt Polly were still alive, and with a rap of one thimbled finger could make grown boys mind. No good appealing to his sister Mary. She thought both Tom and Sid had hung the moon and stars. She believed the whole world could do no wrong. The federal soldiers on our streets now had been a sorry revelation. Some didn't care if they elbowed a lady aside, or helped themselves to your eggs or the chickens themselves. She prayed for them every night, a missionary in her own backyard. Anyway she'd been terribly ill, coughing hard the last few weeks, and I didn't want to make her worse with a new worry. She'd been hiding the red-spotted evidence, burning her old hankies, but I'd found the charred scraps.

Trailing my quilt like a cape, I followed Sid to where our sons slept: Gage on a rope trundle, baby Tyler in a low oak cradle. He was getting too big for it; soon I'd have to move him to a real bed. Perhaps the sight of them would change Sid's mind.

But after he'd leaned over the crib, and brushed the hair back from Tyler's forehead, he straightened and turned away. I stood my ground in the doorway a moment, then stepped out of the way. Followed him like a barefoot, patchwork ghost to the foyer. Maybe outright accusation would slow him down. "Oh, I see. You were just going to leave without a word."

"I aimed to write a note," he said, looking miserable.

"Wait. I can boil up some coffee."

Sid shook his head.

What else was left? I hugged my husband to me, then thrust him out the door and down the steps with his pitiful suitcase full of useless things. I might stoop to guilt and treachery and the distraction of my body, but I did not want him to see me cry.

After a few minutes I blew my nose and went to the kitchen to make coffee. Mary wasn't up yet, but my little one would soon be climbing out of the crib. Easier to get things done, especially if they involved heat or fire, before he was toddling around.

At last I sat with my enamel mug steaming in the gold morning light. Unlike farther South, we still had a bit of real coffee, even if it was nothing like the rich, dark beans from Brazil my mother used to have ground twice and boiled up slowly for my father. *Judge Thatcher likes his coffee strong and hot, and set in front of him first thing,* Mother always reminded Trenny, our cook. Who would purse her lips and nod thoughtfully, as if she hadn't been doing that very thing for almost thirty years already.

I wished Mother were with me, then didn't. She would've been beside herself at Sid's leaving, shiny-eyed and proud. At least, if he'd been going to fight on the other side. Though from what I'd heard, Union was as bad as Confederate. And either only a tad better than the abolitionist raiders from Kansas or renegade secessionist gangs. The whispers of bloody atrocities being committed out in the deep woods and up in the mountain regions by all sides made a body feel like running in circles, pulling her hair, and screaming.

A war certainly brought the vermin out of the woodwork. If gentle, honest Sid had to face such scoundrels . . . soon he'd be climbing the steps at headquarters. A brick building down on Main, it used to be our town hall. Now its wood parquet floors were roweled furry by spurs. The velvet curtains were falling from the rods, heavy with dust. Sid told me the old clerk had spirited the town records away in the dead of night. All our births and marriages and deaths, crammed into apple boxes, were hidden in one of the hillside caves, to stop the soldiers using them as tinder for the huge old iron stove.

I sat at the table worrying, wishing I hadn't thrown Tom Sawyer into Sid's face. Wishing I hadn't thought of his name at all, for now I couldn't pry him out of my head. We hadn't seen Tom since Sid and I had married, though he must've passed us all the time, piloting up and down the Mississippi. Of course the war had commerce all but suspended, and he never came ashore here anymore. But Tom could always hold a grudge.

Once I would've followed him anywhere, well beyond the childhood scrapes he'd dreamed up for Huck and Ben and Joe, and my cousin Jeff Thatcher. And then for me, too. But after what happened in McDowell's Cave, it was never the same between us. I'd pretended for a while his lie didn't matter. But not even Tom could make me forget a man had died. Maybe not the best of souls, but innocent of what the law had wanted him for. When Tom could have saved him . . . yes, I could hold a grudge, too.

That wasn't the only grievance I'd hoarded like pennies, nursed deep in my heart nights while Sid lay asleep and unaware beside me. But it was the worst one, the sin I could least imagine Tom doing penance for. The one I believed I could never in this world forget, or forgive.

Two

I FIRST MET TOM SAWYER when my family was newly arrived from St. Louis. My father had accepted the judgeship of Marion County, awarded by the governor himself. My Richmond-schooled mother, a true-blue Virginian in heritage and pretensions, was ecstatic about the honor. At least until she peered from the train window and got a good look at downtown Hannibal.

"Oh my dear Lord God," she gasped, lifting a hand as if to cross herself, then apparently thinking better of it. She fell back in her seat with such hard despair that puffs of dust rose around her. She turned to my father and whispered, "Your profession has brought us to the ends of the civilized world, Judge Thatcher."

"Buck up, Mrs. Thatcher," he said cheerfully. "This lonely outpost is reputed to be a bastion of your native culture. An island of slavocracy surrounded on three sides by free soil. On your left, across the mighty river, behold Illinois—"

Mother slapped him with her folded fan, a thing she often did when he was joking too much. Except this time the Judge winced and rubbed his wrist. "Forgive me, Louisa," he muttered.

I gave up puzzling over this odd exchange and craned to look out at the Mississippi, a flat stretch the color of tan mud. Two steamboats were trying to nuzzle into place first at the pier of a warehouse, like twin calves tussling for their mother's udder.

I leaned forward to peer through my parents' dust-streaked window at a large clapboard building nearly innocent of whitewash. Its crooked wooden sign proclaimed we were stopped at the HANNIBAL & ST. JOSEPH DE-POT. A porter began slowly unloading our trunks onto the platform. Trenny, who'd had to ride back in the Colored car, hurried up. She worried after the man, scolding and darting in with dogged persistence as he hoisted our things onto a wagon.

As other Coloreds got off, two men holding rifles stepped up to look them over. The debarking Negroes produced little slips of paper and kept their eyes downcast. The men scrutinized the papers closely and returned them grudgingly. I felt anxious then, because I had no paper on me at all, not even a train ticket. But when I asked, my father only laughed and pulled one of my braids.

The loaded baggage wagon pulled away. The Judge helped Mother and me into a phaeton. I sat next to Trenny, who attacked my face with a hankie, as if I'd been playing outside in the dirt instead of trapped in clean boredom on a train seat for hours. I stood this treatment for a moment, then squirmed away to look out the window again. We creaked over a narrow wooden bridge that spanned a creek, then rattled off and passed a lumberyard. Stacks of planks stretched away west as far as I could see. I marveled they had any trees left at all on the humped hills that flanked the town like lumpy, sleep-ing giants.

"Now, this here is Main Street," said the Judge, rousing himself to play tour guide along a broad unpaved avenue. "You see, it is not so bad after all. We have in just one block Grant's drugstore, a newspaper office, a millinery shop, and a general dry goods with quite a window display. Why, look at the boiled sweets in that big jar!"

I sat up alertly then, but my mother kept her face resolutely forward, as if the inside of the phaeton was of far greater interest. We turned onto Bird Street, which sounded funny to me. Then, onto Fourth.

"Let's see, what is this," my father mused, gazing at a huge white-block building on Fourth. "Why, of course. The courthouse! I'll be working right inside that place, my dears."

I squinted at a gathering on its front lawn. A man was waving his arms, making a speech from atop an upturned crate, while more people milled about. As our carriage paused to let a dray wagon pass through the intersection, I heard a deep voice bellow, *"What about the damned slave thieves?"* Then, much cheering and catcalls.

My father frowned, but kept talking all the way to his brother's house. My aunt and uncle Thatcher and my cousin Jeff lived on North Street in a three-story place of brick with crisp white trim, its big yard bordered with catalpa trees. They'd be good for climbing, I reckoned. As the Judge helped first Mother, then me to get out, a trio of boys galloped down the house's wide front steps. They streaked past, whooping, shirts flapping, faces painted up like savages.

"Why, here's your dear old cousin Jeff," the Judge said heartily.

I was looking at the tallest boy instead. He had a snub nose, red-gold hair, and freckles plastered everywhere. His eyes were greeny-gold, slightly slanted like a cat's. When he saw me staring, he grinned and saluted with his homemade tomahawk. I felt mocked and stuck out my tongue, earning a pinch from Trenny.

Cousin Jeff turned from his friends with a dramatic groan, and dragged over to say hello. The other two glanced at each other, and disappeared into the shrubbery.

Then we were enfolded in the welcoming arms of our Missouri kindred, who pulled us into the house, all talking each at the same time. Except for Trenny, who again had to go around back to the kitchen. Which seemed foolish, since we'd all end up in the same place anyhow.

Inside it was dim and cool. Upstairs starched, ironed linen and oak washstands awaited us. These last were set with fat china pitchers of pale tan water, river sand still swirling in the bottom. It smelled like wet fall leaves. We put these things to good use and then, refreshed and damp, came down the stairs for tea and lemonade and cookies.

HANNIBAL SEEMED AT FIRST MERELY a whitewashed town sleeping at the edge of a great river in the August heat, like a cat sprawled on a sunny window ledge. Comfortable, but after one look not much else to see. I soon missed St. Louis. We were to stay at Aunt and Uncle Thatcher's drafty old place till the new, modern house Papa had planned for us over on Center Street, near the courthouse, was finished. Meanwhile, I knew no one. Jeff avoided his lowly girl cousin as if I carried yellow jack and leprosy both.

Mama seemed unhappy, too. But it was hard to recall her as ever being content, even before we left St. Louis. "Mine was too perfect a childhood," she confessed to me the day after we arrived, as I sat on the edge of the bed patting her hand. She was prostrated with neuralgia. "The very perfection of my early life has spoiled me for any other," she added.

"I'm sorry, Mama," I said, for I knew I'd been one of her greater disappointments.

"Your dear papa tries his best, I suppose," she whispered in the darkened room. "But you see, my dear, I'm doomed to be forever melancholy with life's offerings. Always looking toward my first home, though I am a grown lady with a daughter of my own now."

Well, that made me feel like a terrible burden. If not for me, she could head right back to Virginia, to Grandmama and Grandpa Smallwood's big tobacco farm in Suffolk County. She could lie happy and snug in the big sunny room they'd kept just as she'd left it the morning she'd married the Judge. Her polished, ruffled shrine.

I couldn't seem to cheer Mama up those days, much less please her. So I took to hanging about Papa's study, a parlor my aunt and uncle had offered up as a temporary law office. I had to be quiet there, too, but that was all right. I loved to read, and there were crates of books—new volumes shipped fresh from New York, along with familiar ones from our last house. Papa set up a little table and called it my desk. I had an inkpot like his, and the blank side of his used paper to write and draw on.

I didn't stay inside all day, though. A swing hung at the corner of the front piazza. My aunt Mamie's cats liked to sleep there in the sun. I sat on it and read and swung, and petted the cats with one bare foot, all through the last days of August.

In September, my first day of school turned out exhausting. The other girls hung back, watching me warily, whispering behind their hands. My specially ordered St. Louis dress was fussy as a ball gown next to their plainer calico and gingham. No one, boy or girl, said a word to me. I sat alone while the others ran and shouted in the schoolyard. I pretended not to care. The shady front porch loomed in my mind like the threshold of a distant Heaven. I got back home at last, and came out again with a book, headed for the swing.

Just as I reached it I saw a pair of legs waving wildly, upside down, out in the middle of the street. I set my book on the swing and went to the top step to look. It was Cousin Jeff's barefoot, grimy friend, the cat-eyed one who'd saluted me with a rigged-up tomahawk on our arrival. The same boy who, I'd already discovered that first day of school, sat across the aisle from me. A rascally sort, one the schoolmaster kept an eye on always. Now here he was in front of our house, walking on his hands like a circus dog. I laughed out loud. He turned and wobbled back my way, then turned again.

So he'd come here to parade up and down and show off, just to impress me.

That made me take a step back. I'd never yet had a sweetheart, being only eleven. I wasn't sure I wanted one this disreputable. But it was admirable the way he was going at it out there. When a dray wagon rattled past he didn't flinch or drop back to his feet. Just kept on, as if to prove he could live upside down from here on out, if he wanted.

I began to envy him. No girl could've gotten away with such a stunt. Oh, my father was indulgent and newfangled—Mama always said so. He'd taught me lawn tennis and riding and archery, and the names of all the stars and planets. And I could climb a tree as well as any boy. Just the night before, when Cousin Jeff had tried to trip me in the dining room, I'd given him an Indian burn that made him holler. But if I ever tried to venture out into a public street walking on my hands with my legs in the air and my drawers showing, Papa would've snatched me inside so fast, my hair ribbons would be left in the dust.

I went down a couple steps. Lord God, the boy was so dirty, he needed a coat of whitewash, while I had to take a bath every other night. I began to feel a mighty impulse to knock him down, and was headed to do just that when my mother called from upstairs.

"Becky! Rebecca Thatcher!"

I looked up at her window, then back to the street. In a flash the upside-down boy dropped to his feet, smiling. He walked off whistling, as if he'd gotten exactly what he came for.

Before I turned to go in, here came little Sam Clemens, a neighbor boy from the next street over, rolling a hoop past the house. When I called his name, he stopped and trudged up the walk, hoop under his arm, thumb corked in his mouth.

"Who was that, Sammy?" I asked, pointing down the road.

He goggled at me, aghast, then popped the thumb out. "Why, that's Tom Sawyer. Ever'body knows him." He'd shot me a pitying look, then picked up his barrel hoop and stick, and ran off after his hero.

I FINISHED my first cup of coffee, then got up and poured another. Mary came into the kitchen carrying Gage, whose legs hung to her knees. She tickled his sides until he shrieked with laughter.

"Sit down," I said. "Don't tax yourself picking him up like that, Mary. He's a big boy, too heavy for you now."

She lowered my son into one chair and slipped into the other across from me. Her cheeks held bright spots of color, but she didn't look so feverish. I poured another mug and set it in front of her. "Here. My coffee will cure anything."

"Oh, it's not that bad, Becky," she said. When I rolled my eyes, she laughed. "All right, it's the most terrible stuff ever brewed in liquid form. Next to Dr. Parker's Cure-All Tonic."

"But it is Dr. Parker's Tonic," I said, deadpan. "I just pour it in the pan and heat it up."

I laughed much harder than that paltry joke warranted, while Gage looked puzzled. I meant to lighten our mood, hoping that when I told Mary about Sid, perhaps it wouldn't sound so bad. Anyhow, I planned to make her eat something first.

I took boiled eggs off the stove and set them in front of her, along with the little box of salt. I should have been practical and saved it for baking, since the price was going up. But a naked egg without salt is a travesty.

She looked down and bit her lip. "Two?"

"Aunt Polly's old hens are still laying. Or at least, their granddaughters are. The doctor said you should eat as many as possible. And rare beef and mutton, too."

"Oh, Becky, I *feel* like an egg. I'm turning into one. And *mutton!*" She shuddered and rolled half her breakfast across the table. "Here, you take one."

I cracked and peeled and sliced it up, and put it on a plate for Gage. No sense getting upset over a small brown hen's egg, when there was worse news to tell.

After Mary finished grimly chewing and wiped her mouth, I said softly, "Sid left this morning. He's truly signed up and gone."

She stared at me. "He what?" But the way the brightness drained from her cheeks, she'd heard well enough.

"I tried to keep him here, but he wouldn't stay. Says he has to go, that it's a duty."

She covered her mouth with one hand, and I braced myself for another round of terrible coughing. But she only shook her head as tears spilled over her lids and rolled down her cheeks, which were flaming again. "Ah, Sid," she whispered. "My little Sid."

Her brother hadn't been little for a long time, but I knew what she meant. Mary was the eldest. She'd always been kindhearted, and soft for Sid and Tom. She'd make a good mother, a much better one than me. But Old Doc Bonniwell had told her she shouldn't marry. That she must not even dream of having children; that it would kill her and the baby both. So her younger brother would always be her child, Little Sid to her.

"Don't worry." I stretched a hand across the table to pat one of hers. But even to myself I sounded like a fool. Only a stone would not fret under such circumstances, and Mary was most unlike a stone. She began to cough again.

"You'd best lie down," I said, scooping the salt box out of Gage's grasp. He protested loudly, and from upstairs the baby joined in. I rushed off to get little Tyler, and brought him down to the kitchen.

"Sid's gone off to war all alone," Mary whispered. "If only Tom was still here!"

Oh, why did folks still insist on worshipping at his feet, as if he were the Second Coming? I was growing sick of the sound of his name, though I was the one who'd brought it up lately. In his long absence he'd only become more famous, more talked-about than ever. Tom Sawyer loomed over Hannibal like Paul Bunyan without the ox, more legend than man.

"Tom, Tom, Tom," I snapped. "We're well rid of that son of an undertaker. Strain the lies out of him and he's no bigger than your hat."

Mary gaped, eyes wide. "You don't mean that, Becky. Why, he's your cousin, too, by marriage. You can't mean it!"

"Forgive me. I'm upset about Sid, I don't know what I'm saying. You're right. Tom didn't cause the war; he's not even here. Who knows where he might be?"

At that her eyes filled again and her lower lip trembled, imagining her cousin in danger, or sick out on the Mississippi.

"Lord God," I said, jiggling the baby, who was joining in loud on the chorus. "Don't upset yourself so, Mary."

But it was me and my impatience that'd done that. With Sid gone less than an hour, I was already turning into a harridan, a carping fishwife.

Above the din I heard a knock at the back. "Come in," I shouted. "If you dare."

Heavy brogans rasped at the boot-scraper, the door swung open, and Jim stepped in, pulling off a squashed felt hat. The sight of his big blunt-fingered hands and broad shoulders, his shy, pleased smile, made me feel better. His coffee-hued face was as dear and welcome as any I could think of, especially just then.

"Morning, Miss Becky. Miss Mary," he said.

"Oh, Jim," Mary sobbed, grabbing his arm. "Have you heard? Sid's gone. He's gone off to be killed."

Jim looked down at her, eyes wide with shock. "Do tell Jesus," he whispered, clenching the hat and twisting it like a dishcloth. "That's terrible. What'll we do without him?"

I couldn't stand it if he cried, too. "Mary Hopkins!" I ordered. "You must go back to bed right now."

She ran from the room sobbing. I set baby Tyler on the floor. Gage slid from his chair and threw his skinny arms around Jim's knees, and commenced to pitch a conniption. Bawling like a spring lamb, the baby crawled over and eagerly joined in. Such a riot would've never occurred in my parents' house, which had ever been quiet and orderly. My mother and father and Trenny would not have allowed it. Well, I was a failure at order, unlike

Trenny. And not one bit a lady, unlike my mother. And God knows I hadn't inherited that gently serious manner of commanding folks, like the Judge. Instead, I just lost my temper.

I took a deep breath, resolved not to do so this time. "Well then, Jim," I said firmly. "Looks like I'll be in charge. And you'll be the man about the place now."

I can't say he looked pleased at this sudden elevation. He squinted a little, expression cautious. "What do that mean, exactly?"

I sighed. "That you and I shall be doing more work."

He looked glum then, and who could blame him. Jim was our regular handyman, and we paid him weekly wages. Though Mary had warmed to the idea of setting him free, it'd taken some doing to convince Sid. "We've always taken good care of him," he'd said. "Isn't he better off this way than all alone?" But I kept at it, pointing out how Jim had wanted to be freed so much, even Huck Finn had noticed, way back, and tried to do something about it.

I wondered sometimes if I had insisted so hard because I knew it would please my father. When he and Mama had married, her trousseau had included two slaves, Trenny and Custis, wedding gifts from her parents. The first thing the Judge had done after they'd crossed the Virginia state line was to free them both. "I won't own another person, Louisa," he'd told my horrified mother. "It's a biblical abomination, a burdensome curse on the white race."

Mama had cried, because she'd been taken care of by Trenny all her life. Being freed, Custis immediately went North and was never seen again, but Trenny stubbornly stayed on. Even though, Mama had told me, the Judge did everything but shoo her out the door like a wandering chicken. Finally he'd insisted on paying Trenny wages and giving her Sundays off.

"She won't respect you, Mr. Thatcher," Mama warned.

"Nonsense," he'd scoffed. "I'm going to make Trenny into a capitalist. She'll have a bank account to rival any Missouri shopkeeper's."

I didn't know Trenny's current balance, but I did know that bit by bit my father had become nearly as dependent on her as my mother. For one thing, Mama couldn't cook. She burned the simplest dishes, and never got the hang of measuring ingredients. Every Sunday dinner of my childhood had been a miserable surprise: food either raw or charred, or some worse thing in between, and all of it tasted abominable. I hung around the kitchen to sneak leftover biscuits late on Sunday nights, and in hopes of learning some cooking skills myself. From an early age I itched to get my hands on Trenny's big wooden spoon and the thick, grease-spotted cookery book. I didn't want to starve when I grew up and had to run my own house.

And here we hadn't starved. We were all well fed, including Jim. Following my father's example, I paid him each week, though we couldn't afford much. Jim also did odd jobs for neighbors, just as he had while still a slave. Only now he kept all the profits. At first much of his money went toward the fancy clothes he left here wearing on Saturday nights. The rest Sid said he dropped into the church plate the next morning to atone for his "Wilderness Expeditions."

Jim was genial, and every man's friend. But two years earlier he'd fallen in with a rough crowd, stokers from the docks. One night he came home with a split lip and a black eye. A couple dockhands came around afterward and loitered in the street, waiting for Jim. But he swore he was off such company, and wouldn't go back for pie.

"But with Mr. Sid gone," Jim mused, shaking his head, "who'll run off troublemakers? I don't want to be no Yankee conscript. Lord, if they come around . . ."

He didn't need to finish that sentence. We both knew that if any passing federal should decide to take him for a slave, and us for rebels, they'd "liberate" him to dig trenches for the army—thanks to the proclamation of martial law made in St. Louis four years earlier. If the rumors were true, it wouldn't matter that Jim was free. I couldn't stop them; no one could.

Suddenly I was enraged at my husband for leaving me with a sick sister-in-law, a seven-year-old boy and a toddling baby, an honest but vulnerable hired man, and a large house to run. The same thought came to mind: What would Tom do in such a case? This time I wallowed a moment in self-pity, for I knew he would've sided with me. He and Sid had been archenemies, growing up. Two people could hardly act less alike and still share the same blood.

"Well, here's what you'll do right now," I said to Jim, lifting the screaming baby. "Please split me some firewood for the stove."

Jim nodded. "Right. No sense getting all wrought up yet."

He chucked Gage under the chin, patted baby Tyler's head, and escaped out the back door a bit too eagerly.

"And as for you, howler monkey," I said to the baby. He screamed back in my ear like a steamboat whistle; I'd be deaf by lunchtime. "You and your brother will go play with your aunt Mary."

I left them sitting on the bed with her, engrossed in some yarn scraps and a bunch of old stockings, making puppets. I went up to my room and pulled on stays and a decent dress and buttoned my boots fast as I could. Then closed the door quietly behind me and went down the street toward the militia headquarters. Maybe I could catch Sid before his train left; maybe he'd changed his mind in the last hour. Maybe my distressed state would bring him to his senses. I pushed tears away with the palm of one hand. To stiffen my spine, as I walked I went over the household accounts. Did we have sufficient money in the bank to last until he returned?

You mean if he returns, whispered a nagging voice in my head, which sounded like my own. Perhaps I should ask for an advance from my father, in case of an emergency. Were our accounts up to date? I had no idea. Sid paid the larger bills, and I took food and clothing and pocket money out of the sugar jar he kept filled like a magic ceramic bank. But how would I know who to pay? What were the outstanding debts?

By the time I reached headquarters, my skull ached with sorting numbers. I climbed the steps, cursing the stays that dug at my ribs, breathless after the fast pace. A blue-uniformed guard tipped his hat, but not so it actually cleared his head. I ignored the insult and swept past, trying to act as if I knew where I was going.

The town hall was a dim, dusty tomb filled with uniformed men sitting, standing, or—in one case—lying across a desk. The velvet drapes were not only falling but hung in shreds, as if they were used for bayonet practice. Horsehair stuffing leaked from a spur-torn settee. I nearly turned back, then decided it best not to take notice. My boot-heels rang too loudly on the bare floor.

In the center of the room was the desk where our town clerk used to sit. Now a stranger with black hair, his long thin nose jutting above dull brass buttons, had taken his place. Behind him stood a fat soldier whose jacket was so tight, his neck bulged over it like a goiter.

"Pardon me," I said, clutching my reticule so hard, my fingers were turning numb. When I loosened my grip it fell, and I dived awkwardly to grab it up again. "I'm looking for my husband."

Someone snickered behind me and I felt my face heat up. The man at the desk rose and bowed politely. "Yes, ma'am," he said in a pleasantly deep voice. "I'm Lt. Hiram Dickenson, United States Volunteers. How may I assist you?"

Now that I could actually see his face, it took me aback. A long red scar ran down the right side. In healing it had puckered at the corner of his mouth, drawing it up slightly, like a one-sided smile.

"Well, uh," I stammered. I'd expected him to whine and twang at me like an ignorant Kansas plainsman, but he sounded grammatical and educated, even if Northern. "I just . . . I need to speak to my husband, Mr. Sidney Hopkins, before he leaves. He's just signed up with . . . with you."

"Tall man with dark hair and a mustache? Wearing braces and a gray coat?"

"Yes," I said eagerly. "That's him."

"He's no longer with us."

"No longer—?" I grabbed the edge of the desk to steady myself. How could it have happened so soon? I squeezed my eyes shut, opened them again to swimming black dots. "Did you just say he is no longer . . . alive?"

He stared, seeming equally amazed at my words. "What? Oh—no, ma'am. I only meant that he's left this building. By now he should be at the train station. Headed to Arkansas. Bentonville, I believe. Where he'll join up with—"

I was already running out, hiking my skirts as I clattered down the steps. The insolent hat-tipper had guessed my true nature after all. Outside the horse and wagon traffic at Main and Lyon streets had greatly increased. Every soul in Marion County must be suddenly in town and out on business. The Hannibal & St. Joe Depot appeared an impossible distance away. I hovered at the curb, waiting for a lumber wagon to rumble past. Then I dashed out, just in time to slam into the withers of a sweating horse. The impact sent me reeling. I dropped my reticule again and nearly fell, but someone jerked my arm up, nearly wrenching it from the socket. When I regained my balance, I looked up to grudgingly thank my rough savior.

The man who sat astride his horse as if he'd sprouted from its backbone was tanned dark as an Indian. His young face was lined about the eyes from sun and weather. He wore a motley assortment of civilian pants and slouch hat, antique uniform jacket and new cavalry boots. His pale blue eyes stared down at me and narrowed. I'd met that cool, unfriendly look before.

"Huck," I gasped. "It *is* you, Huck Finn!"

"Don't throw a man's name about so careless," he said, glancing over his shoulder. "It ain't like I don't know you, too, Miss Becky Thatcher."

"Not Miss or Thatcher anymore," I pointed out, more primly than necessary.

"No, I s'pose not. But it'll always be so to me. You still don't look a day over fifteen, anyhow."

I drew back a step. What fine soft words from a wild man, like kittenish purring from a mountain lion. Yet Huck had always disliked, even hated me. I was so often in the way, obstructing his view of the great Tom Sawyer.

His horse danced sideways. Huck had a huge smoked ham slung over his saddle horn. I thumped it with one fist. "Planning a big dinner?"

He smiled. "Just wanted to see how high on the hog I could eat. Maybe you know a good recipe."

Slovenly dress was nothing new for Huck, but the eccentricity of the various items he wore made it appear he'd gone door to door on a scavenger hunt, borrowing a piece at a time to get outfitted. And the ham—it was so large, it would take one person months to eat it. And his mount, I saw now, had a U.S. brand.

As if he'd noticed my quick inventory, Huck straightened and clucked to the horse. He tipped his black felt slouch. "Nice to see you again, Miss Becky. I gots to be going."

I grabbed the reins. Horses didn't scare me; I'd ridden plenty. "Somebody waiting for you, Huck? Is it—?"

Then the shrill whistle of a locomotive jerked me out of the past, so I recalled what I'd been about before we'd collided. "Oh, Lord. Move this beast. I have to run!"

And I did just that, lifting my skirt again as much as I dared and pounding down the wooden sidewalk. I arrived at the station panting like a winded horse, and saw no sign of Sid. At the ticket counter I asked the clerk which particular train was scheduled to carry troops south and west. He frowned at me from under a crooked green eyeshade, licked his thumb, and slowly paged through some papers. "That'd be the, uh . . . hmm, the nine-oh-five. No, hold on. I s'pose it might be—"

I heard another whistle. At least one train was pulling out at that moment. "Oh please, can't you hurry?"

I reached for his list, leaned down to look, and bumped an ink bottle next to the papers on the counter. I lunged for it a second too late. The clerk muffled a curse and snatched the bottle from me.

"Oh, mercy. I'm so sorry! Never mind, I'll go look myself."

I ran from the waiting room out onto the platform and looked all around. Men, women, and children. Soldiers in uniform. No Sid. A locomotive pulled in, skirts of steam trailing its iron wheels like torn petticoats. A man got up from a bench along the wall and stepped out, carrying a beat-up valise, about to board.

"Sid, wait!"

He stopped with one foot on the step and squinted through smoke and steam. "Becky! I didn't expect—is something wrong at home?"

"Yes. You aren't there. Sid, please reconsider."

He grasped my fingers, turning my hand over and looking at the palm intently, as if something might be written on it. He smiled faintly, and I wondered what he thought he saw in the lines etched there. "Too late for that," he said. "I've put my name down in black ink on their muster list. If you break me out now, they'll shoot me as a deserter. You wouldn't want that, would you?"

He kissed my forehead. I grabbed his arm, not caring if anyone noticed how we were carrying on in public. "But what should I do?"

He frowned. "About what?"

"I don't know. Everything!"

Bless him, he nodded and didn't laugh. "Don't worry about the bills, I've paid them all. Taxes on the house are due in a month, but I've arranged for the Judge to take care of those. There's housekeeping cash in the sugar box, enough for a long time. Have Jim do the heavy work. Please just take care of Mary and the boys."

Then I had nothing else to ask; nothing more left to say. He wouldn't listen to reason, and I was not skilled enough to outtalk a lawyer. "I'll miss you so. We'll all miss you."

He swallowed. "I wonder . . . will Tyler remember I'm his father when I get back?"

"I'll show him your picture every day. The tinted wedding daguerreotype."

He nodded, squeezed my hand, then climbed the steps and disappeared inside. A moment later he was leaning out a window, his carefully pomaded hair a mess, blown by an ill wind from the South. The train lurched, then slowly clanked forward.

When it was nothing but a vanishing ribbon of smoke, I turned away and went back through the station, pushing past hurrying travelers who frowned and looked at me sideways. I didn't mean to be rude, but had to get out before I lost my composure. Sid was really gone; I'd seen it with my own eyes. I looked down at my hands, smudged and spotted with black ink from the clerk's desk. I walked slowly out onto the street, rubbing hard at the dusky smears as if I could clean them away.

I'd always been careful with ink; I had a horror of spilling it. Papa had taught me my letters when I was four, and he'd been strict about not leaving smudges. I was a very neat correspondent. Then, one afternoon in my second week in sixth grade, years ago, when we'd just come to Hannibal, I'd slipped back into the schoolroom at recess to look at a book. The schoolmaster had shown the class a picture from it, then gone off to eat lunch and left it on his lectern. A most wonderful book, full of color-tinted engravings of wild creatures in darkest Africa. I had to see those pictures again; we had nothing quite so exotic in our home library.

While I was standing on tiptoe, turning pages, a noise startled me. Not the master. Only Tom, the show-off boy, sneaking in after me. Still, my hand had jerked away and struck the inkwell sitting near the book. Thick India black splashed across the page I'd just turned to, a bright rendering of a long-necked giraffe.

"Oh!" I'd cried, thinking of how angry both my father and the schoolmaster would be. And then, to my shame, I lost my nerve and dashed past the boy. Out in the schoolyard I scrubbed my fingers clean with sand while the other children shouted and laughed and played at tag and blindman's bluff.

Now, leaving the train station, I rubbed and rubbed my spotted hands to no purpose. Either it was a superior article of ink, or else we were long past that childish time when such stains rolled off our skin.

Three

I RETURNED HOME FROM the station feeling breathless and wild, the clerk's ink still with me. The dark smudges on my skin felt less real than my recollection of that long-past day at school when I'd scrubbed my fingers until they bled—not minding pain much, but fearing humiliation like the devil. These new stains mattered little, except they made me daydream of the past when I ought to be considering the future, and what might lie ahead. I resolved to remove the ink even if it meant scrubbing my hands raw. I didn't fear bodily hurts; it was the other sort I could never seem to cope with.

By the time we moved to Hannibal I'd already fallen off a pony and broken my arm. I'd skinned my knees to raw meat, had needle-pricked my clumsy fingers countless times and never cried. My father greatly approved of stoic behavior. He would spend time with me if I didn't weep or whine or complain. If I did, he'd escort me out and shut the door to his study.

But I had never been beaten, or even spanked. By the age of eleven I'd never been struck by anyone, at home or elsewhere. The Lydia Parks Female Academy for Young Ladies in St. Louis had not believed in corporal punishment. If any student misbehaved, they gave all of us mending to do. Piles of it.

I'd once seen a whipping, though. Not a child's punishment, but the flogging of a full-grown man.

. . .

WHEN I WAS FIVE my mother and I had taken a coach from St. Louis to
visit my grandparents' farm in Suffolk. They'd been waiting at the station in
a gay little rig pulled by two bays, driven by a smiling black boy in a bright
red jacket. After we exchanged greetings and got in, Grandmama had
leaned over and told me I must call their dark-skinned helpers servants, not
slaves. "You see, they're part of the family, Rebecca. And we take very good
care of them."

At least ten Negroes of different ages were lined up outside the house
waiting to greet us and take our trunks inside. I began to wish I had a little
servant of my own, the way Mother had had Trenny. When I told her so,
she'd smiled strangely and glanced at my grandmother. "Well, then. You
must certainly tell your father that when we return," she said.

The next morning we went for a short ride in the foothills. My fat little
piebald pony had been Mother's as well. He was old but still lively, and we had
nice broad green fields to ride. Afterward, as we trotted back into the farm-
yard, I saw one of the servants was tied to a post that jutted from the smokehouse wall, his arms pulled over his head. As we neared, the overseer stepped
out with a black snaky whip.

"Oh dear," said my mother, though she kept on toward the barn. "Turn
your head away, Rebecca."

But I didn't; I couldn't. As we passed I stared, smelling rank sweat, the
metal stink of fear. This slave—for I could not think of him as a servant
anymore—wore only ragged, dirty pants, not a nice clean uniform. He
twisted against the ropes, screaming each time the whip took a bite from
his back. But somehow it was worse to look at the overseer. His face was
tranced, contorted, no longer human; he'd turned into a pain-dealing machine. Yet just that morning the same man had laughed as he'd boosted me
onto my pony, then chucked my chin. He'd given me a whole handful of
peppermint sweets from a bag, and joked about not eating them all at once.

I'd quickly gobbled every one. Now the boiled sweets rolled over in my
stomach. I leaned out and vomited onto the ground.

"Rebecca, what on earth?" scolded my mother. I slid limply from the pony's back and she rushed me into the house, so I could be turned over to a servant for cleaning up.

Trenny stripped off my dress and shift and pantalettes. She wiped my face with a cool damp cloth. But she wouldn't look at me, or smile. Or even tell me, as she usually did, that I'd feel better soon. Her face was still, her full lips pressed into a thin line. She seemed to blame me for some unspoken sin. But I hadn't gotten sick on purpose.

That is one of my most detailed early memories. I recalled it clearly when the old schoolmaster, Mr. Cross, had stood up before the class and announced that someone had defaced his book, deliberately ruining an expensive color engraving. He slapped a heavy ruler against his other hand as he talked.

"Now, I demand the culprit confess," he hissed, spraying the front row of students with a mist of spittle, as he always did when angry or excited.

Sweat gathered on my upper lip. Beads of it rolled down my sides, under my chemise. Soon this schoolmaster in the rusty black coat, who smelled of old sweat and boiled onions, would grab my arm and drag me up front and beat me like my grandparents' overseer, until his long greasy hair flew about his face. The sweet taste of peppermints backed up in my throat, though I hadn't eaten a single piece of candy all week. The Judge could buy the man a new book with no trouble. But it was clear from the quivering anticipation on Mr. Cross's face that a new book wasn't really what he wanted.

No one had been in the schoolroom when I'd upset that ink pot—except the wild boy, Tom Sawyer. I gritted my teeth. No doubt he'd be entertained to see me beaten for my clumsiness. Just as I thought this, Tom glanced over. His mouth curved in a smile. No wonder; I was in his power.

I'd never fainted, though I'd seen my mother and my aunt and even ladies on the street crumple like sun-wilted flowers and slide to carpet or grass for no discernible reason. The wave of light-headedness, the queer floating sensation I felt must be the first warnings. Little black spots jumped and quivered before my eyes. To fall out right then would be as good as a confession.

Out of the corner of one eye I saw a hand shoot up. Swaying in my seat, clutching the sides of the bench, I took great care to face front and breathe deep and slow.

"Hmm. Mr. Sawyer," said the master, with a pained, disappointed look. "Are you confessing to this crime?"

"That's right," said Tom. "It was me done it." His voice was deep for a boy of twelve, and laced with a twang, as if he'd come down among us from the Ozarks like a brown bear determined to try out civilization.

I turned my head to look at the rough hand-walking fellow who was volunteering to take my punishment. But why? I held my breath as he unfolded himself and slouched to the front. The master lifted the ruler, then slashed it down in four savage blows that should've broken Tom's hand. Yet he didn't flinch. His face barely changed.

"And that shall be a lesson to you, boy," Mr. Cross fumed, but without much conviction. Tom went back to his seat, dropping into it as if he hadn't a care in the world.

Deep red marks crossed his grimy palm. Waves of admiration and envy emanated from all the other boys, the small ones in front and the great big ones hulking in the back. The effect on the girls was more complicated. Those who went barefoot and wore patched gingham dresses openly swooned on their benches. The ones in smocked shifts, or fancier pinafores and buckled shoes, appeared torn between thrill and disgust. Who knows what my own face conveyed, but inside I was convinced Tom Sawyer was extraordinary. He'd read my mind like a spiritualist, had seen my deepest fear and understood it. Then he'd stepped in with no fuss to save me from it.

At that moment, he won me over entirely.

BUT NOW I WAS A GROWN WOMAN with responsibilities, less inclined to hero worship at twenty-six than I'd been at eleven. I might long to escape to blissful childhood memories, but 1864 was no time to daydream. Some goods were growing scarce. More federals had come to town to lodge, and they were so thick underfoot, it was all a body could do not to step on one. Men in blue were prone to turn up at your house at any hour, demanding to be fed. No one dared refuse.

We still got our eggs from Aunt Polly's good hens, since they hadn't all been requisitioned away. We had things stored up in the cellar—preserves, apples, some potatoes and onions. These would not last long, though, with four to feed plus the baby. He needed milk, but who could say how long we'd have our cow? Everyone kept one in town, for no milk was sold here, as in big cities. Yet more than one afternoon I'd watched federals lead some neighbors' livestock down the street, requisitioned for Father Abraham's army.

"War don't never stay so glorious as it starts," my elderly neighbor Mrs. Tate said, looking after the shifting haunches of the latest disappearing cow, shaking her sun-bonneted head.

She was a storehouse of practical information, having grown up in Missouri when it was still the doorstep of the Western Territory, and St. Louis only a raw-plank settlement. She'd lived through the Black Hawk Wars, which she said were a massacre, for the Indians. The oldest daughter of a trapper, she'd known those same Indians as friends, and had also had to hide from them. She'd helped her mother with the chores and children. She knew how to *make* the things we'd become accustomed to buying at local stores. Even medicine.

Mary and I became her acolytes. Under her direction we took walks into the woods along the riverbank to pick dogwood berries for quinine. We'd send the boys running—or in Tyler's case, toddling—ahead to scout for likely looking patches of nuts or blooms or berries. In their age of innocence, it was only a game, these preparations for possible disaster. They tumbled on piles of leaves and played hide and seek while we dug wild blackberry roots. Those we later boiled and fermented to make a cordial good for dysentery. Wild cherry and poplar bark brewed up into a tolerable remedy for chill and ague. And a syrup from the roots and leaves of the mullein plant and cherry bark had a salutary effect on Mary's persistent hacking.

Like many, we cultivated poppies in our garden. Mrs. Tate warned us that, should the war drag on much longer, drugs like laudanum would be unobtainable, all supplies sent to the battlefields. She showed us how to cut the flower pods and milk out opium, and how to dose Mary for cough and baby Tyler for teething. Other than that, we'd had no need of soporifics to treat anything more serious than headache. I hoped each time I added another brown bottle to the medicine shelf in the pantry that we never would.

Around town, people began to talk of what would happen if the fighting came to Hannibal—if the armies clashed at our doorstep, or a troop of raiders or bushwhackers took over the town. Horrors from our western border were still reported in the papers. These stories were greatly exaggerated, I hoped. Surely not even horned abolitionists from Kansas could hate so hard, they'd really drive old men and boys from their homes to stab and shoot them, then burn the house before the eyes of their horrified wives, mothers, and daughters. Yet there it was, in black and white.

Crowds used to gather at the courthouse to speechify on slave escapes and the crimes of abolitionists. They'd created vigilante committees, militias to catch runaways, raised funds to pay rewards for the recapture of escaped property. Any strange white men were detained and questioned. Negroes who couldn't produce passes were whipped and jailed until someone claimed them. Slaves continued to escape—some west to Kansas, some north to Wisconsin, but mainly across the river to Illinois. The meetings had become more crowded, more shrill, and eventually took to featuring brass bands.

But now the courthouse lawn was quiet. Small, doleful groups gathered on street corners, discussing the war. In its first year, talk had been confident, bright, interested. The conflict was seen as an affront and an inconvenience, but not our fight, and anyway unlikely to last over a month. In the second year, folks began to chafe under the restrictions and hardships imposed by the federal occupation. Fewer waved the Stars and Stripes when blue-jacketed troops marched through town. Plenty of boys who'd signed on for the Union got fed up with fighting for Lincoln when their families were being starved out by blue-coated regiments elsewhere. Some men went home, or joined up in disgust with the other side.

The war had consumed over three years by 1864, and much of the good Missouri had to offer. Our previous Christmas had been sparse: a wizened orange and a handful of walnuts in everyone's stocking. An India rubber ball for Gage. This year I wondered if we should even bother.

I went out to try to buy some flour, and heard an old man complaining to his cronies on the bench outside the dry goods store. "How is it we ain't even in the blasted Confederacy, yet here come the blue-bellies still, to occupy us as iffen we were?"

His friend to the left spit a wad on the floor, then gazed on it as if divining the future in its shining slick. "Well, sure enough," he drawled at last.

"Might be some secesh sympathizers in Missouri. But Hannibal ain't secesh. Ain't it yet a free country out here? We got a right to our views. Who'll keep an eye on the politicians, iffen it ain't us?"

Nods all around. Then a squad of federals strolled in to buy tobacco and candy. Silence fell, along with furious, impotent glares from the graybeards.

I privately agreed. You had to be careful what you said to your neighbors these days, for anyone could settle an old grudge with a whispered accusation of treason in the right ears. But most of my concerns were less philosophical. The week before, we'd run out of salt and sugar, and so had McMullen's grocery. Real coffee and tea were somewhat available, but the price was dear and going up. Coffee beans rose to thirty dollars a pound, then higher. A skilled craftsman might make twenty or thirty dollars a day now, and get work from the army, but it meant two days' hard labor to buy a pound of coffee beans, assuming that much could've been found on any grocer's shelf.

Mrs. Tate had taught us to make a passable cup from the seeds of okra plants, nicely browned, just in case. "A less palatable brew can be coaxed from parched yams," she said, nodding until her bonnet strings trembled. "A worse substitute from burnt corn. Though I recall the Indians liked it well enough in '34."

I shuddered. We'd simply go without in that case. Tea was easy. We dried raspberry leaves and brewed them, since a bunch of the vines had long been cultivated all around our garden palings, for jam.

On my way home I stopped off at my parents' house. After I kissed the Judge on the cheek and sat across from him, he said, "What a surprise. And a pleasant one this time."

"What do you mean, Pa?"

"Only that yesterday I was visited by a federal officer, my dear. He accused me of being a secesh sympathizer."

This idea was so patently absurd, I laughed. Apparently so had the Judge, which hadn't set well with the captain. "The man grew red in the face and threatened to arrest me that minute. I told him that nearly thirty years before, I'd freed the only two slaves ever to fall into my hands. And that I'd been sworn in under a federal president and intended to uphold the laws of the nation as usual."

My father had then proceeded to lecture the whole uniformed delegation about the ways some soldiers mistreated townsfolk, taking away too much, even things the army had no use for, like portraits and jewelry and china, all under pretext of requisitioning. He was particularly incensed that some local men were abusing positions of power they'd been assigned by the occupiers.

Now the Judge grinned at me like a cocky boy. "I told 'em one militia officer was requisitioning my neighbors' horses and selling them at a profit to the army, passed off as his own. And that others were helping themselves to the china and silver as well, when they dropped in on our citizens to be fed."

I could imagine how that had been received. "Lord God, Pa. What did he say?"

"He assured me I was mistaken. So I presented the case of Mrs. Hamlin's missing silverware, inherited from her grandmother, safe in the dining room lowboy until she'd fed a detachment of soldiers who'd dropped in and demanded grub."

My father sometimes forgot he was not always in court. But perhaps on the strength of this speech—for he'd ever been a fine turner of phrases—the federals backed off. Still, the captain had promised to return.

My father shook his head. "Before he bowed his way out, the fellow told me he hoped the rest of my relations and associates were as spotless in character."

As I sat in his study, anticipating a cup of rich, dark, real coffee for a change, I wondered how the federals might view me, the wife of a man who'd signed on to fight for the Union. What could they find fault with in our case?

Trenny came in carrying a tray. "Miss Louisa, she's about ready to go, Judge."

"So soon," he said, pushing back from his desk. "But I'd thought . . . ah, very well."

"Sorry, we got no cream today," Trenny said to me, then turned back to the Judge. "Yessir, she nearly packed and all. Right after them men leave, she start me on filling up the steamer trunk."

She set out cups and saucers and a small bowl of molasses. So even Trenny had been unable to find sugar once McMullen's had run out. As she worked, she continued to address my father. "Miss Louisa ain't studying on waiting till tomorrow, Judge. She going to head back home now, she says, while we can still get there."

I looked at him sharply. "You don't mean Mama's going back to the farm? To *Virginia?*"

He pressed his lips together and nodded.

"But—but she didn't tell me." Why in the world would she go South now? It made no earthly sense. "Why didn't you forbid it, Pa?"

An absurd idea. The Judge had never forbade Mama anything—except her old dowry, the slaves whom he'd set loose after the wedding. And he'd been only half-successful then. She still held that failure over his head.

He shrugged and looked away. "She's concerned about her dear parents, and of course the farm. And she feels . . . unsafe here, now that so many men . . . are gone." He flushed, clearly ashamed to admit to his daughter that his own wife doubted his ability to protect her. "She didn't want to upset you, my dear."

"Upset me?" I laughed and shook my head. "Well, I *am* upset. Quite upset to be treated like a child when I'm a full-grown woman with a family and responsibilities, damn it."

I heard skirts rustle into the room behind me. "Ladies never use profanity, Rebecca."

My mother was pulling on her kidskin traveling gloves. I got up and faced her. "Well, they should, if the situation calls for it."

"No situation on earth ever calls for a lady to use foul language."

And Louisa Thatcher was unfailingly polite, her tone well-modulated always. She would never utter even a mild curse, or raise her voice to a shriek, even if she were being cut into small pieces by naked savages. I supposed she thought any roving blue-bellies on the road to Virginia could be frozen in place by a contemptuous half smile and a cutting word. My mother was ever a lady, but I'd failed to master that arcane art. She refused to admit defeat, though, and still pretended we shared some mysterious feminine ideal of grace.

"Why go now?" I cried. "Surely the war will be over nearly before you get there."

She *tsk*ed at my outburst. "Your father has arranged for an escort. I will not spend another day in this benighted wilderness. Trenny and I are going home for the duration."

Home. That had never been Missouri, not for her. But how could she travel all the way to Suffolk, Virginia, and leave us—leave me—here? Perhaps we weren't close. And maybe I rarely asked for her advice, because it invariably involved keeping silent, or smiling and looking agreeable, or wearing tighter stays—none of which I could endure for long. Still, she was my mother. The idea of her being so far away made me suddenly feel orphaned.

She patted my cheek with one cool gloved hand. "But you may come along, dear. In any case, you should certainly send little Gage. But I simply can't cope with a baby on such a long journey. You must realize Gage would be much better off at the farm, in the country, away from the vulgar behavior of the invaders who litter our streets. You don't want him imitating such low men."

"He's barely seven," I said, dropping back into my chair. "He's too young to go off anywhere without his mother."

I would never send my child away without me. Surely with all the plantations and farms in Virginia, the armies would be even more numerous there, even more bent on subduing secesh rebellion. And now on freeing the slaves—since Lincoln had ordered it so just the year before, in his Proclamation. Strangely, as Missouri had not seceded, that order did not affect our status. Union troops here still rounded up runaways and returned them to their owners. But then we also had two governments, Union and Confederate, issuing conflicting orders. Two invading armies, north and south. Plus crazed bushwhackers, Jayhawkers, and George Hoyt's Redlegs, all of them John Brown's murderous heirs.

Kansas abolitionist raiders had often profited greatly from riding across the state line to burn farms, steal goods, and assault and kill witnesses. But now they could no longer be bothered to distinguish between a slave operation and a simple homestead. And so sprang up new secessionist gangs headed by Bill Anderson and William Quantrill. People said Quantrill was a gentleman, even if he'd come from Ohio. But Anderson was a devil red as any wild-eyed Kansas abolitionist. All of them were prone to burning, looting, and even killing. None had come near Hannibal yet, but no one could tell the future. So perhaps Mama was right. Maybe Gage would be safer with her. If she tired of his childish demands, there was still softhearted Trenny.

"No," I said, taking pleasure in denying her, since I'd rarely had a chance to do so. I'd even married the man I knew she'd prefer for me, not— But all that was beside the point now. "No," I repeated, tasting that single hard syllable, enjoying the way it pressed my tongue hard against the roof of my mouth. "Gage and Tyler shall stay with me. They need their mother, and will be quite safe here. We have Jim, after all."

The flare of her nostrils made clear what good she thought the company of a lone black freedman would do us. Because even a free Negro wouldn't dare raise a hand to, much less contradict, a white man. My mother didn't say any of this; she didn't need to. She only bowed to me coldly. "As you wish, my dear."

But things weren't as I wished. "Oh, Mama," I said, and rushed up and took her hand, wanting for once to just throw my arms around her. But she held me off, touching my cheek again with those cool impersonal fingertips, then tucked a stray curl back behind my left ear.

I rode in the buggy with them to the station. While the Judge and Trenny checked the trunk, Mama and I went to the ticket counter, then the platform. I wished her a good journey. She even smiled at me. Then they boarded to find the ladies' compartment, so Trenny could make Mama comfortable before the journey began.

The Judge asked me to stay for dinner, but I begged off. "Who'll cook it, anyhow?" I had no doubt Pa would soon be turning up at our house around suppertime.

He looked astounded. "Why, of course it's all taken care of! Your mother has engaged the Postens' cook to do for me. You recall her, Sadie Bell Lucas. I shall be comfortable in my bachelor's quarters."

Of course. She always saw to every detail. At least, the few not already handled by Trenny. "That's good, Papa. We shall have you over for dinner this week, as well."

I kissed his cheek. He smiled, then turned eagerly back to his papers, as if he were already alone.

. . .

I WALKED SLOWLY HOME. Before I opened the front door I knew something was wrong. The house was too silent. No ringing cries, no squeals of children at play. And it was too late for Gage or Tyler to be napping.

"Mary? Hello! I'm back."

I heard the thud of hurried footsteps; then she burst into the room, Tyler in her arms, her hair straggling around her face. "Oh, Becky, thank the Lord it's only you."

Her face was so pale, I stopped feeling for pins in my hat. "Who else would it be?"

"The ones who came for Jim!"

I pricked a finger on a concealed hatpin and swore. "What? Make sense, Mary. They had no flour at the store, and . . . did you say someone came here for Jim?"

She nodded and began to cry. Tyler tightened his grip around her neck until I thought he'd strangle her.

"Where's Gage?" I asked. "Here, give me the baby."

I took him and he pressed his wet, sticky face into my neck, grabbing fistfuls of my hair, jerking it from the tortoiseshell combs so hard, I yelped. "All right, now tell me. Where's Jim? Who was it came to see him?"

"Not to *see* him," she snapped, blotting her eyes with a hankie. "Aren't you listening? He's been conscripted. Or . . . or requisitioned, I think they said. Like a side of beef!"

She began to cough in long, racking bursts. "They took him for Lincoln's army, to do their hard work. Lord God! What'll we do?"

I stared at her over Tyler's hot, damp head, for Mary never cursed. That alone was frightening. "You're fooling. Tell me you didn't let soldiers in here."

"When six of them bang on the door with the butts of their guns . . . poor Jim. He didn't want to go. I begged them to leave him alone. They said, He ain't your nigger no more, ma'am. I told them he most certainly was not, he was his own man, and they couldn't haul him away like a sack of flour or eggs from the coop. Then they all stared at Jim until I thought he'd faint. At last he allowed he'd go along. But he looked back at me so pitiful, as if I'd failed him. So I ran out into the yard and begged them to leave him be. I said I was sick and needed his help."

That was certainly true enough. "Yes, and then what?"

"The devils *laughed*. Said we secesh partisans would have to learn to do for ourselves now. Then they hustled him down the street. Becky, one of them slipped Mama's good sugar bowl into his pocket on the way out."

"And they definitely wore blue uniforms?"

She frowned, thinking back. "Yes. Well, mostly. They said they'd seen Jim about town, that he was too big and strong not to be doing his part with a shovel. But do you think . . . Becky, he's not cut out for fighting!"

I knew that, but our opinions no longer meant much. "I'll go down to the headquarters," I said. "To talk to them about . . . about setting him free."

How many times would his freedom have to be declared before it took? Poor Jim, indeed.

Four

I ARRIVED AT HEADQUARTERS out of breath. A different guard stood at the door, and this one tipped his hat properly. I barely nodded, in too big a hurry to keep Jim from being shipped off to dig trenches and get shot at. I approached the front desk as if in a recurring dream. Those same falling-down, dusty curtains, the trampled and scarred floor, the torn upholstery on the armchairs. The same thin, scarred, beak-nosed man behind the desk.

"Pardon me," I said. "I'll need your assistance."

"Yes, of course." He was already rising from his chair, which squeaked badly, its spring in need of oil. He bowed. "I'm Lt. Hiram Dickenson."

"So you said before."

"And how may I help you this time, miss?"

"It's missus. I was here two months ago, when my husband . . . I am Mrs. Sidney Hopkins, come to get back Jim. That is, I wish to recover our . . ." I paused, having almost said *servant,* which to him would mean "slave."

He waited patiently and I began again. "Our *hired* man, a Negro named Jim Watson, has been taken against his will from our house."

He pursed his lips and jotted something on a paper. "A slave has been stolen from your property?"

"Not at all. Jim's been free for years now. Officially manumitted by the heirs of the Widow Polly Hopkins. Witnessed by— Oh, never mind that. While I was away, a group of your men came into my house and forced Jim to go with them. They're the ones wanting to make a slave of him. If you see what I mean."

When he frowned, the scar by his mouth twisted downward, as if he didn't see at all. "Why do you say it was my men?"

I was too impatient to hide it. "They wear blue coats, don't they?"

He inclined his head. "So do many others these days, with less reason. Our troops may come to a house for a meal, or to be billeted. But they do not kidnap Negroes."

"Well, these did."

We glared at each other a moment. He looked as put out as I felt. At last he sighed, and said, "I suspect your *hired* man may have been taken by roving vigilantes. Or perhaps even some of the home guard. But not U.S. Army troops. We have no orders to commandeer any forced labor at the moment."

"But you may in the future?"

He took a breath, exhaled sharply. "I may be asked to do anything in the future, God knows." At least he had the grace to redden before he went on. "However, I will inquire into this. Just to be sure there was no mistake. And whether anyone from this command was involved. Which I doubt."

When he stepped from behind the desk—tall, long boned, broad shouldered—he put me in mind of newspaper engravings of Lincoln. Though the lieutenant was not nearly so ugly, even with the scar. His hair was neatly combed back, and less greasy than the first time I'd seen him. No doubt he'd commandeered some family's bathtub since then.

He was also lame. His gait had a lurch, a painful twist, as if someone were turning a knife in his hip socket with each step.

I gave him a description of Jim and repeated what Mary had told me. He took notes and nodded. At the end he bowed politely and escorted me to the door. The guard stared from under a bent hat brim.

"Thank you," I said to Dickenson.

"I'll see what I can find out." He frowned at the overly curious sentry, who took his time looking away, not concealing a smirk.

This time the mood at home was quite different. Mary grabbed my arm, jerked me over the threshold and inside, fairly jumping up and down as she thrust a paper rectangle under my nose. A letter from Sid. I hadn't had one since he'd left.

May 1864
Dearest Wife,

I miss you more than you can know, and long to see you and both my little Sons again. But a Reunion must needs wait, it seems, until this strange War has ended. How long seems less and less clear, the more I see of it, but the sooner we find a way to make Peace the better. Sometimes its hard to know who is the Enemy, after all.

Yesterday we came upon a parcel of Bushwhackers at the Arkansas border, and along with a militia unit we charged. This put them to skeedadling in earnest. I rode up so close on one he jumped off his horse like a jackrabbit and ran into the woods, which seemed comic to the whole bunch of us, tired as we are these days. We laughed for the first time in days.

Still, some occurrences lately make a body wonder if God may be on anyone's side. Two nights ago six men dressed in plain clothes went to the home of an old man in Lexington, where we camp as I write. They called the poor fellow out of bed, telling him to follow. His daughters begged him not to trust them, but he was forced away. The girls clung to his arms, but when the Ruffians got him a few yards from the house they shot him six times. His neighbors tell us he was a Southern man, yet never said a word nor took up arms against the Union and stayed home the whole time. Two of his sons are in Lincoln's army.

Late at night, before I sleep, I wonder how I would explain such things to my own Sons when they are older. I confess I have yet to think up a way. Forgive me, Becky, for writing depressing Tales. If there were glorious Exploits and Honors to report you might like my letters better. But I told you at our marriage I would not lie nor prevaricate.

I think I must also tell you another reason I left home. I could no longer abide being compared to my illustrious cousin, and found wanting. Not just in whispers by townsfolk, but silently, by those closer to me. I am come here not simply to defend Missouri, or to make you

proud, Becky—but so I may face down anyone after this, including my-
self.

Well, my bowels are in fine working order, at least. A poor fellow
just last night died of dysentery. I would much prefer a bullet to that,
but will try to stay out of harm's way, and well, for all our sakes.

Your husband,
Sid

He usually signed his notes, *Your Loving Husband.*

I couldn't sleep that night. How could Sid think I always compared him
to Tom, after so many years? Yes, I had brought his name up, but just lately,
and just the one time. I tossed and turned, and at last got up and did an inventory of the pantry. A mistake, since there was less in it than I'd hoped. I
needed a calming distraction—a good book, someone to talk to. But the
whole house slept, so all I could do was inventory what was left of my family.

Mary, lying on her back with arms crossed over her breast, as if she'd
composed herself for her funeral. That made me shiver.

Gage and Tyler, the baby on his stomach with his little rump in the air,
wet thumb sliding from his mouth. Gage, lanky arms and legs sprawled to
every corner of the low rope bed we'd moved from our room. The Big Bed,
he called it. The crib was the Baby Bed. He was proud to have graduated
from it, and happy to let Tyler have his old crib. I tucked the covers around
them both, for it was cool. Then I dragged back to my own room, because
everyone else was getting some rest and I'd still have to wake up with them,
whether I slept or not.

It was fear keeping me up. Fear of simple yet terrible things, not vague,
childish terrors. When would Sid return? When would we run out of money
and food? When would soldiers or bushwhackers from one side or the other
take away our home, or burn it—a favorite way lately of teaching folks a
"lesson." When would I hear from my mother? I knew that, despite the letter on my dressing table, my husband might lie dead already. And where on
earth was our Jim?

What if I was already alone and just didn't know it?

I lay on top of the quilt and, though I'd shed my corset hours before, couldn't catch my breath. My heart tried to pound its way out, to squeeze from between my ribs and gallop away like a spooked horse. All I could think to do was look back to a time when things to be feared lived only in the dusty recesses beneath the bed.

I HAVE ALWAYS BEEN a light sleeper. As a child I'd often wake late at night or in the small hours. When I was little, I headed for my parents' room and tried to talk them into staying up with me. They never took to that idea, only bundled me down the hall and back under my covers, with orders not to stir again. Trenny was no more sympathetic to my nocturnal wanderings. So by the time I was eight, whenever sleep had fled I knew better than to involve adults. I'd quietly get up on my own, and amuse myself until I felt sleepy again.

One night, after my parents and I had moved to our own new house in Hannibal, I stood in my nightdress at the bedroom window, peering through my father's telescope. I was spying out the stars I could name— Sirius and the dippers—while also following first the gyrations of swooping bats, then the secret night-life of our neighbor's cat. I tired of watching the orange tom pounce on invisible things in the grass, turned my glass back to find the bats, but then heard an inquisitive meow. I swung back to the cat, but he was still busy with his prey. Besides, the meow had sounded strange, too deep and loud.

At a furtive movement in the alley, I turned the glass that way. Fiddled with it, adjusting the focus, then saw the wild boy from school walk up to greet someone: a ragged-looking fellow skulking in the dark, his silhouette strangely lumpy, because he seemed to be wearing many layers of clothing. His coat hung to the ground; his pants bunched at the ankles, and he kept swinging something on a string. Tom seemed to be imploring for a chance to do the same. At last the other boy passed the prize over. I saw with a thrilled shudder it was some sort of dead animal. Why were two boys out long after midnight with a dead animal on a string, when children were all supposed to be asleep?

Of course I wasn't in bed either. Perhaps I had more in common with the Sawyer boy than I'd imagined. But it had never occurred to me to actually leave the house so late; I'd stuck to entertaining myself indoors. So I'd grown familiar, then bored, with all our books and games. Even with the few forbidden adult treasures I could lay hands on while the rest of the family slept. The realization infuriated me. So much time wasted peering out like a prisoner! I could've escaped into the night. How wonderful to have a friend to share the dark hours with—someone you trusted enough not to tell.

I contemplated how I might learn what they were up to. My best plan was to sneak out and follow them until sure I wanted to join in. But there was the matter of getting out of our house. Not only did three different boards in the upstairs hall squeak underfoot, so did two of the stair risers. And the front door always gave a horrible groan when you opened it, no matter how often Trenny rubbed the hinges with bacon grease.

However, a perfectly good oak grew right outside my window.

I laid the telescope on the bed, then raised the sash as high as it would go. I boosted myself onto the sill, leaned out, and grabbed a thick branch that grew so close to the house, it scraped the clapboards when the wind blew. I stuck a foot out until my toes gripped bark, then swung the other out and did the same. I balanced like an organ grinder's monkey, then righted myself and shinnied along the branch.

I dropped into grass and dirt that felt wonderfully soft and damp beneath my bare soles. I crushed a leaf from a nearby bush between my fingers; it smelled so sharp and spicy, I nearly sneezed. I plucked a blossom and tucked it behind one ear, feeling both worldly and childish. But I would enjoy this freedom as much as possible, for I was not allowed outside unless properly dressed, and never without shoes.

A few feet away, the neighbor's cat pounced. He delivered a death blow to his prey, then sat back and narrowed his eyes at me. I hissed and he ran away. I laughed out loud, then wiggled my toes, dug in my heels, and scuffed along through the grass. Then I recalled the real object of my descent. But when I turned to look back at the alley, the boys were leaving. I hitched up the skirt of my flannel nightgown and dashed after them.

They turned the corner at Main and loped down a side street. I did, too, just keeping them in sight. I caught a stitch in my side and was about to give up, but then there they were again, pushing a raft into the water at the end of the street. By the time I reached the banks, one was poling out into the river while the other reclined, a thin stream of pipe smoke trailing after them. I could smell it where I stood, sweet as a fall bonfire of grass and leaves.

I hid behind a water oak and watched. They looked so at ease, relaxed, yet wild as foxes. I could see from where I crouched on the bank that they neither needed nor wanted anyone else along. Oh, I wanted to stamp my feet and scream and curse, though the only injustice they had done me was not to notice me sneaking behind, full of envy and admiration, bent double and pained with it.

The next day at school, I waited to speak to Tom Sawyer at the edge of the school yard. His younger cousin Sid smiled shyly as he passed. I nodded, then turned away and ignored him. He wasn't the one I had to speak to. But Tom didn't come, and finally the master rang the bell and we all trooped inside. We recited our spelling words, then started on arithmetic. I glanced up from my slate just in time to see Tom stride in briskly, looking about as if he were on time. He flung his hat at a peg and himself into his usual seat.

Mr. Cross, who'd been leaning back in his rush-bottomed chair, gazing out with satisfaction at all of us bent to his will, sat bolt upright. "Thomas Sawyer!"

Tom looked up and blinked, face bland and innocent as a pan of fresh milk. "Sir?"

"Up here, young man. Why are you late yet again?"

Tom stopped in front of the desk, then looked back over his shoulder as if one of us might save him. When his gaze reached me, he winked. "I stopped to talk to Huckleberry Finn, sir."

The master rose, looking terrible as God. "You did *what?*"

When Tom repeated himself, Mr. Cross scowled, reached down, and jerked a switch from the endless supply under his desk. It was thick as a pointer finger. "Take off your jacket, you young rascal."

Tom hung the muddied wool from a corner of the desk as if it were made of finest silk. He turned to face the class, no trepidation on his face.

One of the littlest girls began to cry loudly. Two older ones put their heads down on their desks. Susy Harper, the most kindhearted girl in the school, covered her eyes. Even Joe Harper, the boy nearest me, winced. I heard a dry click as he swallowed. But Tom wasn't looking at Joe or any of his friends. He wasn't even looking at pretty red-haired Amy Lawrence, the girl some said was his sweetheart. He was staring at me as if an invisible thread linked us. I stared back, even when the master raised the switch overhead. I would show Tom Sawyer I was not afraid of anything either.

The schoolmaster beat him so hard about the back and shoulders that dust, or perhaps smoke, rose from his shirt. When the first switch snapped, Cross grabbed another, and plied it until his arm tired. "Now then," he panted, tugging his frayed, graying cuffs back into place. "You may take your seat, sir. But with the girls!"

A rare punishment, dreaded by the boys more than any other. Because all day, sometimes all week, the offender was to be addressed as "Miss" by his friends and enemies alike. Tom simply smiled and headed down the aisle to the only empty seat on the girls' side. The one next to mine.

"Hmph," said Amy Lawrence, her voice so loud and bitter, the master raised his head and looked around like a cat tracking birds. Sid, who sat up the aisle from me, glanced back and frowned. He opened his speller with a thump.

As we bent to our work again, Tom pulled out a slate and began to draw. He made a house with two stick people, then added a dog. I ignored this crude artistry at first, but once I glanced over, I was fascinated. The gables and lightning rods on the boxy-looking place he'd drawn showed it was my house. Tom quickly sketched in a third figure, comically sticklike, walking on the road in front of it—but on its hands, upside down. I clapped a hand over my mouth. Then he concealed the bottom of the slate with his palm and wrote something else.

"Let me see," I whispered.

He shook his head. I slid an elbow over and knocked his hand aside, to see *I love* written there. "Love what?" I persisted.

Tom grinned, flipped the slate, and started doing arithmetic sums.

At the noon recess, he whispered to follow him back to the school yard after the others went home for lunch. "I'll give you a drawing lesson."

The first time we would be alone together, I wanted badly for him to like me. So I copied the fluttering mannerisms of the other girls. I spoke in a soft voice, professing mortal fear of rats. I lowered my eyes each time Tom looked my way, and tried hard to blush. I even giggled quite sickeningly as we shared an apple from my lunch. Before we'd eaten it to the core, Tom insisted we get engaged. He handed me his favorite possession, a beautiful carved brass andiron knob. It glowed warm as gold, as if he polished it daily.

"Oh my. Where'd you get this?" I asked, turning it over to admire the design.

"I'll tell you someday," he said. "It's a secret."

But no matter what it says in Mark Twain's damnable novel, I never cried when Tom told me he'd done all this before with Amy Lawrence. And I kissed Tom first, without being asked. But just as my lips touched his, I spotted Sammy Clemens hiding in the bushes, spying on us. The amusement on the little thumb-sucker's face made me realize I'd made a terrible mistake: Prissing and simpering would never earn me a place in Tom Sawyer's gang.

So I jumped up and ran off. "Becky!" I heard Tom calling behind me. "Hey, wait!"

But I would not. He might not know yet what was wrong, but I did.

Tom finally caught up. "Here," he gasped. "Damn, but you run fast—"

"For a girl?" I spat, rounding on him.

He grinned. "For anybody. Here, you dropped this." He tried to press the cherished andiron knob into my hand.

But a simple knickknack could never make up for the foolishness I'd just engaged in. "I don't want it," I gritted from between clenched teeth, turning my back so he wouldn't see the tears running down my cheeks. Why, oh why, did I have to cry when I got angry! It was the most girlish, infuriating thing about me.

After a few moments I heard him scuff away through the dead leaves. I threw the brass knob as hard as I could into the weeds. The school bell rang, but Tom didn't turn up there the rest of that day. I suppose it was that last insult, that sudden rejection, that drove him off. I had the rest of the day to realize that wasn't what I wanted. So after the master rang for dismissal, I went back into the woods, picked up the knob, and brushed the dirt off. I'd thought it over all during arithmetic and spelling, and reconsidered. As long as I had that smooth, cool brass ornament in my skirt pocket, I knew I'd see Tom Sawyer again.

. . .

I HAVE IT STILL, that beautiful, round, ornate ball of heavy carved brass. During my married days in Hannibal I kept it tucked into my glove box, hidden away so Sid would not ask why I'd cherish such a thing. He wouldn't understand. Or perhaps he would. In either case, he'd have felt hurt.

Still sleepless after making my rounds of the house, I got up and felt around in the dark until I found it, then climbed back into the four-poster and put the knob under my pillow. I stroked it each time I felt another attack of nerves coming on. And when my whole body tensed and shivered as if it no longer belonged to me, I gripped the andiron knob to remind me of the brave girl I used to be. The one who'd follow a pack of rough, dirty boys anywhere, and sometimes lead the way.

But I was grown now, with children hanging from my skirts and too much to lose. I wouldn't be following the boys into the wilderness this time. The far-off adventures would all be theirs. I'd be home waiting with the other women, with the children, hobbled by yards of skirts and petticoats and narrow-heeled boots that pinched like the devil if a body tried to run. I think I understood then how Aunt Polly must've felt when her boy disappeared for days without a trace. Helpless, angry, afraid to hear what might be happening beyond the safe walls and lanes she'd thought she knew so well.

Five

THE NEXT AFTERNOON, when I lifted Tyler out of the crib after his nap, his hair stood on end, damp and fuzzy as chick fluff. Mary and I laughed at the sight. But at the table he turned his head and refused to drink the fresh milk Mary had just brought in from the cowshed. I poured it in his favorite china mug, but he knocked it over, then cried, rubbing his eyes as if they were full of sand.

"Does he look flushed?" I asked Mary.

"Let me hold him," she said. But he pushed away from her, arms and legs stiff. When she tried to soothe him, he screamed louder. She turned pale and began coughing.

I gathered Tyler up and rocked him. His eyes closed as if he still felt tired. When I went up to put him back to bed, his skin felt hot. His flannel was damp with sweat. So it was a fever coming on, and no doctor in town, since the army had taken ours.

"Hush, hush, sweet baby," I whispered. When I laid him in the crib he was quiet, only whimpering when I wiped his face and under his nightgown with a cool, damp cloth. I gave him a spoonful of Mrs. Tate's cherry and poplar bark tonic, but he spit it out. After that he clung so hard to my finger, I dropped the spoon and cloth on the floor and crouched beside the crib until he slept. When I finally dared get up, I nearly collapsed; my legs had gone dead with pins and needles.

We took turns watching over Tyler, one sitting with him while the other looked after Gage and cooked meals or cleaned. Through that day and into the night, Tyler's skin grew so hot, it burned our fingertips. I filled a wash-tub with well water and gently dipped him in. He screamed, face blotching red, then purple. But when I laid my wrist against his forehead, it seemed the bath had brought down his fever a bit. At last Mary and I both fell into our own beds, exhausted.

At dawn I woke, but not to a baby's cries. The silence seemed more omi-nous than screaming. I leapt from bed and ran to his crib. Tyler smiled up at me, cheeks still flushed, though he wasn't nearly so warm. Relieved, I took him into the kitchen and heated some grits from the day before with a dab of butter. By the time Mary came in, yawning, the baby was babbling and eating as I spooned grits into his mouth. Gage gobbled his own portion, then begged to go outside.

"All right, but don't go far."

I wished he had someone to play with, but our neighbors on the south side had moved to St. Louis; the husband had been appointed to some military post there. Their Thomas had been only a year older than Gage, and they'd become great friends. No noisy gang of boys played in this street now; they were all grown and gone—some to the army, some to war. No Tom Sawyer or Huck Finn for Gage to tag af-ter. I told myself I was glad; he didn't need to hero-worship such good-for-nothings. In the end it hadn't benefited me, or any of the boys who'd followed Tom.

Huck had always been wild, but now he was some sort of outlaw, by his looks. Joe Harper ran off with Tom and Huck once, to an island, to be a pi-rate. Everyone in town had been sure they'd drowned, then frightened to death when the boys reappeared one morning in church, alive and well. Yet poor Joe had grown up to drown after all. He'd taken up gambling on river-boats, and got knocked overboard by someone who hadn't liked losing at cards.

My cousin Jeff had been another of Tom's acolytes. He'd joined the federals at the start of the war, and was serving under a border commander named Ewing. Quantrill's raiders had burned Lawrence, Kansas, a week earlier in retaliation for a bloody abolitionist raid. Now the latest news was that something called Order Number 11 had been handed down. Ewing's men were to evacuate all Missouri folk, disloyal or not, along the Kansas border, the newspaper said. And to shoot them if they refused to go.

That afternoon I heard a weak knock and found my aunt Mamie Thatcher swaying at our door, white-faced and trembling. She clutched a piece of paper to her heart as if she'd been wounded there.

"Your cousin Jeff has written me about the latest developments on the border," she quavered as I drew her inside. Mary brought us some strong, hot raspberry tea. My aunt was so distraught, she just set the cup rattling back into the saucer and handed me his letter, unable to tell it, or to read aloud.

Dear Mother,

I am well though the Food is terrible and I have no clean linen. If I had been raised like some here I would just steal some off a line, but you and Pap always tanned me good for my Sins and the lesson has stuck. Our troops are inflicting a world of misery on our own, evicting folks right and left. Soon we shall make a Wasteland of the whole western border. Some like this Work a great deal, but I have had my fill. Yesterday we were in company with a troop of Kansas federals who dragged an old man from his house and three times hung him to a tree. They searched the place for silver, used an axe on locked doors, threw over trunks and ripped up bedticks. At the last they knocked the lid off a Casket where his deceased Wife lay. One cut the dead woman's finger off for her gold Wedding band, and pocketed both. Then our captain told the two daughters, "If you want to plant the old lady, drag her out now, for we aim to fire this ranch to the ground." I helped the girls carry the coffin out, unable to abide anyone to treat a Mother so. I got a reprimand, while they ran out and cut down their father, pretty near dead, too, by then. No wonder some folks ride in the Night without uniforms. They may have the right idea after all.

I Remain
Your Loving Son,
Jeff.

"I fear he may join up with secesh raiders," said Aunt Mamie. "Perhaps William Quantrill's wild bunch."

"Mr. Quantrill is said to be kind to women and children," I offered, for lack of any other comforting words. "And he doesn't kill his prisoners."

"Oh, but he's an outlaw, nonetheless!" She began to cry. "My poor boy. He wasn't raised to be a criminal."

I patted her shoulder and pointed out that as far as we knew, Jeff was still in the U.S. Army, not an outlaw at all. "If things get worse, perhaps he'll merely resign and emigrate West, like Samuel Clemens did."

Then I told her how Sam and two others, all riverboat pilots, had dutifully reported to a general in St. Louis early in the war. But when Sam discovered they were supposed to go up the Missouri River in pursuit of our own governor, he'd slipped out a window and run to our house. "I told 'em we's *Mississippi* pilots," he railed. "It ain't a bit the same."

"What now, Sam?" I wondered. "Won't the army be looking for you?"

He shrugged. "I can disappear into the woods good as any fellow. I'm headed to Ralls County, myself and some others, to form our own unit. I won't swear to any damned secessionists, either."

All that summer they'd hid out in a waterlogged camp, drilling in motley clothes with squirrel rifles and shotguns. Sam got a boil. He sprained his ankle. Next we heard, he'd gone West to Nevada with his brother Orion.

"I suppose any young man could do the same," I told Aunt Mamie. She looked vaguely cheered at this benign possibility. I walked her home, where she lived all alone since my uncle had passed away. I sat awhile as she talked of Jeff, and the old days before the war. Her voice was soft and filled with longing, and gradually my mind wandered.

This was the first house I had lived in when we moved to Hannibal. In its front yard I'd first encountered Tom Sawyer, in Indian garb. From my parents' house down the street I'd spied on him and Huck, and followed. Those two had seemed to represent freedom and bravery and invincibility: all the things a girl would be denied in this world. Then one night I'd discovered they were no braver than I, for all their boasting and posing and playacting.

TWO WEEKS AFTER I'D LOST them at the river, I heard from my window the same strange hoarse cat's-yowl. I shinned down the tree and followed Huck and Tom again, trailing them to the old slave cemetery on the far side of town. As they walked along, I heard Huck telling Tom about a wart he had.

"I aim to get rid of it for good," he said. "Or I'm witched."

"But what way?" Tom asked. "Not the toad cure."

They argued about the best method, moving farther into the pale forest of crooked wooden crosses and simple rounded headstones. I found no cover except an old shed inside the entrance. I tried to open its door quietly, to slip inside out of sight, but the rusted hinges gave a ghostly moan. I froze and glanced back, sure I was discovered.

"You hear that?" Tom clutched Huck's sleeve.

Huck nodded. "Ha'nts, sure enough. We best run for it."

But still they stood, as if paralyzed. I slipped around the back of the shed, making a deal of noise pushing through some untrimmed box bushes. Then, in a high, faint voice I called, "Oh woe, oh woe is me! Is someone there?"

Both boys groaned with fear. I ducked and crawled around to the gate again, then stepped out in plain sight. "Why, hello," I said.

They gaped at me, then pretended to relax.

Huck squinted. "Becky Thatcher! What're you doing here?"

I shrugged. "About to ask you the same. This here's my regular stop."

They snorted and elbowed each other. "But you're a girl! They don't go out at night," said Tom.

I crossed my arms and smiled. "So you say."

The wind blew again, and the shed door's cast-iron hinges set to howling. The boys flinched, but when they saw me still acting cool, they held their ground, for it'd be a blow to their dignity to run.

"Oh, pshaw. That old ghost," I said. "Haunts that tumbledown shed night and day. I'm tired of hearing it."

Tom swallowed hard. "It's prob'ly the spirit of a dead slave."

"Prob'ly his master beat him clean to death," Huck agreed. They both were sweating, but still working hard not to show how miserable and scared they felt. And when I recalled the slave beaten at my grandparents' farm, I shivered, too. "Say, I know a way to get rid of it," I told them.

One of my father's new books was all about spiritualists and how they exorcised unfriendly spirits. And how some of them were frauds who rigged up fancy wires and strings and phosphorous cloth to sucker fools out of their money. But the most useful part was the mumbo jumbo spells these charlatans chanted to impress their customers. I'd gone around for a whole day repeating the bogus incantations to myself and laughing, until Mama said I was driving her to distraction.

"Stay here," I ordered. "Don't say a word or you'll ruin it."

In front of the shed I raised my arms and waved them. "Magister Hokum Kabala Sephor!" I cried. "Haunts begone, come back, uh, nevermore."

I wrenched the door open, then slammed it so hard, it stuck fast in the frame. We wouldn't be hearing any more from it that night. I dusted rust flakes off my hands, then strolled back over to the boys.

"Well, I say we make her a Freebooter," Tom proposed. "She's got useful talents."

Huck protested, "She's a girl. Girls drag you down. They want to decorate things and drink tea. They bawl when they get a pinkie scratch. I'm agin it."

But Tom prevailed. I suspected he usually did.

"Now, the initiation. Here's the thing a Freebooter must do," he said. "Give me your blade, Huck."

He grabbed my hand and turned it over. Huck passed him a barlow knife, smiling as if he would relish using it on me. Or perhaps he only hoped I'd scream and run away. Well, I wouldn't, nor did I flinch when Tom made a small cut in my palm, then one in his own. "Now you, Huck," he said.

Huck hesitated, then took the knife and cut himself deeply, looking indifferent when blood welled up, filled his hand, and dripped to the grass. Tom dipped a finger in his own blood, then in Huck's, and solemnly drew an *X* on my forehead. "The pirate's cross," he said, and even Huck looked reverent then. "It has to be made with the blood of two members."

"But what about my blood?" I asked, raising my palm.

Tom said, "You got to draw a cross on each of us with it. And say these words: *Hoodoo conjure man bind my tongue.*"

I took my turn, feeling Huck's skin shiver and crawl under my hand like a wild animal's pelt. I managed to say the words without snickering once.

"Just one last thing," said Tom.

"There's more?"

"You got to strip to your drawers and run around the graveyard," said Huck, grinning.

Tom rolled his eyes. "No she don't."

He spit in his hand and told me to do the same. "Come on now, Huck," he said. Together we executed an awkward three-pronged handshake so complicated, I doubt I could ever repeat it. I resisted the urge to wipe my bloody hand on my dress. Imagining what Trenny would say on laundry day when she saw the grass stains and dirt was bad enough. Then we went home, the wart cure apparently forgotten.

So I was one of them at last. Still, I didn't feel as excited as I'd expected to; knowing I'd fooled them made it less of a triumph. And I didn't like the way Huck glared at me whenever Tom wasn't paying attention—as if he hated me more than school, even more than he'd hate to be made to dress up and act civilized. Not that he was dangerous. But Huck wasn't a person who'd do what you expected most of the time. He was ragged and unmannerly and proud of it. The motherless son of the town drunk, he'd raised himself like a wolf cub in the woods. I'd seen him be kind to a stray dog on the street, then steal apples from the grocer. All the way home he glowered and sulked. I understood he'd jump at the first opportunity to make Tom hate me.

I also knew better than to tell any of the other girls I was one of Tom and Huck's gang. But somehow word always gets out. The girls at school, who'd all known each other from birth, had never been very friendly. Now they shunned me, aside from Susy Harper. Her father was the town librarian, and she loved books as much as I did. All that reading had broadened her; she despised simpering and preening and rocking doll babies, too. Though unlike me she did dream of being a fine lady someday, and running a charity for orphans.

The others made fun of her spectacles, saying too much reading had ruined her eyes. When Laura Wheeler and Amy Lawrence turned their backs on me, and pointed and laughed at Susy, we went off holding hands, talking about books. We organized a walking club with just ourselves as members. Even so, I didn't dare tell Susy I sneaked out at night with boys, either. If she ever told her parents, they'd surely tell the Judge or Mama. So there was no one I could share my triumph with. No one at all.

"YOU'RE MILES AWAY, DEAR," said Aunt Mamie, making me jump. "My, don't you look peaked, too. I swan. With all the men gone, we'll just waste away to nothing."

I had to bite my lip. Aunt Mamie was no featherweight and in little danger of wasting, even after days without sustenance. Nor were we all that desperate, not yet. I made my good-byes and went home, after promising to write Cousin Jeff to remind him of his Christian duty to his mother, and of his law-abiding upbringing. Life in Hannibal sounded dull indeed put that way. I began to envy him even his slim choices, for day by day it seemed ours were dwindling fast.

THAT NIGHT I DREAMED Sid was lost in a dark wood, calling for me. But when I woke, it was Gage crying down the hall, in the grip of a night terror. I rolled out of bed, hissing at the chilly bare wood floor. We'd stopped adding to the fire before bedtime, trying to make what firewood we had last awhile, with no one to cut more except me.

I hurried down the hall, shivering, rubbing my arms under the flannel nightgown. I slid into bed with Gage, pushing Marmalade, Polly's old orange cat, farther toward the footboard to make room. "What's wrong, pumpkin?"

"The bad men," he gasped, clinging like a possum. "They tried to put me in a box." My son peered up, as if to judge whether I understood the seriousness of this. And why a big boy of seven was right to be frightened. "It's dark in there, Mama."

"Of course it is. And you don't have to get in. I'm here to chase them off."

I whispered a made-up story about a boy who lived in Hannibal and owned a magical talking cat that protected him. They had to get rid of a giant who was walking through town, squashing things.

". . . so the cat found a gun which was so enormous, it didn't load with balls or shot, but with anything big you could stuff into it. Like a smoked ham or a fat lady's corset."

Gage clapped a hand over his mouth and snorted. I smiled. Men, young and old, were so easily entertained.

". . . then together they dragged the gun downtown," I continued, "and propped it up high on the church steeple. So when the giant came their way, they aimed it—"

He clutched my arm. "But *what* did they stuff in it?"

"Oh. Well, this time, a whole herd of fat porcupines."

His eyes widened. "But how?"

"Very carefully. Now let me get on with the story. So when they fired the gun, the giant was stuck up all over with very mad porcupines and so he went crying home to his mother. And the boy and his cat . . ."

I glanced down at Gage, whose head was nodding. "Well, they were great heroes. And lived happily ever after, and didn't play with guns ever again."

I slid carefully from under the quilt, shivering again immediately. I tiptoed out, stepping over the squeaky board at the threshold. I went across the hall to Mary's door. Her breathing was slow, only a bit labored.

Still a nocturnal creature, I often roamed the house while others slept. Reassured to see my family safely in place, even if the viewing cost me yawns throughout the day, and shadows beneath my eyes like bruises.

I moved on to baby Tyler. He lay on his stomach in a shaft of moonlight, thumb sliding from his pursed mouth. He was still covered, which was unusual. I tugged the blanket up to his neck. My littlest boy looked like a bisque angel, skin fair and smooth, his upturned cheek plump and curved as a cherub's. I wanted to touch that sweet dreaming face, but Tyler was a light sleeper and everyone needed their rest. So I smoothed the wool over his back and turned to go back to my room.

At the doorway, I hesitated.

The baby was such a light sleeper, he often woke in the night if an owl hooted, or the neighbors several houses down hosted a cat fight. The least noise could set him off. A bit earlier, Gage had been wailing for me at the top of his lungs, yet I'd not heard a peep from Tyler.

I rushed back to the crib, feeling like a ninny. Hadn't he looked fine? He'd been well all day, eaten a good dinner of peas and sweet potatoes. He'd smiled when I put him down in the crib, and made no fuss. Just looked up and said, "Mum-Mum," his name for me.

I reached out to pull the covers back, to soothe my fears. My hand stalled halfway there. Go on, I told myself. Go on, wake the baby and everyone else to prove you're a fool.

His little cheek was so white in the moonlight. Too cool under my fingers. I flipped him over quickly, then hauled him up out of the crib. "Dear Lord," I whispered. "Dear Lord God, please."

Even through his nightgown, he felt faintly warm. But he didn't wake when I whispered in his ear, or when I pinched his fat little wrist, or even when I shook him gently. I rushed to the window, where the silver moonlight was strongest. His eyes were open just the slightest bit, but they were looking at something beyond this world.

My screams brought Mary running. She snatched Tyler up and clutched him so hard that, had any life still been in him, he would've screamed in outrage. The only noise was coming from me. At last I stuffed a fist in my mouth to stop those terrible sounds. So poor Gage didn't hear; so he wouldn't wake and wander in, and be cursed with worse nightmares than he already had.

Six

THE COLOR BLACK HAS ITS own dull weight and smell. It stinks of dead crows and musty frock coats and the sticky pitch that oozes in some spots from the yellow Missouri dirt like the Devil's blood. My baby Tyler lay cold and stiff in the small back room behind the kitchen, and I stood stirring an iron wash pot in the backyard. The cauldron held a witch's poison, dye that bubbled black as Hell. Our best dresses, mine and Mary's, swirled round in the sickening vortex, offering up their lilacs and greens and rose pinks for grief.

Surely the world would know at a glance we were mourning. How could it matter what we covered our bodies with now?

Still I stirred like a clockwork mannequin, until my wrists and shoulders screamed. Until sweat sogged my chemise and mixed with lifting gray steam to glue my house dress to my skin like wallpaper. Until I went away somewhere, a foggy place where I knew no one and no one knew me, or expected me to move or speak or even breathe more than necessary. At last Mary came out, took my arm, and led me inside. She made me chew a cold biscuit and drink hot bitter coffee—also black, for there was no more cream. The cow's in mourning, too, I thought, sitting at table with a mouthful of dry, bitter crumbs.

Out in the yard Mary was wrestling with the paddle, fishing the heavy cloth out, wringing each piece and struggling to throw the wet black dresses over the line, then peg them in place. I should've helped, but I only sat and watched. As if my sister-in-law were an actress performing in a play, and I was the audience, with no responsibility beyond the price of the ticket. Oh, yes, that price had been more than enough for me.

How would I ever tell Sid? Impossible to shape the words on paper, string them in a sensible line where they could be seen and not denied. I looked back on my childhood and saw nothing that might've prepared a person for this. God was a Holy Monster to let children sicken and suffer, to let us worry and wring our hands. And then—oh, then!—he let the poor babe recover. Let us mortal fools drop our guard and heave a sigh of relief, so He could swoop on black wings and steal away what we loved.

Of course children sometimes died. But the only one I'd known up till then was Jimmy Hodges, a boy who'd gone to the Hannibal school with me. He lived in the house behind my aunt and uncle's, an only child like me. His mother had screamed when they came to tell her. Screamed so long, she lost her voice, then refused to speak or to leave the house at all for six years after Jimmy drowned.

How was it a child given all the care and good food and love in the world could die, when an unloved, orphaned stray like Huckleberry Finn survived, even thrived on neglect? The day before, as I'd straggled down Main Street to the undertaker's to choose a casket, I'd seen Huck standing motionless, shadowed by the post office awning, battered felt hat clutched to his chest.

Earlier that day he'd left an offering, a lopsided black wreath, on our front step. Mary had seen him prop it against the door and sidle away. It was as if he were watching over us, though why he should take such trouble was beyond me. Perhaps since I'd married Sid, Huck counted me as family to Tom. And I was no longer likely to come between him and his best friend again.

Not that I'd ever held so much influence. Despite Huck's disapproval, I became a member in good standing of their sacred band, the Freebooters.

Included in the weekend war games and secret nighttime wanderings, when I could get out. The first time, Tom talked me into meeting him at the foot of Cardiff Hill, where the whole gang would be gathering.

We both arrived late. The boys had already begun their game, a higgledy-piggledy cross between Robin Hood's Merry Men and Pirate Blackbeard's Revenge. To play it, they'd stripped off trousers and jackets, some even their shirts. So when we came up the hill, and this skivvy-clad bunch of desperadoes saw a female was infiltrating their ranks, they ran shouting away, yanking shirttails down to cover their skinny asses. I tried not to laugh, but couldn't help it.

Slowly, with much grumbling, they returned more fully dressed. Without raising a finger or saying a word, I'd become a damper on them, on the whole heart of the game. Like an unwanted chaperone. Like a mother.

"Strip off whatever you like," I said, yawning. "Makes no difference to me."

They looked at each other, aghast.

"And what d'you aim to strip off?" said a jeering voice. Huck, of course.

"Not a stitch, for I'm afflicted with a rare condition. Too much exposure to fresh air, on a day when the moon will come out full later, causes me to turn wild. Fur grows on me like a cat, and claws, too. My folks keep me inside those nights, so I do no harm to any unsuspecting soul whose path I might cross."

I gambled none were readers of the Farmer's Almanac, since I had no idea of the moon's phases that month. Anyhow, these boys believed in the most blatant superstitions: that if you buried a marble in a secret place, and said incantations over it, all the marbles you'd ever lost in your life would gather there, in a rolling, clinking reunion. I'd heard them discussing this scientific phenomenon outside the schoolhouse.

After I'd explained my condition, a silence fell. Sammy Clemens goggled like a redheaded frog. Then Tom began to laugh. The others joined in, while still casting cautious looks at me.

Tom retrieved a wooden broadsword and a homemade bow and arrow from a clump of brush. I claimed the bow, since I'd had archery lessons at the Lydia Parks Academy back in St. Louis. I'd done so well, Papa brought the target and bow set from our old home, and had set it up in our new backyard.

After each person was armed, we began to play Freebooters of the Mississippi. The game mainly consisted of some boys claiming to have killed others by some pretend means, and then their pretend victims would hotly deny it. Now and then someone did get hurt. Then they either set out for revenge, or broke down and cried, depending on age and disposition.

After a half hour Jimmy Hodges got thumped on the head by Joe Harper with the blunt end of a sword. "I quit," he yelled, blubbering. He threw down his own sword and ran off, while the older boys jeered and called insults. Then my cousin Jeff got a bloody nose from one of Ben Rogers's wild swings, but he only paused to wipe it with a handful of dried grass, then went on flailing away again. Though I hadn't been aiming for him, I hit Joe Harper in the back with an arrow—they were blunt and sparse on feathers, inclined to shoot off in any direction. Tom rushed up to finish him off. But even after he'd been beat energetically about the shoulders with the flat of Tom's sword, Joe stayed stubbornly on his feet.

"Fall," cried Tom. "Dang it, Joe! Why don't you fall?"

"Fall yourself," said Joe hotly. "I give you the worst of it, last duel."

"You know I can't," Tom reasoned. "I'm Robin Hood. He never falls. Says so in the book."

Joe thought on this, and was persuaded by weight of the printed page. He stiffened and toppled, clutching his chest, kicking up clods of dirt and leaves. He lay still a moment, then leapt up. "Now you got to let me kill you. That's only fair and square."

"Well, I can't," Tom insisted. "See, it ain't in the book."

Their jaws were moving faster than the game. I yawned and wandered off, drawn by the sound of running water. On the far side of the hill was a branch that, upstream, fed into the Mississippi. I'd worked up a sweat. So a nice cool wade sounded more entertaining than a round of legal arguments. I hiked up my skirts and slid down the bank.

Leaning over to take off my shoes and stockings, I saw him. A boy, floating inches below the surface, face up. His eyes were open, but he seemed to be looking beyond me to something astonishing. His arms drifted at his sides, as if he might lift from the water and take to the sky at any moment. His jacket and hair rippled like water weeds. "Oh!" I said, so stunned, I lost my balance and sat down hard on the bank.

Perhaps I should've been afraid, except I recognized him. "Jimmy Hodges," I whispered. "What's happened to you?"

Jimmy was a bit of a baby, but nice enough. He liked to throw a ball against our fence, and haul himself up on my aunt's rose trellis, peer over and talk to me.

I inched nearer. A ripple in the water, which might have been a catfish or the tide from upstream, caused one of his arms to lift in a lazy salute, as if he were taking his leave of me. He rolled slowly, slowly, in the current. That broke the spell, and I went scrambling up the bank for the others. I feared they wouldn't believe, due to my earlier story, until I'd taken them down and shown them.

I got Tom to stop the game. We all trooped solemnly to the branch. Jimmy had drifted farther out. "Somebody must go in and get him," said Tom.

The boys looked horrified. Their gazes wandered to each other's pale faces, then skittered away. Tom leaned out and poked at Jimmy with a long branch. "He's caught on something. Here, we'll draw straws."

Jeff collected twigs. I was elected to hold them in my closed fist as one after another we drew lots. When everyone had taken a twig, Huck suddenly scowled and pointed. "How come *she* ain't taking one?"

Before Tom could open his mouth, I said, "Because I get the one that's left."

We all compared twigs. I was terrified mine, which looked very small, would be the loser. Instead, the shortest fell to Sammy Clemens. He looked greenish, but swallowed and nodded. He paddled out and dived under, groping around until he'd freed Jimmy's shirt from whatever'd snagged it.

Sammy burst up out of the water gasping. I heard him vomiting into the weeds as two of the bigger boys waded into the shallows, grasped Jimmy's limp ankles, and dragged him onto the bank. There he lay like a landed catfish, belly-white.

The smaller ones began to cry then, and want their mothers. I yanked on my stockings, which stuck like flypaper to my wet legs, as the boys struggled back into their clothes. As I buckled my shoes, I saw my companions had dragged on any item that came to hand, getting the wrong size shirts, and britches on inside out or backwards. We ran fast as we could to town, the older ones dragging the younger by the hand, for no one wanted to stay and sit with poor Jimmy.

We grabbed the first adult we saw on the streets—the Dutch black-smith, Hans Bledel. He grinned at our raggle-tag, mismatched crew. But when I'd caught my breath and blurted out what we'd seen, he swayed on his feet. His face and wheat-blond hair were suddenly the same shade. It took me a while to understand why: The terrible news had been lifted off our shoulders, and put on Mr. Bledel's. He would have to break it to Jimmy's parents. I think that was when I truly understood Jimmy wouldn't sit up back on the creek bank and laugh at us for running off. That this was no adventure, or even a ghost story, but the blackest day in the lives of people I actually knew.

I WAS LEARNING MORE of blackness almost twenty years later, under-standing all too well what it had felt like for the Hodges family, back then. The Judge arrived half-shaven, looking as if he'd forgotten how to dress himself. His suspenders hung down behind; his collar stuck out on one side like a broken wing. Trenny was not here to stop him a minute and do up overlooked braces or buttons.

By noon neighbors were turning up with pickled eggs and skillets of corn bread and pies. Or baked yams and shaved bits of salt beef, all some had left to offer at this point in the occupation. The ladies wanted to hold my hands and comfort me, and talk about their own losses. Our house was a cave of whispers and drifting dust motes, of silence broken by muf-fled sobs. Mary had walked Gage down to the Bixbys earlier, so he could play with their dog, out of the way. I hadn't wanted him to see us wash and dress his little brother, then lay him away like last season's clothes in the tiny coffin delivered to our back door that morning. It might seem too much like the box the bad men of his dream had tried to wrestle him into.

The next day we all walked to the church under a constant mizzle and a gray sky. The rain did not let up when the time came to proceed to the cemetery. As we waded down the muddy street, white and black town folk stood at attention along the way, faces long and sorrowful. All blurs behind the black veil on my hat, a curtain I'd drawn against the world. Then I didn't have to look at anyone, even if he was talking to me. I was free to pretend this ceremony was a formality, or a dream that still might not come to pass.

The minister droned about God calling a little lamb to his side. I counted up all we'd lost; my mother hiding in Virginia like a child, my husband and my cousin off somewhere fighting rebels, or maybe raiders, or perhaps dead by now, too, Jim, more family than employee, wrenched away by unknown persons, for some unknown purpose. And now Tyler.

My father, the respected judge renowned for his quick wit and deep intellect, for the many opinions he'd flawlessly written, stood next to me slack-faced, lost as a child. Gage fidgeted on my other side. My oldest son wouldn't feel the full loss of his brother for years—if he recalled him by then. When I stroked my father's hand, the skin felt loose and aged.

The day after we'd fished Jimmy Hodges from the creek, I climbed Holliday's Hill alone. I hadn't wanted to go with one of the boys, because I felt like crying, and that was something I couldn't do in front of them.

Jimmy was dead. I truly felt it as I looked down the hill to the surging tan waters of the Mississippi rushing to the sea. If he'd been carried by the creek that far, we'd never have known what had become of him, or where he'd ended up. I supposed Jimmy—his soul, that is—was up in Heaven, as my mother had said at dinner the night before.

"Is that right, Jimmy?" I asked out loud.

Of course he didn't answer. I hadn't expected his voice to pour down on me, like God's own, from that blue china bowl of sky. Yet somehow the silence made me fear Jimmy's soul was not in Heaven at all, but trapped in the cold still body that lay in a varnished pine casket in his parents' parlor. I felt a strange, terrible guilt for not saving him. For simply being alive when he was not. Yet even as I felt these things, beneath that guilt had pressed an unseemly joy that I was not the one who'd drowned.

But now, standing in the rain at our son's funeral, I knew that furtive guilt, that sneaking joy, would never come. I would've traded places in an instant with Tyler, whose innocent soul must surely be in Heaven.

Is that right, Tyler?

Only when my father gripped my arm, and I glanced up to see shocked faces all turned and staring, did I realize I'd said it out loud.

THE FOLLOWING MONDAY I put on my black dress, which still reeked of acrid dye, and returned to headquarters in case Lieutenant Dickenson had news of Jim. I climbed the steps so slowly this time, my dress might have taken on the weight of lead along with its coloring. The sentries on the steps again looked me up and down boldly, until I lifted my veil and stared back. Then they became suddenly engrossed in the tarnish on their buttons.

As I approached his desk, the lieutenant kept at his work. Head down, he merely held out one hand wearily. Perhaps he'd been expecting more papers, or his pay envelope, or a ham biscuit. When I didn't move he glanced up, then flinched and shoved back in his chair. The wooden wheels squealed as he struggled to his feet.

"Please don't bother," I said. "Is there any news?"

He sank back, wincing. "Some recruiters are rumored to be dragooning freed slaves into the army, and pocketing the bounty cash. But it's only rumor."

"Not to Jim," I pointed out. "And, as I told you before, he's not a slave. He was freed years ago. By us, not Mr. Lincoln."

He smiled without humor. "That was magnanimous of you."

I leaned over and slapped him, a dull smack as my gloved hand connected with his cheek. "You know nothing of me. Or my family. Don't speak about any of us."

He rubbed his jaw. "Beg your pardon. You're right, of course." He did look sorry, and also tired, the circles under his eyes even darker, the skin around his scar paler.

"They took Jim's mule, too," I said. "He paid a hundred dollars of his hard-earned cash for it. Slaves don't earn wages, in case they didn't teach you that in Yankee Land."

"They did. But apparently they neglected to tell the fellows who took him. If indeed they were our boys. Won't you have a seat?"

We stared at each other as if in some sort of contest. "No," I said, laying my reticule on the edge of his desk, like a weapon.

Dickenson leaned forward, hands clasped, elbows on the desk. "Mrs. Hopkins, some things in this war are not, strictly speaking, from Hardee's *Tactics*. I don't like them any more than you do."

"But I'm not roaming New Hampshire emptying your pantry or setting fire to your house."

He nodded. "True. But my home's in Massachusetts."

I didn't care if it was in Hades. "You have my address. If you hear of Jim, tell me at once."

I turned to go, but his voice stopped me. "The Department of the South *has* let their agents impress Negroes—boys as young as fourteen, men with families. Their excuse is Lincoln's executive order from last January. That able-bodied freed slaves may now be enlisted to fight the rebels, by navy or army. I know the Massachusetts Fifty-fourth—"

His eyes narrowed, as if suddenly noticing some difference. "Your dress. Pardon me, but have you had word of your husband?"

"I'm not a widow, so far as I know. The mourning is for my baby. Our youngest son."

He bit his lip and fiddled with some papers, aligning them with the corner of the desk. "Please accept my condolences. I have a new daughter back in Boston I've not yet seen."

I didn't want to picture him as a father, a husband surrounded by children. To think he had a wife sitting at home worrying as I did about Sid. All I wanted was information. And to be left alone.

"As you said, the war has come to us. And we must go along." I turned and walked out quickly, so he couldn't lurch over awkwardly to take my elbow or follow to bow me out. I almost wanted to stay and ask more questions; I actually felt a vague interest in his opinions. I had to smother the urge to tell him more about Tyler. But then I might beg the lieutenant to reveal, if he knew it, the secret of how to bear such a loss and yet stay sane.

I hurried out, staring straight ahead. Descending the steps I saw a familiar figure in front of the apothecary: Huck Finn, bent to tighten the girth on his saddle. He slowly turned his head, as if he'd been waiting for me. He, too, wore a blue jacket with brass buttons. Of course, as the lieutenant had noted, so many did these days. But by the time I reached the street, Huck was gone.

Seven

H UCK WAS BECOMING a living haunt, or at least an unwelcome
mascot. I felt certain he'd never stopped hating me, yet now I
saw him often. In the old days, if you spotted Huck, Tom wasn't
far behind, and vice versa. But Tom had been gone a long while, and there
was no reason to expect him back. Especially considering what had happened the last time we'd met.

I still carried the letter I'd written to Sid about Tyler, and though I would
rather spare him that terrible news, it needed mailing. I crossed the street to
the post office and stood in line behind two men in the mud-splattered boots
and bib overalls of farmers. We all waited for Bill Walter, the postmaster, to
finish selling penny stamps, one at a time, to old Miss Nita Kennet, as she
complained in a shaky tremolo about the ever-rising cost of sending a parcel.

The man right in front of me cleared his throat, then looked around; I
supposed for a spittoon. At last he gave up and hawked onto the floor. "Hear
our riverboat pilots is in as high demand as ever," he remarked to the fellow
ahead of him.

The other man nodded. "A line of work beats farming every time. They
say as how commerce is stopped. But I tell you, goods is still coming in for
those what got cash."

The other snorted. "I ain't talking 'bout goods, now. Don't you know they wants 'em to pilot boats up and down the river? Ferry troops. You know, for the War."

"By damn. Who does?"

"Why, the federals. And the secesh, come to that. All the good pilots been snapped up. Why, there's Bixby, and Dick Kennet, and—"

"And Tom Sawyer, don't forget."

The first man looked nervous. "Nah. He ain't working for nobody now."

"The hell he ain't. I tell you, I saw—"

The first tilted his head and cut his eyes in my direction. His companion glanced at me. They snatched off hats and mumbled apologies.

I smiled faintly. "No, it's all right. I couldn't help but overhear, though. Did you say Tom Sawyer was piloting for the federals?"

The first man shook his head vigorously. "No'm. He ain't been heard of for some time. Could be he taken off for the West."

The second man opened his mouth again, and the first elbowed him hard in the ribs.

"That's right," the second one gasped. "Wouldn't surprise me none if he's gone off to Californy."

Miss Kennet turned from the window and walked out, lips pursed, counting her spondulicks. "Next," called Bill Walter wearily from the barred wicket.

After the first man went up, I couldn't draw his friend into conversation. He worked hard to avoid my gaze while smiling at whatever I said. He finally commenced whistling "A Mighty Fortress Is Our God" very far off-key.

By the time I left, there was still no sign of Huck. But I hadn't imagined him lurking there, pretending to adjust his saddle. Why was he shadowing me like a bashful, smitten suitor?

I scuffed home slowly, for being indoors now made me so heavy with sadness, I could scarcely lift my head. If I went out early and moved along at a brisk pace doing errands, for short spaces I could briefly forget there were no longer two boys waiting at home. I could still imagine them together in Aunt Polly's garden: Gage stalking the grizzled old tabby, Tyler lurching awkwardly behind, big for his age. His tottering gait and clumsy swipes at the cat's tail predicting that he might never be so quick or agile as

Gage. And his round-cheeked face and sweet smile, assuring us it would not matter.

But a grim silence had fallen over Polly's old house. No high-pitched shrieks; no answering shouts of brotherly rage. Gage still played with those cherished lead soldiers, which his baby brother would never again snatch away. But he did so listlessly, all battle sounds subdued. He'd asked twice yesterday about his brother, and each time I sat and explained. "Remember our talk yesterday? Tyler has gone from us to be with God."

He'd nodded, looking interested. "But when will he be back?"

I tried again. "He isn't coming back, because he's so happy up there." Then I had an inspiration. "But we'll be able to join him later."

This new information seemed to alarm Gage. His face crumpled and he clutched my skirt. "But I don't want to die! When Papa comes home, he won't be able to find us."

When you could barely lift your own head, or move from room to room to accomplish everyday tasks, how exhausting it felt to explain to a seven-year-old even ordinary things, much less the intricacies of Christian theology. I pulled Gage onto my lap. "Oh, darling, I only meant we will see him again, but a long time from now. You aren't going to die. Not for so many years that we needn't worry about it at all."

He wiped his nose on my skirt and looked up again. "A hundred years?"

"That's right."

I thought I'd reassured him, but he still looked pale and worried. He didn't seem to be having nightmares, yet he refused to get into bed unless I sat in the rocker until he fell asleep. When the Judge came for a meal, Gage climbed in his grandfather's lap and clung to him, all clutching arms and gripping legs. He dogged Mary and me from room to room as if afraid to be alone, even in daylight.

I understood, though. It wasn't just Tyler's death. Too many things were changing around us, enough to make adults uneasy, even frightened. How must the talk of war, the absences of beloved fathers, the grim-faced soldiers in our streets all seem to a child? I wanted to be comforted, too; we all did. But my husband had marched away, and making sure we had three meals, firewood, enough water—the bare necessities—took up most of my time. Comfort, physical and spiritual, had become a luxury.

I had no one to talk to. No close female friend since Susy Harper had married and moved to South Carolina before the War. No letters from her lately, either; I could only imagine what she must be going through down there. Of course there was Mary, but my sister-in-law was so sweet and optimistic, not a person you wished to burden with dark fears. Unlike me, she'd always been good—and certain everyone else was, too. How could I tell her I hated living in this silent, grieving house, eating cornmeal and dried apples, enduring the pitying glances of neighbors? I couldn't complain about such things while Sid was undoubtedly in worse circumstances, perhaps wounded or ill.

I couldn't tell Mary that sometimes, late at night, I still heard my baby crying. That during the dark hours I feared Tyler was calling me to come get him from a cold, lightless, faraway place. And most frightening, that once I'd woke and found myself downstairs long after we'd all gone to bed, wrestling with the locked front doorknob, desperate to go somewhere at three o'clock in the morning.

My churning thoughts frightened me so at times I wished for a sensible, practical man to talk to. Then I might be able to feel brave, to behave like the woman of the house. Mary would assume I only pined for Tyler, and for Sid. It would never be possible to confide that I still thought, sometimes, about her beloved, absent cousin. Or that the comfort I craved, and the person I longed most to talk to was not her, or my own mother, or the Judge, or even—most shamingly—my own dear, absent husband.

No, God help me. It was still Tom Sawyer.

DESPITE HUCK'S DISAPPROVAL, Tom and I had become friends, and finally sweethearts. Huck didn't go to school, so Tom and I walked home together after class. He waited outside for me the first day. His cousin Sid followed me out of the schoolhouse, talking about a story we'd just read. I hadn't minded; I liked the way Sid had read his part aloud, not mumbling and halting and mispronouncing all the words like most boys did, but in a clear, sure voice, as if he really might be one of the characters.

When Tom spotted Sid, he snapped, "Go on home and play with Mary. I hear her calling you."

Sid held his ground. They were about the same height, though Tom was bigger in the shoulders. "You can't tell me what to do," Sid said, frowning.

"Go on now, Siddy." Tom took a step forward. "You ain't no Freebooter."

"Neither are you," Sid shot back. "It's just a stupid game." But he turned abruptly and walked off, shoulders hunched. I felt a little sorry to see him go, for Tom never wanted to talk about books. Soon, though, he had me laughing, and I forgot about their quarrel.

Gradually, grudgingly, most of the gang—Ben, Jeff, Joe, the worshipful Sammy Clemens—had accepted me. Only Huck stayed sullen, and sometimes flared out openly hateful. He tried everything to run me off. But when he slipped a dead frog down the back of my dress, I shook it out and borrowed Tom's barlow knife. Then I showed the Freebooters how to properly dissect an amphibian, telling them the names of each internal organ, the way my father had taught me.

Another time Huck pushed me into the branch in December, its waters so freezing cold, they burned my skin. I whooped and laughed and splashed, pretending to have such a good time paddling around all the others jumped in, too. All but Huck, who stood glowering on the bank. His eyes, his clenched fists, every part of him hating me.

He didn't seem to understand that his sour moods drove Tom away, and made him want to spend more time with me. But I could see it, and it was sweet revenge to do nothing to make life easier for Huck. Maybe I should've felt bad about coming between two old friends. But Huck was so hard and cold and hateful, I didn't. I rejoiced in the growing notion that I knew Tom better than Huck, better than anyone else in this world ever would.

One day when Tom and I were out alone on Holliday's Hill, we decided to play at soldiers and redskins. "But I got to be the soldier," he said. "And you run through the woods whooping till I catch you."

"You were the soldier last time," I protested. "Come to think of it, the time before, too. No, I believe I'll be the soldier today. You can put the turkey feather in your hair this time. That's fair, Tom. You know it is."

He bit his lip and looked away. "No."

I pushed the bedraggled feather into this hands. "Oh, don't make such a pernickety fuss. Put it on."

To my amazement, his eyes reddened and filled with tears. My first shocked instinct was to make fun, for I thought he must be joking. Tom Sawyer never cried. Not even when the schoolmaster beat him until his hands bled. But still uncertain, I forced my laugh back down. "What is it?"

He sat down suddenly and put his head in his hands. "I never told nobody."

I dropped beside him, though the ground was mucky and the damp immediately soaked through my wool skirt and petticoat. "Tell me, then. Aren't we sweethearts? And they tell everything, just like married folks. And then are sworn to secrecy."

He lifted his head a little, but still didn't look at me. "Or hope to die?"

I nodded solemnly. "That's right."

He sighed and glanced away, at the hills. I thought he wasn't going to say anything after all, but he blurted out, "It's because of my folks. And how they died."

I knew he'd lived with his aunt Polly since he was hardly more than a baby. Sid and Mary were Polly's children. She called Tom son, but he was in fact her nephew. I didn't know how this arrangement had come about. Other children in town might have only one parent, or a stepmother or stepfather, because their real mother or father had died. But Tom was the only one in Hannibal I knew of who had neither father or mother. Even Huck had a daddy, as worthless a scoundrel as old Pa Finn was.

I laid a hand on Tom's forearm; his rough cotton sleeve felt warm from the sun. "You can tell me if you want. But you don't have to."

He shook his head, then slowly nodded. "Well, see, it's just this. I don't come from here. I was born on the western border."

"Oh, over near Kansas? I didn't know that." It wasn't so unusual. I'd come to Hannibal by way of St. Louis. Sammy Clemens had been born in a tiny Missouri village called Florida, before his folks moved here. Several of the other girls came from Palmyra, up the road. So clearly there had to be more to it.

I waited, and at last Tom told me. "My folks moved from Palmyra out to the border in '36, to start a farm. They were making a go of it by the time I was born. But when I was still just a toddling baby, my ma and pa were murdered in a red Indian raid."

That sounded odd, though. The Indian Removal Act had happened further back, in 1830. I knew because the Judge had been one of the few white men who'd disapproved of it. The Big Swindle, he still called it: our government purchasing so much Indian homeland for a thousand dollars. And the Judge scoffed at any mention of the so-called Black Hawk Wars, during which he said a band of vigilantes had hunted down and butchered unarmed Indian women, then shot their silent, terrified children from the trees like windfall fruit. The pitiful remnants of the Sauk tribe had then been forced west, to reservations in Kansas.

"Real red Indians," I said slowly, carefully, for I didn't want Tom to think I was scoffing. "In '38. You sure?"

He scowled. "I weren't nothing but a baby. They told me it was Indians, and I got no call to misbelieve."

I started to suggest something else. For decades Kansas abolitionists had been coming across the border to set slaves free, and raise a ruckus for their cause. They often burned down barns and homes, sometimes even killed folks. In Missouri back then an abolitionist was likened to an earthbound demon with claws and a forked tail. From what I'd heard from gossip and church sermons, abolitionists also dressed up like savages in paint and bear grease, and killed people even on Sunday.

But I didn't know if they'd been doing such things that far back. So I thought better of mentioning it and closed my mouth again.

Tom cleared his throat. "Besides, my folks was kilt in such a way that . . ." He sniffed, and dashed at his eyes. "They was cut up, and . . . and scalped, don't you see? Who else but an Injun would do such as that?"

I shuddered at the visions this conjured, and had to allow he must be right.

"I still dream them in the night," he said, voice choked with unshed tears. "Their red faces painted like Hoodoo masks. They drag me from under the bed and start peeling my skin off with a knife, a little bit at a time. Then . . . then they start to cut off my head, and I wake up."

This fact of Tom's history was not known to any other child in town. Perhaps that's why none of Mark Twain's readers will find it in his famous novel. So imagine how I felt, trusted with the knowledge of Tom's secret demons, privy to the night terrors that made a hero cower and weep and call for parents dead and gone over a decade.

This time when I laid a hand on his arm, he jumped. The way he stared around, I understood something else about Tom Sawyer, the boy unafraid of man or woman or beast. As I'd noted in the cemetery that night, he was terrified of ghosts. But they were the red-skinned phantoms who'd burst into his childhood home with tomahawks and drawn knives, to shed blood while he cried for his mother.

"Tom. *Tom?*" I shook his arm and he turned away, so I wouldn't see he was crying at last. "Tom, I think you're as brave as you are because you cheated death once. And now you ain't scared of it at all."

He looked back at me sharply, to see if I was pulling his leg. "You think so?"

I leaned over and planted a kiss on his cheek, which was gritty with dirt and tasted of salt tears. "I know for a fact." I jumped up and held out a hand, then yanked him to his feet. "Come on," I said. "Get a move on. I'll race you to the top of the hill."

I turned and ran off. Not waiting, deliberately not looking back to see if he would follow. And sure enough, after a moment, I heard him running behind me, gaining ground fast.

IN THAT SIMPLE WAY I had once comforted Tom. Now I could've used similar treatment. But there was no Tom, no Sid, no one else here to give orders or to baby me. I was left in charge, and Mary, Gage, and even my father were relying on me. As for poor, kidnapped Jim, I didn't know if he was alive or dead, or enslaved in Lincoln's army, or sold South by some greedy, bloodthirsty raiders. I had even less clue about his fate than I had about my husband's.

As a child I'd once heard Reverend Sitwell describe the curious institution of human bondage as righteous and sacred—God's plan for protecting the Children of Ham. A condition, he always assured the congregation, for which any right-thinking Negro must truly feel grateful.

Yet even at twelve I knew he was a hypocrite. For just the week before our preacher had sold off a young child born to a slave in his own household. Susy Harper and I had been walking down by the landing when a steamboat started backing off from the pier. Sitwell's cook, Hannah, stood at the water's edge calling for her lost child, who was being carried away on the boat. She wailed and tore at her clothes, shrieking out her grief in cries so wretched and heartbreaking, Susy and I had looked at each other and burst into tears. I ran home to tell the Judge, certain he would do something about it.

He'd listened, looking more and more grieved. He stood, and sat me in his desk chair. "My dear," he said, "you will find this hard to believe. But there is nothing in our law forbidding such crimes against nature. And so, nothing I can do."

The following Sunday I saw my father shake his head as Sitwell preached about the naturally degraded condition of Negroes, and our sacred duty to keep and protect them.

"God-damned Bible-beater," the Judge muttered. My mother had laid a hand on his sleeve. Then he crossed his arms and glowered, but said nothing else aloud.

I'd wanted then to turn around in the pew and look behind me. To crane my neck and gaze up, up to where the black folks, slave and free, sat together in the loft. To see *their* faces when they received this wonderful news. For wouldn't the truth be stamped right there, if they weren't too afraid to let it creep out? But fidgeting earned me a peremptory rap on the head from Mama. A second trespass would mean a full day of tedious chores while I reflected on my errors. So then I, too, sat still.

How confusing it had seemed that if my father was right about slavery, our minister must be wrong. Yet there we sat, listening as if it all made sense. Later, with Tom on Holliday's Hill, it occurred to me that if my father was also right about the Indians, then what Tom had been told so long ago was probably wrong as well. But if my father was wrong and Tom was right, then what else might I have believed all my life and taken for granted that wasn't really true?

A WEEK AFTER I MAILED my letter to Sid, I finally received one from him. I tore the envelope eagerly, nearly damaging the note inside. He was alive, and we were actually having a conversation again! But as I scanned the page, I saw no mention of Tyler's death, no words of grief . . . and it was dated in May, so he'd not yet received my letter. I felt behind me for a chair and lowered myself into it. Sid wrote that he'd been wounded slightly at Centralia, grazed in the side by a minie ball, doctored in the field. A mere flesh injury, he claimed.

I am doing fairly well, and the wound seems to be healing by first intention.

He was recovering in a makeshift hospital in a railroad boarding house. So it was likely he'd be marching again soon, to the southeast. *But perhaps with a different outfit,* he stressed, underlining those words. Twice he mentioned Sterling Price, the former Missouri governor and general. Price had been a solid Union man before federal troops had fired on a gathering of civilians in '61. Since then, he'd been fighting the very government he'd once revered.

Was Sid trying to tell me something about his own allegiances? Surely not, for he'd also be telling the Union agents who were no doubt reading our mail, as a prerogative of war.

He ended the all-too-short note, *Please kiss my dear sons for me.* So he'd not received my latest letter. But was it not more merciful, perhaps, that his youngest child still lived in his mind a few more days?

I slipped the letter back into the envelope, fearing some new insanity was brewing. My husband had gone off for a loyal outfit, not some rebel bunch. Perhaps his wounds were graver than they sounded, the fever so bad, he was delirious. I rose and paced the confines of our parlor, thinking I ought to go to him. But Neosho was far away, in southwestern Missouri. I might even arrive to find they'd moved him.

Then a new thought hit me. If the federals *had* read this letter, Sid might be put in prison, wounded or not. That would either mean Alton, in Illinois, as he was an officer, or else terrible Gratiot Street Prison in St. Louis. Where, along with captured soldiers, women and children were held for feeding husbands or fathers rumored to be rebels, or for cutting telegraph lines, or simply for having the bad luck to be distantly related to a southern raider like Quantrill or Bill Anderson. I vaguely recalled the old prison building on Gratiot: a grim heap, a rats' haven. Full of vermin, damp enough to grow crops of mushrooms, undoubtedly rife with consumption. I thought of all that could befall Sid there, not the least being smallpox.

Well, then, I would have to get to him first. Summer weather would soon give way to fall, and that season in St. Louis could be bitterly cold.

I tied on my bonnet, left Gage with Mary, and set out for federal headquarters again. I would visit once more with Lt. Hiram Dickenson, would
happily endure quaint tales of his old Massachusetts home and smile at all
the appropriate times. If, in exchange, he'd tell me how to find Sid and bring
him home again.

Once I discovered what had become of my husband, I'd bring him back,
public opinion be damned. Even if I had to search the whole state, and tie
Sid to a horse and lead it home. For I was sure only he could get us through
this terrible time. A lawyer, he would know where and how to look for Jim.
Because if I had to face any more silent, pleading looks from Mary, or impatient questions from my father, or think of new ways to reassure Gage—
for there were no decent, satisfying answers to his innocent questions—I
might simply run out into the street screaming.

Eight

WHEN HE GLANCED UP from a ledger and saw me, Hiram Dickenson blinked, then shoved his chair back so quickly, it nearly toppled. He recovered and bowed over a tilting rubble of papers and ink-stained coffee cups and the butts of half-smoked segars. "Mrs. Hopkins. My pleasure again. How may I assist?"

So I told him. He had news, none of it good. I hadn't realized how out of touch I'd gotten, worrying over daily trials such as where to find cornmeal without weevils, or how best to cut new clothes for our family out of the old.

"You do understand this state is under martial law," he said. "There is rebel activity everywhere. You can't just go traipsing around the country-side. No, I can't advise that at all."

"What about St. Louis? And farther south."

"It's not truly safe. There have been skirmishes around Doniphan and Rollo."

"Oh, well, that area," I said, trying not to sound too interested. "What else do you know of the situation?"

He studied me a moment, then looked down at his hands, rubbing at an ink or black powder stain between thumb and forefinger. "You know your governor Jackson and the state legislature wanted to take Missouri out of the Union. Your old home guard's a regular secesh army now. Union militia are our men, and always on the alert down there. It's a hotbed of rebel sentiment, and women with shears tucked under their shawls. They cut the telegraph lines."

Oh yes, Union militia. I knew some here. Riverfront riffraff, mostly; the good men had already gone for the army when it came time for the federals to impose a militia on us as well. What did a man from Massachusetts know of who was a local scoundrel and who a solid citizen? These days I felt only sympathy for any woman who needed to go about armed with shears. Even if they felt inspired to disrupt a Union telegraph carrying dark messages like the ones Missouri had been receiving lately.

He raised one eyebrow. "Have you had some unwelcome news?"

I straightened in my chair and frowned. "I hope you're not implying my husband could be disloyal."

He shook his head. "I'm implying nothing. Only, it's happened before—a complete change of heart. The good news for those who've switched sides is, the Confederates control southern Missouri right now. Any of those captured would be our prisoner. Is he an officer?"

I nodded, mouth too dry to speak.

"Then he'd be sent to Alton, across the river, rather than Gratiot. He could write when he got there, if that happened."

"But he's wounded! In no condition to be sent to such a place," I blurted out without thinking.

The puckered scar at the side of Dickenson's mouth tightened. "No, ma'am. But then hardly anybody is."

"There must be something I could do, if it came to that. My father could write the authorities. He's a judge."

"Ah." Now both eyebrows went up a notch. "I don't suppose he might be Judge Thatcher?"

I nodded. Dickenson had been in town for months; I should have known he'd figure out family relations sooner or later. Or had he made special inquiries?

He ran a hand through his hair until it stood up like a black meringue. "I hadn't quite realized . . . Begging your pardon, Mrs. Hopkins, but I wouldn't have Judge Thatcher write to them."

I drew up to my full seated height, considerable for a woman. It didn't put me quite on eye level with him, but made me feel more in control. "And why not, sir?"

He tapped one stack of papers on his desk. "Tell the truth, we've had complaints," he said in a low voice. "Your father has said unfortunate things to the wrong people. Certain of those have taken offense."

Despite my fear, I almost smiled. The poor man had no way of knowing my father would say anything, to anyone, if he took the notion.

"And then there's the oath," he murmured.

"The loyalty oath?"

"Judge Thatcher refused to take it when I suggested that as a remedy. Your father seems to me perhaps well-meaning, but an outspoken sort."

"He's more loyal than you or I or anyone," I insisted. "An appointed judge for over thirty years, and he upheld the law, federal law, for all that time. He merely hates injustice, and has strong views."

He nodded. "Well, in wartime people often attach great import to things they'd overlook normally. I advised your father to be wary of how he criticizes the U.S. government and its local representatives. Or at least to have a care whom he does it in front of. Or . . . or things might not go well for him."

I felt a coldness creeping into my hands, slithering down my back. The threat was veiled, but a threat nonetheless. How could it be that both Sid and my father might be locked up by the very government they'd honored all their lives, and tried to serve in one way or another? The world made less sense all the time. "I'll remind him you said so. And what would you suggest I do about my husband?"

"Go home. Wait for another letter. And advise all your family to keep in mind the consequences of speaking unwisely around your more flighty neighbors."

I thanked him and left, shoulders dragged down by disappointment. Dickenson was not going to solve my problems that day or any other. The sort of help I needed was not included in his conception of duty.

THAT NIGHT I DREAMED I was boarding a huge black train to go to Sid. The passenger coach was empty, save for me. A fine dusting of soot coated everything. Spiderwebs clogged the corners. I sat anxiously on the edge of the faded bench seat until at last the driving wheel spun, screeching iron against iron. A handful of sparks blew past. We lurched forward, gouts of steam and flakes of ash obscuring the platform outside my grimy window.

A man wearing a shabby uniform staggered in through the storm door. He stopped, legs braced against the rocking, his face shadowed by his hat brim. He held out a hand for the ticket I suddenly realized I'd neglected to buy. But when I fumbled for my purse, he shook his head and tipped his billed cap, and I saw that it was Huck. Too stunned to speak, I craned to watch him amble down the aisle and go out to the next car.

We tore along, rocking side to side, metal plates creaking, tender trucks clattering. Bolts popped like gunshots. The hammering, banging racket grew louder and louder, until I woke and sat up in bed.

Someone was pounding on the front door.

I yanked on a wrapper and ran for the stairs. Still dark out, that gray-quilted light that comes an hour before dawn. Who would knock so early, and so loud? A wonder Mary hadn't heard; her room was closer to the stairs. But she sometimes used our homemade poppy concoction at night if her cough was bad.

I stopped at the foot of the stairs, thinking of one likely, chilling answer to my question. Soldiers sent to turn us out. I thought longingly of the Judge's pistol, which lay far away, in another house, in an unlocked drawer in his desk. But that was the madness of being still half-sleeping. Murdering soldiers was no solution; hundreds more would only take their place. We saw them on the streets every day, multiplying like pond mosquitoes.

Besides, behind the etched glass of the front door stood just one slight figure outlined in moonlight. Surely they'd send more than one, or at least a larger specimen.

The door shuddered again under the pounding. No use trying to sneak up and peer out, since through the window and sidelights, the caller would see me as well. So I crossed the foyer, undid the latch, and opened up a crack, ready to slam the door shut at a moment's notice.

A dark distorted sliver of face and a white eyeball thrust up to the slim opening and stared at me wildly. "Love of God, Miz Hopkins. It's Sadie Bell Lucas. Let me in!"

"Sadie? What on earth!"

My first thought was my father must be ailing. I yanked the door open and she stumbled inside. Sadie Lucas was the free woman of color my mother had hired to look after the house and get the Judge two hot meals a day. She was married to a slave on the old Douglas place, which belonged now to the widow's nephew. Sadie made her living hiring out to various families in town. She'd told me the first week at my father's house that she was saving up to purchase her man's freedom. I'd felt dismayed, for surely it would take a lifetime of hoarding nickels and dimes to buy up the papers of a strong, healthy Negro man. And, if by any chance she'd meant me to feel sympathetic, it had worked like a charm. Ever since, I'd given her fifty cents a week more than my mother had promised.

"It's the Judge," I guessed, crossing the room to light a lamp, trying to figure some way to get a doctor. No, what was I thinking . . . there were none left. "His—his heart?"

Sadie was always neatly dressed. But now I saw her shawl hung twisted on one side and her snowy head scarf was crooked. She was panting; clearly she'd run all the way. She snatched up my hand, squeezing it so hard, I cried out.

"I so sorry, Miz Hopkins. I shouldn't never have opened that door. The soldiers come in and took him away. And the poor man barely dressed. Lord Jesus, I was so scared!"

"What soldiers? Where'd they take him?" I thought of Dickenson's warning. I'd spoken to my father about it. He must have lost his temper since then and said something foolish to the wrong person again.

"Palmyra, ma'am. They done hauled him off all the way to Palmyra."

"This time of night! Whatever for?"

"They say he a murdering secesh, and that he help kill a man. 'Please, wait. I got to tell his daughter,' I beg the man givin' orders. I say, 'She my boss lady.' But the soldier only ax me if I be a slave to the Judge. And I say, Lord no! But then I's too scared to ask twice. So I run up and look out the window upstairs. I see they got two other men tied up, sittin' in the back of a wagon. They shove the Judge in beside them. The driver lash those horses and take off down the street. Now that ain't no kind of way to treat an old man! Why they do him like that?"

She stood wringing her hands, looking at me as if I had the answer.

"I—I don't know. But I aim to find out," I said at last. "Wait here, please."

I ran to the kitchen, fished two dollars out of the housekeeping jar, came back, and folded them into her hand. She shook her head and tried to give the crumpled paper back, but I jerked both hands up out of her reach. "That's an advance, Sadie. I want you to keep the house up for my father, until I get him back here."

She nodded and pushed tears away with the back of one hand. Then she tugged her head scarf straight and pulled her shawl tight around her shoulders. "Yes'm, I will. He a nice old man, that Judge."

"Not everyone seems to agree with you," I noted.

After I'd closed the door behind Sadie, it struck me I was remarkably calm considering my father had just been hauled off like a criminal in the night. Of course, Dickenson had warned me of this possibility, but not what to do about it. I entertained the idea of bribing some soldier of low rank to give me more information. But I recalled the dirty, leering fellows slouching around at federal headquarters, and could imagine all too well what sort of payment they might demand. Safer to board a train for Palmyra myself.

Or . . . I could ask the lieutenant to intervene. Surely my father had been home when this killing was done; he never went anywhere, anymore. I'd swear to that. But how much weight would my word carry?

And then, perhaps because I'd seen him about so often lately, I thought of Huck Finn. Like Tom, he always seemed to know everything. And Huck certainly got around. But I had no way to send him word.

Dawn came slowly, but I made good use of the time. Mourning for Tyler the last few months, I'd cared little for appearances, and I cared little still. My beauty regimen was to rise and splash cold water on my face without a glance in the mirror, quickly pin up my hair, then go about my business. Now I wondered if it might matter how well I looked. Would Huck or the lieutenant, both men, notice or even care? But it seemed to me, as a judge's daughter, that looking starved and desperate might not be the best position for bargaining for favors from an adversary, old or new.

When I dragged Aunt Polly's old pier glass over by a sun-glazed window, what squinted back at me in the harsh light was shocking. A thin, pale face, haggard as a haunt. My faded black dress hung on my bones like an old night wrapper; my long uncombed blond hair was dull and dry as winter grass. Frizzled wisps escaped two tortoiseshell clips I'd shoved into place carelessly, as if my head were any old pincushion.

Not much now I could do to put meat on my bones. But I got out pomade and a boar-bristle brush and worked at my hair until it gave off a little shine. Then I pinned it up, centering a loose chignon as best I could without someone to help with the back.

Some better. And not much need for a corset with no padding over my ribs. Still, a lady wasn't dressed without that rigid underpinning, so I struggled into one, swearing when the laces tangled and one broke off short. Then I plundered wildly through the wardrobe looking for a finer dress. I discovered an old watered silk frock I hadn't worn since my teens. Out of style, yes, but it fit again. It was cut low in the bodice for current tastes, and this gave me pause. But I trusted a man not to track fashion. It was women who noticed such details, and used them against you.

My stockings were thin in places and mended over, but they wouldn't show. I rubbed lampblack on my boots to cover the worn spots where the leather was scuffed or cracked. Then stood back to assess the overall effect. The dress fit nicely after so many years. If I tilted my head and smiled so my cheeks filled out, I looked ten years younger than twenty-six.

But would a heartfelt plea and fair looks be enough to enlist help? Plenty of women were without men in Hannibal. Some, it was rumored, had no qualms about entertaining military men, invaders or home grown. The lieutenant, or Huck for that matter, could no doubt find a younger, adoring, unattached girl who'd offer up sweet compliments and a chance to be of service. And perhaps more.

I sat down on the bed abruptly, suddenly short of breath. Was that where I'd gone wrong, back with the lieutenant? Perhaps I'd missed my cues. Perhaps I'd signed my father's warrant without even knowing it. I looked at myself in the glass again, and dropped the hairbrush on the bed.

I didn't even know whether I could do such a thing—flatter and flirt with a strange man, perhaps offer favors, even to free the Judge. The northern lieutenant was scarred about the face, but otherwise not terribly unattractive.

He had certainly been attentive. His underlings already seemed to infer we had some sort of unsavory arrangement.

No, what was I thinking? A married woman, with children—no, a child. *A child you've always pretended belongs to your lawful husband,* I reminded myself. For the truth, which I somehow managed not to face very often, was not so pretty, nor was it so savory, either. I'd already done things a woman of bad repute might blush at. Yet even now, in the mirror, my face appeared pale and composed, not the least bit flushed with humiliation. Apparently over the years one could lose all capacity for shame, along with the veneer of normality. Under certain circumstances.

Strange to say, this all felt more interesting than shocking. As if I were a material being in one of the nature experiments my father used to conduct with frogs or water bugs, designed to sharpen my female mind and fill a girl with curiosity. I supposed I might blame my current weakness or indifference on a lack of good food. I preferred that to any other explanations that came to mind.

I APPROACHED HEADQUARTERS this time with my hat brim boldly tilted back, a faint smile pasted on my face. I looked directly at the guards on the steps. The younger one blushed and glanced away. The other returned my gaze, but I swept past as if they were stone gateposts.

Lieutenant Dickenson was not at his desk for once. In fact, no one was about in the main room. I paced, peering closely at everything, as if the torn upholstery on the benches, the dusty cobwebs festooning the mirrors, the badly rendered oil painting of some fat, forgotten governor were all new to me, even interesting. When still no one appeared, I finally ventured a few paces down the hall that used to lead to the clerk's office. "Hello?"

That, too, was deserted. Nonetheless, it felt as if someone was near, watching. I turned back suddenly and collided with Lieutenant Dickenson as he came in through a side door. His hand strayed to check his trouser buttons. Perhaps he'd been to the privy around back.

He cleared his throat. "May I . . . Oh, Mrs. Hopkins. You honor us again."

"I'm afraid so," I said. "It's about my father."

"I heard he'd been involved in some unpleasantness in Palmyra."

"On the contrary. The Judge is innocent of those charges. He was home all night, when the—"

Just then some soldiers blundered in the front, laughing and elbowing each other. One shouted something, wheeled about, and went out again. But the others stayed, speaking in loud voices, stomping up and down.

"If you don't mind, I think we'll be better able to talk in here." He took my arm, walking me a few paces farther down the hall, looking as anxious as I felt. He pushed open a heavy door and bowed me in, then made a great show of propping it open several inches with a chunk of marble, the broken half of a carved bookend. Inside, ladder-back chairs sat in a crooked row across from a sagging divan, but he didn't offer a seat. Not that I would have taken one.

I explained how my father had been dragged off and loaded in a cart like livestock. And that I knew beyond a doubt he was innocent.

"Any other witnesses to his whereabouts at the time of this killing, and would they vouch for him? Not that your word isn't good, Mrs. Hopkins," he added hastily. "But you are related, of course, and that wouldn't be seen as impartial."

That meant my aunt Mamie Thatcher wouldn't be able to swear to Pa's whereabouts, either. Who was left to stand up for the Judge? I thought of the empty house across from us, the owners gone to Nevada after both their boys had been killed in a skirmish on the border. And the neighbors on the other side who'd stopped speaking years ago, after the Judge had sent their oldest son to jail for a week for stealing an expensive hunting dog.

Whatever the lieutenant saw on my face must've been adequate answer. "I see. Well, I could send a message to the provost in Palmyra. Except, without any others to testify . . . well." He turned his palms up and looked at me expectantly.

So I'd been right. He wanted to be convinced, with more than words, that he might do our family a great favor.

In my girlhood I had devoured novels in which heroines fainted with impeccable grace, then were revived by men who became smitten with their gently heaving bosoms. Falling out in this calculated way had always seemed to me a noxious ploy, yet I had no better plan. I stepped closer to the lieutenant, until only inches separated us. He smelled of tobacco, spiced hair oil, and faint male sweat, all scents so reminiscent of Sid that I actually felt drawn. Could even imagine leaning my head on his chest, to inhale those comforting scents more deeply.

"You mean you can't help us?" I murmured. "That my father will be wrongly charged and there's nothing I can do? Nothing at all?"

I lifted my face to his. Perhaps that was too bold. His eyes widened and he leaned away a little, jamming both hands in his pockets. The look on his face wouldn't have been out of place on a muskrat caught in a trap. Still, he didn't step back.

"Tell me, then, please, what would convince you of his innocence?" I asked.

Without waiting for an answer, I closed my eyes and made my knees buckle, my spine go limp as rope. It nearly killed me not to throw out a hand to break my fall, and when my hip and shoulder connected with the uncarpeted floor, I bit down on my tongue and tasted blood. The pain in my side was uncanny; I longed to moan or swear.

I felt him standing above me, shocked to an equal silence. Then came the creak of his knees as he knelt beside me. He whispered, so close, my own hair tickled my ear, "Mrs. Hopkins? You are upset, or unwell. Mrs. Hopkins, can you hear me?"

Despite the killing pain in my side, I kept my eyes closed, my face loosely composed, and said nothing, hoping I wasn't drooling on the floorboards.

He rose again. I heard his footsteps cross the room, and hinges creak as the door thumped into the jamb. I was dying to know what he was doing. Before I risked a look, he returned, slid his arms under and lifted me. It felt uncanny, too, to be hoisted blindly through the air, carried like a child. I breathed shallowly as possible, because the scent of this stranger seemed so familiar, I had to remind myself not to respond. To let my limbs dangle as if I had no bones.

I was half-slid, half-dumped onto a lumpy, prickly shelf that must be the horsehair divan. Dust billowed around, filtered up my nose. A sneeze was being forced up, and with no way to head it off, I concealed the sound with a loud groan, then let my lids flutter open briefly.

Dickenson was kneeling beside me. He took both my hands in his and rubbed them. His fingers felt more calloused than Sid's, but his touch was as gentle and as hesitant. "Mrs. Hopkins?" he said again, then let go. I almost jerked away when I felt him fumbling around my ankles, but he was only unbuttoning one of my boots. He slipped it off and began to rub my stockinged foot. The one with undarned holes in both heel and toe. Damn.

At last he stopped massaging my instep and laid my foot back on the divan. Still I felt him hovering. A finger pressed my throat for a pulse, which was probably racing like a startled mule's. His breath smelled of tobacco and, faintly, whiskey, as it warmed my face.

With my eyes shut I could imagine this was Sid come home, leaning over me. That the scars marking Dickenson's face were the same healed wounds I would see on my husband when he returned. I wished to trace their disfiguring course with my fingertips and to make them disappear. Tears started under my lids, because now I'd have to tell Sid of Tyler's death. Yet I was so happy to feel him alive and back home that instead of speaking, I put my arms around his neck. I wanted Sid to kiss me, lay hands on me again. To open my eyes and see at least one thing was still as it should be.

I suppose the lieutenant could not really be blamed if all this inspired him to lower his head and kiss the hollow of my throat, just above my unbuttoned collar. The lips pressed to my skin felt agreeable, dry and soft and warm.

But a dream is always harder to hold to in daylight, when you aren't truly asleep and know very well the difference. I let go suddenly. He was halfway across the room stammering apologies by the time I sat up.

"I do regret, that is, I sincerely apologize—," he said in a rush.

I got up, too, wincing at the pain in my bruised hip. "I don't know what you mean," I said firmly. "I felt weak all of a sudden. And then, nothing."

"Ah. Well, you fainted," he said, sounding torn between accusation and regret. "And so, I . . . I put you on the sofa there. Thinking you might've been injured when you fell." He rubbed his mouth, and smiled nervously at me.

I began to wonder if he knew I'd been playacting. But why would he go along with such a charade? I was still hobbled with the lack of a shoe, but he kept his distance as I searched around for it. He offered no help, only more apologies, inquiring whether I needed smelling salts or a glass of water. He paced and rubbed his palms on his trousers.

"Oh, I'm quite well now," I said. "Except . . . when I think of my poor father, locked away in Palmyra when he's ailing. Do you think if I came again tomorrow, you might have more news?"

He looked alarmed, even horrified. "No. Not at all. I think I have all the information I need, Mrs. Hopkins. My message to the provost will assure them they have the wrong party."

"But the friendly witnesses," I reminded him. "Shall I come again in the morning and see if you've found any?" I had to know he was sincere, not just looking to be rid of me.

He shook his head. "No need. I shall say several citizens have sworn to it. But only, you understand, because it occurs to me just now that I myself saw your father in town around the time in question. I believe he was sitting out on one of the benches in front of the hotel."

His tone verged on pleading. I knew my father wouldn't have been downtown at such an hour. He'd gone to bed faithfully at eight each night since mother had returned to Virginia. But I had to acknowledge for the first time that the man across from me was fully human, perhaps even good. He had mentioned a family. Like any man, he might feel tempted to take advantage of an unforeseen opportunity, yet he would no doubt wish also not to betray his wife and children.

At our first meeting, Hiram Dickenson had reminded me of Lincoln: the tall, vengeful Father who'd sent troops to punish Missouri even though we had not seceded from his Union. But Dickenson was not in command; he was as trapped in war and circumstance as anyone. Even more so, for he was sworn to a military code, and I was not.

He turned politely away while I lifted my hem and refastened the boot he'd removed. He remained turned away as I buttoned my collar and smoothed my skirts, which looked as wrinkled as if we had indeed gotten up to something shameful. He held up a hand to keep me in place while he opened the door wider and glanced out, checking the hall. After a moment he motioned for me to hurry out. When he took my elbow this time, I felt both like snatching it away and leaning into his supporting hand.

He stopped in the hall, looked at me, then away and murmured, "I do hate to ask a lady to leave by the back door. But perhaps it would be best. People have a way of noticing things and misinterpreting them."

I nodded. "It's a small world here in Hannibal."

He smiled. "A small world everywhere."

I wanted to say something in farewell, but nothing came to mind that could decently be offered by a lady to a gentleman, without going so far be-yond propriety, neither of us could keep up a pretense any longer.

"I'll be going, then," I said at last. "I thank you for listening to my troubles."

"By tomorrow we shall hope they're solved," he replied. "So that you needn't bother to return again."

I felt us both droop a little at that. Though an hour earlier I would've sworn I'd never miss the sight of that office, or of Lieutenant Dickenson, if they had both been blown from our landscape and carried off by a twister.

"Yes, I agree." I set off, picking my way across the muddy back alley, holding my breath against the stink from the outhouse, which the wind was blowing our way. I did not look back. But by the time I reached the corner and turned toward the street, I still hadn't heard Hiram Dickenson close the door behind me.

Nine

J UST BEFORE SUNDOWN someone banged as hard at the front door as Sadie Bell Lucas had the night before. But this time when I opened up, my father toppled into the foyer. A wagon was clattering away—not government issue, but requisitioned from some farmer. The driver was hunched, unidentifiable under a dark cape and battered hat. I helped the Judge to a chair in the parlor, then set a lantern beside him to add up the damage. He'd been beaten hard about the face; one eye was swollen shut. He yelped and cursed when I prodded his ribs.

I offered a verdict. "Well, Pa, you're bruised but alive." Then I hugged him very carefully, and set to work feeding and bathing and bandaging. Gage wandered in as I was wiping his grandfather's face with a clean rag dipped in water.

He came over to stare, mouth open in surprise. "What's wrong with Granpoppy? Did he fall?"

"You might say that," I told him. No use frightening a child who had no say over the folly and misbehavior of adults. "Now run get your aunt Mary, sweetie. I need her help."

Mary rushed in, took one look at the Judge, and shrieked like a pounced-on rabbit. "Dear Lord Jesus," she gasped.

"I need less religion and more hot water," I said. "You can pray over him all you like once we get the worst of it patched up."

We set to work and soon the Judge looked better, if not pretty. Then, with us supporting his arms on either side, we walked him up the stairs and put him to bed in Tyler's room, which I hadn't entered since he'd passed away. It hurt to see everything looked as it always had, as if the baby would be back to play with his ball and wooden blocks, then sleep in the crib with carved rails Sid had made.

We lowered Pa onto the larger bed's feather tick. "Don't you stir, now," I warned. "And be more cautious who you talk to. It's not like the old days, Pa. Think whatever you like, but you can't just say any old thing out loud. Our government has seen to that."

"Travesty," he muttered. "Outrage." Though whether he referred to his treatment or current politics, I couldn't tell. He closed his eyes and turned away from us, as if weary beyond reckoning.

THE NEXT WEEK I HEARD at the post office that more supposed rebel sympathizers had been hauled off to Palmyra. They hadn't been as lucky as the Judge. Ten were to be executed, shot for the murder of Andrew Allsman, a provost guard. He'd been too old to serve with the Third Missouri Cavalry, so had made himself useful as an informant, one quick to doubt the patriotism of fellow citizens. The federals relied on him to track and point out whomever he deemed disloyal. Allsman was efficient, having lived in northeast Missouri his whole life. He knew all the hiding spots in town or woods, including those Joe Porter's Confederate militia liked to use.

"It's a fact," said the postmaster to the woman in front of me. "He wan't popular with most folks around Marion County, not just Joe Porter."

I got up to the window to take my turn.

The postmaster pushed over three stamps—all I could afford—while still talking to the other woman. In addition to mail service, he offered all the latest news right at his wicket. "They say Joe Porter's militia carried off Allsman from his home. The ones arrested they claim was Porter's men."

Including, I supposed, my father. Who had not ridden a horse outside our town limits in ten years, thanks to galloping rheumatism.

I paid and moved on to the grocery, where the Palmyra executions were also all the talk. A woman in an old-fashioned bonnet said the accused had been forced to kneel on the grass between pine coffins. "Then," she added, "a preacher had at them one last time. And each had to sit on the foot of his own casket, facing the muskets, and be blown to glory, one by one."

"But only two took a blindfold," said Mr. Murphy, the grocer, with some satisfaction, as he wrapped up my three cubes of pork in brown paper.

The firing squad hadn't been so dead-keen as the average Hannibal rabbit hunter. Several prisoners had to be shot yet again, then at last put out of their agony by some officers who'd been standing by with revolvers.

"Confederate enlistments'll go up from here on out," said an old man at the end of the counter, clutching a plug of cheap tobacco. "Reenlistments, too. You wait and see if they don't." He spit a black wad into the sand-filled cuspidor, grabbed up his hickory cane, and thumped out.

I came in the back door at home and dumped my few parcels on the pantry shelf, then turned to pump a cup of water at the sink. That's when I spotted the large redheaded soldier sitting at my kitchen table. I screamed and dropped the cup clattering into the sink.

The giant raised huge empty hands and rose, dragging off his hat. "Mum. Sorry t' startle you, I'm sure."

So that was the way it was. Dickenson had only humored me. Now he was going to arrest my father and imprison him again. I opened my mouth to tell the man off, looking around for a likely weapon, a butcher knife or toasting fork.

Mary hurried in. "Oh, you're back. Did I hear a shout?"

I pointed to the soldier. "This, this is—"

She glanced at him and nodded. "Yes, Mr. O'Brien. He'll be staying with us. Your Lieutenant Dickenson sent him."

I recalled the dusty, evil-smelling davenport at headquarters and felt blood rush to my face. "He is not by any stretch *my* Lieutenant Dickenson. What did he send this fellow for?"

She smiled at the hulking stranger in blue, who still stood at attention, cap clenched between big grubby paws. "He's to look out for us, Becky. We're his billet, you see. I'm putting him in the sewing room, on the big davenport."

She lowered her voice, leaned over, and whispered, "To make sure your father behaves, is what I think."

"Oh, for Lord's sake. He's enormous. He'll eat us into ruin."

But I couldn't simply order him out. We no longer could play master or mistress in our homes. And O'Brien had come complete with a croaker sack of U.S. dried beef, flour, beans, and even salt, which was getting scarcer than Hannibal men below the age of fifty.

SO OUR PANTRY WAS ENHANCED, but my father was livid, near speechless with rage. At first he refused to sit at the same table with the trooper, muttering things like, "So now *He* has quartered soldiers among us."

At mealtimes Pa took to citing laws and amendments pertaining to the military, so I fed O'Brien in the parlor, because he flat refused to eat in the kitchen by himself.

"For that's the place secesh feed their slaves," he said, nodding knowingly.

But he was terribly messy in the sitting room, spraying crumbs, dropping bits of food that called up mice. We couldn't afford to have rodents eat up our cornmeal and flour, so I brought him back to table and told Pa he must put up with it.

I set them at opposite ends. The Judge was good for a day or two, only flaunting his bandages at the table by rolling up his sleeves and leaving his collar undone, a lapse of etiquette that would've been unthinkable before. But gradually he began to grumble aloud again, berating the federals over greens and pork and corn bread for the way they were handling the war, and conscripting all Missouri's grain and livestock.

"Leaving loyal citizens to starve, sir!" he would bellow, pounding the table with the butt of his knife. "And what do you say to that?"

O'Brien took it in stride. For all the attention he paid to veiled insults, and even obvious ones, he might've been made of locust wood. Perhaps in previous assignments he'd been abused even worse. Clearly Dickenson had chosen him with great care.

"Aye, takes verra many goods to feed an army," O'Brien would reply, if he said anything back at all. "Shame dacint folks be done such a turn, but how else do you fight a war, man?"

His calm remarks infuriated the Judge, until Mary and I broke in to direct the conversation elsewhere. I tried to save up any news I could find in town and hijack talk away from the Union, and war. But how strange it felt, when my father had been a loyal citizen who'd abolished slavery in his own house, that now he'd switched sides—at least for argument's sake. I suppose prison and humiliation, not to mention a terrible beating, can change a man's outlook.

Since what everyone took to calling the Palmyra Massacre, more men were slipping away from their homes, even their Union posts, to sign on with the nearest Confederate regiment. Or even a vigilante band, such as Reeves's Independent Scouts, for anyone who cared to travel as far as the southeast corner of Missouri to try to find them. They were a regiment that had returned from a campaign in Kentucky two years earlier, having mutinied against both Union and Confederate armies. They'd sworn never to leave the Ozarks until they'd returned the state to its rightful citizens, invading armies of any stripe be damned.

After three weeks or so, the Judge finally hit on a topic O'Brien could not ignore.

We'd just sat down to chicken and biscuits and fig jam. I'd chased down the old rooster with a hatchet, fed up with being spurred each time I went to the hen house to gather eggs. That morning, swinging my basket to fend him off, I'd given final notice. "Think you're too tough to fry, you feathered devil? Well, you'd still make a mighty fine stew!"

He'd flown right at my face, and flogged me again. But, as Trenny had so often said, "A rooster always be a rooster."

Anyhow, we were sitting down and enjoying the miscreant bird for a change. And for another change, the Judge was silent, spooning up stew and smiling to himself. That should've told me something, but I was glad to have peace for once, if only briefly and limited to my own house. I'd just gone round with seconds when my father suddenly looked up. "Say, I heard a joke at the barbershop this morning. Quite a good one."

"Tell us, then, Judge Thatcher," said Mary. "A little humor is never unwelcome."

"Yes, tell it. Tell it, Granpoppy," said Gage, drumming his heels on the rung of his chair.

"Don't talk with your mouth full, son," I said gently. "Well? Don't keep us in suspense, Pa."

He smiled, puffed out his chest, and began. "It goes like this. Two men meet on a street in Boston. One has black skin, the other white. Greetings, brother, says the black man to the white man. And greetings to ye, the other man replies. But why call me brother? Sure and I don't know you. And see, we canna be related. Look at your skin, and look at mine."

Mary's eyes were shining. She hung on the Judge's every word, no doubt expecting some sweet riddle on brotherly love. I felt as if I'd swallowed the wishbone and it'd lodged north of my gizzard. I didn't know this particular joke, but clearly it would have something to do with O'Brien.

"You know, Pa," I said suddenly. "Maybe we should—"

"Don't interrupt, daughter," he snapped, shooting a frown down the table. "As I was saying: Look at me own skin and look at yours, the pale fellow says. Jesus, Mary, and Joseph! How you figger we're related? And the dark fellow replies, Lordy, ain't you Irish? That I am, says the pale one. Well, there you go, says the other. Ever'body know Irish just niggers turned inside out!"

The Judge slapped the table and grinned.

Gage looked puzzled, then forced out a loud laugh, obviously to please his grandfather. Mary bit her lip and stared at her plate.

Before I could rebuke my father, there was a crash. O'Brien stood so abruptly, his chair had gone over. "Ah, you bleedin' little Reb bastard."

The Judge pushed back from his place, too. "What did you just call me, sir?"

"Mary, take Gage," I said quickly. She scooped him up and scurried them both into the parlor. I heard him asking querulously why he had to leave the table before pie, and her voice murmuring back, low and soothing. Then she started coughing, which she hadn't done all week.

Damn you, Pa, I thought, even as I tried to get around the table before O'Brien killed him. Why did he have to keep on goading and pricking? As a child, I'd thought the Judge perfect. Of course, I'd noticed flaws as we both grew older. But this smirking, selfish man-child was no father I knew, or wanted.

O'Brien reached the Judge first, and lifted him out of his seat by the scruff like a misbehaving puppy. If I'd thought the corporal would only shake him, or smack him with a rolled-up paper, I might have left them to each other. But O'Brien had murder in his eye. His face was red as flannels and he shook like the town drunk, though far as I could tell he'd never touched a drop since he'd come to stay.

"Corporal O'Brien, I do beg your pardon," I shouted. "My father spoke rudely and foolishly. I fear his short, unhappy stay in Palmyra has addled his mind."

As he rose slowly in the air, Pa snatched up the fork from his plate. He drove the tines into O'Brien's forearm. The Irishman grunted and shook his head like a wet dog. He lifted Pa higher, as if he meant to throw him across the room. Perhaps the Judge deserved it, but with his broken ribs and the general frailty of old bones, such a jolt would surely kill him.

I grabbed my father's knees and hung on. Still growling, O'Brien lifted him higher. At this rate, we'd tear Pa in two. I was thinking to let go and run fast for a weapon, when a dull thud sounded. Suddenly I was sprawled on the floor, pinned to it, the Judge's bulk squeezing the breath from me. I rolled him off, grabbed the seat of a ladder-back chair, and pulled myself upright. There stood Mary, clutching Aunt Polly's iron corn bread skillet like a war club. She was staring white-faced at the prone O'Brien, spread-eagled beside the table.

"Dear God, is he dead?" I asked, trying to jerk my skirt free so I could stand.

She looked even more stricken then, and threw herself on O'Brien's body, sobbing. "Lord God, why does everyone have to fight so? See what comes of it!"

I pulled free at last, leaving Pa to right himself like a turtle if he could. When I knelt to see if the Irishman was yet breathing, Mary was covering his slack face with desperate kisses. "Poor Corporal O'Brien! Please speak. Tell me I haven't killed you."

"Mary," I said, looking at her in astonishment. "Are you and Mr. O'Brien—?"

Just then he groaned, and she laughed and grabbed my hands. "Look, Becky, he's alive! I thought we'd killed him, the whole family together."

I squeezed her hands, then ran my fingers through his thick, springy red hair until they encountered a knot on the back of his head. Sticky, but only a little blood stained my fingertips when I pulled them back. "Let's get him up," I said.

I didn't want to ruin Mary's joy in the corporal's revival. But all I could think of—once it was clear he'd live with nothing worse than an aching head—was that our position vis-à-vis the occupying federals would now be very poor indeed. Surely Lieutenant Dickenson would be justifiably angry. What could I say to save my father this time? That it wasn't he who'd goaded the placid, patient corporal to a frenzy? That yet a different family member had tried to club the poor man's brains out? At this rate, we'd all be in Gratiot shortly, Gage included.

Any Missourian was suspect to one clothed in federal blue. And any brave patriot might report me for so much as sneezing near the flag. The army or militia could empty my pantry and smokehouse without permission, requisition our home, or burn it if they took the notion. So far, I'd been treated more than fairly by the lanky lieutenant from Massachusetts. But greed and corruption also hid behind that uniform. No one could be trusted to tell the truth anymore if it would profit them to tell a lie.

Gage peered into the sewing room at the man we'd draped over the sofa. "Mama," he said in a stage whisper, eyes round and huge, "shall I get my pistol?"

I could've laughed till tears slid down my cheeks, but I forced my quivering jaw to talk instead. "No, darling. Auntie Mary and I aren't in danger. Corporal O'Brien has a hurt on his head. We're going to bandage it for him."

As for the confusion in the dining room, perhaps I'd lie about that, too. For as much as I claimed to hate falsehoods, I'd told my share in the past. What did it matter what manner of tale I devised now? None would ever overshadow the biggest and most unforgivable of my own lies, one that concerned Gage and Sid.

When we next saw each other, I would have to tell my husband his beloved baby Tyler was dead. That terrible loss would make the truth I'd held back since our wedding day even harder to bury within me. But bury it I would. For I had no intention of ever confessing to Sid that our eldest and now only son was not truly his own. Oh, the family resemblance was there. But it had come down to Gage slantwise, through his real father. Through the blood of Tom Sawyer.

. . .

IN THE END, TOM AND I HAD fallen out because of a lie.

After I joined the Freebooters, we roamed Hannibal by night for years, he and Huck and I, and never were caught. Huck was a cat's shadow: long and lithe and battle-scarred. The sun had colored his skin the tanned gold of a panther's pelt. He wore layers of ragged shirts and trousers and belts and wilted slouch hats. He was bundled and swathed like a living patch-work, yet the rest of us were never so quick or light-footed or silent. We talked too loud in darkened alleys; we sometimes set off watchdogs when we fell out of trees or bumped into rubbish bins. All the more reason to leave the town proper on our late night revels and trek to Holliday's Hill or the old Baptist cemetery, so the sleep of respectable folks wouldn't be disturbed.

I'd earned my place with a pretend knowledge of Hoodoo to chase off ghosts—plus the mundane but welcome skill of borrowing a fry pan and a slab of bacon from Trenny's pantry, and cooking up a late supper in the woods. After a year or so, Sammy Clemens joined us and made *his* mark telling stories on dull nights when rain or snow confined us to an abandoned warehouse or a nearby cave. That's right—the author of *Tom Sawyer* might have called himself Twain. But he was that same Sam Clemens who knew firsthand that all the Freebooters of Hannibal weren't boys. Though you'd never guess it, to read his books.

The first time Sam joined us, it was cold; an icy wind gusted off the river. We were on a low bluff in a fishing shack, a bit above town, sitting in a circle and already bored.

"What shall we do tonight?" I asked, hoping it wouldn't be tick races again. A stupefying game, but boys never got their fill of watching the bloated vermin crawling slowly around in circles while they made bottle-cap bets like swells at Saratoga. Even an old story told by candlelight would be better. We could lie on our backs and listen, while the wide Mississippi churned by below.

Instead, Tom announced he had a wart—he always did in those days—and Huck went out and came in with another dead cat, this one not so fresh as the last. He had as plentiful a supply of those as Tom had warts. Then the four of us set off for the graveyard for the traditional ceremony, which involved swinging the deceased tabby overhead and chanting mystical phrases.

"It's a guaranteed cure," boasted Tom.

"Who told you so?" I asked, interested in scientific credentials.

"Old Mother Barker," said Huck. "Ain't she a witch?"

Sam and I fell about at this. "A witch!"

Huck scowled. "Laugh yourselves sick, but she's bona fide. Witched my pap so he rolled off a shed and broke his arm, because he pitched a rock at her once on the road."

"But why'd he pitch the rock?" asked Sam.

" 'Cause she give him the Eye, a course."

Everyone nodded sagely. A bad fate to be stricken with such a glance; it meant ruin and death and lost fortunes. Folks would go far to avoid it. I'd learned of this danger only after moving to Hannibal; it wasn't well known in St. Louis.

"So old Mother Barker says to swing this cat like a lariat," I asked. "And that's it?"

"A course not," fumed Huck. "You're bound to stand on the grave of some wicked, fresh-buried person, and say the spell. *Devil follow corpse, cat follow devil, warts follow cat, I'm done with ye!*"

"Well, I never saw a live cat with warts. Why would Tom's wart follow a dead one?"

Huck glared at me silently, jaw clenched, trembling with rage. More and more we'd been goading each other. But it seemed less a game to him.

"Why not just draw it out with a bean?" suggested Sam, who'd early on been frail, and was still sometimes sickly. I suspected he feared going out to the cemetery again.

Tom snorted. "Aw, that old bean spell don't work. It ain't proven."

So much for alternative cures. We started again for the cemetery.

Its gates were rusted wrought-iron tortured into gothic curlicues. The enormous hinges screeched like wildcats if you moved them, so mostly they stayed propped open. I stepped in behind Tom, but he stopped so suddenly, I collided with his back. "Somebody's here afore us," he hissed.

We all dived into the thick hedge just inside, pushing and shoving to get the best viewing spot. I ended up crouched in front of Tom, who'd let me in first. I allowed Sam to crawl up front, since he always looked as if he might break if you knocked into him.

Three rows away, two dark figures crouched beside an open grave. What drew my eye most wasn't them, though, or the cracked lantern casting a feeble glow over the upturned dirt, or the rusty handbarrow with pick handles sticking out. It was the dark bundle stretched out on the ground beside them, unmoving.

"By golly, it's a funeral!" blurted Sam before I clapped a hand over his mouth.

"No, it ain't, Sam," whispered Tom. "Nobody holds a burying at moonrise."

Something smelled terrible, probably the dead cat. I was losing my taste for nighttime entertainment, thinking about sneaking back through the bushes and out the gate. Then a third man strode into the cemetery, passing by so close, I could've reached out and tugged his coattail. He was in an almighty hurry, nearly running over to where the others stood by the grave.

He stopped, panting, and gestured at the mound of loose dirt. His words came clearly to us, for he had a cultivated voice. "Hurry up now and fill it in, boys. The moon's up and somebody might pass by." He sounded familiar, but I couldn't place him.

The first two quickly spaded dirt into the hole, cursing when their blades rang on a stone or a shovel-load missed the hole. Then they heaved the body into the barrow, though the bundle was so long and awkward, they had to fold it like a wallet. As they did, the tarpaulin slipped from the corpse's face, which gleamed horribly pale in the moonlight.

Sam whimpered and put his hands over his eyes. I patted his shoulder. The men covered everything and tied the tarp down.

"Dang. They went 'n dug up Hoss Williams," whispered Huck with disgust. "And no wonder. It's Muff Potter and . . . that tall one there, ain't that Injun Joe?"

Tom had been breathing noisily in my ear. When Huck said that, he was suddenly quiet. His arm, leaning hard on mine, tensed up.

Injun Joe was the town drifter, a dark, stringy half-breed who spent some days at the docks loading cargo or firewood onto steamers, and spent others merely laying out drunk. He was harmless and good-natured, known for spinning a fanciful yarn to anyone who'd stand him a whiskey. But Tom had always hated him. He used to kick Joe's shins if he saw him passed out in a doorway. Once he stole Joe's old felt hat and flung it in the river, laughing to see it whirl away downstream like a misshapen little boat.

Loud voices drew my attention back to the men. The new arrival sounded angry. "Another five?" he shouted. "Robbery! I paid in advance, the precise sum you set beforehand."

This time I placed the voice: Odell Robinson. He'd traveled up recently from St. Louis, and had stopped for dinner at our house the week before. He was to take over old Doc's practice, my father had told me, once he finished his medical studies. We always had a doctor or two in town, before the war.

"Well, now it's five more," said Injun Joe, rubbing his arms as if they ached. "On account of the devil of a time we had getting him out. They dint call him Hoss for nothin'."

"You sons of bitches," said Robinson, his tone worlds different from the polite murmur he'd used to thank my mother for a second helping of potatoes. "Not another red cent!"

"Then he gits planted back," said Joe. "Watch your mouth, Doc. You come to us, remember?" Joe picked up a shovel and began opening the grave.

Tom nudged me. "Move over! I can't see."

"Move yourself," I shot back, for I could hardly see a thing either, with Sam's bushy red hair sticking up in front. I grabbed his narrow, bony shoulders and forced him flat.

Dr. Robinson cursed and snatched at the shovel. He lost his balance, arms windmilling, and knocked Joe down with him. Muff Potter danced around in agitation, then snatched up the other shovel. He swung at Robinson just as the young doctor tried to rise. The blow made a terrible wet *thump*. A ripe melon that'd fallen off my aunt's kitchen table once, onto the brick floor, had sounded the same. Dirt flew up as Robinson hit the ground.

"They God," breathed Huck, rustling the crisp fallen leaves all around us.

Injun Joe jumped up. "Jesus and Joseph! Why in hell you do that, Muff?"

"I only meant for to stun him," Muff whined. "You said not to let him take no advantage."

"Just on the *haggling* part, Muff. I dint mean kill him!"

Potter mumbled something I couldn't hear and Joe smacked his face. "Damn fool. Gravy for brains! You always ruin things. I never said to kill nobody, never. And now we're out five dollars."

"Help me out or I'll say you told me to! Hell's bells, I'll say you done it yourself," screeched Muff. "Law'll take my word over a red Injun's any day."

Joe stopped pacing, and raised his hands palm up, slowly, as if Muff were a growling dog. "Whoa, there. Maybe we can tell the sheriff it was self-defense."

Muff scratched his head. "Say what?"

"Sure. Young doc asks us to meet him out here for a job of work. Then tries to get us to break the law, dig this fellow up for some crooked experiment. He holds a gun on you—"

"What gun?" cried Muff.

"Never mind the gun! All right, a knife. Sawbones always got knives."

"Be Jesus!" Muff subsided to the ground, head in his hands. "I hate knives. What if somebody seen?"

Joe swept an arm to take in the cemetery. "Nobody here but us. You spot ary other soul?"

"Okay," said Muff. "I got it. He had him a knife. Long as we're not seen, we're okay. We'd be bound to do away with any witnesses. You'd help me out there. Right, Joe?"

The boys huddled around me stopped breathing. I knew this because I heard only silence over my own held breath. The clouds covered the moon again, and the solid dark was a shroud pressing on us all.

All at once Sammy Clemens bolted up, wheezing in terror, trying to fight his way out of the bushes.

"What's that?" said Muff, whipping around toward us. "Who's there?"

The Freebooters flushed from cover like quail exploding from brush. I grabbed Sam's arm and hauled him backward through the hedge, branches scraping us raw. Sam's curls caught on twigs; they stood on end as he gasped and panted behind me. I hardly felt the cuts and scrapes as we fled—just kept running hard, Tom and Huck behind, shouting, "Run faster, God's sake, faster!"

At every step I thought I heard men cursing, heavy work boots pounding closer, but I wouldn't have looked back for all the gold in India. We scrambled away home to the respectable streets of Hannibal, leaving nothing behind but a medicinal dead cat.

I FINALLY FELL ASLEEP that night only to jerk awake every few minutes, legs twitching as if I were still running in the dark. At the breakfast table I drooped swollen-eyed over grits and ham gravy.

My mother shook her head. "My word, Rebecca, you are a sight. Did you brush your hair a bit since yesterday? Oh, for—! Look here, Mr. Thatcher, at your only daughter's hair. Why, there are *leaves* in it! Trenny, don't you ever make this child bathe?"

Trenny scowled and slammed the fry pan down on the stove lid. "You know I do, Miss Louisa. You seen the dirty bathwater, and that hairbrush that need a cleaning. Seems to me some youngins attract dirt like flypaper."

I was pointed up the stairs, and came down again in better order. Just in time to see a deputy leaving by the kitchen door, and to hear my father remark that Muff Potter had been arrested at the cemetery. "Seems I must charge him with murder this very day." The Judge shook his head. "They found the fool lying out drunk next to his victim, the deputy told me."

"Mr. Thatcher! Little pitchers," whispered my mother.

I felt safer, anyhow. At least Muff Potter was behind bars where he belonged.

You can imagine my surprise two days later when the Judge came home and told Mother, over dinner, "Guess what, my dear? A new development in the Potter case. Young Tom Sawyer and the Finn boy witnessed the crime. They've given evidence that a drifter actually committed the murder."

I couldn't imagine why they'd say that, when they knew what had happened. "What's his name?" I asked. "Is he local?"

My mother frowned warningly at the Judge. "Mr. Thatcher—"

"Oh, just a town ne'er-do-well," my father said, spearing a forkful of pole beans. "Called Injun Joe."

I dropped my fork clattering to the plate. "No!"

"There, you see," said my mother, rising to lead me from the table.

"You've upset the poor girl's sensibilities. I told you she's quite delicate. Come along, Rebecca."

I was so stunned at what Tom and Huck had done, I allowed her to lead me up to my bed without another word of protest.

BY THE NEXT DAY, the two were town celebrities. Everyone in Hannibal seemed relieved to put the crime off a white man and onto a red one. I couldn't get Tom alone until the day after they'd let Muff Potter go free. I finally cornered him that Monday just before school. Huck was with him.

"Tom, why did you say Injun Joe murdered Odell Robinson?" I demanded. "You were stuck behind me; you couldn't even see."

"I seen clear enough he's a murdering Indian. Muff was too drunk to do a killing."

Huck was chewing a blade of sweetgrass, leaning against the schoolhouse wall. Eyes half-shut, as if ready for a nap. He wouldn't look at me. "And you say Joe did it, too?"

He shrugged.

"Well, do you?" I persisted.

"What Tom said. He's right."

I glared from one to the other. Huck had told the Freebooters stories about his own father; how old Finn drank and beat him. How he'd had to feed and raise himself like an orphan. But a judge's daughter knew, just from eavesdropping, what rank violence a drunk could do, even after two bottles of rectified whiskey. "Well, I saw everything," I said. "Clearer than either of you. It isn't Injun Joe that's guilty, it's Muff Potter."

They stared at me stonily, a silent, united front.

"Now look, fellows." I would leave off the vinegar for now, and try my mother's oft-recommended approach: honey. I smiled, tried to pitch my voice as sweet as Laura Wright's. "You all really ought to tell the sheriff he already had the right one. You know you'd feel bad if the wrong man hung for it."

They seemed less shamed than annoyed at this statement, exchanging covert glances. "Ah, well, maybe when we see the sheriff this afternoon," Tom mumbled at last.

"Good," I said. "I'm glad you see the sense in it."

Instead, later in the day Tom and Huck swore again—this time to the sheriff—that Injun Joe had killed young Dr. Robinson. I don't fully understand why. Maybe Tom felt he finally had the chance to get revenge on an Indian, even if it wasn't one who'd orphaned him. Even though the killing of his parents had nothing to do with Injun Joe.

The next afternoon I rushed out the schoolhouse door when the master rang the bell, not looking back, not waiting for Tom for the first time in a year. At home I stayed indoors, because though he might look for me in the yard, he wouldn't knock at the door and ask. It was hard to sleep that night. I felt as grieved as if my best friend had died; I suppose in a way he had.

The next day, before the bell rang, I found Tom in the school yard. I still hadn't given up on changing his mind. I knew he was really good and honest, only stubborn.

"Becky, you just mind your own business," he said as soon as I walked up. "I told you what I saw." He'd somehow come around to believing his own words. To recalling the night all catabiased, with him having the better view. "Besides," he went on in a wheedling tone. "Muff Potter's a white man, ain't he? And Injun Joe's only a half-breed, a Injun and a nigger."

"What's that got to do with it?" Then a new thought struck me.

I knew Muff supplied the boys from time to time with tobacco. They'd bragged he even gave them whiskey once. "Made us sick, but it was worth it," Tom had claimed. Perhaps those past favors demanded loyalty in their minds. Misguided loyalty might explain why he'd lied, and why Huck backed him up. But they still had time to recant. Injun Joe wasn't jailed yet, or even caught. Until the sheriff found him, I might yet talk sense into Tom.

I'd considered going to the Judge and telling what I knew. But if I did, I'd also have to explain how I'd come to be in out in the cemetery near midnight, with a bunch of boys, including Huck Finn and Tom Sawyer. Would anyone even believe my story?

If they did, it would mean the end of my nights of freedom. Even if the boys would still speak to me afterward, the Judge would probably put bars on my window. Trenny would watch me like a jailhouse guard. My mother would worry herself into fainting fits that no one respectable would ever speak to our family again. That no one would ever ask to marry me. She despaired already of me ever acting like a young lady. Which meant to never get dirty, to hide from the sun, to stay inside like a hermit. To sit with ankles crossed and stitch on a stack of samplers and pillowcases already dotted with blood from my pricked thumbs, trying not to scream or go cross-eyed.

I didn't want to fill a trousseau chest with fussy linens. To sit so still, spiders could spin webs between me and the wainscoting. The meetings on Holliday's Hill had made me hopeful there might be more to life than curling my hair and never tearing my petticoat. That there might still be some sort of freedom out there for a girl like me. To tell would cost me everything. For Huck and Tom to admit the truth would mean no punishment at all. Boys were expected to slip out, to tell fibs, to cause trouble and cut up from time to time.

But if I didn't reveal Joe wasn't the murderer, wouldn't I be guilty, too? I didn't want to admit this back then, and have to give up being the only female Freebooter in existence.

In the end I would, though. And give up Tom as well. But that second part was much harder, and would take me more than one try.

THESE CHILDHOOD RECOLLECTIONS, the things I still had to confess to Sid someday, all tired me out. I left Mary to tend her battered corporal and went back to the dining room to pick up. I'd figured to begin with my father, but he'd already righted himself and was back at the table spooning up chicken stew, as if we always did away with a blue-belly or two during supper.

I stood beside his chair and folded my arms. "You caused a right mess this time, Pa. I think you're a fugitive from justice and don't know it yet."

"Is that so? Well, pass the salt," he muttered.

"All we've got is what Corporal O'Brien brought. I'm sure you're above using that."

He looked annoyed but kept forking up bits of potato and chicken, chewing vigorously. Even in a crisis, there was nothing wrong with his appetite. I gathered up Gage and got him to sit down again and eat as well. But my taste for dinner was gone. All I could think of was the plain truth: I had to get my father out of Hannibal, or better yet, Missouri. Not just for his sake but for all of us. Once I admitted this problem and its solution, I felt as if the giant hand that had been squeezing my chest had just let go.

So I must find Sid and convince him to leave as well, before we were deemed disloyal and arrested. President Lincoln and the Republicans seemed bent on leveling every state that was slave or southern. Soon there'd be nothing left here but strange northern faces above blue wool. And no doubt a few civilian ones waiting for a chance to turn in a friend in exchange for a greenback dollar.

Why couldn't we go West like the Robbins family had? I'd seen them off a few weeks ago at the depot, brokenhearted, mourning the boy they'd lost to a minie ball in Tennessee. Still grieving, but they were breaking clean, looking to a new beginning. People went off and started over every day. That wasn't giving up, just knowing when to lay down your cards on a losing game. Sid would surely see the sense of it; he'd never relished fighting and intrigue like Tom did. Surely he must be sick of doing war by now. I'd find him and make him come home. We'd pack up, sell what we could, and go. Mary and Gage could stay with friends while I made the arrangements.

I looked at my father, who was crumbling corn bread into his chicken stew. He didn't say another word, but his face had taken on a chastened look, as if he knew he'd gone too far. Who knew how long this contrition would last. No telling what he might get up to if I left him here while I was gone. In the event, I needed help locating Sid, too. We couldn't simply gallop aimlessly over Missouri looking, as Lieutenant Dickenson had pointed out. So Pa would have to come along, which meant I'd need a guide and escort who could double as a keeper.

But there was hardly a local man left who was over thirteen or under sixty. If you added the pull of enlistment to the subtraction of imprisonment, the war had left us a village of women and children, punctuated by the odd grandfather here and there.

Then the answer hit me, someone other than the government I could ask for help. A fellow never hog-tied by regulations or bound by codes and oaths. One who always walked a shadowy path and didn't give a damn what people thought or the law said.

Huck Finn knew the woods and river and back alleys of eastern Missouri better than the lines on his grimy palm. His in-town lurking and trailing of me had finally inserted him even into my dreams. I didn't know what his game was, or how honorable or low his intentions. But he'd shown an interest. Huck had always dressed motley. Now such half-official getup implied a connection to one of the shabbier units, maybe even raiders. But if anyone could find Sid, it was Huck Finn. If anyone had news of what was happening in the rest of Missouri, or where Sid might be, that would be Huck as well.

A ne'er-do-well quietly following a respectable married woman around town was something polite society might ignore, but not for long. And if the man was coarse and low, for that woman to seek him out would be the gravest breach of decorum. But times had changed. With no male relative to do the dirty work and protect my delicate sensibilities—the few I'd ever had—the choice was clear. I'd go look up Huckleberry Finn and take advantage of his newfound fascination with our family.

Someone had to deliver my father and my husband from the attentions of the United States government. After burying one son, I did not intend to lose more men—or any of my family—because of this war. Not if there was any way under God to prevent it.

Ten

THE NEXT MORNING I TRAIPSED downtown, stopping at the grocery, the dry goods, then the millinery shop to browse, as if out for errands and in no hurry. A different kind of fishing expedition than we'd engaged in as children. I hoped Huck was watching out regular; shadowing me on some sort of schedule, so it wouldn't be necessary to roam for days on end, until I just happened to run into him. It put me in mind of the old days, when we ran in a pack as the Freebooters. An uneasy alliance, three wolf cubs shoulder to shoulder, each pretending not to eye the other's dinner.

But morning passed, then noon. My feet began to hurt, for the worn soles of my boots were skinned to paper. I stopped for a cup of whiskey-pale tea at the hotel's tearoom. Whatever the shredded brown herbs at the bottom of my chipped china cup, they weren't the Darjeeling touted on the chalkboard. More likely rabbit tobacco picked out back and dried in the rafters.

I decided to head home. That was when I finally saw him. He might not dress as well as a gentleman, or even a clerk, but I had to admit that under his eccentric dusty attire Huck Finn had grown into a fine-looking man. He was outside the hotel, and the only reason I was able to sneak up on him was the auspicious moment I'd picked to exit. Huck had his back to the big plate-glass window, leaning away from the wind, hands cupped to his face to light a segar.

When he straightened, I stood in front of him trying not to smile, gripping my reticule. He didn't look startled, only tilted the gray-brimmed cap he'd dressed up with a bluejay feather in the band. "Well, hey there, Miz Hopkins."

"Mr. Finn," I said in an admonitory tone. "Why are you following me, sir?"

His eyes crinkled; he looked very pleased with himself. "You never once called me sir when we was swimming jay-naked in the river."

I blew out a breath, trying to hold on to my temper. I had never swum *naked,* least of all with Huck. Fifteen years later, he still made me feel like throttling him with the nearest thing at hand. The hankie balled in my fist might be turned into a makeshift garrote, but I restrained myself. "Never mind the river, Huck. Those old days . . . I'm not . . . look here, I need to ask a favor."

He glanced down at the slatted wooden sidewalk, but interest had kindled in his eyes. He fished a shred of tobacco off his lower lip and drawled, "Ask away. I ain't in no hurry."

Slowly at first, then pouring out like the big river's own course, I spilled my troubles, both recent and remote. It was comforting to look into a face from my youth, which lately in my dreams had taken on the glow of a lost paradise. In the midst of my tale, Huck offered a supporting arm, and I took hold. We set off, strolling down Main Street.

". . . and the Judge said that to a Irish corporal?" He looked impressed. "And then Mary, with the iron skillet. You wouldn't be making any of this up, now?" He threw his head back and laughed. "Wait'll I tell Tom!"

I dug in and dragged him to a stop. "So you do know where he is."

He leaned around me to spit into the dusty gutter. "Didn't think I was playing your shadow for my own benefit, did you?"

I turned my head so he wouldn't see me blush. "Of course not. But why would he send you to do such a fool thing?"

At the crux of the issue, same as he always had, Huck clammed up. "Didn't ask. He don't tell me nothing. But what you aim to do about this mess with the Judge? It ain't my concern, you know. Tom never said nothing about taking you anywhere."

"But Sid's his brother!"

"Cousin. And they weren't never the best of friends. But blood kin, all right."

"So of course Tom would want him rescued," I insisted. "If he knew, that is."

Huck grimaced. He scratched his scalp under the hat, and looked down at the dirt searchingly, as if an answer might be inscribed in the dust, or on a paper scrap. At last he blew out a hard breath. "I s'pose, iffen he's truly in trouble. All right, then. What's your plan?"

I'd had most of the night to think on that very question.

FIRST I ASKED HUCK to find my father temporary shelter, based on a kindness the Judge had done him years ago, when Huck had come into a little money. He'd been a favorite of the Widow Douglas, and she'd remembered him in her will. All I wanted for myself was a way clear to Sid. We'd figure our own passage West. Mary could come along, and welcome . . . though perhaps she and O'Brien had other plans.

Huck contemplated, then slowly nodded.

In the end, I had to tell the Judge a lie to get him to come along. I said his services were required at a made-up murder trial in St. Louis. I told Mary most of the truth, though. That we'd go on the train, be away some time, and return soon as possible. I didn't say Huck would be meeting us at a livery there, and that we'd continue south on horseback to find Sid. I didn't want to get her hopes too high.

I left everything else to Huck. I'd never been south of St. Louis. From what I'd heard, southern Missouri and the Ozarks were still wilderness. And now, a zone of skirmishes between angered residents and various invaders, Union and otherwise. Compared with the few villages down there, and the embattled citizenry, Hannibal was probably an oasis of peace and prosperity.

WE BOARDED THE HANNIBAL and St. Joseph line two days later. Rocking along, Pa fell asleep quickly in the seat next to me, leaning heavily on my shoulder. I tried to read Miss Austen, but the perils of finding a husband in the bucolic English countryside didn't hold my interest. I suspected it might be easier than finding one lost in the bedeviled land of Missouri. I looked out the window awhile, then picked up the newspaper Pa had found on a bench at the depot. The *Missouri Democrat,* three days old, but still the latest news I'd seen in weeks. I scanned the casualty lists, biting my lip, but found no familiar names. Then I glanced at an article titled GENUINE ROMANCE IN REAL LIFE. I grimaced and decided to skip it; if I wanted romance, Miss Austen had surely done it better. Just before I turned the page, I noticed the engraving that accompanied the article. It showed a woman wearing, of all things, a federal army uniform. I shook out the creases and began to read.

The anonymous female was the orphaned daughter of a Michigan family who'd followed her older brothers to war. She'd been a nurse initially, but grew unhappy with that work. So she dressed in some of her youngest brother's clothes and joined their regiment as orderly to the major—who was willing to conceal her identity, since he was her cousin. Both brothers were killed; then she was wounded. Recovering in the hospital, she'd fallen in love with a medical officer. When she revealed her secret, he proposed. Her only bad experience impersonating a soldier had been when a fellow enlistee realized the hoax and threatened her virtue. She'd been forced to shoot him in the face.

Well. I read on.

The irony of the thing was that when she came to St. Louis to plan for the wedding, she'd been arrested due to an ordinance against women wearing men's clothing in public. At the end of the article, the reporter gushed compliments. "Her appearance, manners, conversation, and beauty place her far above the ordinary class of woman who affect the garb of the opposite sex."

I'll bet, I thought. Imagine wearing trousers and suspenders, running around a battlefield shooting with one hand and fending off lecherous fellow soldiers with the other. It was preposterous. The square-jawed, steely-eyed woman in the engraving didn't quite appear the fresh flower the reporter had described. I folded the newspaper, picked up Jane Austen, and read until we reached the junction of River des Peres and the Mississippi, on the outskirts of St. Louis. Carondelet was a sprawling marine works bristling with cranes and tracks and sheds, rolling mills and sawmills. A black pall of coal smoke hung over everything.

The town, just outside St. Louis, was served by three stations. We got off at Robert Avenue and the docks at Davis Street, since our train also carried a freight of iron ore to the Carondelet works. The conductor told us to catch a horse car on Broadway Avenue. At Meramec Street we could connect into St. Louis. The line operated twenty cars, so the only problem was keeping an eye on my father. We got aboard ours, and took a seat.

The car was pulled by a mule so slow, I figured the army requisitioners had wisely passed him by. Carondelet seemed a mighty diverse place. Our fellow passengers spoke English, French, German, and languages I couldn't even name. Near the ironworks, a bevy of Irish got on. I'd forgotten how bustling and dirty St. Louis was, how many buildings and shops and factories it held. People thronged the sidewalks and crossed in front of our horse car recklessly. Everyone was in a big hurry; it was not a bit like Hannibal. I wished Gage was along, so he could see the place his mother came from.

We passed the huge Anheuser-Busch Brewery on Pestalozzi Street, next to a liquor warehouse and a soap factory. Then the St. Louis Hotel, the Varieties Theater, and a pawnbroker. Next, numerous physicians, small shops, eating houses, more hotels, an apothecary, two dentists, and a chocolate factory. Shops selling shoes and furniture, and a butcher's booth. Steam whistles shrieked, cabdrivers cursed, and scents rank and sweet, choking and tempting, some such as I had never encountered, drifted to us. From eating places, onions and meat, yeasty bread, but also strong, sharp spices I didn't recognize. The sour, mildewed scent of old hops. Lye and perfumes from the soap factory.

So many sights, sounds, and smells were overwhelming. I was glad to get off at the Casey and Doyle livery stable. Huck had been waiting there for hours. He paid the proprietor, and we were given two horses. Huck had his own roan gelding.

Pa balked at first. "I shall be late for my court appearance," he said.

"They've postponed the hearing," I told him. "So Huck is kindly taking us on a nice little jaunt."

Pa looked dubious, but mounted up. He'd drawn a hammerheaded nag that looked part mule. My mare was a paint, black and white, sleek and well-muscled, with trim hocks and dark, intelligent eyes that looked at me directly, with curiosity. When I stroked her nose, she nuzzled my shoulder and nibbled my pockets. "What's her name?" I asked the livery hand before we rode away. Huck rolled his eyes and clucked to his mount, clearly ready to leave.

"Cleopatra," the boy said. "On account of she think she a queen."

"Maybe she is." I leaned down and whispered in her ear, "I'll just call you Cleo."

We rode out onto the main street, then turned south to leave town.

Not quite September yet, but as we left the city limits, the air gradually became cool. We stopped overnight at a rambling, tumbledown place Huck called a boardinghouse. He seemed to know the smiling, broad-hipped widow who owned it. If anything, they seemed overly familiar. After dinner, when I realized all three rooms upstairs were occupied by me, my father, and the widow, I asked no more questions about sleeping arrangements.

The next few days we rode hard through drifts of fallen leaves, avoiding towns and pikes, keeping to woods trails and farmland, moving after dark and sleeping days to avoid the attention of federals, bushwhackers, and any overzealous local militias. The sidesaddle felt awkward at first. I hadn't ridden since before Gage was born. I hadn't, in fact, been on a horse in years. Married women go in carriages or on wagons. They don't gallop hell-for-leather over the countryside with children clinging to their waists. Now nothing lay between me and a fall but the grip of my right knee, crooked around a leaping-horn.

"Go easy on me, Cleo," I said. "I'm out of practice."

My arthritic father straddled the balky, lop-eared animal Huck had provided with little trouble, though he complained every mile of the horse's habits and demeanor. "This beast is half mule," he griped. "I believe it has taken a great dislike to me."

"Oh, Pa, that's impossible," I snapped, trying not to think of the ache growing in my own backside, the cramp from the weight dragging on my cocked knee. "You know mules can't breed."

"Nevertheless, one has," he fumed. "And this sorry cut of dog fodder is the result. My kidneys are jolted into my throat at every dip and stone. The spavined beast has a gait like a broken porch rocker."

Huck glanced back. "You sure know horseflesh, Judge. It's the spawn of a jenny mule and a busted wheelbarrow. I'd offer to swap, but this horse won't abide nobody but me on his back."

When we crossed a branch of the Big River south of Camp Jackson, the water was so cold, it numbed my feet. So deep, it soaked my legs through my heavy stockings and my feet through my lace-up boots. Pa's mule-horse balked on the bank, planting all four hooves in the mud like tent stakes. It stood head down, refusing to wet its hocks. Huck had to lash it with a lead line to get it moving again.

As the land rose gradually to signal the Ozarks were ahead, the red-turning leaves of oaks and sycamores and dogwoods gave way to green. To pines, and more pines. The view might be monotonous, but out from under the looming arms of the giant turning red oaks I felt warmer, more cheerful.

We camped overnight off the stony trail, under a stand of butternut hickory. I piled armload after armload of leaves on the fire. "To get it hotter," I claimed, rubbing my hands together as if I were cold. But it was really for the sweet, woody smell.

After a scant dinner of bacon and day-old biscuits, we turned in. It had never before occurred to me that a saddle might make a good pillow, but the smell of honest horse sweat and old leather was soporific. I slept heavily, better than in months. I rose once to draw a scrap of old saddle blanket over my legs, to ward off the first of autumn damp and chill.

I woke at that time of night just between dark and dawning. Someone was creeping around the camp not far from where I lay. I held my breath, trying to think what to do, how best to alert Huck. I kept my eyes half-shut, trying to make out the intruder without giving away that I was awake. It did cross my mind Huck might've taken some notion about my intentions, or come to claim payment for his help. But when I rolled over easy like a dreaming sleeper, both he and Pa were still lying at opposite sides of the fire, the Judge sawing logs with every breath.

The intruder stepped on a dry leaf, not making much more noise than the muted crinkle of paper a room away. But Huck sat up suddenly, a glint of steel in his hand.

I've always disliked knives, even the kitchen variety, since my imagination never fails to summon a vivid picture of what a sudden slip might do to unprotected flesh. I drew my feet under me, preparing to kick and claw and bite, or at least to run. Then Huck stood up in plain sight, as if there was nothing to fear, and greeted the shadows. I saw that more than one person had invaded our camp.

"About time," drawled Huck, and one of the others laughed. I recognized that sound, the low, pleased rumble of it. I checked to see I was all buttoned and covered, then got up.

One intruder, the tallest, dropped an armload of branches on the coals. The fire blazed up. When he backed away, the orange flare lit his face. Broad jaw, straight nose, long, slanted eyes. A thick head of auburn hair that needed cutting. And though in such poor light I couldn't see them, I knew there were freckles on every inch of him.

"Meow," I whispered. Then, louder, "Tom Sawyer. I might've guessed it was you sneaking around in the dark."

A PARTY OF SIX NOW, we traveled deeper into the woods, down through a wet, swampy bottom to cross a narrow, icy creek. Then, over a barrens of untrampled oat grass that the horses gazed at longingly until we reined them in hard. As the sun rose, we headed back into the trees on a rutted trail so worn and narrow it must've been trod not only by Shawnee Indians but their ancestors as well. "Is this the Spanish Trace?" I asked Tom.

"Naw, it's older," he said. "Some folks call it Atchafalaya."

The camp we finally reached was not what I'd expected. I had imagined it would be romantic as a Barbary pirate outpost. That Tom and the others had finally gotten to live out their boyhood dreams of exotic adventure. Instead, I saw a no-nonsense lean-to and some Sibley tents with a big fire going before them. Something stewlike bubbling away in a huge iron pot. Two skinned deer hung from a tree for butchering. A regular picket line of horses off to one side, and hobbled mules grazing on browning fall grass. Ragged scarves of smoke caught and hung in the branches like Spanish moss. Underneath sat a group of men, mostly young, who gave us quick sideways stares.

Soon the Judge and I were settled before the fire, cradling tin-mug breakfasts of venison stew. Tom came back and squatted there, gazing at me. "You look real good," he said at last. "Hardly married at all."

I couldn't think of a comeback to that. It was disconcerting, being so close to him after so many years apart.

"Tell me about Sid," he said. "He was wounded?"

"A little, though he claims it's not too bad. But I still need to bring him home. I—that is, *we* want to go West."

Tom didn't look surprised. "Most Missourians have had a bellyful of martial law and looting. Don't blame you." He took hold of my sleeve. "And what've you been up to, Bec?"

His touch, even muted by cloth, felt warm and good, maybe because the wind through the trees was so chill. When he slid the hand down farther to take hold of mine, I wanted to pull away, yet still hold on. I settled for giving his fingers a quick squeeze, then drew back with the excuse of getting a better grip on my mug of stew. I thought of Gage, back home under Mary's care. Right now, if I wanted to, I could let Tom know about his son. But how did one open such a conversation after so many years?

"Oh, the usual," I said at last, shrugging. "Doing the wash. Putting up preserves. Outrunning the Union militia. And you?"

He laughed. "War put the hex on river commerce, and most pilot jobs. I went with the Union first, figgering to stay on boats. Only I got tired of ducking all those sharpshooters on the banks. Then I started out for the West."

"But you're still here," I observed, worried about the reasons a man like Tom would've turned back from the very trip I was planning. "Don't tell me Tom Sawyer turned tail at the sight of a little wilderness."

He shook his head. "What happened was, near the Pottawatomie a farmer named Doyle sheltered me in his barn. Middle of the night, I hear a commotion; Redlegs ridden over the Kansas border. They shoot Doyle in his yard and start plundering the house. While the women are out in the yard on their knees, crying over the bleeding farmer, I crawl to get my gun, and try to count Redlegs."

"How many?" I asked.

He smiled. "You know I ain't good at sums. All I can think to do is open up from the barn. To shout out, 'Come on, boys, we got 'em now!' Like there's a whole army hid in the hayloft with me. Them Redlegs hightail it, but on their way they torch the house.

"The widow and girls was burnt out, so at daybreak I took them to a neighbor. Saw farm after homestead after farm in the same shape, over the next few days. Before I hit Aubrey, Kansas, I turned back. Didn't see how I could just ignore the War, after all that."

I glanced around. "All these others. Who're they?"

Tom started to answer, then just grinned and jumped up. "Say. Hold on a minute. We got somebody I know you want to tell how-do-you-do."

He was back in a minute with a tall bearded Negro man in work boots and overalls. I took a close look at his good-natured brown eyes, about all I could see above the tightly curled beard, and then I jumped up, too. "Jim!"

He wrapped my outstretched hands in his two warm, big ones. "Miss Becky. Sure glad to see you's okay."

"But—but what're you doing here? Mary said militia or federals or . . . *somebody* took you off to fight."

He nodded solemnly. "Yes'm, that's right. Some raggedy men bent on mischief. But Tom's bunch was up near Palmyra then, and overtook us on the road. They stopped and set me free. Tom said I ought to head on up north if I wanted. But I decided to stick around here a spell."

That seemed an odd choice. "Wouldn't you be safer north, in a free state? Like Illinois."

"Oh, I'll get away by and by. But they conscripting us for the army up there, you know. So I tell Tom and Huck, I gone to stay here and cook. After the war finish, I head up north. You know somebody got to be responsible for these wild boys."

Well, I couldn't argue with that. Back in Hannibal, Jim had been in Tom's company most of his life. A few years older, he'd watched out for Tom when he was little, then humored Tom when he got older and was full of pranks—letting Tom think, at least, that he was smarter. Jim had also spent time with Huck on the river, though he never spoke of that. He'd not made it to freedom on that trip, and I wondered if he'd ever regretted his trust in Huck. But Jim only looked troubled and changed the subject if anyone ever brought it up. Back then the two of them had been running from different demons; demons they must still carry even now. But Jim had always been a good and true friend to all of us, and was only proving it once again.

I came back to the fire, where Tom and Huck and a few fellows were sitting around smoking, spitting, passing a stone jug. Other men were playing cards, or whittling, or casting bullets.

"So are you north or south, regular army or guerrilla?" I asked Tom. "I can't keep up."

"We answer to nobody," he said. "Though we ride sometimes with Reeves's Scouts."

Timothy Reeves and his Fifteenth Missouri Cavalry held a personal grudge against the Union's home guard down here, and the guard returned the favor. Reeves and his troops had been persuaded to leave home only once, to fight in Kentucky at Perryville. In their absence, the militia came back into southeast Missouri, raiding and looting and burning. When they heard, the Fifteenth had turned home, vowing never to leave again. According to the newspapers, they'd been skirmishing with militia and federal troops ever since.

Tom and Huck thought Sid might be with a unit south of their camp. So we rested; I mended a tear in my skirt, and one in Pa's trousers. I saw to our horses. My father and I ate an early dinner with the men. We finished our meal; then I got Pa bedded down under some blankets that were not only wool but U.S. government issue. Stolen, I supposed. But who would quibble about accommodations at such a time? I went back out to the bonfire, and we sat around it, companionably silent for a while. Then, as if at some invisible signal, the stories began.

"Come home after Perryville to take care of my wife," said one graybeard suddenly, from the other side of the fire. "Bella got the wasting sickness, wrote she was too weak to mother the young'uns. When I got there, house and barn was naught but ash. Wife and babies gone, too. I found them at last, thrown down the well. While I was off fighting like a man ought, they wiped my family off this earth like soot from lamp glass."

His companions nodded. One by one each recited his own account-sheet of what the War had cost. Farms owned for generations burned to cinders and scorched brick. Fathers and brothers and sons shot or stabbed or hanged in their front yards, while the women and children screamed and cried and were made to watch. Sisters and mothers and daughters, at a word from anonymous informers, rounded up and packed onto trains like cattle, shipped to Gratiot Prison, where they scrubbed clothes for their jailers, lived in damp filth, and died slow of consumption.

The man next to me, really a boy of about fifteen, raised his hand as if he were still at his school desk and needed permission to speak. He began hesitantly. "My brother Frank? He was with Price's men, and come home after the fighting at Wilson's Creek. The Guard come and arrested him. Mama got him off by persuading him to sign the oath. Then he run off with Quantrill's bunch. Now I reckon he's with Bill Anderson."

In the firelight he was handsome, with brown hair and dark eyes, though he also had large, prominent ears, and a fading purple bruise on one cheek. His shoulders were drawn up tight, as if he'd been struck from behind and was expecting another blow.

"What happened here?" I said, reaching out to gently touch the mottled bruise.

He ducked to evade sympathy, as any self-respecting boy would. But my interest seemed to loosen something in him, for his shoulders relaxed and the words poured out, tripping over each other. "I wanted to go fight, but Mama said I was too young. So I was home when some federals rode up looking for Frank. They meant for Dr. Samuel, my stepfather, to tell where he went. When he wouldn't say, they tied his hands, wrapped a rope round his neck, and pulled it over a tree limb till he dangled off the ground. Haw haw, they said. Let's see how well you dance. And they choked him over and over while Mama begged them to quit."

He glared at the fire as if seeing it all unfold there again. "Finally they let her cut him down. He was bad off. She dragged him to the house, but then they commenced to beat me. Just kept on and on, no matter how I said I don't know nothing. And they did . . . other things I can't even say. After my ribs knit up, Mama sent me here to my cousins. But I left them. I'll sign up with Bill Anderson, or maybe Quantrill. To revenge what they done to my folks."

He frowned and looked around with his lower lip stuck out, as if some grown man might contradict him. His expression so reminded me of Gage, I wanted to hug him. But a boy his age would resent that. So I only said, "You were brave to suffer all that. What's your name?"

"Jesse, ma'am. Jesse Woodson James."

"What a nice name. Pleased to meet you, Jesse," I said.

He nodded, then drew up his knees, propped his chin on his folded arms, and stared silently into the flames again.

"I slept in the tall grass by day," said the last one at his turn to speak. "I lay in the woods and skulked like a varmint by night, looking for food. I was hunted, while all my kin was made to suffer for my sake. This war has changed me from a man into a wolf. I got no country, I got no flag."

He spat into the fire. As if that was a signal, they all got to their feet, yawning and scratching at patched vests and ragged coats. They retired to the tents or sheds or corners where they slept curled up, half-wakeful, like boot-scarred mongrels. Finally only Tom and Huck and I were left at the fire.

"I'm turning in," said Huck, yawning. "Being odd man out and all."

I wondered just what he meant by that as I watched him go. Tom bumped my shoulder, leaning into me so hard, I nearly went on over. "Nice to have a woman around here for once. Nicer-smelling to sit by, anyhow. Ever think we'd sit around a campfire again, so many miles from Hannibal?"

I scooted a couple inches away, but not because I wanted to. "I've done a lot of things we never imagined when we were young. I may yet do more."

He put an arm around my shoulders and hugged me companionably to his side. This time I didn't pull away. His wool jacket felt rough against my cheek. It smelled of woodsmoke and grass and the horse he'd been lately riding. "I used to think we'd end up together," he whispered. "Though not like this, exactly."

I smiled in the dark, knowing he couldn't see. "Oh, you mean in a nice little white cottage with six children inside?"

He tensed. "Well. I guess I don't know what way exactly."

"One of us is married, anyhow," I said. "And tomorrow we'll go after Sid."

He grunted, but said nothing else, which worried me. "Tom. You *will* help?"

"Oh, sure. He's kin, ain't he."

Still, I worried. Tom had never hidden the fact he disliked Sid. And I didn't really know Tom well anymore. Eight years had passed since I'd last seen him. That'd been the day of my wedding, when he'd stood outside the church like a ghost come to haunt me. Then the War had rolled over us, just as it had torn and scarred and hardened the whole country. Now Tom rode with desperate, disillusioned, maybe murderous men, who swore allegiance to no one.

Once I would've trusted him through anything. But that was before we fell out over Injun Joe, and our different ideas of right and wrong. So I had to wonder as we sat side by side: Could I trust him now to keep his word?

I'D LOST MY WHOLEHEARTED faith in Tom not all at once, but slowly, over the course of my thirteenth summer. It began on a sunny Saturday afternoon that fell the week after they'd let Muff Potter out of jail. I sat under an arbor in the backyard, reading a novel by somebody named Acton Bell, called *The Tenant of Wildfell Hall*. I'd borrowed it from my father's library without permission. It was new, not yet on the usual shelf but thrust under a stack of newspapers on Pa's desk. I was a few chapters in, engrossed in the hapless but courageous Helen and her dissolute, profligate husband, Arthur. By then I'd realized if Pa saw it, he'd take the shocking book away in an instant. So I was hunched in the wicker lawn chair, guarding against that event, when a man fell over our back fence.

He crashed down onto Mama's fairy roses. I leapt up and saw someone thrashing and yelping in the flower border. I ran over to help, expecting it to be Tom. He favored a dramatic sort of entrance. But when I grabbed his arms and dragged him out by the coat sleeves, it turned out to be Injun Joe.

He might've been on fire, so quick did I let go and back away. Before that night in the cemetery, I'd only seen Joe in town. I'd nodded at him once when he'd tilted his greasy, misshapen hat to us. Mama had ignored him, grabbing my arm and jerking me along as if *Indian* were a catching disease. Who knew what he'd do if he'd found out I'd been in the cemetery that fatal night?

"Please," Joe said, hands outstretched as if to show he had no weapon and meant no harm. "I don't want trouble from no one, young miss. I need your help."

He looked like he needed help. His face and hands were torn and bleeding from rose thorns. Blood threaded down his neck and was soaking into his collar. But it wasn't just that. He was thin as a willow switch, and his dark eyes looked haunted. One side-seam of his black coat gaped from a tear, and his shirt appeared dirtier than usual. His right sleeve was rolled up over a long, deep gouge that looked like it was mortifying. He held that arm away from his side, as if he couldn't bear to have it touch anything.

This was the fearsome Injun Joe, the so-called Cemetery Murderer. And we children had brought him to this pitiful state. I swallowed past a hard knot in my throat. Fright made me breathless, like I was on a swing going too fast and couldn't stop. But my fear was slowly replaced by horror, then disgust. And yes, pity. If an animal had wandered up in such shape, I'd hurry to take it in, to fuss over and nurse back to health again.

I was just as much to blame as Tom and Huck. I hadn't spoken up, and so had badly wronged the man, too. If the boys saw him now, could they still tell their slanted story? Adding up these pitiful details, my fear drained away. "I can get cotton-lint and a sticking plaster."

He clasped his outstretched hands in a pleading gesture. "Some food instead, mebbe? Old Joe, he ain't eat in days."

I bit my lip and nodded. "Wait behind the garden shed, where no one can see you. I've hid there myself plenty of times."

I slipped in through the back door. From the upper hall rolled the long, deep notes of a gospel song, which meant Trenny was up there waxing furniture. Mama was shut in her room for her regular afternoon nap. Just as I was supposed to be, but it was no big feat to slip down as soon as her startlingly unladylike snores began.

I tiptoed past the foot of the stairs and ducked in the pantry. Inside were leftover ham biscuits on a plate under a cotton dishtowel, and a new wheel of cheese big enough to carve a few slices from without anyone noticing their absence.

Joe ate like a starving stray, bolting the food in ragged gulps, hardly chewing. It was sickening, but still I felt sorry for him. He swallowed the last of the bread and sliced ham, and washed it down with a mug of water from the well. "You're a kind young miss," he said. "You know old Joe didn't hurt nobody. But most white folks, they sure think so."

"Well . . . I don't," I said slowly, unwillingly. Fighting the fear that remained of him as a sly, shiftless Indian, as a dirty half-breed. Not clean, not like us. The kind my mother always favored with her frostiest condescension, when she wasn't pretending they didn't exist. Up close, his eyes were not small and black and hateful like I thought a red Indian's would be, but green flecked with brown and gold. The hands that tore at the food were sun-browned and grubby-nailed—but then, so were mine. His were slender for a man, with long tapering fingers. Graceful-looking, the kind that might play a piano, or doctor a person. Or, I supposed, skillfully shuffle a deck of cards.

He was still regarding me keenly. "You don't feel scared to be out here with old Joe?" he said, wiping crumbs from his face delicately as a cat.

"I don't know," I said, which was true. "It doesn't feel any more dangerous than climbing Holliday's Hill, or wading in the branch."

He nodded. "I seen you before. With Tom Sawyer, and the other. The Finn boy."

I tensed again. Did he mean in the cemetery? Perhaps he had come to silence me, then. I edged away one step, ready to bolt for the house. "You have?"

"They was out at the old cemetery that night. Or so they says. But what they swore to the law, that ain't the way it happened. Not saying they be lyin', exactly. Just confused, like."

I nodded, too worried to speak, thinking of what else he might've seen.

"Sheriff don't know it, but Joe does. Mebbe somebody else was hid out in the cemetery, too." He looked me in the eye for so long that slowly, unwillingly, I nodded. "Mebbe you can talk to 'em, and they'd see sense. Tell the sheriff old Joe ain't the one done it. Old Joe, he's afraid to be took in agin. Some folks around here are still hot about Indians. Some folks, they always had a mind to lynch Joe."

I stared at him in horror. "But why?"

He regarded me silently a moment. "You ain't from here. But Joe's old mother, rest her soul, was full-blooded Sauk. White men run all our tribe away. Government bought their land up for a thousand gold dollars. They didn't want no Indians around. No more'n folks here want old Joe. But Joe, he got no place else."

"I—I'm sorry."

He smiled a little. "See, I think you know better. So you'll talk to them boys for Joe?"

As he made this speech, I wondered why he always referred to himself that way, as if he were talking about someone else. It almost made me look around for another man named Joe.

I shrugged helplessly. "Already tried that. Maybe I can talk to Tom again at the picnic next Saturday. There's a tour of the cave right after."

Joe looked surprised, then thoughtful. "The one three miles below town? McDowell's Cave."

I nodded. "My father has a steam ferryboat chartered. A treat for the Sunday school classes. My mother thought it up."

He rubbed his hair until it was even more snarled and disheveled, then shoved his hands into his pockets and paced around behind the shed. "If Joe happen to be at that cave, too, maybe Tom Sawyer might listen? That boy, he got it in for old Injun Joe, can't figure why. We got to get this whole mess straight. But Joe can't show his face to a crowd. Not when white folks is in a hanging mood."

I thought a minute. How I could save Joe from the noose, and Tom Sawyer from a lie. And, of course, myself from being locked away for years by my shocked and angry parents. "Maybe I could steer him to one particular spot," I suggested.

I still thought then that Tom didn't really mean any harm, that he was mistaken, somehow blinded by his tragic past. If he saw Joe up close, pitiful as he was, surely Tom would come to his senses and tell the Judge and sheriff the old Indian was no murderer.

So Joe and I made our plan. He smiled and stuck out a calloused hand. And though it was unwashed, the nails broken, the creases grimed with dirt, I took it in my smaller, slightly cleaner one and we shook on it. Then I helped him drag a wooden crate over to the fence. He scrambled back over and was gone quick as a shadow on a cloudy day.

Eleven

S ATURDAY MORNING YOU'D HAVE THOUGHT everyone in Hannibal was gathered in our front yard. The little ones raced around playing tag and squealing. The older children divided up, boys and girls, then each group worked hard to pretend no interest in the other. Finally my mother and Trenny came out onto the piazza, looking flushed and harassed, and handed out huge wicker picnic baskets. These were carried by some of the bigger boys, and by our chaperones, three young ladies from church, who were assisted by a couple of single gentlemen.

At eleven we trooped down Main Street in a high-spirited parade, the girls a tide of white lawn dresses and blue ribbon sashes. The boys all wore short pants, though some even had shoes on. Tom hung back, scuffling along barefooted with Joe Harper and my cousin Jeff. But when I got near, he fell in beside me without a word. When we passed the Widow Hopkins's, Sid was at an upstairs window, gazing glumly down. I tugged Tom's sleeve. "Why's he staying at home?"

"Ain't you too mad to talk to me?" Tom asked. He glanced up and shrugged. "Ah, he's sick with a bellyache. Mary stayed home to keep him company. She's a saint."

"Poor Sid. I wish he could come, too."

Tom slapped viciously at a horsefly that had zoomed in for its own picnic. "Well, I don't. I hate the sorry little do-gooder."

"Oh. But why, Tom?"

Instead of answering, he started to whistle off-key.

It would be very late when we returned, so I'd been invited to stay the
night with Susy Harper, along with two other girls who lived far from the
landing. When I told Tom, his eyes gleamed. "We'll go up to the Widow
Douglas's house later, then. She has ice cream every day."

"I don't know," I said. "Maybe." That kind of subterfuge would normally
appeal. But just then the idea of hoodwinking my parents didn't hold so
much attraction. Maybe it was recalling what bad shape Injun Joe was in,
thanks to Tom and Huck's tale. Or maybe I was tired of living a double life,
even at such a young age.

We all crowded onto the ferry, a broad white vessel with red-painted
railings and plenty of brass fittings. The crew was a tall, balding Negro man
and a muscular white fellow with a withered arm tied up in a sling. At last
the huge blackened stack shrieked out a burst of steam. The wheels cranked,
throwing gallons of muddy Mississippi, and the boat lurched away from the
pier. The passengers sent up a shout of joy and hung over the railings, waving Hannibal good-bye.

Three miles below town, we chugged through the shallows to the mouth
of a woody hollow. The children debarked and raced off to run up and down
the craggy forest slopes until we were near collapsing from heat and black fly
bites and hunger. Then we sat in the shade and dug into the wicker baskets,
which held a feast of fried chicken, cold baked sweet potatoes, tart apples,
Trenny's deviled eggs, and thick slices of sugar-frosted devil's food cake. Then
the chaperones insisted we sit in the shade for an hour for our digestion. That
produced a lot of whining and scowls. They looked young, but in the end had
turned out to be no better than parents. After squirming under this enforced
rest for a half hour, Tom leapt up and shouted, "Who's for the cave?"

I felt a jolt almost like fear, worrying whether meeting Injun Joe would
shame Tom into admitting the truth. He might hate me for planning this
confrontation. He might not believe I meant well, and wasn't against him.

Tom pulled me to my feet. We all climbed the hill to McDowell's, the
youngest ones scampering on ahead, the oldest carrying bundles of fat

white candles. The cavernous mouth of the cave was shaped like a gigantic triangle, a giant capital A. Someone had already been up and unbarred the massive oak door that normally sealed it off.

Two young gentlemen heaved the door open on its squealing hinges. The first dim chamber rose tall as the foyer of a giant's castle, and felt cold as an icehouse. Its limestone walls sweated frigid pale droplets. I peered into the deeper gloom of a side corridor that stretched off without end, then glanced back over my shoulder at the green-and-gold sunlit world waiting outside. For a moment I wanted to run back to the ferry.

Then Tom had hold of my arm. "Here, Bec. Take a candle, and I'll light it."

All around me, people were lighting candles, fending off others who rushed up and grabbed at them. Many lighted tapers were knocked down and went out, or were blown out, before the harried chaperones were able to restore order and form us up in a respectable line. By and by we went filing down the steep descent in reasonable order. The main avenue was eight or ten feet wide, but our feeble lights didn't begin to reveal the ceiling. Our flickering rank of candles was a mere procession of fireflies, or Wee Willie Winkies dwarfed by the vast gloom of the cave's moonless night.

The air farther in was colder than a springhouse packed with Maine ice. I shivered and wished I'd brought a shawl. From time to time we passed crooked offshoots that led who knew where, for this cave was a labyrinth neither Theseus nor a Minotaur could ever have navigated.

Tom leaned to my ear. "Folks say you could go down and down and find nothing but more tunnels." We all were whispering, for the sheer size of the place made a body lower his voice. "Down and down," he repeated. "On into the belly of the earth, and it'd be all the same. No end to it."

I shivered from cold and from too much imagination. Tom had been here a hundred times, or so he said. I supposed he knew this cave as well as anyone. Yet he'd just admitted he could never master it, should we get lost. What I knew of its history made me feel no better, either. A St. Louis doctor named Joseph McDowell owned it. Folks whispered that he did medical experiments on dead bodies, and used the cave as his laboratory. They said he kept his own daughter's corpse preserved in alcohol somewhere inside, in a glass coffin. It gave me chicken chills, wanting to see such a terrible thing as much as dreading it.

We strolled down Grand Avenue, pausing to admire the oddity of Alligator Rock, and then a formation like a huge cross, and next one that looked just like a birch-bark canoe. That got me to thinking about Injun Joe again. I tried to steer Tom away from the group, toward where Joe had said he'd wait for us. When the others stopped to exclaim over the glittering surfaces of a stone called the Spring, I saw the Straddle Alley turn was next. I slid my hand into Tom's and raised a finger to my lips, then pulled him away.

He didn't resist, only asked, "Where we going?"

"I want to see the Gypsy's Crystal. You know where it is, don't you?"

He hesitated a second. "Well, sure I do," he said at last. "Next to Tom Thumb's Bed."

So we went on, and he made careful marks now and then with a stub of chalk probably purloined from the schoolmaster's supply. After two more turns we spotted that perfect little four-poster made of dripping water and minerals, fancy enough for a midget pasha's repose. I was impressed. "Let's climb up on it."

"Sure. Here, I'll write our names on the wall." He stood on top, using the smoking candle to black our initials on stone. "Now we'll be together forever. Once you've writ your names in McDowell's Cave, you made a lifetime pact."

I was about to ask how he knew that, when I heard the faint echo of footsteps.

"Somebody's coming," said Tom. "But how'd they get ahead of us? And . . . hey, wait. They're coming from way off inside."

We looked down the narrowing corridor, which sloped downward. At a light that slowly grew, bobbing as it approached. I felt Tom tense beside me, and put my hand in his. Perhaps he thought it was a ghost, or the corpse of the doctor's daughter, escaped from her glass box.

At last the figure drew close enough to see. There, holding a lantern, was Injun Joe, trudging uphill from deep in the cave. He didn't call out or look around, just plodded on with grim determination. Maybe that's what scared Tom so bad. That dogged inevitableness of Joe's walk might've seemed like one of his nightmares come to life, like the silent red men who'd sneaked into their cabin to kill his parents. Perhaps he thought Joe *was* one of them, come back to finish the job. Or to revenge himself for a lie.

Tom leapt off our perch on the limestone bed, and bolted down a side tunnel, dragging me along behind in a grip so tight, I knew it would leave bruises. Behind us I heard Injun Joe shout. "Wait!" I cried to Tom. "Don't run! Joe just wants to talk to you."

Tom looked back as if I'd lost all reason, and ran faster. He zigzagged through tunnels and crooked, canted rooms studded with gleaming swords pointing floor to ceiling. We dodged rocks and razor-sharp outcrops of minerals. Until I finally dug in my heels and pulled back so hard, he had to slow.

But by then, we were already lost.

TOM STILL CLAIMED HE KNEW the way out. We wandered for hours, becoming weary and thirsty. Every time he thought he heard Joe, Tom dragged me deeper into the labyrinth. By then his fear had become contagious. In the candle-shadows, horrible things lurked around corners, making faces, ready to jump. He led me behind a lacework waterfall made of dripping limestone and down through a wide crack in the wall that opened into a huge space like an empty ballroom. Across the stretch of wet, glittering floor, a glass box hung suspended from chains. It seemed to glow on its own, as if it held phosphorus.

"What is that?" I asked, squinting into the dimness, though I thought I knew.

Tom seemed calm now, swaggering as if we hadn't just raced through the dark like field mice fleeing a hawk. "The millionaire's daughter," he said. "So beautiful, old Doc McDowell couldn't bear to put her in the ground. Instead he made her grave here. I reckon the cold might keep her, anyways. But the coffin's filled with spirits."

"She's saved under glass, like Snow White," I whispered.

He nodded. "Go on, have a look."

Fascinated and repulsed, I took three wavering steps forward. Then three more. My fingers brushed one side of the cold, slick glass. A girl floated there in clear fluid, black hair drifting around her face, the hem of her white dress floating around her bare ankles. Suspended forever, a mermaid trapped in a wasp jar.

"One day," Tom whispered from behind me, "Huck and Joe Harper and a boy from Palmyra all come in here. On a dare, I climbed up and lifted the lid. The Palmyra boy reached in and dragged her up by the hair and kissed her lips."

I looked again at the vague, perfect face a few inches from mine, floating dreamily, as if she'd crawled into a giant bottle and fallen asleep. White dress, white hands, no color at all except for that long dark hair. As I gazed at her, so clean and perfect, I thought: *That's the way they'd like me to be. My mother. The schoolmaster. Even my father. Silent. Clean. Bleached out and colorless. Good all the time.*

I could imagine her shifting slow and graceful, turning that white face to look into mine. Smiling. Inviting me to climb in. I backed up a step, and then, though I wouldn't ever run away in front of Tom, I turned my back and walked quickly to the far side of the room. "Let's go. We got to find the others."

I'd given up on fixing things between Tom and Joe. My plan had been doomed from the start, for Tom's fear and hate were so great, a single meeting would never overcome them.

We moved on, but it seemed we were only going deeper, that the ground slanted ever downward under our feet. After hours that felt more like a day and a night, I grew weaker and weaker. If only I'd eaten more of the abundant food at the picnic! But I'd been too nervous things would go wrong. Well, they certainly had.

You, dear reader, probably know what had been happening with our companions, back in the blessed light. Sam Clemens's book told that: How the other picnickers at last left the cave, group by group, panting in exhaustion but still full of hilarity, smeared with tallow drippings, besmirched with clay and soot. Pleased with their adventure and so worn out, the chaperones forgot to count heads as they boarded the waiting steam ferry, as its bell clanged to call everyone. They never missed us.

It would have been near dark. By then I sat in a heap on the floor of the cave. At first I imagined them noticing our absence, rushing right back to find us. Except no one would come all the way back where we were, a secret place where the descending tunnels had taken us a good piece down toward Hell. I was thirsty and tired and hungry, but at least we still had light.

Then something swooped at my candle. A black wing knocked it out of my hand. The burning taper rolled away, then dropped off the edge of the walkway. It fell, but I never heard it hit bottom.

We got up and walked again. I had to light my last candle off of Tom's. Each new corridor we came upon, he would reassure me. "Oh, it's all right. Now this ain't the right one, but we'll come to it by and by."

The sixth or seventh time he said this, it hit me. I turned and looked into the dark with horror. "Tom. You didn't make any marks. Not after we left the casket."

His voice came to me low and shamed. It was very dim, but I could still see that he was slumped against the wall, face turned away. "I was such a fool," he whispered.

We grabbed each other then and cried so long and hard, I thought we'd lost our reason. I didn't want to stay down here forever, to keep company with a dead girl, to wither and turn to dust while she floated there for eternity. "What kind of father would pickle his own daughter like a beet?" I gasped through my tears. And then we were suddenly laughing like fools, which of course we were.

At least we'd got some of our spirit back. But all we could do was keep moving. It wasn't until Tom blew out my third candle that I realized how much time must have passed. That he was trying to save it in case no one came. I thought he still had one or two left in his pockets, and some stubs as well. But all my hope was draining off like water. Those candles might measure how long it would be before we were rescued, or found our way out. But when they were gone, we were as good as the walking, hungry dead.

It was so cold. We lay down for a while and I curled in a ball, shivering. At last I fell asleep. When I woke, Tom turned out his pockets; he had a crumbling piece of cake left from the picnic. We washed it down with some strangely sweet-tasting water that trickled in a stream down a nearby wall.

"This is the last candle, Becky," he said, and held up half a tallow stick.

I began to cry again, pride forgotten. Bitter tears that burned my cheeks. I dreaded dying in the utter dark, without stars or moon, while the dead girl in her glass box swung slowly, slowly from her chains, staring with colorless eyes.

No good hoping I'd be missed that night. Mama and the Judge thought I was spending it with Susy Harper. Susy would think I'd changed my mind and gone on home. We sat and watched the last candle melt and puddle until the wick winked once, then went out.

We slept again and woke hungry enough to eat a wax candle, had there been any left. Later, I don't know how long it was, I heard faint, far-off shouts.

"Tom, someone's coming. They've found us!"

"No," he said dully. "That's nobody. Just the Injun."

"Even so, he must know the way out. He just wants to talk, that's all. I swear it."

Tom snorted. "How would you know, anyhow?"

"He told me so. Tom, he came to my house. He looked so pitiful, I gave him some food. And I talked to him about the killing. And . . . and you."

I told him about the conversation I'd had with Joe that afternoon. I could hear in his voice he didn't believe it one bit. But I argued and goaded until he agreed to move toward the sound. We had to go slow, since there were pitfalls and now we couldn't see them. Once he dropped a rock off the side of the path, into a gap that seemed to stretch out on either side. But no clink of stone on stone, no hollow thud of it striking bottom ever came back.

The shouts came again, fainter. The voice seemed to be on the other side of the huge pit. Tom whooped until he was hoarse. I'd already lost all power of speech but a raw whisper. After a while the other voice, or voices, faded away.

Tom found a string in his pocket and paid it out as we roamed, still looking for a way out. At one turning, he shouted in fear.

"What?" I gasped, clutching at him, at the air.

"Injun Joe's hand!" he gasped.

I peered into the darkness. "Where?"

Tom was backing away, shouting out threats and curses. I heard someone running off. Or was I only hearing things, too, making up new terrors in that endless maze of night?

"But he might've shown us the way out," I whispered, turning around in blackness. Feeling dizzy, as if I'd suddenly been hung in darkest space like an unwilling star. I flailed at the nothingness all around me, thick as a blanket thrown over my head. I couldn't breathe; I was choking on the cold stale air, groping until my fingers slammed into a wall of rock, shredding the skin over my knuckles. I sucked the blood away, frightened by how good the trickle of warm liquid tasted, how sweet it felt going down my parched throat. I squeezed my eyes shut to try to stave off the screams pressing at the back of my throat, eager to burst out and show me how crazy I'd soon be, forever.

I didn't want to go mad, or to die. Which would be worse? I blinked back tears and lifted my face, ashamed of my cowardice. If we were going to die here, I should be on my knees, praying, saving my eternal soul. Yet all I could think of was food, and how nice it would feel to have a hot bath and lie on my own bed. Clearly, I was not only bad but not much of a Christian either. A little bit of suffering and I fell apart, and could think only of bodily comforts.

A low moaning sound lifted the fine hairs at the back of my neck. What was it, that ghostly groaning? I looked over, sensing more than seeing that Tom had fallen to his knees. I reached out and my hand collided with his face, hot and slick with tears. He groped for my hands like a blind man and gripped them so hard, I cried out. If Tom Sawyer had given up, then what hope was left?

I dropped to my knees beside him. The shock of the hard rock beneath them felt like a small atonement for my pride and cowardice. For thinking that I had the answer; that I alone could make things right and save us all. Above all, I promised myself, I would not go mad, nor would I cry hysterically or cling helplessly or give in to despair. Mark Twain has written this scene otherwise in his novel. But the truth is, I did not give in. I resolved to be strong for both of us.

I lifted my face, eyes still shut. I don't know how long we actually knelt there, two miserable human beings huddled in the dark. But gradually I became aware of a cool breath on my face. I froze for a moment, not even breathing, for I realized what it was I felt: a faint current of fresh air moving over my skin, lightly caressing my neck.

For air to move in there, for even the smallest breeze to blow, it had to have a way in.

Carefully holding my face up so as to feel it, I followed the caress of that tiny draft, knee-walking over sharp rocks and lurching into holes, one hand always on the wall nearest me, praying not to fall. I lost track of the breeze once and my heart nearly stopped with the bitter horror of a last chance, gone. But I kept on, and as the stone wall curved away I felt that thread of air again, then a small gust. And saw, with my face still lifted, a glowing thread above me. I scrambled on hands and knees back around the curve in the rock wall.

"Tom," I whispered hoarsely, kneeling beside him. "Tom, somebody ran a line in here. We can feel our way out."

"What," he mumbled. "Where is it?"

But no, it couldn't be a line, a rope or string way up there. It ran away from us down what must be a corridor. The darkness there was more a dull gray. And the line or string must actually be a thin crevice, a faint chink of light.

I dropped to hands and knees again and felt my way across the cold damp rock over to him. "Come on, get up," I said.

He jerked away, but I kept tugging at his arm while he batted at me with both hands. At last he stood. Then, leaning hard on each other like old people, we stumbled along. Always looking up, keeping the near-invisible glow in sight. And always keeping one hand on a wall, hoping not to step wrong and tumble off a ledge to fall and fall forever.

Just as I was wondering if I had the strength left even to hold my head up and keep track of that teasing glow above, Tom rasped out, "Another one, I see it. It's a crack in the rock!"

We moved along faster then, nearly falling, tripping over our own feet and each other. The line of light seemed to come closer, to dip down toward us. I began to wonder if we'd already died, and were walking toward the secret crevice in the night sky that led departed souls directly to Heaven. "Wait, stop here," I said at last. "Lift me up."

Tom squatted and I got on his shoulders. He stood again, staggering like Muff Potter on a drunk. I braced myself against a wall and stretched a hand up to the light. I thought my fingers were only inches from it. "Go on, walk," I commanded. Donkeylike for once, Tom obeyed, carrying me along the corridor as I groped up at the teasing light. After a hundred steps or so, my fingertips brushed the pale crease, blocking part of it out.

I dropped to the ground again, and we trudged on. Now we didn't need to keep a hand on the wall to guide us, for the crack widened and we could actually see shapes, then our own hands before us. Then I could reach up and touch the lowering ceiling of rock, feel the wonderful sharp edges of the opening, where fresh air warmer than the air of the cave was blowing in with a faint whistling sound.

We must've walked for miles. And yet, now that we could see again, we didn't look at each other. Only up at the dawning light, at the door gradually opening back onto our world, the simple, holy thing that would save us.

In the end we had to bend over, then crawl on hands and knees, and I began to worry we'd never get out, but die flat on our backs looking up at a slice of sunlight and glimpses of green leaves. A grave with a view, I thought wildly, and giggled. But when Tom looked over at me, puzzled, I managed to be quiet again. We rounded a bend, sweating now, scrabbling up a slope. A gust of air scented with pine resin and river mud hit me in the face, and I shrieked with joy. Here, I could rise on torn, bleeding knees and poke my head out of the cave into light so intense, so dazzling, I could easily believe I'd been lifted to Glory.

For a moment all I did was rejoice, blinking like a blind person suddenly gifted with sight. I slid down again and grabbed Tom; we laughed and shouted and embraced. Then, after all that rejoicing, hauled ourselves up and fell out onto the warm, rocky ground littered with acorns and sticky sweet gum pods. We were so weak by then, we had to sit still just to avoid fainting. At last, when we could look each other in the eye again, we grinned in relief to be free of the dark. It felt like being born again, as if nothing bad had ever happened to us, or ever would.

After resting we half climbed, half fell down to the riverbank. I soon realized we must be nowhere near the mouth of McDowell's, where our group had come in. For this was a low area, and there was no trail like the one cut into the bluff below that great iron-banded door that guarded the cave. We picked our way down to a ledge near the water. By then I was truly dizzy, not from fear but from some illness, a swamp fever.

How long I lay with my head in Tom's lap, I don't know. In a sort of delirium I heard voices, and the splash of oars in water. My father told me later that two men in a skiff came by, and Tom hailed them. They lifted me first into the boat, then Tom, and took us to a house where a kind-faced, toothless woman fussed over us and tried to make me eat. That was the last thing I recall, until I woke up in my own bed in Hannibal.

I didn't realize, when I opened my eyes again to the familiar comforts of my own room, that four days had passed since we'd pulled ourselves from the roof of the Underworld. Our escape route had put us on the riverbank, in the next county south of our own.

Once I awoke, the first thing that happened—after my mother had tottered out of my room, overcome by migraine and the joy of my survival—was that my father came in and sat on the edge of my bed. The Judge took hold of my hand and told me how glad he was to see me awake and well. Then he told me McDowell's Cave had been sealed up for good.

"So no one else can get lost, as you did, my dear. And perhaps die in there."

"Sealed?" I whispered. "But . . . wasn't anyone else inside? Did they check to make sure no person was . . . living there?"

The Judge looked at me oddly. He carefully felt of my forehead. "No one lives in a cave, Becky. Not these days. Are you quite sure you feel well enough to sit up?"

I had to speak out to save Injun Joe's life, if he was trapped there. But what if he wasn't, and I only gave away that he was still here, around Hannibal? Then he'd be hunted again, captured, hanged for a murder he didn't do. And—for I couldn't make myself forget this, no matter how selfish it made me feel—I would be in a great deal of trouble, too.

As I fell silent, my father patted my foot through the quilt. He got up to leave, then turned back at the door, smiling as if he knew a great secret. "By the way, a young gentleman's here to see you."

Pa leaned out into the hall and motioned to someone. Like a sunburnt vision, Tom Sawyer was suddenly in the doorway, clutching his hat, looking uncertain. "Hi, Becky. How you feeling now?"

I dragged myself up straighter in the bed, and grimaced impatiently. "I'm fine. But Tom, listen to what my father says about the cave. Pa, tell him."

"Oh, that," said the Judge. "I already told Tom we'd sealed it up. Two or three days ago. You've been away that long, my dear, in a manner of speaking. Delirious with fever."

I stared at Tom. "You already know? Then you told him about—about—"

When he raised his head, it was clear he was struggling. But with whether to tell about Joe or not to, I couldn't figure. "No," he whispered at last.

I understood then he was not the boy I'd thought he was, no hero, but a liar and a great coward. And now, the next thing to a murderer.

I turned from them both to stare at the wall. "Tom," I said bitterly. "Tell the Judge about what we saw in the cave. The other person."

"Other person?" My father came back to sit on the bed again. "What other person? Lord God, another lost child, do you mean?"

Tom cleared his throat. "That's why I come, Judge," he said then, but too loud, as if he were on stage in a play. "You know when you asked if I'd seen anyone in the cave? Or even any animals."

The Judge nodded. "That's right. You said none."

Tom looked at the floor, his face reddening. "Well. But I forgot, while we was still in there, Becky and me, we *thought* we might've seen someone else."

"What?" cried the Judge. "But this is terrible. Who was it?"

"We thought . . . I think maybe it was Injun Joe," Tom told him.

My father rose and looked between us, dumbstruck. "So that's where he was hiding. Come with me this minute," he snapped at Tom.

As they rushed off, I tried to climb out of bed. It must've made a great thump when I fell, for both Trenny and my mother rushed in. All I could manage was to crawl over and pull myself up enough to look out the bottom pane of the window, down at the front walk where Tom and my father were hurrying off. Tom must've felt me watching, for he threw a look back up at me, over his shoulder. A naked stare full of shame and anger.

Within a half hour, skiffloads of men with guns were on their way downriver. The ferryboat steamed after, packed to the gunwales with gawkers and busybodies.

THEY FOUND HIM SOON as they unbolted the door, after chipping away the mortar they'd sealed the edges with. He was stretched out at the threshold, dead, it said in the Hannibal paper the next day. I wasn't allowed to read it; my mother had ordered that edition thrown away. I sneaked downstairs and found the *Courier* stuffed deep in the trash pile, where Trenny stored scrap paper and old rags. I read every word.

It said Joe's face was turned toward the door, close as he could get, as if he wanted to be as near as possible to the light and freedom that lay inches away on the other side. He'd hacked for days at the foundation beam, the thick interior sill of the doorway hewn from a giant oak. How he must've despaired to find, then, that outside a natural sill of solid stone kept the big door hard and fast in place!

Imagine the hopelessness he must've suffered. I could, from my own stay in the dark. His knife lay by his hand, broken in two. Gnawed strings, the wicks of candles, lay scattered around him. He must've found stubs left by tourists and eaten the crumbs of tallow. His only drink was from a shallow basin of limestone hollowed by moisture dripping from the ceiling. It fell, the reporter said, at a rate of about a drop every three minutes. Imagine watching a drop collect and bulge and hang, until at last it fell, the writer went on. And when it did, there was barely enough to dampen your lips.

I stuffed the paper back into the bin and climbed the stairs to my room. How thin and ragged Injun Joe had looked the day he'd tumbled over the fence into my backyard. How grateful he'd acted for the simple food I brought. He'd thanked me over and over as he wolfed it, while his hands shook from exhaustion and hunger. A healthy man would've lived long enough to be freed by the group that rushed back to the sealed cave. But Joe had used up all his strength hiding and running, trying to escape a false accusation of murder.

And Tom Sawyer, who could've saved him—not once, but twice—had not spoken up. Tom had not told the truth when he'd testified to the sheriff about who'd killed young Dr. Robinson in the cemetery. Then had lied again when he'd had a chance to tell the Judge the cave was not empty. We both knew where Injun Joe was, but only Tom was awake and aware, and could've spoken up in time.

I turned these bitter thoughts over and over in my mind. They skittered and scuttled like a shiny hard-shelled pest unearthed from under a Missouri rock. But I couldn't look away, or excuse Tom Sawyer, or forgive him. I looked and looked, until I understood just how small he was, how mean and vicious, how heartless and cruel. I pulled the covers up over my head and lay very still, but didn't dare to cry, for Trenny had the sharpest ears and an even sharper, inquisitive mind. How could I tell her I'd ruined my life by falling in love with someone as evil and unrepentant as Tom Sawyer?

No one could bring Injun Joe back to life. But Tom must pay for his sins. Otherwise, his soul was lost. He had to confess and at least clear the man's name. And I was the only person left on Earth who could see to that.

Twelve

I DECIDED TO CONFRONT TOM right away, and not let him off so easily as my father had. But when I said I needed to see him, the Judge shook his head. "Poor boy's suffered a great ordeal, Becky, and isn't over it yet. Did you see how white his face appeared after his visit? I had Doc Porter look him over to make sure he didn't need to go back to bed, too."

My father didn't understand why I was so upset. Had the dead man been anyone in town but Joe, would folks have been so easy with his death? His funeral, held three days later, became a sideshow. Someone had conceived a grisly notion to bury Joe right at the mouth of the cave. When word got out, people flocked in boats and wagons from towns and farms and hamlets for ten miles around.

"As if it were a circus." My mother sniffed, shaking her head until the curls over her ears bounced. "How common and vulgar they behave in Missouri! A funeral or a hurdy-gurdy show; it's all the same to them."

She would never get over the differences between her beloved Old Dominion and the blunt and practical West she'd been transplanted to.

"Yes, yes," my father murmured from behind his newspaper. "A circus. Or a hanging, which most folks find nearly as satisfactory. And exactly what the poor devil would've gotten, had he lived."

I had not seen Tom in a week. School was out for the summer, but I managed to get into town by volunteering to do errands for my mother, who looked surprised and pleased, though Trenny peered at me with suspicion. I finally caught up with Tom two days later outside the General Mercantile, where he and Huck and Jeff Thatcher were playing a cutthroat game of marbles that involved barlow knives and quantities of spit.

I pulled him aside at Huck's turn up. "Why did you lie about Injun Joe? He died because you didn't tell he was in there!"

Tom rocked back on his heels and looked away, as blank as if he didn't know me. "He was a good-for-nothing. An Injun to boot. That killing was as much his fault as Muff's."

"But Muff Potter's been set free, while Joe is dead! Besides, that's not how it happened. I was there, remember?"

He shot a glance at the porch where the other boys played, then dragged me farther away. "Not so loud."

"Your turn, Tom," shouted my cousin Jeff.

"Becky, look here. Even if the Injun didn't stab the doctor, he was a bad character. He stole things, and laid out drunk. I bet he killed heaps of folks when he was on the border."

I stared at him then. Tom seemed to have got Joe mixed up with the Indians who'd killed his parents near the Kansas border. I supposed a person might never get over such a thing, that he would carry the scars of it forever, and perhaps look for vengeance whenever he had the chance. Then feel justified, even pious about it. But I couldn't go along with such half truths. Yet I also couldn't imagine turning on Tom, exposing him publicly as a liar, and also as a sort of killer himself. Even if I did, would anyone listen? The Judge and the sheriff had believed Tom about Injun Joe, while I was not yet recovered and still, to their minds, possibly delirious. Whatever Tom had said, they seemed also to believe he'd single-handedly saved me. He was a hero. I was only a prop in his play—as I would be in Mark Twain's novel, many years later.

I thought Tom right about one thing: No one in town would miss Injun Joe. He was redskin trash, a lump of horse dung in the road. What an improvement cleaning it away would make to the scenery in Hannibal.

His funeral was the entertainment of the summer. It'd tied up the thrilling tale of a graveyard murder under a full yellow moon with grisly justice done in the end. Even though Muff Potter was no better than Injun Joe. In fact, I knew he was worse. But he looked more like the rest of us than had the dark-skinned, sharp-faced Indian.

Tom took my arm and shook it. "See here, Becky. You're my girl, ain't you? Yet you're taking up for a lyin' old layabout, a half-breed scoundrel. Over me!"

"*You're* behaving like the scoundrel," I said.

He pushed me away and sneered. "I should've known a high and mighty girl from St. Louis would look down on Hannibal folks. Think us a bunch of ignorant savages. Go on, then. Huck was right about you! Take up with someone else. Like that damned prissy-mouth Sid!"

He stomped off. His friends stared openmouthed after him, then shifted speculative gazes to me. I turned and walked slowly home, ignoring the questions they called out about what in the world was ailing Tom. His ailment was nothing I could fix, or explain, or live with, either. We were no longer sweethearts, no longer even friends. It slowly occurred to me that we wouldn't be spending our lives together, as we'd often imagined, and I did cry then. But by the time I walked up our front steps, I made sure my face was dry, my expression composed.

That summer I saw Tom no more, except from a distance. No one meowed beneath the windows, calling me to nighttime revels. I spent July and August helping my mother plant a fashionable moon garden, and reading the newest books my father had ordered from Boston. Susy Harper invited me to stay over one night, but her brother Joe—a great friend of Tom's—gave me such evil looks over dinner, I slunk home the next morning before anyone else was up, leaving a note claiming headache. I was still the outsider, the come-here, and Tom the local hero.

When school started again, Tom rarely showed. The few times he did, he was late and hadn't done his work. He stood up front righteous as a martyr and took his whippings silently, staring coldly ahead, meeting neither my eyes nor the gazes of his admirers. He must've been planning his escape onto the Mississippi even then. As fall turned to winter, Mr. Cross gave up whipping him for his sins. I think the man's arm simply gave out.

The following March, Tom stowed away aboard the steamer *Prairie*, captained by the famous Isaiah Sellers, a giant among riverboat pilots. Jeff—one of the few boys in town still speaking to me, and only because we were kin—informed me the ship had real staterooms. And that Tom's silver tongue had talked Captain Sellers into training him to be a pilot, instead of booting him off at the next town.

All the news I had of Tom Sawyer after that came from others. He never wrote, but of course I hadn't expected that. A year or so later, I began to spot him occasionally, usually in Huck's company, whenever the fabled *Prairie* made port here on the St. Louis run. Tom always acted as if he didn't see me as he lounged around the dock in his uniform, the commerce of the port whirling and shouting and sweating around him. He was the sun orbited by admiring younger boys, telling stories about his adventures up and down the water. Perhaps he spoke as loud as he did in the hope I'd overhear, or at least be curious and ask about him. I still wanted to be part of the circle that always grew up around him, that followed and laughed and hung on his every word. But I had forfeited my claim by putting justice above loyalty.

Over the next five years, I finished my schooling. When Tom dropped into town from time to time, it made me despair that he could act so cool, so remorseless about letting a man die when he could've saved him. And yes, it galled me that Tom had thought he could still make me do as he wanted—still love him and forget such horrors. The few times we did encounter each other, I cut him dead. His pride made him bow ostentatiously before I swept past, him smiling ironically, lifting his shiny new pilot's cap.

Charming and flawed and some ways a devil, that was Tom Sawyer. And oh, how I missed him! For the first time I wondered if it was possible to love another person too much. One less stubborn might've given in—but not me.

I don't think I'd truly understood all this until many years later, as I sat beside Tom in his secret camp full of desperate men. As once again I breathed in his familiar scent of pine resin and horse and oiled leather and smoky woolens. It was hard not to lean on him or cling to his arm before that big campfire. Many years had passed since we'd savaged each other's hearts back in Hannibal. And not just once, but twice, for Tom had returned one last time. Though no one else knew about that final visit, and I had long ago decided no one ever would, for much was at stake.

So now, when Tom was suddenly with me again, all the joy I felt was turning gradually to bitterness. For face-to-face, I could no longer pretend that both the happier time we'd shared before this infernal war, and the young man I'd once thought of as mine, were not lost to me forever.

I STROLLED DOWN THE LINE of horses, found Cleo, and fed her a leftover biscuit. Then I rolled myself in a blanket underneath the pine-limb lean-to where my father lay snoring, arms crossed over his chest, as if he'd been laid out for burial. At the rate I was worrying over him, and Sid and Gage and Tom, heart lunging at every new problem, I might precede him to the final rest. I determined to get some rest, to try not to think of sitting there at the fire, so close to a long-lost love.

I lay quietly, waiting for sleep. Night sounds closed in until the forest seemed a roaring city full of racket and complaint. The songs of a million peepers and bullfrogs, the testy arguments of raccoons in a nearby tree cursing each other roundly. The high chirruping of the last crickets of the season, which punctuated the sporadic, loopy screech of some demented night bird. And then, just as I was finally drifting off, I heard the faraway choir of a wolf pack. Though they sounded hills and ridges distant, it silenced all the other animals around me.

My eyes refused to close. These were not the benign woods of my childhood, the tame slopes of Holliday's Hill. I had plenty of time to muse on this difference between savagely churning thoughts. But even if I had to lie awake all night in a freezing forest full of wild beasts and stubborn, damaged, snoring men, we had to get an early start in the morning. To find my husband, to whom I'd solemnly pledged love and loyalty. It had been so many months since I'd seen Sid, as I lay there cold and wide awake I could summon up only parts of his face. A square determined chin; a long straight nose, so unlike Tom's short Irish one; dark serious eyes that didn't snap with mischief but rather paid uncompromising attention.

Arrange these bits as I might, I couldn't piece them together whole. I'd no sooner pin down his nose than the eyes would vanish. This failure made me clutch at the prickly army-issue blanket, mutter curses, and finally sit up again. The ground beneath me was nothing like a feather tick, or even a straw one. It hurt when I threw myself back down. How desperately I wished to feel familiar with Sid's face once again. To love it still most of all.

I slept eventually, and dreamed that a man who smelled of woodsmoke and oiled leather and horses had slipped beneath the blankets next to me, sliding warm hands beneath my clothes. He whispered my name in my ear, over and over, as if he'd just learned how and wanted to keep on saying it.

It was, of course, no dream. But when I gasped and lunged away, a rough hand pulled me back while another clamped my mouth. "Ease up. It's only me," said Tom's voice, husky and amused. He kissed my ear, then my neck. "Go back to sleep. Dream."

When he let his hand slide away from my mouth, I whispered, "If I call out, the Judge will hear."

Actually, that was unlikely. My father was snoring like a sawmill and dead to the world. I rolled away again, but not quickly enough. Tom had always been fast, and he knew me better than anyone, in all ways. "Didn't you miss me, Becky? I thought about you on the river. Out here, too. All these years. I sent Huck sometimes to see what you were doing."

"Tom, you have to go," I said firmly. Why couldn't my words sound more forceful, more convincing? If he didn't leave, I feared he'd be proved right: I would not refuse the dream, when it appeared so temptingly in the flesh.

He caressed my face, my neck. Ran warm hands down my sides, and up again, over my bosom. I gasped and sat there stiffly, unmoving. But I didn't pull away.

"You're still hot at me about that damned old Injun," he said at last.

That was a dash of cold water. I shoved him away hard. He got up and stood looking down at me, shoulders slumped, arms hanging as if I'd defeated him in one of our old contests. "Well, if you are, you're right to be," he said quickly, as if he feared I'd turn away before he was done. "It was stupid and mean, even if I was just an ignorant boy. I don't expect you to believe I'm a changed man. But I regret that thing, Becky. It haunts me. I just don't know any way to make it right again. Not now."

I wanted to believe he meant it. And though the next morning I would ride to find Sid, the man I was married to, I didn't send Tom away. I had been married to him first, in my heart, bound to him long before I took those public vows with Sid. Tom and I could never be together as husband

and wife. But I wanted him, just once more. It would have to last me the rest of my days. So I pulled the blanket back and let him crawl in. And we were sinners then, yes. But not against nature.

THE NEXT MORNING I WOKE GROGGY and alone in the lean-to, in a tangle of blankets. The Judge was already up. I found him at the fire, gnawing on a wizened hunk of smoked venison. I looked away quickly, for breakfast has never been my favorite meal, nor was deer my favored meat. The coffee smelled good, though. I took a stick and hooked the pot off the fire, then poured some into a tin mug I'd polished clean on my skirt. I sat on a stump to drink it, and after a few sips I was wide awake and could no longer refuse to recall what Tom and I had done the night before. I set the mug on the ground and rubbed my face, hard.

Lord God. I had turned into the kind of woman people cut dead on the street. The sort who inspired real ladies to twitch their skirts aside in passing, so as not to be contaminated.

I couldn't think of any way to salvage my character just then, not out in the woods and facing a more important mission than improving myself. So after a moment of despair I raised my head again and picked up the cooling coffee. At least I might try to avoid Tom altogether until we had to leave. In fact, I decided, I would not even speak to him again.

"Pa," I asked. "Where's Mr. Sawyer?"

"Tom? Oh, he went off some time ago. They heard militia was camped over the next ridge and have gone to see about it."

"What?" I set the coffee down so hard, it sloshed on the hem of my skirt. What a fool I'd been to think the man would stick around long enough to face blame or regrets. "But he's supposed to ride with me to find Sid!"

"Change of plans," said Huck's voice from behind me. "I'm bound to take you now. Better get suited up."

I looked down at my wool skirt, my heavy cotton waist and merino jacket. "What do you mean? I'm all dressed."

He smirked. "Not for the ways we'll be going, you ain't. 'Less you like branches and brambles in your drawers. Besides, we don't want the kind of folks we'll meet thinking you're a *lady*."

I didn't like Huck Finn talking so about me or my underclothes, and turned my back. When I glanced over again, he was rigging up a dressing room in the lean-to by wedging an oak branch between two supports and hanging moth-holed blankets over it.

A lady will be treated as well as she is dressed, my mother had always lectured. One who failed to wear a hat and gloves would be classed as common; one with bare legs or no shoes would be cut dead by any polite society. But I was sure Mama had never dreamed I'd someday be camped in the middle of the woods, hopping crow-footed behind flea-ridden blankets, trying to yank on a pair of greasy wool trousers of unknown ownership. I looked carefully inside, then was sorry I had. I shook them out vigorously to pretend that would dislodge any vermin, and hopped around some more, cursing. At last I got them buttoned up.

I took a few turns around the shed, expecting to feel encased like a sausage, and strangled down low. The trousers were indeed scratchy against my thighs. Lying so close to bare skin, they felt improper. They set me off balance, as if I might float away without yards of skirt material to anchor me. Yet I couldn't say they were uncomfortable.

Next Huck tossed over a graying collarless shirt, a raveled knit vest, and a rusty black coat that looked and smelled as if it'd first seen the light during General Washington's war.

"How 'bout a fashion show?" he called. "We got to get moving here soon."

I came out reluctantly. Below all this male finery my narrow, pointed, buttoned boots looked tiny, ludicrous. Huck frowned, rubbing his chin, then rooted around in a burlap sack and produced a pair of broken-soled brogans. They were some big, all right, so I accepted thick homespun socks as well, trying not to think of the feet that might've worn them last.

Huck's mouth twitched. "A lady needs a hat," he said dryly. "Bet you thought I didn't know that." He produced a horrible concoction of felt pierced with a bent pheasant feather, and twirled it on the end of one finger.

"No. Absolutely not," I said, taking a step back. "Anyhow, I'm not a lady, remember?"

"Gentlemen cover their skulls as well." He clamped it firmly on my head.

"I better not feel any crawling varmints, Huck! Lord God. I never in my life wore such a getup."

He inspected me again and grunted, then walked over to the string of horses and lifted the sidesaddle off my paint mare. He replaced it with a worn, regular one. I hoped no one would actually see me straddling a horse like one of those pale inbred women who rode barelegged into Hannibal from the hills, chewing and spitting and wiping their noses on their sleeves.

I ran over to the Judge, and hugged him.

"Merciful Heavens, daughter. What have you got on?"

"A disguise, Pa. I'm incognito, so ill-mannered federals don't bother us."

He frowned. "Well, this is most peculiar, and certainly—"

"Unladylike. Yes, I know."

"But I suppose if Mr. Sawyer and Mr. Finn think it best . . ."

I barely managed not to roll my eyes. "Try to stay out of trouble, Pa. Tom will get you someplace safe. We'll all be together again after I get Sid back home."

He returned the hug and gave me a damp kiss. Then eagerly went over to join a poker game being played on a raw plank set across two barrels.

I MINDED MY ENDANGERED reputation only the first couple miles. The real revelation was how much easier it was to sit astride a horse than to hook one leg around a leaping horn and cling for dear life, trying to ignore screaming muscles and pulled knee tendons. After a few miles, I realized my clothes had a mild case of graybacks. It was unbearable at first, the sudden nips from lice in the most inconvenient places. I scratched like mad, cursing Huck behind his back.

That afternoon we passed a burnt-out farmhouse. A woman and a boy were out scraping in the dirt for something, potatoes or turnips or beet roots. They stopped and gaped as if we were royalty but said not a word. They were so thin, they didn't have to. Huck greeted the woman kindly and tossed her a packet of smoked meat from his saddlebag. The worst thing was looking back and seeing the way they tore into it right there in the middle of the road. After that, I could bear the occasional louse-bite pretty well.

As we rode on, the woods grew thicker, the road narrower. "Where exactly we headed, Huck?" I asked, kicking Cleo up alongside his gelding.

He leaned over and spat into the leaves off the path. "Near Iron Mountain."

"You mean Pilot Knob? But I thought the federals had taken it. How can we—?"

"We'll manage," he said tersely, then fell silent. That gave me plenty of time and quiet to think over last night, not a welcome diversion. How much easier if I could've explained away my transgressions as a dream. I began to repeat that in my head anyhow: *A dream, Becky. Just a bad dream.* But it felt too much like what had happened the last time I'd set eyes on Tom Sawyer, seven years before, back in Hannibal. I concluded that I was not only not a lady but also weak and disloyal, and chronically prone to sins of the flesh.

"Damn it," I said aloud.

Huck started and nearly lost the reins. "What's wrong?"

"Nothing, just a cramp," I muttered, resolving not to think of Tom Sawyer for the next few miles. I turned to Huck again for diversion. "Say, tell me. How is it you can roam all over Missouri and not get arrested or conscripted?"

"Oh, I got papers. I been mustered out of the army for having frequent fits and seizures."

I stared at him. "But you never!"

"No, but I could, if need be. Don't like being told what to do, not by nobody's government."

For some reason, as we rode along, Huck seemed to gradually warm to me. Maybe because Tom wasn't there, and we weren't competing for his attention. As we covered the miles, I began to talk a little more, making sure not to be too wordy or judging. We relived some of the old days, and the mischief we'd got up to. I knew better than to mention the graveyard, or Injun Joe, or even hint that their version of events wasn't the true one. I had my own secrets. Things I could never tell Huck or anyone else.

For I had seen Tom another time, just before our wedding—Sid's and mine. And it occurred to me that Tom might've confided the details of that meeting to Huck years ago. Imagining this, I felt an urge to stare at Huck, to interpret the different ways he glanced over at me. If he'd raised an eyebrow at the wrong moment, I think I would've ridden off into the woods to feed myself to the wolves who'd serenaded us the night before.

. . .

THE LONG-AGO YEARS IN HANNIBAL after Tom left passed quickly. I studied hard, read a great deal, wrote in my journal, weeded the garden, and avoided needlework whenever possible. My parents took me on a shopping trip to St. Louis, and I walked most days with Susy Harper. While I filled the time, Tom stopped in town less and less, rarely bothering to leave his steamship and stroll around. My last year at school I saw no sign of him at all. Just like that, he was gone. I guessed then he'd never cared for me, and never would feel remorse.

Yet I missed him, heaven help us. And me with all my life left to live. This seemed to speak badly of my judgment. I retreated further into books, which made my mother despair even as it delighted my father. He bought crates of them, speculating I might be the first woman he knew to read law.

"There have been one or two, up north. It's not unheard of these days," he said, rubbing his hands gleefully.

My mother wrung hers at the notion I might educate myself into spinsterhood. She went to her room to lie down whenever Pa spoke of it, and kept Trenny running with cool cloths for her head. I felt bad I couldn't please my mother, but not bad enough to sit still and learn to tat lace, or paint daisies on china plates, or entertain the well-bred, carefully selected suitors she hinted about importing from Richmond.

On matriculation day, the school had a ceremony at the best hotel in town. The five graduates were me, Susy Harper, my cousin Jeff, Laura Wheeler, and Tom's cousin Sid. My father had arranged for a nice luncheon in the dining room. As our proud families finished pound cake and coffee, I got up and walked to the front, because I'd been chosen valedictorian.

Sid Hopkins leapt to his feet as I tried to sidle past, and managed to topple his chair. Stammering and blushing, he wrung my hand with his sweaty one. "I meant to congratulate you before," he said. "For beating me out for this great honor by only two points."

His long, searching stare made me nervous. He seemed to be trying to tell me something else—but what? "Well, I'm sure I don't deserve it," I said, looking down at the floor, remembering for once that a lady was always modest and humble.

"Of course you do," he insisted. He still had hold of my hand.

"No, really."

But he insisted on my brilliance, and I continued to demur, until at last even his sister Mary rolled her eyes, and Polly Hopkins snapped, "Land sakes, Sid! Sit down."

By then my palms were sweating, too. But my speech was a dry, flowery, tiresome harangue on truth and duty. I still recall the peroration: *Surely any loving reproof of our friend, Truth, is better than the kiss of an Enemy. For it is Truth which gives us strength to overcome our Natures, and conquer such Enemies. Along with Knowledge and Understanding, those bright Swords which light our way in the dark.*

It all makes me wince now, but my indulgent audience applauded madly, save for Joe Harper's grandfather, who'd fallen asleep, head lolling. They rose to their feet, ignorant of the fact they were celebrating my public rebuke to Tom Sawyer.

The schoolmaster brought me a stiff bouquet of hothouse roses provided by my parents. They beamed and clapped, though my mother just that morning had expressed doubts about the wisdom of so public a display of female intellect. She'd fretted this tiny fame would frighten away all suitable men, assuming there even were any in the state of Missouri.

I had no such worries. My old nemesis the schoolmaster was retiring, going to live with his sister in Rolla. I was to take over the position until a suitable new master—meaning a male one—could be found. I planned to hold on to this job long as I could, blocking my ears when my mother hinted at the eligibility of this or that fellow. I didn't love anyone, nor did I care to. And if a man and a woman lived together without love, how could any ceremony in the world make such a sham a true marriage?

To be tied down for the price of a roof and a wardrobe of nice clothes, glued tight to the side of one who meant nothing to me—*that* would be degradation. I'd noticed, however, that few others seemed to share this reservation. On visiting days I'd heard the gushing compliments my mothers' friends paid each other on their husbands and homes, even when the couple in question fought like rabid hounds and hadn't spoken a kind word to each other for decades. But back then I was young and terribly wise, the torchbearer of truth, an all-seeing eye whose gaze would sear to ash all the hypocrites of Hannibal.

At the graduation, my victims nodded and smiled and clapped, unaware I was mocking them. But as I curtsied to acknowledge their praise, I glanced up and met Sid Hopkins's gaze. He was clapping, too, but so slowly, he seemed to both acknowledge and to mock me in turn. A faint smile suffused his face, as if he'd understood the joke and admired me for it. That shook me, because I'd formed most of my opinions of him through Tom. I had no personal grudge, though, and he was nice-looking. Not tanned and muscled like Tom, but rather with pale clear skin, jet-black hair, and a high forehead like Mr. Poe's. As he clapped, I noticed his fingers were long and fine, like a poet's or a pianist's. Realizing I was staring, I quickly thanked everyone and left the makeshift podium.

The next day Trenny called me downstairs. "Got you a visitor. A young gent'man."

For a breathless moment I thought: *Tom.* I raced to the stairs and galloped down.

In the parlor Sid Hopkins sat stiffly, hat on one knee, the book I'd left open on the settee propped on the other. When he noticed me standing in the doorway, he jumped up. I walked past his outstretched hand, picked up my book, and shut it with a snap.

"Hope it's all right to call, Becky. I should've asked you first. But your mother was telling folks yesterday you were bored and needed an outing."

Lord God, I thought. My mother.

His hands were trembling. He jammed them in his pockets, then jerked them out again, waiting for an answer.

"Oh, I see. What precisely did you have in mind, Mr. Hopkins?"

He looked so taken aback, you'd think I'd just suggested we remove all our clothing and wade into the Mississippi. "Oh—well, that is, I hadn't thought—I mean, that you would, uh, consent." He bit his lip but gazed back at me, earnest and hopeful. He looked . . . honest. The sun through the windows made the pale tips of his neat, flat ears glow pink.

Suddenly I felt old and jaded. The last few years I'd gloried in that sensation, but it was tiring forever playing the Keeper of Standards, the Priestess of Truth. I had nothing against Sid. I'd always admired his willingness to raise his hand and answer questions in class and, unlike most of the other boys, not look ashamed of it.

I smiled at him. "Well, then. Let's go."

When I reached out and took his arm, he dropped his hat, which rolled on its brim like a wheel across the parlor floor.

"Never mind that," I said, dragging him out the door and down the brick walk. We strode briskly down the street, and I steered us toward the riverfront. By the time I slowed at the end of Main Street, we were both a bit winded.

"You were right," I said, turning us about at the levee. "A nice walk was just the thing. Now please take me home."

He looked confused, but dutifully saw me back to my front stoop. "Thank you," he said uncertainly. "I enjoyed the company and . . . the conversation."

I nodded, smiled, and shut the front door firmly in his face.

"You are one rude girl," Trenny huffed. She'd been spying and wasn't the least bit ashamed.

"He'll be back," I said serenely, picking up my book again and reclining on the settee. I knew it was so, for his hat still lay like a bowl full of shadows on the parlor floor.

Sid indeed returned. The following week he escorted me to a hop at the Harpers' to celebrate Susy's nineteenth birthday. I danced with him five times, surprised to feel delight at his arm around my waist, his gloved hand locked to mine.

At last it grew so hot, we went out on the piazza. He brushed off the brick steps and invited me to sit. "How about here? There's a nice breeze blowing from the river."

"All right. Yes, let's." I swept my skirts under me, and settled on the top step.

Sid stood for a minute, then abruptly sat next to me. Without looking over, he pulled off one of his gloves. "I hope you don't mind, but I would like to hold your hand."

That was so unexpected, I surrendered one to him. He folded his fingers around mine, and it wasn't his hand that trembled then.

"Come on," he whispered, glancing back at the windows spilling light and music and noise onto the lawn. "It'll be much cooler down by the water."

We rose and walked down to the promenade. I looked back at the Harpers' house once, then decided I didn't care if anyone was watching. We wandered along the walk until we'd passed out of the golden glow of house lights and into the shadows.

"Your mother's invited me to dinner next week," he informed me. "But I won't come unless you say so."

"Please do," I said. "We could use some new conversation over the corn bread."

One side of his mouth twitched, and he nodded. Then he walked me back to Susy's, and later, after cake and punch, escorted me all the way home. On the steps he took both my hands in his again. I thought perhaps he would try to kiss me, and closed my eyes. But ever-vigilant Trenny yanked the door open and held up a lamp.

" 'Bout time you got in," she scolded. "It's mighty late for a young lady to be out."

Sid gave my hands a squeeze, and let go.

"Oh, Trenny, it can't be," I protested. "We were the first to leave. Weren't we, Sid?"

But when I glanced back, he was halfway down the walk, almost to the street.

School began again in September, and I took over the classes. Teaching was not so easy as it'd looked from the pupils' side. The little ones could be kept track of, and they minded me. The older ones were a different matter, the boys especially. Some became convinced they were in love with me, which involved showing off and mooning around my desk until I shooed them away. Others would go out to the privy, then fail to return at all. Such revelations didn't make me like the old schoolmaster any better, but I did wonder how he'd managed to put up with it for so many years without marching the whole lot down to the river and drowning us.

By the second week, each afternoon Sid was turning up to walk me home after I'd rung the dismissal bell. I began to look forward to the sight of his calm, serious face beneath the dark hat that'd once been left as a hostage on our parlor floor. I also looked forward to the way his eyes lit up when I came out of the schoolhouse at the end of the day. Soon he was eating dinner with us two nights a week. My father approved, and called him a steady fellow. "Not like others I might name," he said.

Of course he meant Tom and Huck, but I only looked up from my plate blankly, as if I had no idea. The Judge liked it that Sid was reading law and hoped to be a magistrate. My mother liked him, too, though she was disappointed my only serious suitor wasn't rich, or at least a landowner, never mind not a Virginian. It was hard not to grit my teeth at my parents' frequent heavy-handed hints. But I liked Sid in spite of them. He was different from most young men in Hannibal, who spent their working time at the sawmill or on the docks, their off hours fishing and drinking and bragging and brawling.

I was surprised one day to realize I no longer wanted to get even with the world. And that I rarely thought about Tom Sawyer at all anymore. It was quite refreshing.

Thirteen

B Y THE FOLLOWING YEAR, I was certain Sid would ask me to marry him. I was of two minds about this. I liked him better than anyone else, and was tired of nursing at anger and righteousness like sweet milk, weary of carrying my heart like a stone in my breast. But I had also resolved, after Tom's departure, that I would never marry. I saw that hallowed state as a trap for any woman who knew her mind and wanted a measure of freedom. Yet the idea of being an old maid didn't sit so well, either. I also noticed that on the days Sid didn't visit, I still looked for him, and felt restless and bored. So perhaps that was love—at least, the reasonable kind.

I secretly consulted the revered etiquette book my mother kept on her writing desk and often referred to. Under the heading MARRIAGE I found this advice: *If a gentleman gives you reason to believe he wishes to engage your affections, seek the advice of your parents.*

That sounded ominous and impractical. I turned the page. *Advances or offers of marriage are made in a thousand different ways; but however tendered, receive them courteously, and with dignity.*

I was sure I could manage that much.

Remember also that no happiness can be expected in the marriage state, unless the husband be worthy of respect. Do not marry a weak man; he is often intractable or capricious, and seldom listens to the voice of reason.

How odd. For while that description was the very antithesis of Sidney Hopkins, it clearly related to Tom Sawyer. Yet Tom seemed anything but weak. Capricious and intractable and stubborn, undoubtedly. But weak? I snorted and tossed the book aside. Clearly I'd have to rely on my own judgment in matters of the heart. Not a reassuring prospect when I looked back on my record to date.

Another six months passed before I was actually tested, though Sid had called on me all through that time, escorting me to concerts and lectures and even to services at the Methodist Church. One evening we were sitting on the porch swing after a July Fourth picnic, sweltering, but hoping for a breeze. I kept us moving by kicking against a post each time we swung forward.

"Becky," said Sid suddenly.

He sounded abrupt, perhaps peeved. I was sure he was going to ask me to stop kicking the post, which made an agreeable thump each time I did so. Instead, when I turned to look at him, he slid off the seat of the swing and onto his knees, facing me. Unfortunately at that moment the swing came forward again, and the edge struck him in the chest. It must've hurt a great deal, but he only grabbed the seat to stop it, and didn't wince. He stared up as if he was about to speak, but then didn't say anything.

"What is it?" I asked at last. "What's wrong?"

"It's you," he said. "I want to ask you something."

Of course then I knew. I had prepared myself months earlier, so this is what I did: I quickly closed my eyes and made myself imagine how I'd feel if Sid got up off his knees, turned away, and walked down the steps right then, never to return.

Immediately panic and loss welled up. I opened my eyes and looked at him. "Yes."

He frowned. "But I haven't asked anything yet."

I could've kicked myself then, instead of the post. Always jumping too fast, that was Becky Thatcher. I looked away and smoothed my skirt demurely. "Why, yes. Yes, it is hot, I agree. Let me fetch some lemonade before you keel over entirely."

I started up, but he caught my hand and grinned at me. "Too late. You've already accepted my proposal."

In all the months past, it hadn't occurred he might be making a study of me as well. Or that he'd come to know what I'd do beforehand, too. That seemed a good omen, at least then. I took a deep breath and sat back again. "You're right, I did."

He drew a small flat parcel from his pocket. "So I'm counting on you not to take this amiss. I was only hoping, not assuming."

Gloves, I thought. Oh, very proper. Or an embroidered handkerchief. Perhaps even a lace mantilla. But when I undid the ribbon and tinted paper, it revealed a slim leather volume, its spine stamped in gold. *A Vindication of the Rights of Woman,* by Mary Wollstonecraft.

I coughed to disguise my laugh.

Sid looked worried. "I chose this because your father said you were interested in law and justice. I haven't read it. Of course we can exchange—"

"Oh no," I said. "No, never. It's quite perfect."

Looking back, that was the best part of being engaged. Because next came telling my parents, though of course Sid had already spoken to the Judge. And then, the excitement of the announcement, and the engagement parties. Frantic measuring and sewing and ordering and planning, and all the other draining, hysterical preparations by Mama and Trenny. I cared for none of those things, nor did I want to be the center of such a frenetic domestic whirlwind. But I had no choice. August passed, then September. As the date drew closer, I had second thoughts.

Four weeks before the wedding, I began altering my route to school, walking slowly past the waterfront. Three weeks before, returning from a visit with Susy Harper, I turned impulsively onto the promenade. And there, as if my very wanting had called him up, coming down the gangway of a huge, grand palace-craft in pilot hat and jacket, was Tom Sawyer. At least I thought it was him. I lifted a hand, but he turned and walked quickly the other way.

Damn, damn, damn, I thought. *Why must he turn up now?* Had I conjured him somehow by walking so slowly past the waterside so often, deep down hoping for this? Yet why would any woman bother with a man so stubborn and capricious and intractable, one who anyway seemed only to hate me? I turned and stumbled off, then ran all the way home.

That night I came to my mother's door and knocked. "Come in," she called.

I stood by her bed and confessed I was having doubts. "So I think it might be best to postpone the ceremony."

She drew me down beside her. "Oh, daughter. All women have . . . well, fears . . . about the married state. We shall discuss what duty one owes a husband, and he you, before your nuptial night."

"No, no, that's not it," I said impatiently, nevertheless feeling my face heat up. As if I hadn't gotten a good idea about what there was to that part already! Every child in town had at one time or another seen horses, or cows and bulls in the fields, or at the least, dogs up to their business right in the street. "It's something more—more distressing."

She nodded and patted my hand, dismissing me. But also sounding undeniably relieved. "Whatever you say. Nonetheless, we will have that little talk soon. Yes, tomorrow, I think."

Oh, I couldn't wait.

So my mother thought me nervous, as young brides tend to be, and maybe she was right. I already felt bound to Sid by my word, and my undeniable feelings for him. And yes, by the rules of that damned etiquette book.

Never trifle with the affections of a man who loves you.

It seemed to me, though, that on the eve of becoming one flesh with a lawfully wedded husband, I shouldn't have such strong feelings for someone else. That night I went to bed early but lay awake while the clock downstairs struck ten, eleven, then twelve. My parents and Trenny had long since retired. My father snored deeply. The even breathing of Trenny and Mama was lighter, but their alternating music was annoying. At last I got up and shut my door. As I turned back to the bed, something white flashed against the windowpane. Before I could make it out, or think whether to scream, there came a low *meow*.

I rushed over and shoved up the sash. A gust of cold air preceded Tom as he dropped from the windowsill onto the floor.

"Hey there, Becky," he said, as if it was noon and we were passing on Main Street. He reeked of segars and whiskey.

I took a step back. "What on God's mortal planet are you doing, Tom Sawyer?"

He shoved his hands in his pockets, rocked back on his heels, and squinted hard at me. "Heard something I couldn't credit, in town. So I decided to come ask you."

So that was it. "Well, ask away." I crossed my arms over my goose-pimpled chest, sure I was exposed through the white cotton lawn. "And close that window. I'm freezing to death."

He slid the sash down in its candle-waxed tracks, firm but quiet, until it settled tight. "Is it true? You marrying Sid, I mean."

"I guess I can marry whomever I please," I said, though that wasn't, strictly speaking, true. The other person had to want to marry you, too.

Tom stepped closer. "But you can't, Bec. Not him."

One thing I'd learned as a girl running with boys was to hold your ground. To never let them know you were nervous. Otherwise, you were lost. "Last time I checked, you weren't my father. You are not my master in any way I can figure. Besides, I love Sid."

He winced and shook his head. "No, you don't." He stepped close, grabbed my arms, and started walking me backwards. I went along to keep from falling on my backside, and never looked away from his eyes, glaring right back to show I wasn't cowed. I could've screamed and brought my father running with his pistol. We both knew that.

He stopped our awkward dance suddenly, scooped me into his arms like a puppy, and dropped me on the bed. Before I could scramble up again, he'd pinned me to the feather tick. We wrestled, panting and hissing curses at each other. I kneed and scratched him, managing to land a good crack on his nose. Me desperate to escape the quicksand depths of my own mattress. Him trying to make me settle and admit defeat, admit who it was I really wanted. Well, I would not do it. I think we both knew that.

At last he stopped fighting and let go of my arms. He lowered his head and laid it on my chest as if he was tired out. His shoulders shook, and I thought at first he must be laughing. It did seem in some ways funny, like one of our old wrestling matches up on Holliday's Hill. But the neck of my nightgown was getting damp. With a great shove, I rolled him off and turned onto my side so we were face to face. "Tom, what is it?"

His eyes were squeezed shut, his lips pressed together. He only shook his head.

"Come on, now. Say."

He took a deep, shuddering breath. "I didn't think you could ever love anybody but me."

I stared, stunned he'd even given it that much thought. "Well—well, neither did I. But don't cry. Please." Years later, I was still a fool for a man's tears.

He rubbed a hand under his nose just as he'd done at twelve. "I'm not," he said gruffly.

Oh, for heaven's sake. I jerked up the hem of my nightgown and wiped his face. But as I leaned down to do this, he got a look on his face. Reached out and cupped one of my breasts. "These are new," he said, grinning.

I slapped his hand away, hard. "Stop that, you damned fool! Hush, or someone will hear. Then you'll be in a fix."

"You mean *you* will. Maybe I want them to hear. Then the wedding will be off, I bet."

For a moment I couldn't breathe. "You'd do that to me?"

"No." He reached up and touched my face. "No, Becky. I wouldn't, not to you. You mean more to me than anything."

What a strange way you have of showing it, I thought to say. Instead I ran a hand over his face, too. It felt different than I recalled. The bones closer to the surface, harder planed. The skin rougher, prickly with stubble about the jaw. Tom Sawyer had a beard now. He was a grown man. And he was in my bed. That should've shocked me a great deal more than it did. I rasped my thumb over the stubble, and tweaked his chin. "Ha! That's new, too."

We were left staring at each other, each with a hand cupping the other's face. And it seemed as if all of the past—our arguments, his lies, the death of Injun Joe—all of it was washed away in that long, longing look. The next thing, which didn't require any thought at all, was a kiss. And then another. After some time of this, my nightgown came unbuttoned, got pushed down around my waist. And his shirt landed in a heap on the floor.

He pulled back and looked down at me. "We better stop now," he said, though his hands kept on with what they were doing.

I didn't answer, just dragged his face back down to mine. Tom Sawyer had never beat me in a dare, or yet told me what to do. I had no intention of letting him start.

Afterward we lay side by side, barely breathing. Not saying a word. At last he sighed and folded his hands behind his head. He glanced over at me, looking very pleased.

"What is it?" I asked, poking his side.

"Nothing much."

I tickled his ribs. "Come on, tell me."

"All right. *All right!* You know I can't stand tickling."

"Shh!" I said, pressing both hands over his mouth. "Go on and tell me, then. But do it quiet."

"It's nothing. Only that . . . you won't marry Sid now. You can't."

I felt a chill, as if the window was still open, even though I knew he'd shut the sash tight. "What did you say?"

He raised up on one elbow and looked down at me. "I said, I'm glad you ain't going to marry him now."

I couldn't think what to reply. For, stupidly, it'd only begun to occur to me that the two things—my marrying of Sid, and my being there like that with Tom—that the one must cancel the other out, like daylight and darkness, or snake poison and antidote. Whatever his intentions, Tom's words were true; it was only fair and right to break off with Sid. And it surely looked as if the desire to be his wife had been loved right out of me by his wayward cousin.

But it didn't seem fitting for Tom to so quickly and jovially point this out. What froze me was, now I had to wonder whether Tom had planned all of this, every bit. From first kiss to the stain on the sheets that, even with nothing to go by but moonlight, I saw as a dark blot standing between us.

I scrambled up on my knees. "Get out, damn you," I whispered fiercely.

"What?" He looked at me wide-eyed, perplexed. "But why?"

"Go on!" I shoved so hard, he tumbled off the bed.

He scooped up his shirt, stumbled a few steps away, and looked back at me. "Lord God, what's got into you?"

You have, I thought to say, except it would sound like a crude barroom jest, and that wasn't the way I meant it. *It's you, like a demon, has got into me again. A lying, conniving, selfish, wicked—*

I ground my teeth and pointed to the window. "Get out the way you came in."

He stood straighter when he saw I was serious. "So you're throwing me out already," he joked. "How come?"

"Think about it. What've you done just now, Tom?"

He frowned. "You seemed to like it well enough a minute ago."

I dug my nails into the mattress to keep from screaming at him. "So this is your new plan, then, instead of climbing out of windows the way we used to. To climb inside them, and wreck people's lives?"

He held up one hand. "Whoa. Nothing's wrecked. Not for us."

So he truly did hate his cousin Sid. Or at least didn't give a good damn for him. I pulled my nightgown up around my shoulders again and carefully fastened every tiny button as I gritted out an answer. "For me, and for Sid, getting married is wrecked, Tom. We can't have a wedding now. Or did you intend to step into his place at the altar?"

He stopped to stare, one arm hung up in a shirtsleeve. "Me, *married*? You got to be reasonable, now," he pleaded, as if I'd demanded the moon in a jar.

"Then you get the hell out of here," I said, tasting the bitterness of each word on the back of my tongue. "Go and leave me in peace to think what's to be done."

I wanted him to at least insist on staying. To tell me it was our problem, not mine alone. That we'd think of a way to fix things. I knew that was what Sid would've done, had their places been reversed. Because Sid was a good man, a dependable one who loved me. But it was Tom standing in my room buttoning his trousers, looking puzzled that he was satisfied with things as they stood, and yet I was not.

He did then what he had always done, ever since he was a motherless boy in his aunt Polly's house. He turned the fault away, shed it off his back like rain. "I don't see why you have to nag me so," he said, voice low with resentment, "and ruin everything."

Then he raised the sash, slid a leg over the sill, and went on out the window.

THE MORNING OF MY WEDDING I sat before my mother's dressing-table mirror, brushing my hair. She stood behind me, holding the heated curling iron. Long, fancy ringlets had been Mama's idea. She said I couldn't go to my own wedding with my hair hanging loose and straight as a bundle of sticks, or stuck up any old way in plain braided twists above my ears. We were still arguing about it.

"You must have your hair done up properly," she insisted. "Otherwise you'll look like a little girl. Or a schoolteacher."

"But I *am* a schoolteacher."

"Lord's Mercy," she snapped. "Just be still and do what I say." As if I were six again and wiggling so she couldn't comb out the tangles.

I put my hands up to my face and began to cry. She threw the brush down and left the room, calling for Trenny. "You try," I heard her say out in the hall. "As usual, I can't do a thing with her."

"All right," I said to Trenny, as if she'd just arrived to hang me. "Go ahead."

"Better I do it anyhow." She sniffed, catching the end of one hank and twirling it deftly around the rod. "She only burn your ears off, most like."

I laughed, and she smiled at me in the mirror.

"Why weren't you my mother?" I blurted out. "You've always been a better one than her."

We stared, gaping, glancing from our mirrored doubles to the open door where my mother might walk in at any time. Trenny recovered first. "'Cause if you was mine, I'd paddle you good. And then keep you home."

I turned and hugged her waist. "When she dies," I whispered into her apron, "I'll set you free from this house. Except you must promise not to move too far away."

"Shoot," she said, catching and twirling another section of my hair with great skill and concentration. "I been set free already, and ain't I still here? That's 'cause you folks so damn helpless. Anyhow, what good come from running off and starting over at my age? As if I gonna get married or some such fool thing."

"I'll loan you my dress," I said. "If you are brave enough, I'll even do your hair."

We were laughing like fools when my mother finally came back, my grandmother's Spanish lace veil cradled like the shroud of a saint in her hands. "I declare," said Mama. "Now that's more like it. We don't need long faces on a wedding day. It's mighty bad luck."

THOUGH IT WAS COOL OUTSIDE, the dressing room on the second floor of the church was a stoked oven. My mother had insisted they fire up the furnace before dawn. "We don't want our guests to catch a chill," she'd chided the sexton the day before. "Spare no expense. Plenty of coal! Judge Thatcher will reimburse you well."

So I was slowly roasting in heavy satin brocade. Beads of sweat trickled down my sides and seeped through the boned corset laced extra snug. When I'd asked Trenny to pull it tight, then tighter still, my mother's eyes had shone. As if I'd finally come to my senses and become a late-blooming southern belle. But the truth was, since the night four weeks earlier, when Tom Sawyer had visited, I'd begun to fear my waist was expanding. Ridiculous, yes, but I had little enough knowledge of how such things worked, then.

As soon as Tom had gone out the way he'd come in, I'd dragged the chamber pot from under the bed and thrown up into it. Then climbed into bed again, shivering as if with ague. I promised myself to see Sid the next morning and call our wedding off. I had no need to consult the etiquette book again; I recalled the entire passage perfectly.

Never trifle with the affections of a man who loves you. Some young ladies will not scruple to sacrifice the happiness of an estimable person to their reprehensible vanity. Let this be far from you!

I didn't have to tell him why. Indeed, wouldn't it be a kindness to conceal the true reason? I could invent something womanly and vaporish and all too plausible, like any other Hannibal girl might. Having decided this, I finally stopped shivering and slept a few hours.

But the next morning I was sick again. My mother felt of my forehead and rushed to get a damp cloth, the height of her mothering skills, her one great specialty. As she mopped my face, sending icy rills into my ears and down the collar of my nightgown, Trenny came in.

"What ails the child?" she asked, frowning down at me.

I raised myself to say I was fine, and vomited across the quilt before I could stop myself, or crawl out of bed to the chamber pot.

"Dear Lord, it's the cholera," cried my mother, clapping a hand over her mouth. "Oh, my poor girl."

"Ain't no such thing," Trenny scoffed, nudging Mama aside. She pushed me flat onto the feather tick, brushing at the sheets, as if to whisk something away. When I opened my eyes again, she was looking me up and down sharply.

I stayed in bed for three days, sweating and shivering, unable to eat. Or at least unable to keep anything down for long. I think I called out once for Sid, which made my mother cry. She must've thought I was dying and longed to gaze on my true love one last time. I only wanted to free him, to tell him we couldn't possibly marry, ever. But it seemed too difficult even to raise my head, much less string coherent words together.

A strange heaviness weighed on my belly, though when I raised the sheet and looked down it was flat, even concave. My hipbones dented the cloth of my nightgown. I didn't know then that when some women become pregnant, they experience signs right away. That those so sensitive, or so afflicted, can tell the very night a child is conceived.

But Trenny saw it all, I'm convinced, and knew. It was in her eyes, and the furrow between them that came and stayed whenever she looked at me. When I finally was well enough to sit up and not lunge for the chamber pot again, and we were alone, I told her I had to see Sid and call off the wedding.

"Huh." She shifted beneath her lower lip the snuff she always dipped when Mama was napping. She sat on the chair by my bed and plunked a basket of mending in her lap. "Think that's a good idea?"

"Oh, yes. I like Sid. Maybe even love him. But I can't possibly marry him." She sniffed. "Seem to me maybe you already did."

I tried to sound puzzled. "Why, what do you mean?"

She inclined her head at me. I realized both my hands were pressed over my belly, fingers down, like arrows pointing out my guilt. My face felt so hot, she must've seen the red flush creeping up from the neck of my nightgown. "Well, I didn't, and I can't," I repeated. "It's not possible."

She didn't say another word. Just lifted one of the Judge's black socks from her basket and inspected it all over. Grunted, and picked a needle out of the pincushion tied to her wrist.

I slid out of bed and padded over to her chair. Sank to my knees, took hold of her hand, and petted it like a kitten. "Trenny? Please tell me. What would a woman do if . . . if the man she was set to marry wasn't, you know . . . if he wasn't the one who'd . . ."

"They God." She threw down the sock she'd just begun stitching. "Woman got no real choice, does she?"

She sounded so bitter, it took me aback. I'd been thinking of my problems, but what was I saying, who was I saying it to? Trenny was free, and my father didn't hold with slavery or any of its public or private peculiarities. But the maid of one of my mother's friends had once had a baby that looked awfully white. I'd just that year been allowed into the adult circle, so I heard them talking. When this embarrassment became public knowledge, all were sorry for the friend, and shook their head at the husband.

Yet it was the slave woman who had to carry his, or any man's child, even if she'd been forced. Even if she had a husband of her own.

"Well, if it was a problem, I mean, of mine . . . I do have a choice," I said, trying to get it straight in my mind. "It's terrible to be forced into doing something. But it's not the same."

"A choice?" She snorted. "And what we gone call this little make-believe baby when it come out? Your folks might not be so pleased with just any old last name a'tall. Do you recollect Miss Rosa Willa Tremain?"

Of course I did. Rosa was a sweet-voiced, red-haired girl with beautiful slanted green eyes; she'd been three years ahead of me in school. But poor Rosa drowned in the Mississippi two months after she'd graduated. Uncharitable folks had whispered she'd put stones in her pockets and jumped in. Her parents had moved off to Palmyra a month later, where perhaps the whispers about Rosa and a secret lover would not follow. Where, it was said, they might not have to recall seeing that swollen belly beneath her dripping dress, when they'd fished her like a dead pike out of the muddy tan water.

So there they were, my vaunted choices. I could be shunned by all of Hannibal, and see my parents shamed before the town. Or, there was the fast-running river. Or lying to Sid. For the rest of our lives.

I closed my eyes and tried to imagine floating down toward New Orleans, dragged to and fro with the current, my hair snagging on limbs, my bones battered soft by snags, by wheeling uprooted stumps. My flesh nibbled ragged by slick wall-eyed creatures that darted in for a quick bite. I pictured my parents standing by like grieving statues on a muddy bank as my horrible remains were pulled from the water. All of us stared at, discussed avidly by strangers.

Being vain, and a coward at heart, I chose the lie.

. . .

THE HEAT THAT BLEW UP the church stairwell felt like a foretaste of damnation. Gasping for just one good breath, I went to the window, where a huge oak shaded the church, and wrenched and hammered at the sash until it rose a few inches. I thrust my head out and deeply inhaled the cool, clean autumn air. Then I looked down, and gripped the windowsill tight.

There among the gnarled, exposed roots of the oak stood Tom Sawyer. He was leaning against the massive trunk, wearing his river pilot getup, apparently here to see for himself that I was really marrying his despised cousin. He was no coward, but Tom might be even more vain and stubborn than me. He could never believe he'd lost unless he'd seen it with his own eyes.

I glanced behind me. Susy Harper, my maid of honor, had just left to find a tortoiseshell pin for a lock of hair that kept slipping down onto my forehead. But she could return at any moment.

How I hate you, I thought, staring down at Tom. With one yell I could've brought him a great deal of trouble. I opened my mouth to scream or curse, but just then he looked up. He lifted a finger to his lips to swear me to silence, the way he'd done when we were twelve. That simple, familiar gesture cracked my heart. How could it be that I still wanted him? Even now, forced into a dress so tight, I could only breathe niggardly sips of air. Even now, as I was about to make a marriage unfair to a good man. Love was supposed to make people better, finer, not turn them into faithless alley cats. For an educated, well-read schoolteacher who knew all the declensions for Latin verbs, who'd been valedictorian of her graduating class, I felt witless and stunted.

Come down, he mouthed at me.

I gripped the ledge, then pulled back inside. I struggled once more with the sticking window, and with a great heave forced it to move. A seam ripped under one arm. I shoved again, until the sash rose higher. Then, corseted and laced and powdered and curled, crammed into expensive white satin like a Smithfield sausage, I climbed up and perched on the sill so Tom could see me glowing in all my besmirched finery. "Why?" I said in a low voice. "Do you plan to escort me inside, and marry me?"

He tilted his head back and lifted a hand to shade his eyes. The cocky look drained away. He bit his lip and looked at the ground, hunched as if something hurt him. After a moment he stuck his hands in his pockets, straightened his stance, and without another word walked off toward the riverfront. The set of his shoulders said plain enough that he was free—of me, of everything to do with Hannibal.

Free being his operative word, the reason I'd noticed and admired him in the first place. So this was the only revenge I was likely to have. I didn't savor it much.

Just then my mother and Susy burst into the room chattering, to announce that my father was pacing downstairs. They'd finally got his boutonniere set just right, and the organ was about to start up, so I really ought to come on down the stairs, where my groom waited.

Fourteen

I HAD NO INTENTION OF TELLING this particular history to Huck as we rode over one Ozark ridge after another. Early autumn threw out frantic, last-chance colors: The barely clinging leaves flaunted dull gold and rusty red, as if the trees meant to give up their lifeblood even faster than the rest of Missouri. We rode through mounds of scarlet and yellow and pumpkin-orange, our horses shying when the wind swirled them into snaky, swirling drifts.

We were below a ridge north of Pilot Knob, which some called Iron Mountain after the local railroad, when we heard the crackle of musket-fire. Huck galloped to the crest and looked down. He waved me forward and I urged my mare to the edge. In the valley below, a bunch of men, some mounted but most on foot, were going at each other like ants skirmishing over a dropped sweet.

"That's Reeves's Fifteenth," said Huck, pointing down. "Them others is Union militia."

How he could tell them apart was beyond me. The swarm below all looked the same. Some were in white or checkered shirts and farm britches, dark trousers, or faded overalls. But most wore homespun butternut, with here and there a flash of dirty blue.

"Might Sid be with them?" I asked. "And if he is, can we go get him now?" Then it hit me: Why was the Missouri Fifteenth attacking other Missouri troops, even if they were militia? "I thought Reeves was defending the state border. That he was *for* Missouri."

Huck looked at me with pity, as if a person expecting anything to make sense these days was not right in the head. "All the regular federals, the army, they got sent elsewhere," he said at last. "Kept getting lost up here, bogged in the rivers and chilled at night. Harried by Reeves's bunch till they finally turned tail. The federal depredations now are done by home-grown misbegottens."

"Oh," I said. At first it had made sense, Missouri claiming to be neutral. Merely defending our home from strangers, even if they'd come from only as far off as Iowa or Minnesota or Independence, Kansas. But we were just as much at war with ourselves as with any government from Washington.

"Here's a thing might make you feel better," Huck drawled. He spat over the edge, watching the trajectory of the pale glob. "Think of our own militia like pirates in sheep's clothes. All the *good* Missouri boys volunteered up right away, and went off to be killed. Leavin' to home naught but the dregs. Thieves, liars, and one-legged mother-killers, all keen to beat and bully and murder. They steal the fat of the land and get paid and petted and praised for it. But how was the damn federal army to know that? They wasn't from here."

"Which side are you all on, then? You and Tom."

"We stand for Missouri," he said. "On the side of folks as mind their own business."

"So that's what he's gone off to do now? Mind his own business."

He laughed. "If you happen to think piloting steamboats is his business, why then I guess he's gone off to do it."

"But the steamers are all taken over by federals, too," I said, exasperated. "By them, or by the secesh. He'd be a slave to one, and a target for the other."

Huck rubbed his chin slowly. "Huh. You think so?"

How I hated that know-it-all look, the one I'd got so used to when we were children. Any time he knew a thing I didn't, Huck was pleased as a slit-eyed cat.

"Well, then, maybe he's gone off to manumit one," he said, and slapped his horse's rump with the reins. He began his descent into the valley.

"Manumit," I called after him. "That's a mighty big word! You sure you even know what it means?"

WE WATCHED THE SKIRMISH from a stand of pin oaks and hackberry trees. A half dozen men in butternut passed within a hundred feet of us, running down three more in blue trying to cross a creek. The blue-clads were losing ground fast, especially one who was so fat, his jacket rode up to expose a hairy belly and jiggling handles of lard. His uniform had obviously been made for someone thinner and shorter. The others looked better fit and better dressed. But when they splashed into the water, all three were caught from behind and clubbed down.

On the far edge of the field, men on horseback sat watching the whole thing like a market-day fair. Officers, I guessed, for one on the left held a rippling flag of fading blue silk with a gold seal in the middle, flanked by cutouts of fierce-looking Missouri bears. The one on the right sat erect, though the black hair that straggled long from under his hat needed cutting. The one in the middle seemed the most imposing: a gaunt, broad-shouldered man in a calvary officer's plumed hat and a jacket patched in spots with leather. I couldn't see any of their faces, shadowed as they were by hat brims.

"C'unnel Reeves," one of the men in butternut called over his shoulder. "What you want we should do with 'em?"

The tall, gaunt officer raised one hand in a movement so slight, it could've meant anything. The butternut soldiers turned back to the bleeding blues. The fat one sat in the shallows cradling his head as his hat floated downstream. The others raised hands, palms out, as if to cry uncle and stop the game. But the butternuts fixed bayonets, then spitted them with economical thrusts. They left the bodies lying in the creek.

I wouldn't look away from the carnage with Huck right there. So I swallowed back bile and glanced at the officers again. The dark-haired one spurred his horse until he reached the wooded area and the enlisteds.

"Colonel Reeves says take them out of the creek," he shouted. "Folks down-stream have to drink that water."

His voice raised my skin in goose bumps. Huck laid a hand over mine, where it gripped the reins, as if he expected me to gallop out of cover and onto the field. I shook him off, but otherwise kept still. I wasn't a complete fool, even if after all these years he still liked to think so.

Grumbling, the soldiers turned and scrambled back into the creek, grabbed the dead men by the arms and hauled them onto the bank. The mounted officer watched this work, then spurred his horse back toward the others.

I knew Reeves now, the one in the middle. The flag bearer was still a mystery. But the dark man who needed a haircut, who sat so straight in the saddle—I'd seen that rigid posture before. The tensed muscles that signified one ready to drop from tiredness, but fighting it hard. I'd seen it close up, at home. The black-haired officer who'd delivered Reeves's orders was Sid.

HUCK AND I RODE FORWARD so he could speak to the colonel. I tugged my hat low on my forehead and reined the mare in a few yards back. Sid watched our horses draw near. His gaze skimmed over me and away. I felt pleased with my disguise, which must've been more convincing than I'd thought.

"We can go on into camp," said Huck. "I delivered him some news."

We took a winding track through the forest. At one point I made to fol-low a wider path, and Huck grabbed Cleo's bridle. "This way," he said, pointing to the narrower fork. It looked overgrown, unused.

"Why this one?" I asked, turning the horse onto it.

"T'other's booby-trapped. Mostly pits and deer snares."

The camp was not what I'd expected. Three cabins made of notched logs chinked with mud circled a huge burnt-out fire ring. Motley-looking tents sat off to each side. Easy to see where the wood had come from; many stumps ringed the camp. The largest cabin even had a door and rough shut-ters. The smaller structures were roofed with tent canvas. One had a rudely scrawled sign: REEVES HOWLERS.

The dining room was the outdoors, with tables rigged from board laid across crates or sawn logs. A faint pall of smoke hung overhead, and the charcoal smell of singed meat.

"Last camp they had bigger huts," said Huck. "But they've had to move. The men always set up a howl when they got to leave home behind."

I saw they'd been resourceful, having added fireplaces to their tents, of broken brick or fieldstone or, in one case, mud and sticks. Some had plank walls to shield the entrances. We walked past men sitting on boxes, intent on a game played on a painted board. Dull metal disks like lopsided gray checkers dotted the squares.

"Bullets hammered flat," Huck said when he saw me looking.

"Huck, that news you relayed. Did you tell Sid I'm here?"

He laughed. "Didn't think Reeves'd be too pleased to know that. Tell Sid yourself."

After we'd tied the horses, I went looking for him. He was standing over a scrawny boy, chewing him out for some infraction. I hung back until he was done. The boy trotted off at last, head down. When Sid saw me lurking, he rounded on me. "What is it?"

"Pardon me, sir," I said, trying to deepen my voice, with the result it shot up and down the scale like a young boy's. "Need to tell you something."

"Go on, then," he said wearily, rubbing his face, not looking at me.

I lapsed into my normal tone and pushed the hat back off my forehead. "Sid," I whispered. "It's me, Becky."

He stopped rubbing his eyes and turned to stare. Then grabbed my arm so hard, I cried out. He dragged me off behind the larger cabin so roughly, my hair came unpinned and went sliding from beneath my hat.

"What the hell are you *doing* here?" he said, shaking me.

Not the reception I'd imagined. But it was clear how tired he was, how useless it would be to take offense. I jammed the pins back as best I could and stuffed my hair under the hat again. "I came to bring you back. You said a few months away, but you've been gone most of a year. We've got problems at home. The Judge is in trouble. They hanged some men in Palmyra, and . . . Sid."

He looked apprehensive. "What?"

This would be the hardest. As if Tyler were dying all over again. I squeezed my eyes shut. "The baby."

"Tyler? Isn't he well?"

My voice cracked. "No. He's not." I tried to get hold of myself. "We lost him two months ago. I suppose you didn't get my letter."

His face slowly blanched to gray. He swayed, turned, and walked a couple steps away from me. Then caught himself and turned back. "No, no letters. We don't get mail anymore, here. But—what happened?"

I told everything, stopping only when one of his men passed by. Sid clenched his jaw and shut his eyes. He lowered his head, but didn't cry. I put out a hand, then quickly let it drop when more troops passed, arguing about whose turn it was to cook the potatoes.

Sid looked up at me again. I'd expected him to be grieved for Tyler, of course, and surprised, even displeased at first to see me. But the complete lack of welcome in his gaze staggered me. "I'm sorry about our—about Tyler." The muscles in his jaw clenched tighter. "But you should never have come. I'll be sticking it out here till the war's over. Reeves is the only barrier between Missouri and chaos."

"Missouri is already chaos," I argued. "I've seen it. No man can change that unless he's Jesus God Almighty. We're still under martial law. The federals don't consider anybody regular army, or even rightful citizens. Just collaborators, traitors, or prisoners."

"Colonel Reeves has a commission from the state to defend this border. He came all the way back from Kentucky to do it. I plan to help him keep on."

"What state? There is none, now. Reeves isn't in charge back home, or anywhere else. Huck said the federals used to occupy these southeast counties, and they will again. Sid, they'll think you're a guerrilla. And that Reeves is a traitor. They'll never let you come home. You'll be shot, or hanged."

He clenched his jaw even harder, until a muscle jumped in one cheek. "Nevertheless."

"Nevertheless what? Have you seen dispatches, heard any news? After four years of war, we're nearly beat, even if we tried our best not to be in it."

He slumped against the cabin, hollowed as a reed flute. I wanted to put my arms around him but didn't dare. For just a moment he'd looked right at me. Now he was gazing through me.

"Then it's the end of the world," he said. "You may as well go on back."

In a way he was right. Win or lose, nothing could be the same again. No more sleeping river towns surrounded by green and peaceful hills, bordered with clear, innocent water. Life had turned to mud and blood and smoke and metal, sharp edges everywhere. Now we knew what horrors we were capable of. Maybe not all men had had holes blown in them yet, but it seemed their souls leaked out just the same.

"Sid, please listen. It would be different out West," I insisted. "Other folks are going. It's worth a try."

"Is it?" That was the only time he smiled, but it wasn't a pleasant thing to see.

He didn't seem the same man at all. The one I had married, and loved. But I wouldn't give up yet. "I won't leave here unless you come with me."

"Then I'll have you escorted from camp."

I decided to call his bluff, if that's what it was. "If you do, I'll pull off my disguise."

"Then Reeves will escort you himself. He'll never let you stay once he knows you're a woman."

He took hold of my arm again. Gentler this time, but a firm grip nonetheless. Then he walked us around the camp, issuing orders. Until at last we came upon Huck, smoking and playing poker at one of the tables with some scouts.

"Mr. Finn," said Sid. "I have someone here belongs with you."

Huck sighed and laid his cards on the table. The others groaned, so he must've been winning. He scooped up a small heap of coins and paper, mostly Confederate. Stubbed his segar economically on his boot sole, then got up and brought the horses round.

Still I hesitated, but short of pitching a womanish fit, I had no great plan to change the way things were going. I glanced back at Sid. How could he send me away and look so cold, so like a figure carved of stone? I slowly put one foot in the stirrup and mounted Cleo again as my husband watched like a stranger, arms folded. I looked away, up at the gray September sky, opening my eyes wider to keep any tears from spilling. Crying would do no earthly good, would gain nothing. I nodded to Sid and reined the mare around to follow Huck.

We aren't through yet, I decided. Even if my husband thinks so.

On the way out, we passed two men in uniform just coming in with a pack mule. When the shorter, stocky one glanced up, it felt like looking in a strange mirror.

So I wasn't the only one in camp.

All the uniforms, blue or gray, were bulky and loose, a terrible fit. Still I could see this soldier had delicate features, fuller hips, small feet. I'd read of women joining up, yes, but had scarcely believed it. Under the baggy uniform blouse, that troop member hid bosoms. Maybe the men in camp hadn't recognized her shape as female, being stuck in the notion that a woman would not dare wear pants. So their minds simply denied what their eyes told them. And what's more, since the trousers had been clearly pulled tight across the hips and she had a bulge out front, that soldier had looked not only female, but also five or six months pregnant.

I said nothing about it to Huck, though. "What now? Or should I only ask what your orders say to do in this case?"

He laughed. "A Finn may tolerate suggestions, but not orders. I'll think on it. In the meantime, we'll go into the next town. Got something burning a hole in my pocket."

"All right." I sighed. "Maybe we'll think of a plan in the meantime."

I'd sold a brooch and a garnet ring before we left St. Louis, figuring I'd need the money. The isolated little town we rode into wasn't much more than a single short street lined with shops of red brick or clapboard. Yet in some ways it looked so much like home, for a minute I felt panic we'd taken a wrong turn.

In any case, I was mulling a half-formed plan. For seeing that other woman at the camp had reminded me of the article I'd read on the train. The one about the woman arrested in St. Louis for wearing men's clothing. Had she not left the army and come to the city to plan her wedding, she might still be in the ranks, fighting. Well, the wilds of eastern Missouri were not St. Louis, and doubtless had few ordinances.

My plan would only require a slightly different outfit. I walked down the street with Huck trailing after, reading the signs and peering in windows until I found a tailor shop. "Come along with me. And tell the proprietor I need a uniform," I said to him.

He snorted and dropped onto a bench. Drew a knife and a stick of pine from his pocket and began whittling. "Tell 'im yourself."

"They might not wait on me if they figure out I'm female. Come on, Huck. Say I'm your cousin."

He laughed. "My what?"

"That's right. Don't you want to be rid of me?"

He grimaced and pulled his lanky frame upright. We went on in the store. While I fingered the single bolt of yard goods and gazed at a handful of bone and jet buttons in a glass case, he spoke to the tailor, occasionally gesturing over at me.

At last he came back. "Told him you was a dummy," he grunted. "Well, go on."

I balled up one fist, by then not in any mood to take guff, especially from a raggedy-ass fence-straddler like Huckleberry Finn. "You did what?"

"Told him how you cain't *talk*," he whispered. "Don't you see? He'll figger you're a man and find you a jacket without expecting you to discuss size and fit and whatnot. But he's still got to measure you. Go on, it'll be pie."

He pushed me forward. I stumbled down the aisle toward the back, where the clothing was hung. The thin, balding tailor lifted his lip and smiled at me like a gap-toothed rabbit. He pulled out a tape and began taking stock. When he came to my chest, I hunched my shoulders and looked at the floor, wishing I'd thought to bind my breasts. He pulled the tape around, frowned, then pulled it around again, tighter. He darted a glance up. I looked away, pretending not to notice.

He hesitated, then went on to measure my waist with a good deal more feeling and clutching than I thought necessary. But I held my tongue. He knelt and slid the tape halfway up the inside of my limb, but his fingertips lingered there, remeasuring, as if he were having trouble making out the numbers. When he slid the hand higher, I kneed him in the face. He went over with a squeal, clutching his bloody nose.

"What in hell now," griped Huck, glancing up from a display of Bowie knives.

He came back and looked down at the tailor writhing on the floorboards. As the man dragged himself up onto his knees, moaning, I told Huck the problem. He heard me out, then turned and kicked the tailor's legs out from under him again. The downed man scrabbled away on all fours, dragging the tape between his knees like a tail.

"Looks like we got to shop on our own," Huck said to him. "Unless you object?"

The man fingered his bruised face and shook his head. He waved us to a wooden rack of used jackets and trousers. While the tailor jammed a hankie under his nose, Huck found me a pair of wool pants the right length. Then a sack coat, fairly clean and only a little loose in the shoulders.

"You kin use the old hat, pulled down low. Just for God sakes, don't walk so damn much like a girl. And you gotta swear every chance you get, see?"

"Well, but I don't have a gun." I threw a wad of my money onto the counter, probably more than the four-handed devil deserved. "I'm no thief," I said loudly. "I mean, no *damn* thief." I spotted a pair of stout-looking brown boots, and picked them up, too.

"A *gun?*" said Huck. "They God. That's all you need."

"Anyone shoots at me, I plan to shoot back," I insisted.

"Whoa, there," he muttered. "Nobody said nothing about you doing any fighting."

"Oh, it won't come to that. It's just until I can get Sid to see sense and come along."

"Becky. You got no idea what you're doing. War ain't no jaunt on Holliday's Hill."

"Oh, Huck. I know it," I said meekly, to win him over. "I'll just hang in the back, and stay out of danger. Until I can talk sense into Sid."

We went out to the horses. Huck still grumbled and swore. He plundered around in his saddlebag, pulled out a bundle wrapped in cloth, and handed it to me. The thing was heavy as a lead doorstop. When I unwrapped it, the long blue barrel was pointed right at my face.

"Lord God," I whispered, quickly reversing my grip to point it at the ground.

"Merry Christmas," said Huck. "It's a nice Navy Colt. I guess Tom'd skin me iffen I left you defenseless. Mayhap he'll skin me anyhow. Now, take some of these here cartridges. And we'll just hope to Goshen you don't never need 'em."

Fifteen

ALFWAY DOWN THE TRAIL that led to Reeves's camp, I pulled Cleo up short. Huck looked back and reined in, too. "Give me your knife," I said, holding out a hand.

I have to admit, Huck Finn never bothered a person with questions. He reached down and pulled his hunting knife from the sheath on his thigh. Then held it out, butt first. The thing was a wicked stretch of curved, polished steel. Huck was vain of this blade and oiled and sharpened it every night.

Counting on his dedication, I swept off my hat and clamped the brim in my teeth. I unpinned my hair, which was tied back with a strip of leather. Huck raised his eyebrows when I laid the cutting edge of the blade just above this leather thong.

When I was eight, I'd gotten a mess of pine sap in my hair while climbing a tree. It'd never been cut up till then, and my mother tried even coal oil, before giving up and handing Trenny her sewing scissors. She'd cut it to my shoulders. I hadn't cared, but Mama wept as if I were on my deathbed. I hadn't cut a single strand since, and it hung past my waist. A terrible nuisance to wash and comb, but I'd developed some vanity about it. Sid had always complimented me on the various ways I found to put it up. He loved my hair.

Too bad. I gripped the heavy horse-tail of it tighter, took a deep breath, and began to saw.

Huck winced. "They God, Becky, you're making a mess. Give it to me."

I let go and handed him the knife. He nudged his horse up close and leaned in. For some reason, the notion of someone else cutting it off made my eyes burn, then fill with tears. I swallowed hard. "It's only hair. It'll grow."

Huck stopped and looked at me. "What? I ain't said a word."

Yet he looked upset, too. He coiled the long honey-colored rope carefully and handed it over, still bound by the thong. I stuffed it into my saddlebag. Then he made me hold still again while he evened up around the ears and neck. "That's some better," he said at last, tilting his head. "But you ain't no work of art."

"I only need to pass for a man, not win a prize," I snapped.

"Then it should do, seeing as how you're tall enough. Got shoulders on you, too. Clap that hat back on, and let's go."

He reined in again at the last fork before the sentries. "This is where I get off." He gazed at me sternly. "You still mean to do this?"

I nodded. "Take care of the Judge till I . . . I mean, till we get back. And Huck?"

The roan gelding danced impatient circles in the fallen leaves as Huck tightened the reins. "Yeah?"

"Check on Mary and Gage. There's still a little money in the bank for them. If things get bad at home, she can move to the Judge's place."

He touched his hat and kicked his horse into a trot.

It felt different riding back to Reeves's Fifteenth alone, dressed as the Scouts had been. The late afternoon was turning chill, a few fall leaves among the evergreen still drifting down onto the path, kicked up by the paint mare's hooves and occasional gusts of wind. It was close to dark. Once I thought I saw a few stray flakes drift down through the scarecrow arms of the trees arched overhead. But it was early for snow. The air felt pleasantly cool on the back of my naked neck, and the revolver seemed to anchor me on one side. I felt dangerous and masculine by virtue of its weight alone.

"You and me, Cleo," I said to the mare. "We'll be about the only women there."

She snorted and tossed her head to show what she thought of my continued choice of company.

When I reached the sentries and halted to be looked over, I said I wanted to see Colonel Timothy Reeves, that I was there to sign on. I waited for pointing fingers, incredulous looks, even guffaws. For them to act shocked or disgusted and run me off. Instead they waved me on. I wasted no time looking for Sid, not wanting to be ejected again before I'd had a chance to join up. Instead I headed straight for the cabin Huck had told me belonged to Reeves.

After he'd gone to sign up in Hannibal, Sid told me an army doctor had examined him. I think he mentioned this to ease my worries, so I'd know he was fit enough to go. As if that was my concern! Out here, Huck had mentioned, they had no doctor. One reason Reeves had lost so many men lately to a Union militia major named Wilson, who also executed any presumed Scouts he came upon, no questions asked. Of course, Reeves returned the favor, when he got a chance.

"Our Old Friend told me Jimmy Wilson's hot for revenge and tired of waiting," Huck had remarked to Reeves earlier, as we'd walked around camp. "Our Friend also says Wilson don't care if anybody gets in the way, uniformed or not. He's this minute over at Doniphan burning up the houses of good southeast Missourians. Turning their wives and children out on the road."

Reeves's mouth had tightened, and he'd gone off. So they obviously needed more hands, and I was determined to tag along until I figured out how to make Sid see sense.

I dismounted, looped Cleo's reins over a rail. Went up to Reeves's cabin, and knocked hard on the plank door. The tall hard-faced man with pale eyes and long brown hair, his worn blouse unbuttoned at the top, yanked the door open. "Damn it all, Lieutenant. Told you I was bound to get some sleep now." Then he saw me and scowled, waiting for an explanation.

"I came to, ah, enlist," I said, trying to pull myself up and look tall and bulky there in the doorway. "Goddamnit."

"Why?" he asked. "How'd you find your way here?"

"Well, I mean to, that is, to defend Missouri," I stammered. "To kill any bastard who invades and attacks us. I come down from St. Louis, and Mr. Huckleberry Finn directed me. I got a damn good sense of direction."

His face lost some of its hardness, and he rubbed his chin. "Finn, eh? Well, I can hear you ain't dumb. Are you blind, deaf, or lame?"

Startled, I shook my head. "No. I mean, no sir."

"Then you're in," he barked. "And welcome."

"That's all?" I felt relieved yet disappointed, as if I'd prepared hard for a test and gotten off too easy. "Don't you want my name? How do you know I'm not a damn Union man, a spy? Not that I am. Hell. But what if I was?"

"Iffen you're lying, we'll take care of you soon enough," he said mildly. "You mightn't have noticed, but we're in the middle of nowhere. So what's your name?"

This threw me a moment; I should've had one ready. "It . . . it's Beck."

He only nodded, and didn't ask if it was a Christian name or a surname. "Fine. Go get you something to eat, boy. Then make yourself useful."

He shut the door so hard, a drift of leaves fell off the plank roof and showered all around me like a treasury of old bills, gold and orange and red.

"All right, then, I will," I said to the closed door, wondering just where to do that. Deep down I must've believed I wasn't going to get away with what I just had. I walked off, hoping to avoid Sid for a while. I asked some men who were whittling where I might find food, then get outfitted.

They looked round at each other in astonishment. The youngest one snorted. "Outfitted?"

A graybeard smiled at me kindly. "Supplies ain't in great abundance just now. But get you some vittles from the cook, young feller."

He pointed me toward the biggest fire, where a fat-bellied man was stirring a pot. The steaming concoction turned out to be a stew of rabbit, carrots, and potatoes. Along with a tin mug of it, the cook handed me a biscuit hard as a striking flint.

I'd worried this independent army would be a men's club, a grown-up version of the Freebooters. That they'd do everything together—bathe, dress, attend to urges of nature. But it was already getting cold that fall, and there wasn't much bathing going on. I saw a man from time to time make his way into the woods, so I only had to act like one of these modest fellows and follow suit. I kept my shirt and jacket on all the time, and watched and copied their movements, taking big strides and spitting, as I'd learned to do with Tom and Huck.

The chief of Scouts told me I was to share a tent with another young soldier, wispily bearded, named Gaylord Scott. Oh, I worried then, but we slept with jackets and shoes on and all. My fear ebbed with my growing fatigue. My tent mate, who suffered odorously from indigestion, slept with his back to me, and snored.

Sitting away from the fire each night, trying to remain inconspicuous, I listened to the men around me talk. They were farmers and sharecroppers armed with shotguns and rifles from home. They had no quartermaster, or a dollar of funds, or any supplies to speak of. This puzzled me, for they also had over a hundred mounts that, along with the men, surely needed to be fed. The few experienced officers must've felt challenged to drill a company of such recruits armed with a kitchen-drawer assortment of weaponry, including old-fashioned flintlocks that threw prodigious sparks when fired. Reeves himself carried an old Mexican War rifle.

The men laughed about how before they'd hunted only squirrels and small game. They carried the same weapons now, and knew how to use them. A powder horn, a cap pouch, a string of patching, and a hunting knife completed their kit. I wondered how they expected to go against the prodigious Army of the Potomac, should it show itself in southeastern Missouri. Probably not a man among them had ever seen a piece of artillery.

Of course, rolling guns through the narrow passes of the mountains and across deep, swift streams would pose a problem for the great and ancient Hannibal himself, even with the assistance of elephants. Yet one day when I wandered back behind the tents and cabins, there beneath lengths of oilcloth lay a small brass fieldpiece and a pile of cannonballs.

No, the Scouts weren't at all what I'd expected a military company to be. Officers and men ate together, so I had to keep well clear of Sid. Not too difficult, since I could usually put fifty men between him and myself. Everything seemed oddly informal. Men spoke to Reeves without an intermediary or even a salute, calling him Colonel. Or just Preacher, since he was also a Baptist minister. I'd been concerned about executing a salute properly, but needn't have worried.

As a lifelong town dweller, living in more-settled northeast Missouri, I'd also assumed the people of the Ozarks to be backward and ignorant, lacking in education, rustics adrift in a misbegotten wilderness. I soon realized a frontiersman had to be shrewd, quick-witted, wary, and cunning, or not live long. I'd heard wolves howling the nights Huck and I slept out. There were also bears in the mountains, and rattlesnakes, and big bloodthirsty cats the people called painters. These last they regarded with particular horror, for unlike a bear, a painter would deliberately stalk a person, even break through a door or window to carry you off. Living beside such dangers, their courage was steady and instinctive.

But it wasn't just the men who were brave. Women at surrounding farms, those who hadn't been burned out by militia, helped feed Reeves's boys at great risk to themselves and their families. These isolated hills, like the rest of Missouri, had thought to stay out while the country gnawed itself apart like a fox in a spring trap. But at last even they had been forced to join the great armed poker game of war.

Two weeks after I arrived, in mid-September, a piece of hot news flew through camp. "Price is coming," Gaylord Scott exulted as we turned in that night. "On his way here from Arkansas."

Toward the end of the month a tattered, much-read local paper brought us word he was nearly to Fredericktown. Maj. Gen. Sterling Price, our former governor turned Confederate, was now in charge of twelve thousand troops, at least half of them cavalry—for what self-respecting Missourian did not own a horse? He and his generals, Shelby, Fagan, and Marmaduke, were the scourge of the federals, harrying their troops through Arkansas. All the newspapers avidly followed the exploits of this native son, painting a thin gloss of patriotic reproach on the accounts to mollify the occupying Union power. But the reporters' breathless style and admiring descriptions of the silver-haired Price gave them away.

"Well, hell, what'll we do when he gets here?" I asked Gaylord. My tent mate was a farrier from Cape Girardeau, and he'd already lost three toes, shot off when the Fifteenth had gone to Kentucky.

"Just take back Missouri," Gaylord said. "Our mission's right here."

He liked to joke about how glad he was to have left only his toes in Kentucky. "I'd be like a monkey hanging wallpaper, trying to shoe horses and work a bellows and hammer steel with only one good arm."

"Weren't you damned afraid, though?" I asked.

"Sure. But I can't wait till we join up with Price," he said fervently. "Gather all our troops like a mighty river and push on east. We'll throw the damn Yankees into the Mississip!"

Listening, I nearly believed him. Men on both sides had killed each other in slaughter that would disgust even wolves, even painters. How could we ever join together again? Families had broken, split apart just as mine had over who was right. Missouri would still be surrounded on all sides by free states and Union troops. Our Kansas border had been burnt to ash by troops carrying out Order Number 11, following on the heels of abolitionists like Anthony, and Jayhawkers like Henry Lane, who continued the bloody campaign of "Pottawatomie" John Brown. Missouri was dying, snarling and clawing at the ground like an old wolf with a broken back.

"So we'll follow this son of a bitch Price and take St. Louis?" I rubbed the handle of the revolver in my belt nervously. "Hell! That ought to be some damned fight."

"Don't worry," said Gaylord, polishing his saber for the umpteenth time. "And don't carry on so, Beck. You curse a sight, but damned if you still don't sound womanish—no offense meant. But we got to pick you up somethin' better than that there wheel-gun."

I pulled out Huck's revolver. "Hell! What's wrong with my Colt?"

He grinned. "Stick by me, and I'll show you what's what. Here, take this canteen. I got an extra. And best think about growing you a beard, son."

I ducked my head and thanked him, putting a hand up to cover my hairless chin.

Reeves strode among us the next day to make a sermon about our duty to Missouri's women and children, in finest Baptist Bible-beating style. He finished the speech with an odd ringing cry. *"Wilson and Ewing and Pulliam Springs Farm!"*

I was puzzled, but all the men roared and took it up. There followed a scramble for saddles and horses. I saw Sid confer with Reeves, then swing up onto a huge dun gelding with flowing black mane and tail. At last, moving in a snaky line, we were on our way north. To Pilot Knob, the rumor came back. Reeves had some men drag brush behind them to stir up clouds of dust, to make any force we might encounter believe we were ten times our true number.

I rode beside Gaylord, hat pulled low, and recalled his comments of the night before. The last thing I wanted was to look or sound womanish. But my curiosity was high, a good distraction from my fear, which was rising steadily. When I leaned to pat Cleo's neck, my hand trembled. She turned her head and looked back as if to say, *Steady there, girl.*

"That thing the, uh, fucking Colonel shouted," I said to Gaylord. "What does it mean?"

He glanced at me in surprise. "You ain't from around here, or you'd surely know of the Wilson Massacre."

"I'm from St. Louis, damn it. So tell me."

"'Twas back at Christmas in '63."

"Last year? Son of a bitch."

He nodded, looking annoyed I'd interrupted, taking the mystery and romance out of the thing before he'd even got wound up good. "Right. All that fall the Preacher ambushed the feds, catching them in creek beds and at river crossings, nailing them good. Making 'em look the fool. Jimmy Wilson brooded all that autumn. And at Christmastime, the Enrolled Union Militia come looking for us."

"And found you," I guessed.

"Damn right. Only not in a fair fight. Wilson, he sneaked up to the Pulliam farm, at the Springs near Doniphan, where the Preacher and friends and families were having Christmas dinner. Our boys had stacked their arms on the ground, and was setting at table for turkey and ham. Unarmed, amongst wives and babies. But Wilson wanted the Preacher bad. So he divided his soldiers up and surrounded the house. Then they opened fire. Besides the men, they shot sixty innocent women and children, and took a hundred fifty prisoners. And them he mostly executed."

"Oh," I said. Nothing else even adequate came to mind. Only images of babies and children and women screaming, torn by bullets, falling across festive tables, their blood mingling with corn bread stuffing and gravy beneath a gray haze of gunpowder.

"The Preacher got clean away. So did a few others, like Sid Hopkins. You met him?"

"Oh, Hell yeah," I mumbled, looking down. "The goddamn lieutenant."

I tried but could not in my mind recast my calm, quiet, orderly husband as a renegade—running, ducking for cover, shooting back—as desperate men and screaming women and children fell all around him in a terrible bloodbath. Could he still laugh, or sleep at night, or touch me or Gage in the same gentle way, after living through such savagery? My heart gave a painful squeeze and I shut my eyes, then remembered Gaylord and opened them quickly again.

"Ah, the lieutenant ain't so bad," said my friend. "Anyhow, Reeves swears there ain't no hole deep enough in this world or the next to hide Wilson. That he's painted forever with the mark of the Beast, and the Preacher will ride him down and cleanse his black soul with fire."

"But how? We're headed off to join up with Price."

"Only fifteen hundred federals holdin' the fort at Pilot Knob, and the railroad at Iron Mountain," said Gaylord. "General Ewing and Wilson are hiding there."

His eyes shining with inner fire, he fell silent. And though I didn't know this man Wilson, when I thought on all I'd heard, I reckoned that he deserved to die.

WE MERGED WITH PRICE'S Confederates near Fredericktown, on the Fayetteville road. Ahead of us, their columns rattled and clanked along, throwing up a wall of dust probably visible for miles. For Gaylord and I riding along in the middle, it was a choking, blinding torment. From a distance Price's columns were an impressive sight. But once we got up close and fell in behind, the infantry we passed, who'd been fighting all the years since Sumter, looked ragged and poorly. They wore tattered shirts and holey trousers. Thousands were barefoot. They carried water in clay jugs. As we rode by, I saw their shirts and pockets bulged with cartridges, because they had no storage boxes or military gear. No tents or blanket rolls, only an amazing variety of rifles. How could they resupply if every man needed a different caliber? They made Reeves's boys look well off.

And this was the army that would take back St. Louis. I felt goose bumps rise. Not from awe, but a despairing chill that radiated from my bones. "God help us," I said without meaning to.

"Oh, he will," said Gaylord. "He will." His eyes still shone. Clearly he saw something else, something not visible to me. Then I realized what it was:

Some of the marchers wore neither gray nor butternut, but dusty Union blue.

Gaylord nodded. "Yup, deserters. They seen the light and come to join us. Hundreds of 'em, see?"

We made camp that evening outside Fredericktown so the generals could confer. Early the next morning I woke to bugles, for Price still had a brass band of sorts. Gaylord was shaking my shoulder. "Get up quick," he said.

"What is it?" I gasped, rubbing my eyes, wondering how I could slip away, with so many men around, to tend to the bursting pressure in my bladder.

"We're marching to Ironton," he announced, rolling up his blanket.

I frowned, confused. "I thought we were to take St. Louis."

"First we'll take the railroad. Then the garrison at Pilot Knob, so they won't come nipping at our flanks."

Ironton was a small railroad town, scarred by artillery from previous engagements. Saloons were still doing business, but there was no time for drinking or to admire the scenery. Our Scouts entered town bringing up the rear of Shelby's column. Price had sent Fagan ahead. We came cantering in just as he was driving the Union pickets from the fort right back into Ironton in a cloud of dust and a hail of shot. Then the tide turned; the relentless pounding of cannon sent the Confederates before us into a panic. We glimpsed some stumbling back. But as we streamed in with Shelby's column and more and more forces, the federals eased back, too.

It felt like a huge murderous cotillion was going on all around me, and I'd never learned how to dance.

The sounds of guns ceased at dark, as if by gentleman's agreement. Nevertheless, I found it impossible to sleep. The ground was rocky, the supper beef raw, and a heavy rain fell without stop, soaking us, our food, and the lumpy earth. I huddled close to the horses, though they afforded no real protection from wind and damp. Gaylord kept whispering opinions on our progress excitedly, as if this were a party he'd been looking forward to his whole life.

We rose and rode the next morning at dawn. The fort lay on the floor of a valley, flanked on one side by tall, sloping green hills. Thousands of us surrounded the walled enclosure as best we could. Fagan's cavalry dismounted and we followed suit. That made sense—horses can't climb walls. I tied Cleo to a pine sapling, my hands shaking so I had to knot the reins twice over.

Word was the federals had at least a dozen pieces of artillery inside. They clearly had plenty of ammunition. We'd have to cross hundreds of yards of open ground just to reach the ramparts. I looked away, mouth suddenly dry. A turkey shoot, and we'd be the birds.

Apparently Price thought so, too. Later in the day, from our shelter in the fallen timber of the foothill, I saw the Confederate artillery moving up the slope behind us, dragging their big guns. "What're they doing?" I asked Gaylord.

He watched a minute, frowning. "Maybe they figger to get up high so they can knock out those guns at the fort."

From time to time our line surged forward, but we were well in the back, so the skirmishes were happening beyond our sight. I heard gunfire and shouts; sometimes the bleating screams of wounded men, the even more horrible cries of mutilated horses. Gaylord fretted it would all be over before he got off a single shot.

Late that afternoon our turn came around. Another wave charged, and this time we were swept up with them. Reeves galloped alongside, shouting a yelping cry that seemed to enrage the Scouts. They answered with yells and whoops and screeches that would've made fiends from Hell envious. Gaylord grabbed my arm and dragged me stumbling along.

No, I can't do this, I thought. *My son is waiting for me at home, if I am killed, then he—*

But I jerked at Huck's pistol to free it from my belt, for there was no way back. Those behind pushed us onward. The line ahead seemed to bend beneath the weight of all the falling shot and shells, the men out front leaning forward as if trying to make headway against a sudden gale. The shells flying overhead had sounded mundane as frying bacon grease at a distance. But up close the noise was deafening, like the flapping of thousands of buzzards in low, desperate flight around our ears.

The Colt dragged my arm down as we ran. Gaylord, just ahead, shouted out a keening cry I could not interpret, much less imitate. In the crush of bodies, I lost my hat but clung tight to Gaylord's coattail, with no idea of when to aim and shoot. I feared I'd kill a fellow soldier ahead of me, rather than the ones we were fighting.

As we moved forward, the ranks before us thinned. But smoke hung so thick a few feet off the ground, I could make out only hundreds of running legs, which for all I could tell had been blown off their owners and were continuing downhill from sheer momentum. Suddenly a huge branch was blasted from a tree. It fell, crushing two men just ahead. Canister rounds exploded, flinging lead balls, while from our own hillside rounds of shot and shell growled and screamed back.

"Howl, ye dogs of war!" cried Gaylord. He lunged forward so eagerly, I lost my grip on his coat. Then for a moment the smoke and dust lifted, and I was far enough forward to see everything.

The field between fort and hills was littered with bodies, most wearing butternut or gray. Price had been feeding Fagan's men to the guns all afternoon. They'd paid the toll for us, but we hadn't been close enough to see until now. I looked around for Sid, for a sergeant, for some kind of direction. All I really wanted to do, as a canister of shot burst like fireworks from Hades and more shells flew over, was squat in terror with my arms locked over my head. I felt horribly small, and wished to be smaller, to shrink into a grain of dust, invisible.

A scream jerked my attention forward again. Gaylord was on his knees, clutching his arm, which now lacked a hand. I started toward him, but someone slammed into me from behind and I hit the ground, rolling up against my tent-mate's legs. He was staring down in disbelief at the bleeding stump where his forearm should've been.

"Come on," I yelled, pushing up off the slick, bloody ground. "I'll help you off the field."

I grabbed him around the waist. He leaned on me as we staggered against a mixed tide of gray and blue still pouring off the hill. Men were balking, turning back to run. When they did, cavalry galloping up and down the field whipped them forward again, shouting abuse. One file-closer beat a soldier with the flat of his sword until the terrified man gave in and stumbled toward the fort again. I was glad Sid wasn't the officer I'd seen on that snorting, rearing horse, cursing like a demon, mercilessly driving frightened men in piss-darkened trousers on to certain death.

"Can you make it?" I asked Gaylord. His whole side was soaked black with blood.

He nodded and grimaced, and we hobbled on a few more steps. Then from behind us someone yelled, "Hey, Reb!"

I glanced back to see a soldier pointing a long Springfield. A boy, his face hairless as mine, so for a moment I didn't raise the Colt still gripped in my other hand. As I hesitated, the youngster raised his rifle and fired a simple puff of smoke at us. Or so it seemed, until Gaylord's skull burst apart, showering me with blood and chunks of bone and clots of flesh and hair. Headless, my tent-mate took another step forward, then slid from my grasp. I went down, too, with the sudden dead weight of him, staring up at the boy soldier in disbelief. He was reloading his rifle, chuckling as if he'd just bagged a rabbit.

Without my consent or participation, one hand of its own will lifted Huck's heavy revolver. I steadied that wrist with the other hand, aimed at the line of buttons on the soldier's tunic, and squeezed. As the recoil knocked me back, I saw a hole open in the federal's blue blouse front. His arms flew up like a doll's, his grin went askew, and he toppled backwards.

I looked down at what was left of poor Gaylord, then back up at the fort. Who would share my tent now, and tell stories, and help me figure what needed doing next? With my friend's blood and flesh sprayed over my clothes, it crossed my mind that I could leave the field, passing as wounded. Then, a thing Gaylord had said as we lay waking all the night before returned to me.

"You wait, Beck," he said, as we sat under an oilcloth that wasn't doing much to keep us dry. "You'll be a new man when they commence shootin' at you. Won't be scared of nothing. All you'll want is to rush into the thick of the fight. And any hurt boys of ours you see, why, it'll only make you crave revenge all the more. You'll be cool as an icehouse then."

Poor Gaylord. I'd not only doubted his words but had thought them the most foolish blather I'd ever heard. Yet as I rose to my knees in the middle of chaos, his blood soaking the legs of my trousers, I calmly reloaded the single chamber I'd just fired. For the gun seemed all mine now, not Huck's, and I felt as if I'd done war all my life. I pushed a new cartridge in place, and thought in that short space of time of an infinite number of things. Of my dead baby's sweet face, gone forever. Of my son Gage's voice, and the million questions he would still need to ask, even though I might not be there to try to answer with patience. And of my husband, somewhere on this same field, perhaps alive, perhaps not. And yes, damn it, of Tom Sawyer— that I might never see, or speak to, or touch him again.

I found Gaylord's knife in his pocket, and slipped it into my own. By then I seemed to have split into two people. One part went on recalling all the dear, beloved things of home, hurt to the core and mourning the loss of every single one. While the Other that was me moved forward, stepping over men without heads or arms or legs, or even their middles shot away. I moved past the screams and groans of friend and foe, squinting against powder smoke, intent only on finding another enemy who needed, this time, to be killed first.

Sixteen

DARKNESS FLOATED DOWN over the Ozarks like a dirty shroud. The firing ebbed away when the sky began to pour rain again, and we all straggled back toward the base of the hills. Something had gone wrong with Price's lines. The remaining troops, those who hadn't been shot down or blown to bits, were milling in confusion, companies mixing with no order. Messengers were galloping flat out, heading north, toward Union lines. I couldn't figure why.

Back on the field it wasn't quiet, either. I went out with some of the Scouts who were combing through the fallen bodies by candlelight, looking for friends and relatives. Our puny glow drew some fire from the fort, which fell short and was easy to ignore. I rushed from one dark, prone shape to the next, peering closely into dead faces, praying not to see Sid's. The bodies lay scattered, blue and gray and butternut sprawled over each other intimately as courting lovers. Some with clothes torn off, others missing limbs or heads. The crown of a skull hung by the hair like an ornament from the limb of a blast-blackened tree. But even that was not so bad as the noises toward the edge of the field, by the woods.

"They God," breathed the man in front of me as he helped another soldier lift a wounded but still-living man. "Damned hogs got a holt of some dead federals."

"Least it ain't summer," said his companion. They turned away and carried the injured man back toward the camp. The others went on searching.

I did, too, for a while, then gave up and tried to find my way back through the battlefield in the dark, sometimes stumbling over a torso or a limb, tripping on things I did not care to examine closely. I heard moaning from time to time but could never quite make out where it came from. At some point I must've made a wrong turn, for I was farther from the hills and off to one side of the field. I cursed when I tripped over what felt like a hand. But this body cursed back.

"Sid?" I threw myself down beside the dark shape, holding my candle up to see.

A low groan. "Who's that?"

"It's Becky. Oh, Sid. Lie still if you're hurt bad."

He sounded amazed. "Becky? Then I am dying. Or dead. But I thought this was Hell."

I ran a hand over him, blinded by both the dark and tears of gratitude, trying to find the wound. "No, you aren't. It isn't."

When I pressed his left thigh, he cried out. "Don't touch that," he begged.

"Don't worry, dear," I said, swallowing back a sob. "We'll get you fixed up. I'll see to it. Here, first let's get you free."

Sid's mount, the big dun, lay nearby. The poor beast had been gutted by a shell. At least he hadn't fallen on Sid. His legs were pinned beneath a dead man. I started to rise, to yell to the boys for help. But then—then Sid would be sent to some overburdened field hospital, patched up and returned to the fight. If he survived the surgeons. Gaylord had told me one night, in a hushed voice, of the terrible pile of amputated limbs he'd seen stacked helter-skelter outside an army hospital. Of the men unloaded from trains like cordwood and left to lie in sun or rain until their turn to be butchered came round yet again.

"But these men here with us can't all be killed," Gaylord had said. "Nor all lose an arm or a leg, either. Why shouldn't I be one who gets away clean?"

Poor boy. He'd been wrong on both counts.

A new idea, born of desperation and disgust at the mindless machinery of this War, was working its way up from the back of my mind. Now Sid was

no good for fighting, so he couldn't object to leaving. And if he had scru-
ples . . . well then, let him think it was only temporary. I loved him enough
to lie. If it was the only way to save my husband's life, I'd lie to anyone, of
any rank or station. I'd shake my fist and lie to God Himself. Oh, I had once
been an apt pupil, but clearly the years had dulled my wits, for it had taken
nearly losing him to make me understand: Nothing in this world mattered
to me more than Sid.

With this in mind, I kept quiet and set to work. I wedged the candle
into the mud. It took much heaving and pushing until I could roll the dead
man off Sid. Then I half dragged, half carried him to a stand of trees with
blasted tops still smoking. Too wet to make a fire, but I found a hollow in a
burnt-out stump. I groped in my pockets for a locofoco and lit the candle
again.

As I bent over him, Sid muttered through cracked lips. "You—you're different. What's happened to you?"

"Same thing as to everyone else: the War. And if you mean my damn—I
mean, my hair, I cut it off. What does it matter now? Lie still, before you
hurt yourself further."

"Oh, Becky." His voice was chiding, as if such a trifle were still of great
import. He reached up and felt the blunt, clipped ends. "It was so pretty."

"It will grow," I said, then began to cry. Tears quickly clogged my nose
and throat so that all I could do was wordlessly lean forward and kiss his
forehead and cheeks, which were smeared with dirt and powder smut, but
uninjured. Then, I set to work.

Our struggle over the field had torn his wound open, for it was bleeding.
The weight of the corpse on his legs must've acted as a sort of tourniquet,
because judging from the flow of blood now, he would've been long dead. I
ripped one sleeve from my shirt and tied it above the tear in his trousers.

"Any water?" he asked. "I thought I'd die of thirst. Saw rainwater in a
ditch, but couldn't reach it."

I'd seen those ditches, too, scummed with blood and clogged with bodies. I shuddered. "Here, drink this." I pulled my canteen from my waist, the
one Gaylord had given me. Sid sucked at the warm, musty liquid as if it
were cold pure spring water dipped from a limestone cavern.

"There, now," I said. "Hold up, that's enough." I had to pull it away. Then

I settled us as comfortably as I could for the night, sure I would never sleep with Sid's head in my lap and the stiff binding of Gaylord's blood gluing my clothes to me. Across the field, someone was singing "Annie of the Vale," mournful as a dirge. But I must have nodded off eventually, clutching my revolver. Because during the night I dreamed a column of shadows went marching past, a rustling, endless line out of the earthenworks of the fort, wrapped in black like wraiths.

Some time later I jerked awake as a huge blast shook the ground. Then, a hellish rumbling, as if a displeased God was come down to tramp out the land, just as the Yankee song promised.

"The magazine!" someone yelled faintly from over at the camp. "Damn fools blowed themselves up with their own powder!"

During all this commotion, Sid lay peaceful. Much too quiet. *Dear God,* I thought. *No.* Not like the baby, like Tyler! Surely He would not take Sid from us, too. I pressed a shaking hand to his chest. It rose and fell shallowly, and he was still warm. I loosened the tourniquet and, when no blood gushed forth from the wound, retied the cloth more like a bandage. I'd look at the damage in the light of morning and see what else could be done.

At dawn the fort was still and silent. A ragged hole had been blown in the rampart. I heard shouting from up where Price and the officers were stationed. But it sounded more like consternation than jubilant cheering. I guessed then the federals had set their powder magazine off on purpose, to keep it out of our hands.

I cradled Sid's head and watched as Price's division entered the broken fort, while Marmaduke's set off in the opposite direction, north. Perhaps they were chasing Ewing and his men. The fort did look unoccupied with the tattered Stars and Stripes gone, the flagpole bare. If Ewing had slipped down the road through three divisions, he was indeed a magician. Or had my dreams made a hole in the seen world for the federals to slip through like black, silent ghosts?

I took Gaylord's blade from my pocket and sawed off the rest of Sid's trouser leg. The cloth had dried stuck fast to skin and hair, but I tried hard not to cause more pain than necessary. In the pinkish dawn I saw an oval-shaped hole as big around as the end of my index finger. The conical shot or ball had punched out a neat circle, like a biscuit cutter. The skin around this was sunken, as if recently pressed by a giant's thumb; the edges discolored, pushed inward. I sat back, washed with relief. It didn't look near so bad as other wounds I'd seen. But where had all the blood come from?

"Have to get the ball out," he whispered. "I might die anyway."

"Nonsense," I said, sounding more certain than I felt. A bit of something fibrous, like torn cloth, stuck up out of the wound. I pinched it between thumb and finger. That, at least, I could remove on my own. "Hold on. Are you ready?"

He nodded. I tugged at the scrap of fabric as Sid gritted his teeth. It didn't move. He flinched when at last I got brave and gave a hard yank. The little strip of bloody wool came free, along with a gush of watery blood. I examined the swelling around the wound. At least there were no red streaks.

"What now," I said, mostly to myself.

Sid answered. "Feel around. See if there's a ball still in there. Sure as hell hurts like it."

"Oh." I bit my lip. "With my . . . fingers?"

He nodded, closed his eyes, let his head fall back against the tree.

I took a deep breath and jammed my index finger into the still-bleeding wound, pressing into warm flesh up to my first knuckle joint. Sid made a choking sound, like someone being strangled. The only way I could keep on with this grisly task was to pretend it was a joint of pork I was fixing for supper. I forced myself not to look at Sid's face, or to listen to the horrible muffled whimpering. I pressed deeper, amazed at how easily my fingers entered another person's body. I felt only ground meat and muscle.

"Nothing in there," I said. "Better look at the other side. Can you roll over?"

His face was pale as skimmed milk, but he did so. The back of his thigh was another story, the hole three times as large, the skin all around shredded, the edges ragged flaps. "Oh my. Think maybe it passed clean through?"

"Better be sure." He took a deep breath and held it.

I used the same finger, and the God-like business of pressing into living, bleeding flesh seemed easier this time. The wound in back was different in all ways. Inside it was not a smooth, slick channel but rough as wood fibers. I felt no ball, no hard splinters of bone. When I sat back to tell Sid so, his face was a deadly white, his breathing hoarse but steady. He'd passed out. I wiped my gory hand on some dry leaves, got up, and wrestled a fairly clean shirt from a body nearby, to bind the leg again.

When he woke I gave him more water. Then we rested under the trees. The smells of woodsmoke and frying meat drifted our way, but I was far from hungry. At last the troops noisily broke camp and marched away. They seemed to be heading northwest. That way lay the capital, but it was hard to imagine these ragged remnants taking it now. I braced myself for objections from Sid, for demands that I report his survival to them. He didn't say a word.

Perhaps, after losing so many, Price had given up his dream of capturing St. Louis. Anyway, his doings were no longer important to us. The immediate thing was to get Sid to where there might be a real doctor.

Just then I realized what else the troops were taking. Cleopatra, my mare. If anyone noticed my absence, they'd likely assume I'd been killed. Poor Cleo. She was too good and smart a horse to waste on a foolish war. I wanted to run after and get her back. But then how would I leave again, or keep Sid's survival a secret? "Oh, Cleo, I'm sorry," I whispered.

At midday I helped Sid up and we started off. I quickly understood Fredericktown was too far away now. We'd covered the distance easily before the battle, but on horseback, and none of us had been shot. Sid could limp along with me holding him up on one side, using a hickory branch as a crutch, if we stopped frequently.

We'd gone only about a mile on the road when we heard someone coming up behind us. I grabbed Sid and dragged him into the bushes. A group straggled by, some talking, others whistling. They wore overalls and denim britches and flannel shirts, and all of them were Negro men of varying heights, builds, and years. The youngest had yet to grow a beard; the oldest looked grizzled as Methuselah. Over broad or narrow shoulders they carried only shovels. Then I understood: this was the burial detail, one of the possible jobs in store for Jim if he was ever taken again.

After they passed, we climbed out onto the road again. I thought first we'd better make for Ironton, but then settled on a little place called Belleview, which was closer. I hoped all federals and militia had been driven off. We stopped on the roadside and ate some biscuit and scraps of dried beef. I'd taken these provisions from the dead, feeling like a thief and a ghoul—a worse grave-robber than Muff Potter, as I turned out the pockets of staring, sightless men. It was crumbled and hard and stale, but still it was food.

We walked slowly, resting often. Until dark, when Sid began to lean so heavily on me, I staggered. His leg had swollen badly. In a sheltered spot near a thread of a creek we made camp. I gathered a bed of leaves and laid Sid back on it, then sat and related how Huck had brought me south. How I'd dressed up two different ways like a man, and hidden among the ranks without him even knowing it.

"You are something, Becky," he mused. "I'll soon be up and taking care of things, so you needn't go to such lengths again."

"Of course you will. We just have to get your leg fixed up. I'll see about a doctor, even if I have to requisition one."

He laughed, then grimaced at some pain. "I don't believe there's another woman in all Missouri the like of you."

"Maybe not," I agreed, not meeting his eyes, for of course I hadn't told the whole of it. I hadn't mentioned Tom Sawyer. But then neither had he.

We spent our second night back together on the bank of that tiny creek. I woke once, frightened by a strange noise. To buck up my courage, I told myself, *You'd not be scared if Tom or Huck were here to see and give you Hell for it.* I decided then not to merely pretend. Instead I would *be* Tom Sawyer; then no one could hurt or outfox me. And soon I fell back asleep.

In the morning I left Sid to scout around, for we needed something to eat. I went down the road a ways, then turned onto a cleared, twisty dirt trail. A neat little cabin sat at the end. "Hello the house," I called, and stood waiting.

No answer. Something about the scene gave me the heebies, though the cabin looked cheerful enough, with a bit of whitewash on the shutters and late-blooming daisies swaying by the front steps. I walked slowly up to the tiny porch and climbed three shallow plank steps. Only as I was knocking did it occur to me what felt wrong: the absolute quiet. What lonely cabin out in the woods would not have at least one dog for company, for sentry duty? But by then the door was already swinging inward on leather hinges, releasing a musty, sick-sweet smell, and a low buzzing noise.

I took a step back, gagging. Inside was dark, but I could see more than enough. The pale bare ankles of a woman, her nightdress hiked up over her thighs. At first I thought her head was missing, but it was only that the darkened blood from her slashed throat had covered her face and matted down her hair. Across the room lay a gray-bearded man, hands frozen into claws, the handle of a butcher knife protruding from his chest.

They must've fought the intruders fiercely, for the single room was a shambles. A broken chair lay beside the man, along with bits of smashed crockery and a fiddle, strings bristling, the neck snapped off. Only a small three-legged table sat upright. On it, like a grisly joke, someone had propped the severed head of a large black dog, jaws grinning, tongue protruding as if it enjoyed the jest. The rest of the animal was nowhere to be seen. When its eyes moved as if to follow me, I flinched back, then realized a mass of flies were crawling over the poor creature's head, busy at their work.

I started again at an eerie moaning sound, then realized I was making it. Somehow this ruined little home was far worse than the carnage I'd seen on the field. I wanted to turn and bolt, but the scene seemed to demand witness. Who had done this horror—federal militia, army, Confederate raiders? Or perhaps Union bummers. Did it really make a difference?

I contemplated burying the poor souls but had no shovel. And Sid lay alone and wounded back by the creek. In the end I only backed away, pulling the door shut firmly behind me. Thinking of the one small mercy: There'd been no children among the corpses.

"Our Father, who art in Heaven," I mumbled as I felt my way backwards down the narrow steps. But fright chased the rest of the prayer out of my head, for it also occurred to me that whoever had done this work might still be nearby. Might even then be watching my slow retreat.

I lost my nerve, wheeled, and ran blind, smack into something that wrapped cold ghostly arms around me. I beat at my attacker until I realized it was only a faded flannel shirt draped over a bush, probably washed and left there to dry by the dead woman inside. It looked plenty big enough for Sid. Gasping, I wrenched the garment from the grasp of thorns and clinging, twiggy fingers. The worn fabric smelled of fresh air and lye soap. Inhaling that clean, homey scent, I buried my face in the soft cloth and sobbed. Then, bundled it under my arm and ran back up the path. I didn't slow or stop to catch my breath till I reached the road.

I made Sid put the shirt on right away, but didn't tell him where I'd found it. Just took his bloodstained tunic and waded into the creek. There I also washed Gaylord's blood from my own clothes, watching the rusty stains swirl away to pink water whirling downstream. Gaylord fading from life all over again.

In neatly patched flannel, Sid looked less like a secesh officer and more a poor mountaineer. I wondered if that was any better. Not much to be done about the slashed trousers, but it was a start. We ate the last crumbs of biscuit, and drank all we could hold from the stream. Clear and cold, though not very filling.

The next day we limped a ways farther; then I walked on into Belleview alone, leaving Sid in a patch of woods just off the road. I saw no doctor's shingle, so I went down the street until I found a mercantile store. Its shelves were nearly bare.

The owner was a nervous little man with stringy brown hair and a round potbelly. He got a sad, resigned look when it was clear I hadn't come in to buy. "A doc? You want Missus Lorna, then."

"There's a woman doctor?" I asked, surprised.

"Nearest thing. She's our midwife, doses folks with herb cures. All we got left. Doctors is following the army, ain't they?"

He directed me to a clapboard house. Whitewashed rocks ringed the bare front yard. A big woman swung the door open as if she'd been waiting behind it, expecting me. Her pinned-up red hair was shot with silver, her eyes flat and gray as hammered bullets, her arms muscled like an Irish washerwoman's. Her sharp gaze paused on my flat belly. "Well, you ain't the party in question," she said, and folded her arms. "But you ain't no man neither, however you might dress, my girl. Don't believe we've met."

I'd thought all the way in how to explain Sid's wound, having no notion of where Belleview's sympathies might lie. I'd settled on a story at last. "My husband's hurt. We were headed to Tennessee, to see family, when a bunch of 'whackers set upon us up the road."

She frowned. "Where up the road?"

"I don't know. I guess Pilot Knob?"

When she didn't answer, I smiled and ducked my head, trying to look embarrassed. "I'm dressed this way because he—I mean my husband—he thought it'd be safer. For traveling."

"Hmm," she said, looking me over again head to toe. "Appears you been dragged through a hedgerow backwards."

"I assure you," I said, hearing my mother's imperious Richmond accent creeping into my voice, "I do not usually choose to dress in so common a manner."

"Do tell," she grunted.

"They *shot* him," I said more insistently, desperate to put her on my side. "And then stole our horses. We've been walking ever since."

At last she nodded. "C'n believe that much, anyhow. Come on in. I'm 'bout as close to a sawbones as you'll get in these parts."

I thanked her. She stuck her head out the door and looked around. "Well, where's my patient?"

I shuffled and looked over my shoulder. "Up the road a little way."

"They God." She stared as if I'd left good sense behind with him. "Whyn't you say so? I'll get the buggy, we'll go directly."

It turned out her full name, when I thought to ask, was Lorna McGill. She drove the buggy deft as a teamster. We found Sid curled up and shivering like a scorched spider in the brush where I'd left him, though the day was mild. She grabbed him under the arms and hauled him up behind the buggy seat before I could help, then whipped the horse back double time.

Her house was as neat inside as out, the broad plank floor scrubbed so hard and often with ashes, it'd bleached to white. Colorful quilts covered the beds, tucked under the mattresses. The kitchen was the one place that looked disorderly, though pleasantly so, its beams hung with drying plants and flower heads. Bottles and jugs and a few jars of preserves lined a long table.

She put Sid to bed off the kitchen, on clean sheets, dirty as he was. She unbuttoned the ruin of his pants, removed my sorry, makeshift bandage. She *tsk*ed at the wound, which had closed like a pursed mouth. The flesh was red and puffed. Sid moaned and tossed as we worked; his skin felt hot as a baked potato. Lorna McGill laid hands on his wounded thigh and stared at it a moment.

"It needs the heat drawed out," she said.

She went into the kitchen and came back with a wooden bowl of gray-white paste. The smell of it was eye-watering, worse than decaying onions. She started smearing it over the wound.

"Lord God, what's that stuff?" I gasped.

"Garlic and violet leaves. Aloe juice. Strong, ain't it? But it'll draw the pus. Like for your man to chew some garlic, too, but he ain't in no shape. We'll get some boneset tea down him, though."

He sputtered and coughed and tried to slap us away when we tried. At last we propped him on pillows and Mrs. McGill held his arms down while I spooned it into his mouth a bit at a time. Most trickled out, but some got swallowed. After this torture, we left him alone to sleep.

"You'll want to bathe," she said. It was not a question.

I felt my face heat up as hot as Sid's. No doubt I stank to the heavens; when had I last been near soap? Apparently my quick dip in the creek hadn't been an adequate substitute.

She dragged a zinc tub into the kitchen and filled it with cold water, then poured in hot from big kettles off the cookstove. While she heated up gravy and put biscuits on a plate, I washed away the grime and muck and mess that riding horseback and sleeping on the ground and being baptized with the blood of misled men had layered on my skin. Then I rubbed myself dry on clean flour sacks, and put on the skirt and shirtwaist she handed me.

"May be old-fashioned, but they's clean," she said. "Ain't about to fit me again in this life."

The clothes were cut in a style long past, high-waisted and lower in the bodice than I fancied. But they smelled of dried lavender flowers and years in a fragrant cedar trunk. Being out of fashion did not stop me wolfing Mrs. McGill's food, while she parted my damp hair in sections and went through it with a fine comb, looking for anything living. She dropped what she found in a saucer of coal oil.

I closed my eyes, feeling drowsy. "I'll pay you, of course."

She laughed. "Don't worry about that just yet. Especially if it's naught but secesh paper. T'ain't worth spit anyhow."

When I lay down on the old sprung sofa in her front room, it felt like a feather bed.

EARLY THE NEXT MORNING Sid's color looked better. He opened his eyes, then wearily shut them again. The wound was draining reeking yellow pus.

Mrs. McGill said that was good. She changed his bandages and dosed him with more garlic.

"Why would that help?" I asked. "It smells evil."

"Don't rightly know, but it clears up puffed flesh right quick. And you can put it in stews and rub it on chickens before you cook 'em."

"Hmm," I said, in such close imitation of the same tone she'd used to me the day before, we both laughed.

We passed two weeks at Lorna's. I went downtown each day to look at casualty lists, which were supposed to be posted on the door of the mercantile. But with paper scarce and the telegraph lines mostly cut, the storekeeper advised me not to hold my breath. If one did come out, I hoped to see Sid's name. If he was thought dead, no one would come looking for him. Not the army he'd signed on with, not Reeves, who might grudge his defection. Not anyone in all Missouri outside our family. That had become part of my plan, too.

Though I felt more respectable in Mrs. McGill's old-fashioned dresses, it was hard to suddenly be buttoned into a tight bodice again. I got short of breath walking into town, unable to inhale freely the way I had beneath a loose cotton shirt and sack coat. I had to take shorter, feminine strides, but since Lorna and I wore different shoe sizes, I still had to put on the old brogans. Of course, everyone was short on fashion, not just me. My hair was a problem, though. I had to pin it back carefully, and rely on a hat to conceal that it was bobbed like a mare's tail.

I was glad to be done with fighting and hiding, but already missed freedom, and not just in attire. At first it had felt shocking to straddle a horse. But how much easier it was to sit one like a man! Anyone who said women were weaker riders had never tried to gallop and jump clinging with just one knee to a saddle horn. My brief career as a young fellow named Beck had put me even farther from being any kind of lady. Yet who could mourn? That hothouse rose had never been me, only the daughter my mother had dreamed of.

One afternoon, at the beginning of the second week, we heard a sudden banging at the door. It put me uneasily in mind of the night Sadie Bell Lucas came pounding to tell us my father had been dragged off to Palmyra.

Mrs. McGill set the biscuit cutter on the floury board. "Must be the

Siegfried baby. Them Joneses—she's a Jones—they drop 'em early. Allus have."

She dusted her hands on her apron, leaving white streaks, and went to answer. She came back a good deal quicker. "Militia on the way," she rapped out.

When she went into the back room and told Sid, he started to struggle up out of bed.

"Lie back, son," she ordered. "You'll get to bleeding again."

"No, Mrs. McGill. They'll kill me anyhow, and burn your house. We must leave."

"What else can we do?" I asked, wringing my hands. "Can we hide him?"

She shook her head. "Those boys know every cranny. Ought to, they requisitioned enough of my hams and chickens. But don't fret. We'll fix you up." She patted Sid's hand, then bustled off. I heard her footsteps pounding up the steep wooden stairs faster than I would've thought possible. I kept Sid still and in bed by telling him I was gathering up our few things. All at once Lorna was back, panting and red-faced, a bunch of clothes in her arms. She tossed them at me. "Put these on him. And be damn quick."

I shook out the bundle, which contained a sizable lady's nightgown, a nightcap, and a rat—a twist of false hair the same red as Mrs. McGill's. I looked up at her, mouth open.

"I swear," she snapped. "Ain't you never seed a switch before? Once they was all the rage. That kerchief is for you, Becky. Tie it over your hair, like the nurses do."

I did as she said right then.

"Now look here," she went on. "Your man's lying in for a hard birth."

Sid gaped at both of us. "What?"

"So we'll pad him out with this." She tugged a pillow from behind his back, then frowned down at him. "Can you act?"

"You mean, like in a play?"

"You're no soldier now, but a young German wife in labor with a breech baby. Trust me, it hurts like the devil, and takes one hell of a long time. But you only got to perform it long and good enough to convince other men. *They* don't know much about birthing, praise God."

He nodded slowly. "Believe I can just about do that." He glanced at me, and his mouth twitched at the corners. "Because I recall how you screamed the roof down the day Gage was born. I covered my ears and felt like a murderer."

"Did you?" I said, blinking back tears. Why had it never occurred to me before that I did not have memories like this with Tom, and never would? "Well, it sure hurt fit to kill."

Lorna McGill snorted. "Reminiscing's all well and good, but militia's coming down this street, checking each house one at the time."

I helped Sid drag the nightgown over his head, then wadded the pillow and stuffed it underneath. I pulled up the quilt again. "Bend your knees and clutch this like a belly. You wouldn't be able to lie so straight."

He did and I eyed the result. "Now let's do your hair."

I pulled the nightcap low on his forehead, then tucked the hairpiece underneath. All fairly convincing, except . . . then I realized what was wrong. "Your beard," I gasped.

Lorna found a razor in the drawer of a highboy. "My papa's. Lord knows he don't need it anymore. Take this soap, and for Jesus' sake, don't cut him!"

I ran back to Sid's bedside and held out the razor, hands shaking.

"I better take that," he said. "Or the federals won't need to kill me."

He'd always hated a full beard, and worn at most a mustache. He'd shaved not too long past in camp, for his beard was barely an inch long. I brought hot water from one of the kettles that sat on the stove day and night, then handed him the tin of soap. Sid pulled the razor over his cheeks while I held up a hand mirror.

He was dragging the blade down his neck when someone pounded at the front door. I jumped, and the mirror jerked. Sid flinched, dropped the steel onto the bed, and pressed his fingers to his neck. I stared, horrified, as red seeped between them.

"Only a nick," he whispered, not looking at me. "Be fine in a moment."

Voices volleyed back and forth in front. It didn't sound like an argument, but not like the guard was going away either. The voices came closer. I slid razor, bowl, and soap under the bed. "Start acting now," I said. He grabbed his false belly and gave a high-pitched howl that sent chill bumps down my arms.

"What in holy hell was that?" said an unfamiliar voice from the kitchen.

"Told you, got a breech birth coming," Lorna shot back. "I can't mess with you galoots all day. Got to attend to God's little crossways blessing on the Himmelfennigs."

I would've marveled at how calm and cool she sounded, but just then a whiskered face topped with a blue kepi thrust around the jamb. It gazed at us, then withdrew.

"Where's her husband? What's their name again?"

"Told you, Himmelfennig," Lorna huffed. "Dutch family. He's dead last month at Little Rock."

The militiaman said ominously, "Rebel fellow, was he?"

A sharp, shocked intake of breath. I could almost see Lorna drawing herself up, glaring, mortally insulted. "He was with *General Steele*," she said icily. "*Himmelfennig*. Iffen you want to check the lists. And can spell."

"Huh, a Dutchman," the militia man grunted. "'I fights mit Siegel,' eh? Beg your pardon, I'm sure." He didn't sound very sorry.

I looked up, and there he was again in the doorway. Staring at me, then at Sid, who was writhing on the bed, clutching his feather-padded middle and moaning piteously.

"Who're you?" demanded the ginger-haired trooper, his gaze back on me again, narrow and mean.

"Aunt Lorna's assistant. I come all the way from St. Louis to train for midwifing under her."

Sid bucked and gasped and clutched my hand, wringing it till the small bones shifted and popped. He threw himself back, clawed at the quilt, and shrieked again.

"Jesus and Joseph," said the militiaman. "Sounds like she's dying."

"Told you, it's breech," said Mrs. McGill from behind him. "Stay if you want. But stand aside so I can do my work. Or I'll be asking you and your men to help dig a grave."

"I just got to ask the lady there a couple questions, is all."

Sid groaned and thrashed; he'd worked up a genuine sweat. I hoped his wound wouldn't open again, too.

"*Questions?*" Lorna cried. "Questions! What sort of heathen devil are you?"

"See here," said the man. "I got orders to check every—"

Just then an inspired Sid thrust one arm out at the militiaman, as if imploring help. He clawed the air, his splayed fingers red and sticky with the blood from his shaving nick.

"Oh my! Baby's coming," I shouted. "Auntie, where's that knife?"

Sid groped at the federal's pant leg, leaving smears of red on the cloth. The militiaman blanched and stepped back. "They God," he muttered. "Damned if this ain't an ugly business."

"It'll get a whole lot uglier," Lorna told him. "Baby's so big and crossways, I got to cut her down below to let it out. Rebecca, more hot water! Oh, and you." She jerked her head at the federal. "You can hold her down while we cut. I'm out of laudanum, and she's bound to kick and scream."

"The hell I will," said the man, his Adam's apple bobbing. "I got work to do." He backed away, turned and stomped through the kitchen and down the hall.

We all three barely held back trembling, hysterical laughter till he slammed the front door. Then with shaking fingers I stuck a plaster on Sid's neck. Lorna went out to harry the remaining federals, who were liberating her laying hens. Hearing a hellish commotion, I rushed to the window in time to see an old Orpington flap wildly into the air and tear spurs-first into a smooth-faced boy who'd had the gall to try to stuff the bird into a knapsack.

IN FIVE DAYS, SID WAS A GOOD deal better, sitting up and taking food more substantial than broth. I didn't want to eat Lorna out of all she had, so I laid plans for our return to Hannibal. We'd go home, collect Gage, and invite Mary to move West with us. As for the Judge, I'd have to either take him along, or somehow send him down to stay with Mama. I'd have to be careful how I presented all of this, for Sid might not agree.

That morning, while he spooned down grits and butter, I talked of home. "I was thinking how Sam Clemens went West, three years back. Now, where was it he headed?"

"Dakota Terrritory," Sid supplied. "He'd just deserted that Hannibal regiment they raised."

Oh, dear. Best to steer away from that topic. "Well, but it was really to be his brother Orion's secretary out there."

Sid laughed. "Actually, I think he had it in mind to pan for gold."

"Ah," I said, then fell silent, not wanting to push too hard. The Clemens brothers had sent back favorable reports in letters to their mother, though since the war had heated up, I hadn't heard more. Nor, I supposed, had Missus Clemens. I wondered what that meant, and whether I was a fool to think we could start again so far away. But what could be worse than the hell of Missouri?

So I mentioned Sam and Orion Clemens every now and then. And from the last of my silver I set aside five dollars to buy tickets to St. Louis at the Ironton station. Of the remaining seven dollars I sewed three into my corset, to get us the rest of the way home. That left four, which I saved for Lorna McGill, though she'd told me she wouldn't accept money, that I was not even to offer. She said it was all worth it for the show Sid had put on.

But she'd laid herself out for us considerably. Had shared when food was scarce, risked her home and more. I would not burden anyone in this way, or take unneeded charity. Those coins were all I had to give. The day before we were to leave, I slipped them into her pie safe.

Seventeen

THE NEXT MORNING, a neighbor of Mrs. McGill's was taking a wagon load of lumber from Belleview to Ironton. We laid Sid on the planks so he could stretch out and rest. Before I climbed up, Lorna hugged me. Then she thrust some papers into my hand.

"What's this?" I said, fearing it contained her own money, or mine, given back.

"A pass. You'll need it to get to St. Louis. More federals up there than plague frogs in Egypt, so they say."

The papers stated we were Mr. and Mrs. George McGill, traveling to St. Louis to attend the funeral of a nephew killed in battle. "Where'd you get this?"

"From the provost office," she said. "My mister's away until next month. So you mought as well be me."

As we pulled away, I looked over my shoulder at Lorna, who stood in the road waving until she was just a doll-sized figure in calico. The next time I glanced back, she'd vanished.

At Ironton I showed my pass to the station agent. He was behind a shelf built up high like a store counter. A tall clothespin of a fellow with sleeves rolled to his elbows and an expression that looked as if it were costing him money to talk to me. He held our pass at arm's length, then pulled it up two or three inches from his face, squinting. At last he gave a sharp nod and shoved it back. "Train runnin' late," he barked. "Got to wait a spell out there." He jerked his thumb at a bench. I handed over four dollars and we went out. Sid sat on the bench rubbing his thigh, until I laid a hand on his to make him stop.

Twenty minutes later the locomotive pulled in, bell ringing, belching pungent white clouds of pine smoke from its bulbous stack. The tender swayed and banged; the couplers crashed and rattled. Four huge bright-painted driving wheels threw sparks as it braked. Just two passenger and three freight cars, and a platform loaded with logs. We boarded the first car. Fine, peppery pitch-pine ash had collected on the seats and armrests, so I spread a handkerchief to keep my skirt clean.

After a few minutes we started off. The car swayed so, I felt sick after a while and laid my head against the seat back. I took Sid's hand and closed my eyes. On my lap sat a basket with the lunch Mrs. McGill had packed. "Does your leg still hurt?" I whispered. "Would you like a boiled egg?"

He was looking out the window, not at me. "I'm fine. And not hungry yet."

Then he was quiet. Perhaps he was angry at me for taking over, for arranging everything. I hadn't even told my master plan yet. I fretted awhile, then laid a hand on his arm. "The station master said we'd be in St. Louis in three hours. If we don't break down, or hit any bad stretch of track."

He nodded, but didn't say anything to that, either.

When we stopped at Carondelet, I saw the ironworks again. The stone town hall and its huge spreading elm looked unchanged since my first sight of it, my graduation trip with the Judge. The plank walks were new. Parts of the Commons, which surrounded the town on three sides, had buildings going up. St. Louis, big and dirty and noisy, was moving ever outward, encroaching on the smaller town, and perhaps one day would swallow it. But on closer inspection, I saw no workmen moving about. The building sites looked abandoned.

At the St. Louis station tides of passengers surged in and out. Sid had to limp along, so we inched upstream, buffeted by thrusting shoulders and swinging bags, by hard knees and elbows. I asked at the ticket counter where to find a decent, reasonable room.

The clerk patted his enormous mustaches, which he'd waxed into swooping gull wings. "Try Hazelton House. Between the Mercantile Library and Collins Brothers Druggists, Second Street and Vine." He tapped a tin sitting on the counter, and I glanced at the label. HASHEESH CANDY, EXHIL-ARENT ORIENTAL NERVINE COMPOUND.

"It's what-all a body needs," he assured me. "Your mister there looks mighty peaked."

I thanked him for the advice, but did not avail myself of the potion. We found the hotel after several false starts and bad directions. Fortunately, they had a room for us. In the morning we would catch the boat. Traveling by steamer was quite risky these days. A number had blown up, and the newspapers speculated Confederates had planted bombs. Also, there were sometimes sharpshooters on the riverbanks. But I thought it might be easier to keep Sid out of sight on a steamer than in the confines of a railcar.

As Lorna McGill had warned, St. Louis was crawling with officers on horseback and troops on foot. So I left Sid in the room to rest and went out to find something for supper.

As I neared the cathedral, a great many people were filing in, all in mourning dress. I assumed some dignitary had died, or perhaps a very rich man. The large crowd soon overflowed into the street, causing horse vans and wagons to swerve, drivers to shake their fists. As people closed around, trapping me in an inexorable flow toward the cathedral steps, I felt panic. "Excuse me," I gasped to the woman pressed against my left side, as a large sweating man lurched into us both. "What is happening in this church?"

She stared as if I had two heads and both had spoken to her at once. "You don't know of the outrage done by the rebels upon a great hero?"

I felt a chill walking my spine. I frowned and shook my head as I lied. "We only just arrived from up the river."

"Then you missed the news. Some secesh traitors murdered a group of Union boys took captive at Iron Mountain. Poor Major Wilson! This here's his memorial service."

Lord God. Wilson, the one man Reeves had hated and hunted above all others, as he'd been hated and hunted in return. This muttering crowd looked primed for blood, while not far from here, up in our hotel room, lay Sid—Reeves's lieutenant. I glanced around, seeking a gap to escape through, but more people moved in, pushing and shoving, craning to see over other heads.

"You might well look upset," she said, peering into my face again. "But have no fear. They'll execute six traitors from the prison in revenge. Mr. Lincoln has ordered it so."

"You mean, the ones who killed the major?" I wondered if I knew any of them.

She smiled scornfully. "No, but what difference? A gracious plenty of 'em are sitting up there at Gratiot. And an eye for an eye, saith the Book. I sure hope they let us in to see it."

I could think of nothing to say in return to that. Just then a gap opened to my right. By giving up any pretense at manners and elbowing as hard as the rest, I managed to get all the way to a news and segar stand, where I collapsed on a bench, gasping as if I'd hiked miles uphill. When I could breathe again, I bought an evening *Missouri Herald*, and found the story.

A boy and some neighbors walking along St. John's Creek had stumbled on six bodies still partly clad in federal uniform, half-buried under a fall of dead leaves. Two were torn to pieces, clothes and all. It was supposed hogs and buzzards had been at them. The dead were identified as Wilson and five of his men. In the article no mention appeared of the many farms the major had burned from Doniphan to Ironton, nor of the men he'd executed in circumstances just as pitiable. But then, this was a Union paper. I tore out that page and threw the rest in a bin.

I passed a barbershop, a haberdasher, and other shops until I found a grocer with cheese and apples and crackers. I hurried back to the hotel, clutching our supper as if I'd stolen it. I didn't tell Sid about the killings or the mob. He needed to sleep, to ready himself for the rest of the journey.

That night I lay awake listening to the crowds on the street, the shouting and carousing, the pop of gunfire now and then. When the sky turned pink, I dressed, ate a cracker, and splashed water on my face. When Sid asked why we had to leave so early, I handed him the article.

He read it and then hung his head, staring at the floor. Just when I thought he wouldn't say a word, he looked up. "Price took them prisoner. Why did he give them to Reeves? He must've known this would happen."

He ran his hands through his hair until it stood in black spikes. "The federals will execute six of the Confederate rank and file, it says here. And a major held at Alton. Innocent men who never laid eyes on Pilot Knob or Reeves's Scouts or Major Wilson. That's what passes for justice in the glorious Union now."

"Well, you had nothing to do with it. Though I suppose they wouldn't believe that."

He only shook his head and lowered it again.

God forgive me, I was glad. Not that innocent men would die, for that was a barbarous injustice, as bad as coldhearted murder. And certainly not because Sid felt responsible. No, I rejoiced he'd lost faith in his revered Colonel Reeves, in the Preacher's hopeless Cause. Perhaps now we could put the dangerous, festering wound that was Missouri far behind us.

We set off down narrow streets toward the riverfront. On the way we discovered that St. Louis was a marvelously filthy town. Even this early, thick greasy coal smoke was banked in a dense canopy that hid the sky. Brick houses and shops leaned over the street, packed together in blocks poured from the same mold, with the same number of identical windows set in arched frameworks of twisted stone. From the river St. Louis always appeared a gold-domed, white-steepled temple to some industrial god. Up close, it stank of coal oil and horse dung and piss-soaked brick. Its gutters were heaped with potato peelings, torn handbills, and the odd dead rat. Every surface was grimed the same gray.

The pavements along the riverfront were even worse, the sidewalks cracked and begging for repair. Everywhere lay an abundance of yellow-brown river mud smeared thick as chocolate. In short, it was much like the riverfront at Hannibal. Even more so now, since the armies of drays and throngs of men and mountains of freight that used to heave and swell and surge along here had all but vanished, leaving less than a hundred men to tend to business. Some wore uniforms and oversaw the loading or unloading of the grim freight of war: Guns, stout barrels and crates of munitions and supplies, and, here and there, a tin shoddy coffin.

During my early childhood, Mama tried to shield my eyes and ears from the loud, hulking Irishmen who lolled about the wharf's warehouses. Some were drunk, some still working toward this goal, and others already unconscious with an empty bottle sliding from their slack hands. Yet those men, and our local German immigrants, had signed up first to fight. Now ragged, sweating Negroes sang chanteys to keep the line moving. As if the setting—plantation or wharf or boat—made no difference.

But the greatest change was down at the water. Before the war, there'd been a line of puffing, whistle-shrieking steamboats a mile or more long, vanishing into the distance either way. But here lay only a dozen or so half-awake specimens, and only two wood-yard men, their stacked cords of split pine and oak much diminished from the wooden towers of my youth.

We boarded our boat, the *Sultana*. Her carved chimney-tops were painted red, the pilot house and hurricane deck trimmed with white filigree and gilded acorns, though the paint all over was wearing thin. The boiler deck was the traditional blue but held no Windsor armchairs like the ones I recalled on most such packets. The skylights were glazed with colored glass, though, and the ladies' cabin had a pink-and-white flowered carpet only slightly soiled down the middle. Our cabin held clean bunks, a looking glass, and a closet sized for doll clothes. I'd hoped for a washbowl and pitcher, but it seemed such luxuries were no longer to be had. Everything was flocked with dust and stank of mildew. The single folded towel left on the bed was worn to gauze.

We'd brought no trunk and so didn't have to submit to a baggage search. Departure time was several hours away. Sid decided to lie down. I was too nervy to keep still in my own coffin-sized berth, so I went up to the deck. Strictly speaking, only ladies of the baser sort would be found alone there. But it'd been so long since I'd been on a steamer, I wanted to watch as we pulled away.

The few boats tied up here were clustered like orphan calves in a pad-dock. We'd have to scrape our way out a hands' breadth from the others. At last the *Sultana* got a head of steam up and backed out. She hung a moment in the current as if undecided, while black smoke piled from her stacks. Then, just as it seemed we'd be swept downstream, she gathered momen-tum and we were under way north, toward Hannibal.

Fog drifted low over the ironed brown water. Trees on the bank thrust black skeleton fingers through silver mist. The landscape had its double in the water, as if two identical worlds existed above and below. The lofty green bluffs on the Illinois shore made Missouri's look low, flat, and mean by comparison. I wondered how a slave escaping to freedom might manage to scale them after a hard swim across the swift current.

We skirted towheads, the overgrown sandbars Tom used to tell me were baby islands. They took their time being born, years and years, the tan mud and silt changing the channel and depths constantly, making things interesting for the pilots. I knew we were about to pass the mouth of the Missouri when torrents of yellow mud began to surge through the calmer Mississippi water, like bluing and lye soap brought to a boil in a wash kettle. The currents dividing around us swept along uprooted trees, massive branches, splintered lengths of lumber, and a dead mule.

"I hear in twenty-five years, the wear and tear will move its banks to within ten miles of St. Louis," said a low voice next to me.

I nearly pitched over the rail, not having heard anyone come up. I turned and looked into the familiar face of a gaunt, dark-haired officer.

He bowed. "Beg pardon if I startled you, Mrs. Hopkins. I thought you'd seen me."

"Lieutenant Dickenson. No—no, I hadn't." I turned away, gripping the rail so tight, my fingers ached. Why, with at least a dozen steamboats still plying the river this morning, did this man have to take passage on the *Sultana*?

He pulled a segar from his pocket. "Do you mind?" When I flapped a hand and shook my head, he lit up. "I trust you're well?"

"Yes. We, ah, we attended a funeral in Carondelet." I bit my tongue and resolved to say no more. He knew Sid had been in the guard, but I prayed he had no idea about my husband's time with Reeves's Scouts.

"My condolences. I trust it was no one close?"

I didn't answer at once, because everything was coming back to me in a rush. The room down the hall of the headquarters, my so-called fainting spell on the dusty couch. His face so near, his breath had warmed my neck.

"No. Not at all. An estranged uncle. We hadn't seen him in years. I must apologize, Lieutenant. I'm not feeling well, and will now go back to my cabin."

He smiled ruefully. "Again, my proximity has had a deleterious effect."

I ignored that, and we bowed like the polite strangers we should have been. Then I walked off as quickly as would not seem to constitute running away.

"Lord God, Lord God," I muttered over and over, earning a startled look from an old lady I passed going within. I locked our cabin door behind me, unbuttoned my waist, and loosened my corset. Then I lay back across from Sid, taking deep breaths to calm myself.

We passed Alton just before nightfall, when hunger drove us up to the main cabin. As we walked by the lieutenant's table, an officer seated across from him said in a loud whisper, "Look here, Hi—if it ain't your lady friend from town. That judge's daughter."

Dickenson answered even more loudly, as if he wished everyone, including Sid, to hear. "Why no, you are mistaken. That lady is nothing like."

Sid's hand tightened on my arm. I shook my head and whispered, "I'll explain later."

I told the older couple seated with us that we were returning to St. Paul, after visiting relatives and attending a family funeral. Then I realized my mistake; they could well be heading that far, too. "But we'll be getting off at Hannibal first, to see my sister's new child," I amended.

"Oh, I do love a baby," said the woman fervently, as if she planned to order one from the steward. She was plump, white-haired, in antiquated striped silk near bursting at the seams. But we'd all been forced to raid attics for castoffs these days, simply to be decently covered. Her husband wore rusty black and a checked vest, and kept pulling out his hunter.

"Herbert likes to keep track," she told us. "He's made a record of the fastest times on western waters."

"Ain't nobody beat the *Eclipse* yet," Herbert said, putting the watch away. "New Orleans to Cairo in three days, six hours, forty-five minutes."

"Is that so?" asked Sid. "My cousin is, or was, a steamboat pilot."

"Wasn't it forty-four minutes, dear?" The woman gently corrected her husband.

He snorted. "What I said, Martha. In '53 it was."

After the large plates were cleared, the federal from Dickenson's table who'd remarked on me came to stand next to my chair. When I looked up, he held out one of the old cotton mitts Lorna had given me before we left Belleview. "Excuse me, ma'am. I believe you dropped this."

"Oh." I took the worn glove. "Why, thank you."

Still he remained, smiling down at me in a scornful way. Then he glanced at Sid. "Sir, I heard your wife say you were from St. Paul. Perhaps we have mutual friends there. May I ask your address?"

Neither Sid nor I had ever been to St. Paul. We knew neither a street nor a person in that entire city. Sid had just put a bite of pie in his mouth. It seemed to me best to conjure up some sort of name, but one not too simple, which might sound even more made up.

"We live on, ah, McGill Street," I said quickly, thinking of the glove clutched in my sweating fist. "Do you know the east end?"

He turned that hard glare back to me. "I confess I'm not familiar with that side. What would McGill be near?"

I opened my mouth again reluctantly. Before I could say a word, the woman in striped silk cleared her throat. "McGill's outside town, actually. A new street, set up just before the war. Course with all the shortages, not much building going on now, is there? It's lucky you finished your lovely house before that happened, my dear."

She laid a soft damp hand over mine, and squeezed. That pressure told me clearly to shut my mouth. I did so with gratitude.

The federal looked, if possible, even more displeased. "Perhaps you should ink your street address inside your gloves," he snapped at me. "Shall I get a pen from the purser?"

Lieutenant Dickenson came over to stand behind him. I gripped both glove and napkin and tried to keep from wringing them. Soon we'd be outnumbered.

"Did you hear those shots outside, Parker?" Dickenson said to his scowling companion. "I've sent Mr. Jamison to tell the captain. We're drawing fire from the western shore."

"What? But we just passed the blasted gunboat," Parker complained.

"What does a sharpshooter care for a gunboat," said Dickenson, smiling down at us. He handed the other man his hat. "Come along, now. Let's tend to duty, eh?"

After they left, I thanked my dinner companion for her kindness. "We're so tired, I couldn't even recall my own address. I feel so very silly."

"Of course not," she said. "While you're in Hannibal, will you please give my regards to the widow Mrs. Douglas? We attended the Female College in Columbia, Tennessee, together. Oh, ages ago. When she was still Miss Harkner."

When I told her gently the Widow Douglas had died years before, she produced a tiny square of cotton from her sleeve, the edges turned and only a little mended, and dabbed her eyes. "Poor Grace. How she loved that old castle of a school. She was such a romantic. And you see, I learned to love the South there, despite its flaws. I wish you and your husband safe passage to your home, my dear."

She did not need to add, *Wherever it really is.* I thanked her again, and squeezed her hand in return. Then we excused ourselves and rose to gather up our things, for Hannibal was not much farther on.

Just as we reached the deck, a deep roar came to us over the river, a drumroll for the end of the world. Low and muffled, some distance away, it reverberated back from the trees for an eternity, as if the whole planet were being shaken. The *Sultana* trembled from stacks to hull.

"The boilers!" shouted someone on deck. "They God, we'll explode!"

A frenzy around us then, as people began running and screaming, looking over the rail desperately, gauging where to jump. I clutched Sid's arm, but he gripped me harder, and held me in place. "Be still," he said. "It's not us. We'd already be flying to Kingdom Come."

I turned in a circle. Past the next bend, over the trees, a sulfurous orange glow tinted the night sky. "Look," I said, pulling Sid around to see it.

Two deckhands ran past, one carrying coiled lines, the other a lighted flambeau. ". . . so Cap'n told the engineer," gasped one, " 'Stop creeping along and cram the steam onto her.' "

"But what in Hell is it?" said the other, stopping to jam the flambeau into an iron bracket.

"Boat burners, I bet!"

We looked at each other. "Sid—"

"You know boilers will explode," he said.

Twenty minutes later, on the far side of the bend, we began to see wreckage floating past, some of it aflame. Everyone rushed to the rail. In the flickering light of the flambeaux, I made out shattered planks, bobbing steamer trunks spilling clothes, scorched bales of cotton, splintered crates. And bodies so mutilated, missing limbs, that none could possibly be living.

Soon we reached the wounded ship herself. The wheelhouse and the part of the deck that still jutted from the black water were being eaten by flame.

Wreckage had been blown into the trees; a body was draped like laundry over an overhanging limb. As we watched, a man flung himself from atop the wheelhouse, clothes smoking, and landed on another fellow already in the water. Shrieks and moans came: the high-pitched cries of women and children, the piteous groaning and bellowing of scalded cattle, who thrashed in the water as they were carried past. Our wheels cracked into soft objects as well.

The captain cried out, "Stop the starboard. Stop the larboard! Set her back on both!"

I turned away, covering my ears with my hands. "Stop," I whispered. "Please stop."

"Come below," said Sid gently. "Little they can do now but try to pull some from the water."

I shook my head. How heartless to go below and start packing up our things, as if people weren't dying horribly a few hundred feet away.

The captain stood on the deck above, directing the crew where to swing out one of the cargo booms over the side, lowering a line to a man in the water. Two crewmen jumped in to help. Below us the deckhands hauled aboard the first survivor. He gabbled out he was the ship's carpenter. "I been sleeping, then all of the sudden I'm flown a hundred feet from the boat, still on my mattress." He was frightened but unhurt.

The next few were not so lucky. They'd been scalded, and were writhing and groaning in terrible pain.

Captain Mason was putting a boat in the water to approach the wreck when a remaining portion broke free with a great rending and cracking of wood. Two women and a child imprisoned in the wheelhouse waved desperately at us, faces contorted with terror. The men hurried to drop the boat, but something jammed. Before they could fix it, the floating wreckage, part of the saloon deck it looked like, sank from sight forever into the muddy river.

I cried out and turned away. As I did, I glimpsed another man in the water, off toward the stern. I gripped the railing and leaned out. He looked like . . . but surely not. And yet, I would've sworn it was Tom.

"Over here," I shouted. "Please, here's one! You must get him out." I waved up at the captain, who turned toward me.

"Becky," said Sid. "Wait."

The captain must've misunderstood me. He shouted orders, and one wheel creaked and began to revolve again. Sid and I watched in horror as the stern swung over sharp—the wrong way. The marching, splashing wheel passed over the swimmer and he disappeared.

"Dear God," I groaned. "Did you see? That was . . . it looked just like . . ."

Sid looked puzzled. "Who? Did you know him?"

"But—didn't you? I was certain for a moment it was Tom."

He shook his head. "No. Not Tom. Don't you think I know my own cousin?"

Before I could answer, the chief mate came by, looking for volunteers to tend to the injured. I said I'd go, and so did Sid. But he looked too pale, and staggered when we set off behind the mate. He seemed relieved when I told him to go lie down; he limped painfully away.

Lugged into the dining room, where the tables and chairs had been pushed against the walls, the injured lay on pallets dragged from our cabins. A harried crewman asked me to tend to a half-naked man whose skin was cooked smooth and shiny as patent leather. He bled from cuts and gashes on his arms and chest; his scalded flesh smelled horribly like boiled ham.

"Us stokers seen the fire coming," he gasped as I carefully dabbed linseed oil on his burns. "We slid onto the boiler, and couldn't get off. Oh, I begged 'em to shoot me."

"We'll take care of you," I murmured. "I'm so sorry for your pain, but perhaps . . ." Yet I couldn't think of anything comforting to say. He was so terribly injured, how could I tell him he'd be well again?

"You look kind. Can't you shoot me, ma'am?" Then he went off raving, shouting at a nonexistent crew to hump themselves, to move faster or they'd never make Memphis by dawn. I laid cotton lint over the linseed oil, until he was swathed in white to the waist. As I tended to him, I thought again of the man in the water, the one who—for a moment—had looked like Tom. Had I only wanted it to be him, to save him, have him back? Of course, I hadn't saved the poor wretch at all. If I hadn't drawn attention to him, he might've made it to shore, instead of being run down by the wheel of the *Sultana*.

Captain Mason walked past as I labored and brooded. He stopped to thank me, saying they'd board a doctor in Hannibal—if one could be found. "But we'll continue to St. Paul. Conditions for the poor devils'll be better there, at a real hospital."

I laid the last piece of cotton on my patient. "Do you know what happened, sir?"

"I suppose this to be another rebel atrocity, like the *Ruth* or the *Robert Campbell*, in '63. But how can one be sure? These are terrible times." He bowed and moved on.

I sat beside the stoker, wishing I knew his name. Mercifully for us both, he'd fainted. From time to time he roused and pawed at the cotton, exposing cooked flesh again, until I gently pressed the dressings back in place.

I don't know how long I sat there, but at last Sid found me and pulled me to my feet. "Come back to the cabin."

Instead, I asked to come up on deck. After the terrible smells of the makeshift infirmary, all I wanted was fresh air, a view far removed from the groaning and shrieks we could still hear. It no longer seemed to matter whether it was an accident, or a hellish punishment inflicted on one group of men by another for no good reason at all.

The breeze was clean now, only faintly tinged with pine, instead of smoke and charred flesh. I stood at the rail, gazing out at the Missouri shore. It looked like peaceful forest, but I knew better. "How can such things happen? And go on happening. God has deserted us."

I expected Sid to rebuke me for this impiety. He'd always been the more fervent churchgoer. But he only put an arm about my waist and drew me close. "Perhaps God feels the same about us these days. At what horrors we visit on one another. On those same neighbors Christ told us to love."

I had nothing at all to say to that, for there was no question my husband was absolutely right this time.

Eighteen

I T WAS NEAR MIDNIGHT when we at last pulled in to Hannibal. Too dark to see much, but that didn't matter. I heard the high, familiar cry of a drayman. *"Steeaammboat a-coming!"*

Back at last. I felt I'd been gone years. Eager to see Gage and Mary, we gathered our few things and went up top. I stopped to speak to the captain, who gravely informed me that my injured stoker seemed somewhat better.

"I'm very glad to hear it," I said, wondering if he was only trying to make me feel better. The man had been so mortally hurt, he'd looked barely human.

A steamboat captain was always the hero and the envy of every boy I grew up with. Ours stood now by the big bell, uniform worn but immaculate, his look calm yet imposing. A deckhand stood ready with a coiled line at the bow. These fellows were admired even more by boys, because they weren't required to wear shoes.

Steam screamed through the gauge-cocks as the captain rang the bell sharp. A lurch, and we swayed on our feet as the big wheels stopped, backed, and churned the brown water to frothy cream. Then what a scramble to get ashore, pushing past a tide of others doing the same to board, and all the while the hands took in and discharged freight over our heads. With so much yelling and cursing in the air, any shipping clerks who'd nodded off in their sheds would be awake now.

I'd expected troops at the levee here, too, but the town looked dead asleep. The local drunkard who always shambled up to bother passengers for a penny was sprawled out snoring by the empty skids. Sid and I hurried through the dark, narrow streets, their silence so eerie, I began to feel like Rip Van Winkle, awake but come home too late. I walked faster, then slowed when I realized Sid couldn't keep up.

He cleared his throat, and the sound echoed off the darkened buildings. "I imagine there's a curfew."

"I wonder if Gage is asleep," I said. "How surprised he'll be to see both of us." I hugged Sid's arm closer to me. Yes, home. I had managed it after all.

I also wondered how the Judge was faring with Tom's bunch, whether they'd taken him South to my mother's people in Virginia, or if he'd simply worn them out, too. Maybe when you've possessed the power of life and death, and can hang anybody who offends the law, over the years it gets harder to put up with not getting your own way.

Sid reached for the front doorknob, hesitated, then pounded on Aunt Polly's door instead of barging in. He shifted, favoring his injured leg. At last I heard someone thumping slowly down the stairs. After a moment, Mary opened the door just a crack, looking pale and apprehensive. When she saw us, her eyes grew round and her mouth dropped open. "Oh!" was all she got out. And again, "*Oh!*"

Then we were both hugging her thin frame to us, until I feared she couldn't breathe and would start coughing. Anyone not local might consider this homely little tableau unremarkable, if they were unaware that the custom in Missouri for either greeting or saying good-bye, even to close relatives, was normally just a firm handshake. In my family and Sid's, I'd never seen anyone publicly kiss another soul, unless it was a child under the age of three.

When I held Mary at arm's length, though, for a better look, she was not thin everywhere. Beneath her apron sat a perfect rounded bulge. "Mary," I gasped. "You look so . . . so well."

She laughed. "I am well. And you needn't look at me *that* way, either of you. I'm a married woman." She held up her left hand, where a thin gold band glowed in the light of the overhead lamp.

Our turn to stare. Finally I said, "I suppose—Corporal O'Brien?"

She nodded, smiling but crying, too. "Only it's Sergeant O'Brien now."

Sid scowled at the notion some man he'd never set eyes on had married his sister and put her in a family way, all while he was gone. "What! Who is this O'Brien? Who are his people? Where are they from?"

Mary rolled her eyes. "Oh, Sid."

I dropped my bag and left her to explain, while I ran up the stairs to see my dear little boy. Gage lay sprawled across the bed, nightgown hiked and wrapped around his legs, thumb plugging his mouth. Drawing the covers up again, I knelt on the floorboards and laid my head on the mattress, face close to his.

"How I missed you, my darling," I whispered. The past few weeks I'd had to think mostly of how best to mind Pa or find Sid, or not be killed myself. To just try to get along. And yet Gage had been there, wrapped in my thoughts like a delicate souvenir I could pull out at low times to gaze on and caress, to raise my spirits. I'd been afraid to do this too often, in case I wouldn't live to see him after all. Or return only to find he'd sickened and died like little Tyler. I'd lived through the baby's death. But to lose both! When I gathered him up and hugged him to me, Gage grumbled in his sleep.

I couldn't have borne losing him. Though I would've had to stand it, as so many others were doing all over the ravaged land—even if instead of a cradle or trundle bed their sons lay dead on a field or in a muddy trench. Or still crouched there alive, hugging a rifle for cold comfort, while Parrott shells screamed overhead. Perhaps Tyler's quiet death at home was in some ways more bearable than seeing a grown child off to be shot at, mutilated, or killed. To discover he had died alone, his life leaking away on a bloody field like Iron Mountain. And for what? Slaves we did not own, a Union that hated us unto death, some old men's idea of glory?

When the War began, everyone said it would be over in a month. Then they changed to saying it couldn't go on much longer. They'd said the same last year, and the year before. The South was starving, wasting, dying. Yet why, after all, should the killing not go on forever? The War continues, its black mouth chewing up an endless line of boys and men, then shitting them out, dead or dying, onto shell-scarred ground.

No, we'd not stay here. I meant to flee beyond the reach of cannons and raiders and uniforms of any hue. But would I get Sid to agree? I looked on my sleeping son and stroked his sleep-tousled hair. Even if we had to depart without his father, we would leave Missouri. Though of course, that wasn't right. We'd be leaving Hannibal without the man who'd fathered Gage in any case. For who knew where Tom Sawyer might be, or what he was doing? Unless I had indeed killed him myself, back on the steamer, with a word. Just as he'd once killed another man with the absence of one.

WHEN WE SAT DOWN together at the breakfast table, Mary served grits and a few slivers of ham. "It's about all we have left," she confided. Besides the greens growing out back, and corn bread, those two staples were always dinner. "Still," she said, "we are more fortunate than some."

On the fifth morning, after Sid had taken the first sip of his steaming cup of okra-seed coffee, and given the usual grimace, he picked up the *St. Louis Herald* I'd bought in town. He turned a page, then with an exclamation held it closer, as if he didn't believe what he was reading.

I'd just forced down a bite of grits, very dry and bland without butter. "What's wrong, Sid? What is it?"

Without looking up he replied, "It says here the steamer sunk in the river south of Hannibal was the *Madison*."

I set down my fork with the next portion of grits still on it.

"You remember her," he prompted.

Of course I did. So that was the doomed boat we'd come across on our way back home. The first steamer Tom Sawyer ever piloted on, after he'd learned the trade from the famous Captain Sellers on *Prairie*. He'd be downcast to hear it was no more. "Do they know how many were lost?"

"It says here, forty-one passengers. And the crew . . ."

Sid paused; a guarded look crept over him. "The crew all killed," he said quickly, and folded the paper. He set it on his lap, out of sight.

Many steamboats, perhaps dozens, had blown up during this War, though certainly boiler explosions weren't unheard of before now. Sometimes captains would tie down their safeties and race, and the end result of that folly wasn't always victory. But the authorities had begun to take notice of the number lost the past four years. There'd been rumors of boat-burners working for the Confederates on the Mississippi and Missouri rivers since the war began. We'd always known there was danger in traveling by steamer, but these days the risk felt greater. From Sid's expression, though, I saw there was more to it than that.

Before I could ask, Mary rose from her place, clutching her napkin. "Sid," she said, voice gone shaky. "I think you didn't tell all of it. What was that list at the end?"

"The list of passengers and crew. And—and there were three pilots on board."

Mary leaned hard on the table, staring at him. "Sid, you must tell us."

I saw his jaw quiver, as if he were about to laugh, or cry. He began talking rapidly, as if he might not have time to say everything he needed to. "Well, one name listed here is Thomas Sawyer. A pilot, it says. A mistake, no doubt. Or do you suppose there could be another with the same name? And the captain, he was Frederick Laclede. A man from St. Louis, an old family—"

"I don't give a damn for the captain!" Mary shouted. She began to sob in ugly gulps, then pushed away from the table, running out of the room with a clumsy sway. I heard a door slam upstairs.

"I should go to her," I said, lips so stiff, I could hardly form the words. But the stiffness was spreading to my arms and legs. Sid's look pinned me to my chair. It seemed grieved but also self-righteous, as if somehow this was all my fault.

Gage dropped his hunk of corn bread on his plate, and looked from one to the other of us, lower lip quivering. "Mama. Papa. What's wrong?"

"I'm afraid your uncle, our cousin Tom, may be dead," Sid said, watching my face all the while. "It hardly seems possible. All our lives . . . I didn't think he could be hurt by anything. Especially not the river."

"Our uncle Tom?" said Gage, sounding more puzzled than sad. "Do I know him?"

"Not really, sweetheart." I stared back at Sid. "But are you sure? Perhaps there's some mistake."

"It says here that he and another man were knocked into the river by the blast. They swam back to pull folks from the sinking steamer. But on the last trip, only the other man returned to shore. So when you thought you saw him—"

I clapped both hands to my ears. A bell was ringing somewhere, perhaps outside, perhaps in my head. The room was turning dark; I couldn't see. I'd have to get up and loosen my stays or else faint. How I hated that, the drugged feeling when you came back to yourself. Everyone staring.

I lowered my head and rested it on my folded arms. Sid scraped his chair back, slid his hands under my arms, and lifted me. Gage was staring down at his plate, picking the pone into crumbs. A tear trickled down his cheek. But perhaps Sid didn't notice, because all he said was, "Finish your breakfast, son. Don't waste good food." As if this were any other day.

He heaved me up. "You'd best lie down. We'd better go see if Mary can be comforted."

In the bedroom he unbuttoned my waist, and loosened my stays quite dextrously. I lay back on the bed, the old rope one of Polly's, which Mary now shared with O'Brien. We clung to each other as she cried in choking gasps, dampening my neck with her tears. She'd always loved Tom as well as her own brother, and had thought nothing but good of him, no matter what anyone else said.

I stroked her hair. My eyes stung, yet no tears came. Instead I felt stunned, betrayed. How could he leave this Earth, and I not somehow feel it? How could he have been dead for nearly a week, and I not know it for certain?

So I was somehow still his. It seemed there was no cure for that, even though I had a husband I loved quite well. This was a conundrum I'd never mastered. Perhaps because I was so weak, or maybe because I was the mother of Tom's first, his only child.

As far as you know. That whispery inner voice crept into my head from all the corners of the room. *For who really knows what a man like Tom Sawyer might get up to in his travels?*

Once it began, the mean words seemed eager to go on and on, accusing and speculating, until at last I forced them down. "I never got to tell him," I whispered into the damp curls stuck to Mary's forehead. It pained me most to think of that; now Tom would never know about Gage.

"What, Becky?" said Mary thickly, through her tears. "Tell who?"

I'd forgotten she was there. "Nothing. I only meant for Sid to see Gage finished eating."

I disentangled myself and got up. Poured water from the washstand pitcher into Aunt Polly's flowered china basin, which was scummed with a ring of soap and O'Brien's red bristly hairs. I didn't much like this sight. Yet the big ham-handed fellow gazed at Mary over supper each night as if his life story were written on her face. He wouldn't let her lift anything heavier than a soup spoon. She'd told me he washed and dried the dishes each night in the kitchen while she put her swollen feet up on a chair. Then he sat and rubbed them, and told her all about his day.

So I ignored the whisker mess and took up a cloth and washed my hot face, then held it to my burning eyelids. Finally I dipped and wrung it again, and went to clean Mary up.

"He's a mighty good man," I said as I wiped her salt-tracked cheeks. "Your Mr. O'Brien."

This home truth seemed to cheer her a little. I left her in bed, still hiccuping a sob now and then in her sleep.

I found Sid in our room sitting on the bed, staring at a child's ball; an old one I didn't recognize. "Where's Gage?"

He didn't look at me at first. "Out back, playing with the cat."

When I dropped down beside him, the old springs screeched.

At last he glanced up. "You loved him."

Perhaps it was wrong, and even more deceitful, but I could not discuss it. Not yet, not then. "Most people did. He had a way about him."

He looked at the floor again and his shoulders twitched, as if he were laughing to himself. He bounced the ball off a plank. "What do you have in mind to do now? For I admit, I'm at something of a loss."

"Leave this house to Mary and O'Brien. I'll close up the Judge's place."

"And then?"

I fell back across the bed, arms outflung, feeling heavy as lead, too fatigued to move. "Sid, please let's go West. It's what any person with any wits left is doing these days. Mary has a new letter from Sam Clemens. He says every fool out there is getting rich digging gold or silver out of the ground with a pick."

Sid grunted and looked away. "West," he repeated, with no inflection.

"Missouri's a corpse in the sun," I persisted. "You know it as well as I do. This hellish state plants raiders and soldiers, and waters the crop with blood. I will not have my son to grow up here."

He looked at me sharply. "Your son?"

"What?"

"You said *your* son. Not ours. Not mine."

I wanted to close my eyes, to look anywhere else, but held his gaze. "You know what I meant."

"I believe I do," he said. He stared back for a long moment, and that gaze showed me many things. Some I wouldn't have expected to see there, before: Grief. Love. Pity and rage. Perhaps even hatred. No doubt he saw some of these mirrored in my eyes as well.

He looked away again. Got up, creaking our bed, and walked toward the windowstill holding the ball, limping from the wound that'd downed him at Iron Mountain. He gazed out on Aunt Polly's overgrown garden, on Gage pursuing Mary's old orange cat through the dying potato vines. "Tell me. What good is a man whose wife must ride out and save him?"

"Sid, you were wounded. I didn't save you, I—I only helped get you home again."

I was about to rise, too, when he said else something in a low voice. He was still facing the window, and the words were muffled.

"I'm sorry. I couldn't hear."

He raised a hand to the glass and ran a finger over the old crack that made a thin new-moon curve in one corner. That flaw had been there ever since ten-year-old Sid had thrown a ball at his cousin Tom in anger— perhaps the same toy he still held in the other hand. The throw had gone wild, and struck the pane. Tom had been wrongly accused and punished for it. He'd taken three painful raps on the head with Polly's thimble, and hadn't said anything. But according to Tom, neither had Sid.

Without turning to look at me, Sid spoke louder. "I said—all right, Becky. We'll go West, then."

I waited, but he stayed at the window, silent. Perhaps grieving for Tom, too; Sid was a good man; he would not rejoice at any death, not even that of an enemy. At last I got up quietly and went from the room, already turning over in my mind what needed to be done to prepare for our journey. I'd gotten my way, and was relieved. But somehow I'd expected to feel more joy of it.

A WONDERFUL THING HAPPENED before we left town—Jim came back. He knocked on our front door early one morning, and when I opened it, there he stood in a frock coat, a silk hat, and striped trousers.

"Morning, Miss Becky." He was smiling as if I'd won a prize and he was it.

"Oh . . . Jim!" Without thinking of appearances, I threw myself at him and hugged his neck; no doubt the neighbors talked of that for weeks. Then I dragged him inside. "Sid! Mary! Gage! Come see who's here."

They came running from all corners of the house and greeted him pretty much the same. And at that moment, seeing Jim still big and strong and good-natured, truly a free man, all my tears unshed for Tom came forth. Jim fretted and apologized, while Mary sat me in a chair and Gage brought a glass of water without anyone telling him to. When I could speak again, I shook my head and said I was fine. "I'm just so happy to see our old friend again."

Gage was chafing one of my hands like he'd seen grown-ups do, as if I'd fainted. "I'm fine now, darling," I told him. "Jim, do you have news of my father?"

"Yes'm. Huck Finn got him safe all the way down to Tennessee last month, and by now he ought to be with your mama. You hear about your grandaddy? He done died last month."

"No—no, I hadn't heard that." I'd never known the old man well, for he hadn't been fond of spending time with children. I recalled only a stern, sun-reddened face and iron-gray hair and the scent of bourbon. But I felt sorry for my mother, who'd doted on her family and their connections to old Richmond and even beyond, to Jamestown and England—as if the main point of life was to be as close-bred as racehorses. My tears flowed again, and I didn't explain it wasn't for the loss of a grandparent. I used Mary's hankie. "Everyone stop fussing and please sit down," I begged.

Jim had heard about the steamboat explosion. He told us he'd gone all the way north to St. Paul looking for Tom, only to be told his body hadn't been recovered. "Lotsa folks was dumped in the water. Tom, he tried to save 'em. But the river take its due."

With a stifled cry, Mary jumped up, rushed to the kitchen, and began banging pots and pans around. We all sat miserably for a few moments, not speaking at all.

Then Jim said, "Say, guess what. I got a new job." He'd started working in the hospital in St. Louis as an orderly, nursing wounded Union soldiers. "It hard, you know. And be harder still when one of them boys up and dies on me. But it suit me, telling stories and making sure they comfortable. Seem like all I can do for 'em, sometimes. They most all just Yankees, but—"

Just then he seemed to remember Mr. O'Brien. He was in uniform and standing next to Mary, who'd just returned from the kitchen. O'Brien had one arm around her shoulders. "They God," Jim amended. "Don't know what I'm saying. Mouth just run away with me."

Mary's eyes still glittered with tears, but she smiled. "Jim, don't apologize. You're doing the Lord's work. And I haven't yet introduced you to my new husband, Mr. O'Brien."

Jim got up and shook his hand. "Pleased to meet you, Captain."

"Aye, well, it's sergeant," said O'Brien, who still did not look unhappy at the brief promotion.

"Yessir. Well, I said I's gone be rich some day. You recall, Miss Becky, I tole Tom and Huck Finn that many years ago? That time with Huck when we raft down the river. And didn't I try to nurse Tom back to health then? Well, listen to this—that hospital in St. Louis pay me five dollars a week!"

We all marveled over that, especially since it would be in greenbacks instead of worthless secesh dollars. Right now a fortune indeed, for one of any color.

We took supper in the kitchen, and after dark Sid and O'Brien walked Jim down to the riverfront so he could take a steamer back to his position in St. Louis. He carried a hunk of Mary's corn bread rolled in a clean old napkin. I watched the three of them go, and worried. The chances of Jim's boat also coming to grief were slim, but I hated to think of him on board and at risk. At least he was happy now, and prosperous.

And Mary was going to be a mother. While Sid and I would soon begin all over again, in the far-off Nevada Territory. Surely way out there the ghost of Tom Sawyer could no longer hang over us, or lurk around every corner.

1864

NEVADA TERRITORY

Nineteen

ONCE YOU DECIDE TO MOVE to a different place, at first the sheer excitement of the coming newness takes over all your senses. I believe this is a survival tactic implanted in the human species, designed to help spread our kind all over the planet. Otherwise, considering the work involved, few would have the energy to leave home, and we'd all live crowded just east of Eden.

During the next week we engaged in a whirlwind of planning, packing clothes and household goods, tossing out old things, and saying good-byes. We sold some of the furniture, every piece Mary and O'Brien wouldn't miss, for we needed the money. But with the departure of each familiar, well-loved chair or bed or table, my anticipation felt less pleasant, and more akin to fear of the unknown. Still we rushed to get started, because the uncharacteristically mild fall weather would rapidly change. And no one in his right mind would journey out to the Territories in the middle of winter.

I fell into bed each night exhausted, trying not to think of the future, trying not to envision the strange country we were bound for, lest it tire me out before we even boarded the stagecoach. I was only partly successful, for we were losing too much to ignore it: Mary, so like a sister when I'd never had one. Aunt Polly's house, my home all the years since my marriage. And my parents' place, where I'd spent my growing years in Hannibal, now shuttered and boarded up against intruders and weather. And yes, even the ruined state of Missouri. No matter how terrible it had become, it was still my native land.

Added to these impending losses was a cool silence between Sid and me. He limped around doing whatever needed to be done, doggedly, steadily, with his usual efficiency. But his heart was not in the preparations. He spoke to me only briefly, and too politely. As if he'd guessed my feelings for Tom, and Gage's true origin, without me confessing a word. I tried to behave as if all were well, for Gage's sake. If the wound to mutual trust and affection was a fatal one, perhaps there was no marriage left. But my clumsy machinations weren't the real problem. That had begun even before we wed, because I could not rid myself of a disease named Sawyer.

Even in death Tom would not let go. Yet the fault was my own. Perhaps that last betrayal had been instigated by Tom, on a pile of blankets in a lean-to shed in the forest. But I'd joined in quite willingly.

IN '64, THERE WAS NO ROAD to the Pacific, and rails across the plains wouldn't be laid for ten more years. Sam Clemens's latest letter warned us about the stage departing the Kansas–Missouri border: he said to remember it allowed each passenger only a very modest amount of baggage. So we'd gritted our teeth and jettisoned much of what I considered essential for starting a new home, then repacked mainly clothes and a few tools and kitchen things.

On the appointed day, a tearful Mary came to see us off at the riverfront, leaning heavily on O'Brien. "Oh dear, Becky," she said, clutching at my arm. "I want to stop all this somehow. I fear I'll never set eyes on you again."

I feared the same. But I hugged her neck, then peeled her hands away and passed her on to Sid. He stood pale but stony-faced as she wept in his arms, while O'Brien patted her back with one great paw and murmured Gaelic endearments.

Finally the whistle blew, and we climbed the gangway to the packet. Then we three stood at the railing, our hands upraised—Gage wildly waving both of his—as Hannibal slowly dropped away at our stern. The *Molly Ina* thrashed south toward St. Louis. We'd change boats there and steam west for

St. Joseph, where we'd catch an overland stage. Soon we'd be away from Missouri and Sid would no longer be Lieutenant Hopkins, but simply one more anonymous pioneer lighting out with his family for the Territories.

St. Joseph was five days away, up the Missouri River. We disembarked briefly in St. Louis, boarding a smaller packet older than *Molly Ina,* and in worse repair. I recall little of the voyage after our boxes were loaded and Sid had tipped the porters, except the thrill of horror I felt whenever the boat lurched or rolled, or kissed a sandbar, or dragged a snag down her side.

Each time, I'd rush up from the ladies' saloon to the deck, towing Gage along, determined to leap over the rail with him if need be. When it became clear the problem was not an exploding boiler, I'd kneel and hug him as we watched the steamer back off bars and butt into them time after time, until one wheel or the other could walk over the impediment, and put us afloat again.

The days were sunny with a chill, cutting wind. I spent much time hauling my son safely away from his observations of whatever open machinery he could glimpse on the lower deck. Gage had a fascination with huge gears and boilers and wheels that I found alarming. When you have but one child to cherish, both man-made machinery and nature seem more ominous and full of threat.

The Missouri River must've been uncommonly low. We ran aground so often, I began to think we'd never get out of the state. But after five days we tied up at St. Joseph and sent our meager luggage on to a hotel. Sid went to the stage office and paid $350, the last money from my father's account, for tickets on the overland coach to Virginia City, Nevada.

St. Joseph sat on the rowdy east bank of the Missouri, and our rickety hotel on Robidoux Street was thin-walled and noisy. A few years earlier this area had still been part of the Platte Territory, inhabited only by Sioux and Sac and Fox Indians. Plus one white man, Joseph Robidoux, the canny fur trader it was all named after. Thanks to the Missouri's westward bend, St. Joe had become the jumping-off place, bustling with travelers and outfitters preparing either to head west or make money off those who wanted to.

Once we got our feet back on dry land, we were swept up in the jostling crowds. Homesickness receded and excitement took over again. Gage raced around our tiny room, squealing and jumping on the bed until Sid made him stop. After two stories and a half hour of cajoling, he finally went to sleep in the trundle rolled from under the hotel bed. We'd come too late for supper, and went to bed starving. I'd promised Gage a huge breakfast of sausages and grits and fried bread, and for myself, as many cups as I could hold of the hotel's coffee. When I'd passed the dining room, it had smelled like the genuine article. That alone was almost worth a trip down the Missouri.

I opened my valise, shook out my flannel gown, and Huck's revolver clunked onto the tobacco-stained carpet.

Sid turned to stare. "Lord God, what're you doing with that?"

The longest sentence he'd said to me all day. I picked the gun up and slid it back into the case. "It's not loaded. Sam says everyone goes about armed out there."

"Even women?"

I bit my lip, determined not to argue, since I'd had my way in all else. I forced an apologetic laugh. "Of course I won't *wear* it, Sid. You can if you want."

"Yes, no doubt I'll need it," he said with so much bitterness, I turned back to look again. But he was facing away, undressing for bed.

We got in facing opposite walls. Gage's childish snores seemed very loud. Even though Sid lay still, I could tell he wasn't asleep. Since Tom's death, he hadn't turned to me once in bed. And I lacked the nerve, or perhaps enough wanting, to lay a hand on his shoulder or to brush his hip beneath the quilt. *So perhaps that part is over,* I thought. *Perhaps there'll be no more children.*

That my husband now had no issue of his own blood pricked my conscience daily. It felt like a debt I owed, a gap in an invisible ledger, a heavenly scale tipped by unequal weight in the pans. I should make that much right, at least, and give to Sid the same I'd given Tom. But I was too frightened to ask whether he still wanted me, or could even bring himself to touch me again. Yet here he lay, still beside me, in a narrow, lumpy bed in St. Joseph, en route to Nevada, pretending to sleep. Wasn't that proof of something?

I reached out in the dark. My hand bumped Sid's thigh, and he flinched.

"I'm sorry," I whispered, thinking I'd hurt him. The scar was raised and red, and on cold days, still painful. He said it ached, especially at night.

But he remained silent. Sid had always been a gentle soul. Aside from throwing that ball at Tom once, he was careful not to hurt human or animal. So it was a great surprise to me when he rolled over suddenly and pinned me roughly to the mattress. If he hadn't clamped his mouth over mine, I would've cried out. When he forced my lips apart, his teeth cut me. I tasted blood and tried to squirm away. He pressed down harder, until I was drowning in a quagmire of feather bed.

He lifted his hips and jerked our nightclothes out of the way, then pushed my knees up and shoved into me so hard, I gasped. My eyes watered but I made no other sound, even when he was so rough, I feared he'd pierce some vital organ. In eight years of marriage, he had never mistreated me. I was certain he'd never think to use even a paid woman so hard. Still, I thought I understood. So I kept quiet, swallowing back blood and snot, trying not to make a sound.

Men are strange creatures. For the first time in our shared history he bruised my skin, marking me as with a brand or notching knife. Perhaps it made a twisted kind of sense to him, to even the score between himself and his dead cousin through me.

At last he stopped moving and shuddered, lowering his head to bite my shoulder, groaning as if he were suffering torments, rather than enjoying what might normally be called pleasure.

HE WAS UP FIRST IN THE MORNING, scraping his chin at the washstand. I wrapped the sheet around me, wincing as I hunted for a fresh chemise and linen. The last time I'd felt so bruised, I'd just given birth to Tyler. It occurred to me we'd be jolting over rocky ground on a stagecoach all day long, too. I stopped, chemise in hand, wondering if that had also occurred to Sid. If so, he was more calculating than I'd given him credit for. Making a day's journey perched on a rocking bench seat would be even less pleasant now, for me.

When I looked up again, I caught him staring.

"Good morning," he said, not quite smiling. When I dropped the sheet, he must've seen the bruises on my legs, the marks of his teeth on my shoulder. He turned back to the mirror. The slow scraping of the razor resumed.

"Morning," I replied, then dressed myself slow and careful. "Save some of that water." I pulled on my corset and came up beside him to get a damp cloth.

He set the razor down. "I believe I am looking forward to this trip at last," he said. I noticed he'd laid the blade on the side farthest away from me.

Gage woke out of sorts, as children often do. But soon he was laughing and looking forward to the journey again. Overnight we'd somehow moved back into a familiar orbit.

Our baggage was weighed at the stage depot, and with a nod the station-master passed it on to be loaded. Behind us a man had to snatch his trunks open and make a hasty selection of the most important twenty-five pounds of his former life. He desperately pulled on extra shirts and vests and stockings as the horses stamped and blew, and the driver muttered imprecations.

We three, and the man swaddled in two season's outfits, appeared to be the only passengers. When we climbed in, the reason became clear. I hadn't taken much notice earlier when the stationmaster and the driver argued bitterly about delayed mail. Now I saw the interior of the stage was full of it. We adults had to sit on the back bench seat, the only unencumbered spot, with Gage in my lap. Across from us, a tower of mailbags rose to the ceiling, the lower ones pressing on our knees.

"Boots fore and aft're full," snapped the driver as he slammed the door. "You all got to put up with twenty-five hunnert pounds of this stuff till we unload along the way."

I unfolded a quilt against the late-fall chill and spread it over our laps. Sid gave Gage a sip from his canteen. Strapped to my waist, under my merino jacket, was a small leather purse of gold from the sale of our worldly goods back in Hannibal. It would have to last along the way, and get us set up in Nevada.

The driver shouted at the horses, cracked his whip, and with a dislocating jerk we were off. Our swaying, scrolled box with painted wood trim rocked like a doll's cradle and threw us about like loose-jointed puppets. We huddled under the quilt as the swaddled man stared forlornly out the window, spectacles caking with dust. Gage read a volume of fairy stories that first my mother, then I, had grown up with. Its tissue-thin pages kept him occupied until I looked down and saw he'd gone to sleep, thanks to the rocking.

So had the stranger. His wire-rimmed spectacles slid farther down his nose until they hung on the tip. Finally I could stand it no longer. I unhooked the earpieces and slipped them into his breast pocket.

Soon we were tearing through northeast Kansas, then a few hours later crossing the plains, a sea of dry grass punctuated with an occasional tilled field. I finally understood why the plains were called *rolling*. Corn or hay or wheat or grass in fall all browned to a single color. It swept up and down in wavelike troughs and ridges, as an ocean might heave after a storm. I'd never seen an ocean, but as we rocked along through the relentless tan waves I began to feel light-headed and dizzy. When I complained, Sid laughed. "You're seasick." He pulled my head onto his shoulder. We rode that way for a long time, the pleasantest part of that day's journey.

Each stop for a change of horses, we leapt out to stretch our legs, and I wished for a feather pillow to sit on. Broadsheet advertisements were certainly misleading. SMOOTH TRAVEL IN ROOMY COMFORT. LUXURY ON FOUR WHEELS. SUMPTUOUS UPHOLSTERY. In reality we were crammed tight, jostled and bumped, breathing gritty red dust, at the mercy of every rock and pothole nature grew. Besides the wall of letters and parcels swaying inches from our knees was another great pile strapped on top of the stage. I hoped our suitcases hadn't fallen off back in St. Joseph.

"Twenty-seven hundred pounds of mail aboard," the driver remarked at the third fifteen-mile change of horses. "A little for Mr. Brigham Young, a bag for Carson City, a heap for Frisco. But the bulk be for Injuns. Whoever the hell learnt them to read oughta be shot. Beg pardon, ma'am," he muttered, tipping his hat.

"Indians?" said Gage, who'd been watching the fresh horses being harnessed. He looked up at me. "Maybe they'll try to scalp us."

"Certainly not," I said, nudging Sid. He shook his head and patted our son's shoulder. Gage went back to admiring the six shining bays who stamped and tossed their heads as if they were impatient to reach a new life, too. I looked forward to more leg room when we delivered mail to the Indians, or the buffalo, or anyone who'd take it.

An hour later we suddenly stopped in the middle of the prairie. The driver leapt from the box and stomped around, raising clouds of dust. The conductor, short and round-bellied in vest and billed hat, climbed down, opened the boot, and threw a dozen bags onto the dusty trail. The two men climbed up again and we went on. Glancing back I saw only tall grass, rolling plains, and the bags humped together in the rutted trail. Had folks written and wrapped brown paper and licked stamps all in vain? No Indians appeared, and soon the forlorn heap was swallowed by dust and distance.

When we stopped, we'd barely figure where we might be at when the whip cracked and we'd lurch off again. The air grew colder. I saw less grass, few trees, more dirt and dust. The steep-banked ribbons of streams we passed seemed a charming feature until the stage raced down the side of one. We landed face-first in the dirty canvas bags, which scraped our noses and made us sneeze. As the coach jounced over the rocky streambed we flew around like dice in a gambler's fist. Gage rolled at our feet, sprawling and kicking, as the adults flung out arms to ward off sharp-edged parcels and mailbags.

As we avalanched from one end to the other, our wicker picnic basket followed, shedding smoked sausages, boiled eggs, and mealy apples that'd cost the earth back in St. Joe. The basket slammed Sid's elbow and punched my stomach. It struck Gage in the face and made his nose bleed. But our funny little boy was pleased, since the injury was good for a piece of brown sugar broken off the loaf in the basket.

That evening the driver blew a bugle to announce a way station. Sam had warned that these would offer sparse comfort. He'd described long low buildings of sun-dried, mud-colored brick, with flat roofs thatched or sodded. The first was topped with a layer of dirt hosting an impressive stand of weeds. "The pasture's on top of that house," marveled Gage. "How do their cows eat?"

"Why, they just climb that-there ladder, son," the driver said, jerking a thumb at a rickety one leaning against a wall.

The largest building was actually a ramshackle barn with room for a dozen horses. The smaller hut turned out to be our dining room, so squat, I could touch the eaves. We had to duck to get inside. The lone window was a square hole large enough for a man to crawl through, with a nasty flap made of some animal's stiff, tanned guts. The floor was packed dirt crisscrossed with the trails of large insects. A smoking fireplace served for both heat and cooking. In one corner a fifty-pound sack of flour lolled; I shuddered to think of mice skipping barefoot through it. On a wooden trestle table sat a dented, blackened coffeepot, a squat tin kettle, a sack of grayish salt, and a greasy flank of bacon that'd gone off some days back.

After we smelled dinner—a pan of mysterious, stringy meat with cabbage boiled gray—we ate our basket provisions instead. Then they wouldn't be bouncing around the coach at every jolt. The serving woman ladled us out a lukewarm murky liquid she called coffee. "Where you folks headed?" she asked. When we said Nevada, she shook her head. "*Tch.* That's a far piece from civilized folks."

An old man sitting at the end of the table slammed his mug down. "Don't know why in Hell that fool Lincoln would make such a godforsaken territory into a state," he wheezed. "Ain't enough people there to turn and spit at."

"Hush, Daddy," the woman said, spooning gravy onto his plate. "Eat your dinner."

"Old Abe needs the money," grunted the driver. "Comstock Lode'll pay for his war."

When the conductor came back, a fresh driver was with him, and a new passenger, a stout lady swathed in black bombazine. Away we flew again.

We spent nights in any pose we could manage, lulled asleep by long smooth stretches, jolted awake by sudden bumps or rocks. The second morning Gage woke us with loud cries. He'd spotted sleek brown rodents standing on two legs, watching us as curiously as we did them. A few miles later Sid saw our first antelope. Then Gage shrieked, "A wolf! A wolf!"

The stout woman traveling to Omaha jerked awake. "Lord save us," she gasped. "Anyone got a gun, for pity' sake?"

"It's not a wolf," said Sid. "Just a coyote. More a mangy wild dog."

We thrust our faces out to watch the panting creature lope along. He looked like an old fur coat stretched over the wrong skeleton. His ribby sides heaved; his bushy tail dragged in the dust as he shot us a furtive yellow glare.

"He's very homely, poor old thing," said Gage sadly. I hoped when we settled at last in Nevada he would not be dragging such vermin home.

Then the driver shouted, and Sid thrust his head and shoulders out. He hoisted Gage to the window and our son pointed out across the prairie. "Oh, look! Do you see it?"

I gazed over their shoulders, and made out a black speck against the lightening sky. It could've been a tree, if a prairie had such, or a lone cow. But this object was moving fast. Seconds later I saw a horse and rider sweeping toward us as if borne on the long yellow grass that rose and fell like the river back home. In seconds came the faint drumming of hooves.

"Mercy sakes, must you step right on me?" the stout woman complained. Just then rider and horse burst past. I caught a white flash of teeth in a wind-creased face tanned to leather. The man raised up in the stirrups and waved and shouted, face contorted. Impossible to catch actual words. Thick yellow dust flew into our coach, along with the smell of horse sweat and damp wool. For a moment he galloped alongside, then in a burst of speed pulled away.

We fell back onto the seat and looked at each other. "That was the Pony Express," declared Gage. "Nobody back home has seen them. Only me."

Sid looked doubtful. "I thought they stopped running a year or two back. It's all telegraph now. Unless somebody cut the wire."

Gage sat up again, looking puzzled. "The Express man's coming again." He pointed in the same direction. "But how'd he get way back over there?"

I ducked to peer out. Sure enough, a dust cloud and a black speck approached from the same quarter. Soon it separated into two, then three, then five. I turned to look at Sid. "The Express don't ride in a group, do they?"

"No." He frowned. "Let me see."

The riders were gaining, but we heard no friendly hails from the driver. Instead the whip cracked and we lurched like drunkards as the horses sprang forward. I didn't want to say *Indians,* lest Gage be frightened. Sid looked back at me again, the crease on his forehead deeper. After a few moments I saw our pursuers wore slouch hats and high boots and dusters fanned out like dark shawls over their horses' flanks.

Now we rocked along desperately fast, the Omaha lady calling on the Lord. I was afraid we'd hit a pothole or boulder, go end over end down a gully, and be shaken out like weevils from a biscuit can. With a high whine, the doorframe splintered, showering us with chips.

"Get down," cried Sid, pushing my head and Gage's toward the seat.

When the praying lady just kept moving her lips, he yanked her down, too. "Pardon, missus, but someone is shooting," he said.

"Jesus save us," she cried, and squeezed her eyes shut.

The rocking of the coach grew less fierce. We slowed to the pace of a walk, then stopped.

"Stay down," Sid ordered, and raised his head. He ducked immediately and jabbed my ribs. "Where's your pistol?" he whispered in my ear.

I pointed at the roof. The gun was in my valise, the one tied up there uselessly with the others. Sid looked now as if he wished he'd taken Clemens's word about the heavily armed fashion in western dress.

Head still bent, I heard the clopping of hooves and muffled voices. Above us the driver and conductor were having a low, fierce argument.

"What did you see?" I whispered to Sid.

"Five mounted men."

"Do they look—friendly?"

He didn't answer, which seemed ominous. I heard the creak of saddles, horses stamping and blowing. "Get off there, driver!" shouted a voice made up of dust and sand and dry brush. "You, too, old man!"

The stage rocked. "Now you passengers!" ordered the same hoarse voice.

Following Sid, we climbed out into a chill wind and a cloud of hanging dust, the Omaha lady still calling on gentle Jesus. I pressed Gage to my side, but he appeared more interested than frightened, avidly taking in the circle of stamping, blowing horses and their dark-clothed, dusty riders. One fellow spurred his dun up front. Slight as a boy, he waved a huge revolver. All five wore long blue dusters and dust-streaked bandanna masks.

"Line up there and kneel on the ground," the slender fellow ordered. When I heard his voice, I looked up. It seemed familiar, but I didn't know any western bandits.

"Now put your hands in the air." He spoke as if reading from a script, voice hesitant, singsong, cracking on the high notes.

"I ain't gonna do it," said the conductor, who stood and glared at him.

The bandit stared as if he couldn't believe he'd heard right. Another of the gang spurred up and whispered in his ear. They argued while the sun beat on our heads and pebbles worked sharp edges through my skirt and into my knees.

"Iffen you don't kneel down, old man, well then," cried the first bandit at last. "I got to send a ball through your skull. It ain't no never mind to me."

With a look of disgust the conductor lowered himself slowly, joints popping. "There. You scurrilous pup."

The bandit sat up straighter. "What you just call me?"

"Leave off, Jesse," the second one whispered hoarsely. "Get the money and sich, and let's go."

Two highwaymen appeared related, with the same dull brown hair and eyes, and large rounded ears poking out from under their kerchiefs. This fact also nagged. At last I placed the voice: it belonged to the young man who'd sat next to me at the fire, at Tom's camp in the Ozarks. He'd said his name was Jesse, and couldn't be much over sixteen. But what was he doing way out here?

Sid, kneeling next to me, had a spot of color high on each cheekbone, so he was furious. As he held his arms up, he looked around from the corners of his eyes, but I saw nothing nearby in the nature of a weapon. Not against these, even if they were only boys. Some carried revolvers, others carbines or Sharps rifles. Knife handles stuck out of boots and belts.

"Listen up, folks," the first bandit instructed. "Put your cash, watches, and jewelry in this here grain sack."

"I served at Pea Ridge," the driver spat out. "You boys is a disgrace."

"Confederate or Union?" asked one gang member.

Jesse rounded on him, and when he looked away from us, I felt Sid tense. "Shut up, Cole," said Jesse.

"Confederate!" snapped the driver. "What the hell you think, *Cole*?"

"Damn it to Jesus," said a third bandit to Jesse. "I told you, don't use names."

Jesse scowled. I guessed from the resemblance the third one might be the older brother he'd told about that night. Jesse swung down off his horse as the one called Cole covered us with a Sharps. Then Jesse walked down the line holding out the sack. The conductor dropped a fat gold watch and a soft leather purse; the driver a messy wad of greenbacks. The Omaha lady, quivering all over, tried hard to pull her rings off and at last succeeded.

When he stood before me, I looked up into his eyes. "Hello, Jesse," I whispered. "Do you recall me? From Tom Sawyer's camp north of Iron Mountain."

He flinched and peered down. "Well, damn. If this don't beat all. You look some different in a nice clean frock."

I nodded, trying to agree. My lips felt too stiff to move again.

"Then never mind y'alls stuff," he said. "We don't steal from old acquaintances."

"This is my husband," I said, tilting my head at Sid, who stared at me incredulously.

"How do," said Jesse. "Your missus here is a kind lady. I feel bad about this, but a man's got to earn a living. And strike out at the tyrant an' the oppressor. So we taken up the highway."

"Like Robin Hood," said Sid. "I guess you do it for the poor?"

"Reckon we do. Ain't nobody poorer than us right now." Then Jesse seemed to notice Gage's awestruck gaze. He strolled over and shook a finger at him. "Now, let this be your lesson, young feller. Don't follow our evil ways. And always take care of your blessed mama." He handed Gage a two-bit piece with the air of a great lord conveying a boon. Our son, open-mouthed, took it between thumb and forefinger. Sid made a choking noise deep in his throat.

Jesse took Sid's purse with a flourish but extracted only a few bills, keeping his back to the other outlaws. He tucked the rest in Sid's waistcoat and leaned to me again. "This here's the first time we ever tried it," he said in a low voice. "How we doin'?"

"You ought to stop now, Jesse," I whispered back. "It's a desperate way to make a living. You'll all be shot or hanged. How will that make your dear mama feel?"

This warning seemed to please rather than frighten him. His eyes crinkled above the handkerchief mask. He swaggered back down the line. When he reached the driver, he returned his wad as well. "Here, old soldier. We's all rebels. We don't prey on them as has faced the cannons what roar for Dixie."

The bandits unhitched the stage horses and fired over their heads, running them off. We watched the James Gang gallop away, then lowered our arms, the conductor and the Omaha lady creaking and groaning and rubbing their knees.

"Well, if that don't take the goddamn prize," said the conductor, spitting off to the side. "A pack of goddamn two-bit secesh trash bandits."

"Hold your damn tongue," snapped the driver.

We set about trying to catch the horses, with the conductor god-damning every rock and gopher hole as we chased the frightened beasts here and there in a mad game of tag. Three hours later we were finally harnessed up and off again.

When we reached the next hole-in-the-wall way station, the conductor didn't report the hold-up, just spit in the dust and looked disgusted. "Ain't no goddamn sheriff for a hundred miles. And anyhow they's probably related."

We spent the night rolled in blankets on a dirt floor. When we rose the next morning, our fellow traveler seemed invigorated by our shared adventure. All morning she volunteered hair-raising tales of bandits and Indians, of outrages that always involved a friend of a cousin or a great-aunt twice removed. Her family and acquaintances seemed to draw fire wherever they traveled. Gage was just waking from a nap when she launched into the Mountain Meadow Massacre, a bloody raid on a wagon train made by Mormons dressed as Indians. I covered my son's ears and asked her to please refrain. She subsided into wounded silence.

At Omaha we bade her farewell, and two young men got on. We lurched off again feeling like seasoned westerners, quite prepared to face the rigors and delights of our new home.

Twenty

FIVE DAYS LATER, as the sun was setting, our team climbed the road to Virginia City, Nevada. The town crouched midway up Mount Davidson. "There 'tis," drawled the man on my left. "We's seven thousand feet above sea level."

The lofty Sierra Nevada atmosphere was so clear, we'd first spotted the city fifty miles earlier. The mountain was so steep, the town was pitched like a slate roof, each street forming a terrace, with a considerable drop to the next one down. The houses were propped with thick posts in back. *Beneath those slopes,* Sam had written, *lies the fabulous Comstock Lode, a richer deposit than King Solomon's mines.* So chock-full of precious metals were the Sierra Nevadas, speculators priced Comstock mines by the foot. In his letter to Mary, Sam had crowed that values were going nowhere but up. *Think of a city,* he'd boasted, *with not one solitary pauper in it.*

Mount Davidson loomed over all like the dome of a gray cathedral; up close it looked dry and barren. A canyon split the foothills below, forming a natural gateway to the desert. A silver thread of river stitched through, with a pale green fringe of cottonwoods for decoration. Snow-topped lavender mountains barred the western horizon. The lowering sun gilded a handful of clouds many shades of pink and gold and rose. "That looks like Heaven," said Gage suspiciously. "I thought we had to die to get there. Like Tyler."

I couldn't answer, for tears suddenly clogged my throat.

Sid drew him close. "That's just a town full of gold nuggets and silver ore, son. A different kind of sparkle than Heaven's. You'll see, when we get there."

That evening we checked into the International Hotel, and fell into deliciously soft beds. The next morning, feeling raised from the dead, we dressed and went out to look up Sam Clemens.

We found him at the office of his newspaper, the *Territorial Enterprise*, but he didn't resemble any reporter or editor I'd ever seen before. The western Sam wore a dusty slouch hat, a blue woolen shirt, and denim pantaloons stuffed into tall brown boots. He'd grown a surprising beard, a riot of curling red whiskers that fell over his shirtfront like a hairy dinner napkin. A navy revolver was slung at his belt. The editor, typesetter, and printer all wore guns, too.

"Sid! Becky! And this must be—hmm." He paused to study Gage, pulling at his whiskers. "But how can this enormous fellow be the baby I saw in Hannibal?"

Gage squirmed and frowned. "I ain't a baby."

I patted his shoulder. "Aren't. You *aren't* a baby."

He twisted to squint up at me furiously. "I just said so!"

Sam showed us around, and we admired the latest edition of the *Enterprise* right off the press. I read several humorous, far-fetched columns. "Sam, who's this Mark Twain fellow? He's quite the wit. I'd never have imagined a shoot-out could seem so amusing."

"Oh, do you think so?" He drew himself up with swelled chest, so I supposed this Twain must be one of his protégés. It struck me I'd heard those words before. Leadsman back home called it out in deep voices, like a chantey. For *by the mark, twain* was a depth measure. And Sam had piloted on the river before heading West.

"Sam—?" But he was already hurrying us out the door, back to the hotel for breakfast.

We took a table near the front window. I unfolded a thick linen napkin and smiled at Sam. "Good to see a home face so far from Hannibal. A city editor! What all do you do there?"

"Mainly I go round town and ask all sorts of folks as many impertinent questions as I can devise. Then I write them out to publish. But I never say,

We have learned so and so; or, *It is rumored or reported thus and such.* No, I am a beacon of unassailable certitude, and always begin any article with, *It is a definite fact that.* Otherwise, people put no stock in their news."

Sid and I laughed, and Gage joined in uncertainly. "I see," I said. "And if you're ever wrong?"

"But I never am! Only once or twice my sources might've been mistaken. And I'm grateful for the littlest event now, whether it's a newly arrived hay truck from the country, or a grisly murder."

"Murder," said Sid, turning a butter knife over in his hands. "Is there much of that here?"

"Well, not so often as the hay trucks, but pretty near. The first twenty-six plots in our cemetery are occupied by murdered men. They were looking for it, no doubt. Still, you ought to get a gun and wear it, Sid. Learn how to shoot it, if you don't know already from the War."

I caught a taint of wistfulness, or envy, in those last few words. I thought of Huck's revolver and didn't meet Sid's eye. When I did glance up, he was nodding thoughtfully, as if he'd come to the same conclusion. Of course, advice is always more authoritative coming from friends, or better yet, strangers. Rather than so unreliable a source as one's wife.

A storkish girl in kerchief and stained apron came to the table and stammered out the day's specials. We gave our orders. Without looking anyone in the eye, she scurried off.

"You go armed in a mining town," Sam told us, "for the rough element is king. A person is not much respected here until he has, as they say, Killed His Man. That's the very expression they use. When a newcomer arrives, no one asks if he's industrious and capable, as in the North, or if he came of good family, as in the South. All they want to know is, has he Killed His Man? A fellow with no blood to his credit is of little consequence."

Sam assured us a lawyer, a doctor, an editor, a banker, a head desperado, a blacksmith, and a gambler all occupied the same social level. "To be looked up to quickly, stand behind a bar and sell whiskey. But if a fellow is both saloon keeper and has Killed His Man, he's revered."

The girl brought us coffee, and a brimming mug of milk for Gage.

"Now, you don't have to worry," Sam told Sid. "I took care to prime your reputation."

It seemed he'd already informed a number of people that Sid had ridden with a special outfit back East, and was a good hand with gun and saber. What's more, that he'd Killed His Man many times over, and was a steely-cold desperado with nothing left to prove.

"Oh, I laid it on handsome, Sidney. I meant during your military service, but no need of such a fine distinction here. And mark me, beyond that, them festivities back East ain't a fit topic, unless you're as hot for the Union as they are here. It's business. The Comstock Lode is paying Mr. Lincoln's bills. Though surely the War's all over but the shouting."

My husband looked taken aback. Perhaps he had killed in battle, though he never spoke of it. But to have Clemens kiting his reputation as a murderer! Still, when in Rome, I supposed.

Sid opened his mouth to say something, but just then the girl came back burdened with big platters of ham and fried steak and bread. "Let's eat while it's hot," said Sam, rubbing his hands gleefully. "This's on me. I've had some great luck with trading lately."

"Trading what?" I asked, inspecting a none-too-clean fork.

Sam slashed at his beef steak. "Mine shares. Buy 'em, sell 'em, swap 'em. People give 'em away on the street like penny candy. I can't be bothered to collect my salary half the time. I'm rich as Croesus on paper, but I don't aim to cash in till things peak."

He stopped cutting and waved the knife. "Comstock wealth runs in golden veins down from the mountainsides, right under our feet. I tell you, we're treading on the fatted calf! Ten thousand souls, and not one solitary beggar in all of Virginia City."

Sid and I glanced at each other in renewed wonder; then we all fell to eating. The steak was big as a dictionary and just as leathery, but the ham and eggs were heaped high. After weeks on a stage coach, with mealy apples and way station grub, it was the manna of the Israelites.

At last Sam leaned back and slapped his belly. "That's right," he said, as if we hadn't stopped talking. "A thousand wildcat shafts incorporated, and the stock for sale. Men digging all day right in the middle of the street! Nothing like it since the world began. Wouldn't Tom just love it, though?"

Sid pushed his chair back and laid his knife and fork on the plate. "I'm sorry to tell you this," he said. "But Tom's dead."

Sam's face fell; he dropped his chair to all four legs. "What'd you say?"

As Sid filled him in on Tom's fate, I avoided listening by fussing with Gage's face and clothes, brushing off crumbs and bits of egg.

Sam looked very low then. He paid the bill silently and left far too many coins for the girl in a coffee-stained saucer. "What d'you plan to do first?" he asked Sid, with less enthusiasm.

"I'm thinking of practicing law, as I did with Judge Thatcher back in Hannibal."

Sam caught fire again. "There are only two lawyers in town! One is a drunkard."

"And the other?" asked Sid.

"Oh, he's French. You'll make your fortunes. Sid Hopkins will be the next governor of Nevada."

Sam talked on, pounding the table in excitement. There was space to let in the newspaper's building, so they left immediately to get a shingle painted. Gage and I set off down the sidewalk for a daylight look at our new home. Coming out we had to step over a man lying on the raw plank sidewalk. At first I feared it must be the latest Killed Man. But then he swore loudly and scratched his half-exposed backside, and I saw he was only very intoxicated. I steered Gage around and ducked into the first doorway, which turned out to be a saloon. A variety of bearded faces—astonished, disapproving, hopeful—looked up from their glasses. We backed out again quickly.

Virginia City was a sprawl of contradictions. Along wide dirt streets square buildings of sawn lumber soared above squat log shops and canvas tents. Only a handful were painted, though, for some reason with an ugly coat of leaden gray. The fancy storefronts with massive cornices were false, as were the upper windows; like stage scenery they fronted humble one- or two-story clapboards with pitched roofs. Proprietors made good use of their front walls to advertise wares. The upper floors all had outside staircases—cheaper to tack up quickly, I supposed.

I was grateful for the wooden walkway, for thick dust, assorted trash, and slops made the street a challenge to cross. Deep blue-gray potholes testified to what conditions could be looked forward to after a rain. All I had to avoid on the sidewalk was glistening slicks of expectorated tobacco. The walls and posts were pasted over with flaming bills promoting claim shares and goods and beer garden concerts.

Businesses clustered along lower Wallace and South Jackson and on C Street, while large brick houses and small wooden ones dotted Idaho Street and the south slopes. I counted several assayers, a grocer's, two Celestial laundries, a surprising number of dressmakers and milliners. Also a book-keeper, a fortune-teller, an upholsterer, a barber, and a flower shop. Most were small, but carpenters swarmed over new, larger shops. Perhaps five hundred buildings all told, but the lack of plan, steep slopes, and the odd architecture gave the town a grotesque look.

Virginia City dwarfed Hannibal, and was altogether different. It wasn't just the lack of trees, or the shining mountains that cradled it, but the air of hurried excitement and dogged intent. I'd seen that on the riverfront back home, but only for about thirty minutes a day when a steamer stopped. Here it was everywhere, all the time: A wild rush to go and do and earn and spend at all hours, day or night.

As we walked, most men, even the rough-dressed ones, bowed politely. A few stared so boldly and rudely, I might've been parading in my chemise. Others pushed past without a glance, clutching shovels and picks or canvas sacks. Sprinkled among the white faces were a number of Negroes, and a few sallow-skinned Chinamen. I saw red Indians loitering down one alley, then in the next several short dark men in wide-brimmed hats speaking rapid Spanish. I supposed they were Mexicans, and failed to get Gage not to point and stare.

As we walked, I began to plan. Our hotel was expensive: two dollars a day. We'd need to find a house to rent, or build one—far from C Street, where the saloons and gaudy dance halls were packed even now, in the day-time. Through big front windows their mirrored shelves reflected bottles of amber liquors. Thirsty men swilled this poison down and demanded more. Near the open doorway of one place, an organ grinder cranked a wheezing box and provoked his consumptive-looking monkey with a stick into a sullen, shuffling dance. Behind another rough, lopsided storefront lay a red-velvet den where a hurdy-gurdy girl showed her knees as she sang shocking lyrics. I turned Gage around to find the International again.

Yet even as we rushed away, I felt less shocked than drawn to what I'd seen. All about us unfolded excitement, avarice, lust, devilry—but above all, enterprise. Things that in Hannibal were conducted behind closed doors, if they were conducted at all.

The first few days I was out of breath simply from walking in the high, thin atmosphere. I felt winded climbing three or four streets to do an errand. On returning, I could've used a set of brakes, to avoid rolling home like a runaway whiskey barrel.

We moved from the International to a boarding establishment in Gold Hill called the Comstock House. But after one night the snoring and shouts, the stinks of smoke, unwashed bodies, and the filthy water closet drove us out. The next day we found a tiny house on G Street for fifteen dollars a month. Wood-framed, its walls were covered with canvas. It had a detached kitchen with stove and cupboard complete with dishes, plus washboards, a galvanized tub, and a flatiron. The pump coughed a gush of water cold and hard as iron over my outstretched hand. The parlor featured a sagging horse-hair sofa and one rocking chair. A smaller room to the side would serve as our bedroom. The privy, rough wood but fairly clean, was of course out back.

As Sid set up his law office, I tried to furnish and feed us on five dollars a month. This demanded so much ingenuity, penny-pinching, and sweat I forgot for days on end there was still a war on back home, and that everyone I knew was far away. Then it would hit me suddenly, a fist to the belly, and for a moment I couldn't breathe.

I kept busy teaching Gage his letters and simple sums, and improving the house. After a few weeks my corset began to feel devilishly tight. First I loosened it, then stopped wearing it altogether. A month later it occurred to me why it'd become so uncomfortable. I'd lost track, but it had been six or seven weeks since my monthly flow.

"Sid," I said that night, after Gage had gone to bed. "You're going to be a father again."

He looked over his newspaper for a moment as if he didn't understand. Then he dropped the paper and rose to give me a kiss. "Becky, what good news! A girl this time, don't you think? I'll make a new cradle."

"Well, babies don't come to order," I pointed out. "But I'll see what I can do."

His obvious pleasure cheered me even as I worried who would deliver this new little one, or help me afterward. Then one day, paging through Sam's *Enterprise*, I discovered "Doctress Hoffmann," who practiced medicine on South C Street. Her advertisement claimed she could cure all female complaints and the common diseases of children. The Doctress had practiced for twenty-four years and held a diploma from the best school in Germany. I wondered if she spoke English. A woman who was also a doctor ought to know more about the female problems than any being on earth. I decided to call on her when my time arrived.

The Irish family on the other side of us consisted of Margaret O'Shaunessy, a round-faced woman a bit older than me, her two small boys, and an older adopted daughter. Her husband had died in a cave-in at the Chollar mine two years earlier. She had some gold-mining stocks in the Ophir, the Hale, and Norcross. She and the daughter did fine sewing, and she took in boarders.

"Only clean white Christian men," she assured me, though I hadn't asked. When she noticed my condition, she took me aside and advised me to get a servant.

I laughed. "We aren't that grand, Margaret." Back in Hannibal you might engage a slave or a workman or a laundress, but only the quality hired actual servants for every day. And though perhaps we had once been so, the Hopkinses were no longer quality. The war had changed that for us, as it had for so many others.

Margaret laid a finger on her chin, considering, then went on as if I hadn't spoken. "Best thing's an Irish girl, of course. Or a Paiute woman, though that face paint gives a soul the heebies. But a Chinaman's a better bargain. They'll do things you wouldn't ask of a white person, and don't gossip family secrets like the girls will."

I told her I'd think about it. But what made us good friends happened one day early the first winter. I'd been sweeping and mopping and my skirt kept flopping around, getting in the way. I finally tore it off in disgust and took up soldiers' togs: a pair of Sid's trousers belted high with a length of hemp. I was dumping a load of sheets in the washtub when I heard a knock. Then Margaret O'Shaunessy came in through the back door, bearing a plate of steaming biscuits.

We both stood quite still as she took in my manly attire. Even in the

West, ladies did not wear trousers. I was wavering between making up some excuse and ordering her out, when Margaret began laughing. She set the biscuits on the sink.

"Mother of God! I thought I was the only one who traipsed around in britches in me own home. Well, now. Since you're dressed for it, would ye like to share a wee smoke?"

I sent Gage out to play so Margaret could introduce me to the evils of tobacco. She rolled two cigarets expertly; then we sat and puffed. She was so pleased at corrupting me, I made sure to pretend to cough, and didn't tell her Tom Sawyer had beat her to it by almost twenty years.

"He's getting to be a big lad," she observed of Gage. "The Sisters of Charity run an orphanage with a school. They take students."

Sid said no when he realized it was a Catholic school, but it was the only one around. So we enrolled Gage there as a day student for three dollars a month. It seemed a good investment. The Sisters, crowded into a large clapboard shack, were saving to build a new schoolhouse and hospital. They'd hoped to get government money, until Sister Frederica informed the state legislature they would not accept black orphans. Since Nevada subscribed to impartial suffrage, the newspapers seized on this.

The *Enterprise* huffed that the Sisters could run their orphanage as exclusively as they chose, but without Nevada's money. The *Gold Hill News* opined that housing black and white children together was contrary to nature. I wondered what both nuns and editors would've thought of Huck and Jim's raft trip down the Mississippi. Or of Trenny, who'd slept on a cot in my mother's room from the time they were both small, who'd ordered even the Judge about, and raised me, too.

Virginia City had been a sight for desert-weary eyes. But what glittered from afar sometimes turns out, up close, to fall short of Heaven. Back East we'd read of stage robberies, gold-appointed gambling dens, red-velvet-draped bawdy houses; of tall, handsome gunslingers and madams in jeweled finery. The bulk of that was fairy tale. For those of us trying to make a living, surviving was taxing enough, never mind putting on any glamour. Buildings were hastily erected with no planning, and the mine tunnels that lay below our feet were shored up with planks. These sometimes collapsed without warning, and a house or shop tumbled in.

This and the threat of fire, above and below ground, were ever-present. Coming out of a store the first week I heard suddenly, from below my feet, a muffled commotion. Wails from hell: the heartrending cries of some miners trapped in a collapsed tunnel. The ground beneath me trembled and then, two feet away, caved in. I dropped my parcels and stumbled back from a dark pit that appeared to plunge to the very doorstep of the Damned. I glimpsed the contorted face of a man whose scrabbling hands lost their purchase, as he slid away from me and forever from the light of day.

"Help, help!" I cried. But shouting rescuers were already bursting past, brandishing picks and shovels. I ran on clumsily, cradling my heavy, expectant belly, calling into every store or café for more help. When I returned, panting, with six more hands, the first few had made a new pit and were digging like fiends. By then crying women and children had gathered around. But no one could reach the trapped souls. They'd have to hold their funerals with empty coffins.

Sid opened his law office for business the second week, but drew few customers. Those he got were rich in schemes but cash-poor. He drew up claims, wills, and deeds anyhow, turning no one away. "Otherwise someone will take advantage of them," he'd say each time. "But it won't be me."

I began to fear he might not be cut out for lawyering after all.

A laboring man's wages were from four to six dollars a day, a tidy sum back home. But here free men worked ceaselessly as Pharaoh's slaves, in three shifts called gangs. Blasting and picking and shoveling went on without stop. All hours, the floors trembled beneath our feet; my dishes danced across the shelves and jumped to their deaths. The city and mountainside were as riddled with mining shafts as a mouse-gnawed cheese. Any man you saw in the City—for there were few women—was certainly a prospector. Oh, he might seem to be running a general store or hotel, or digging wells, or shoeing horses. But he was really only waiting to strike it rich. Some who couldn't pull a fortune out of the ground resorted to con games, or stealing, or murder.

But we also had good things and good times. Picnics and dances and church suppers, the same as back home, though in the Sierras you had to check the sand for scorpions before you spread your quilt and unpacked your basket. Sam felt we should cultivate more exotic pastimes, perhaps a sport unique to the area. One day he hit upon the idea of camel races. "Ten years back, the army brought Bactrian camels to the Territories from the Gobi Desert in China."

"What?" I scoffed. "Whatever for?"

"They hoped to use them as a secret weapon, or some such thing. But the rocks injured the poor beasts' feet. And camels are even more bad-tempered than generals," he said. "So the army gave up and left them out in the desert."

Some enterprising miners began using the animals to haul the huge bags of salt needed for the silver reduction mills. Then, a new problem arose: oxen, cows, and horses were terrified of the sullen-eyed, humpbacked creatures. Citizens lobbied to keep them off the roads between dawn and dusk to cut down on accidents.

Sam felt the camels were getting a raw deal. "Yes, yes, they are disagreeable and bad-smelling," he conceded. "But that only puts them in a class with most of our population."

He felt a festive annual camel race was the answer, and took us out to the Comstock reduction mill one day to evaluate some likely specimens. "It's the sport of kings in Arabia," he told Sid. "And very fashionable."

"I think that's horse racing," said Sid dubiously, eyeing some lumpish, dusty, ten-foot-tall beasts penned in a log corral.

As we leaned on the top rail, a camel wrangler approached the largest one, a white male with some packs on its back. He made noises at it. "*Shhh, shhh, shhh.*"

The huge beast eyed him, then raised its head and gave a bloodthirsty shriek. We tensed, ready to flee in case the creature attacked and tore the poor fellow apart. But the next instant the camel only dropped to its knees, still grumbling, to be relieved of its sacks of salt.

I lifted Gage to better see its poor delicate feet, which had caused the army so many problems. They were huge, with two long bony webbed toes. Above that, knobby knees were padded with fat and callus. Rheumy eyes peered from beneath bushy brows arched like bank awnings. The camel was shedding thick wads of hair in patches, like a decomposing horsehair sofa. I shuddered to think what its breath might be like.

"Oh, splendid beasts!" cried Sam, flinging out his arms to take them all in. "I will race you, and weave fine topcoats of your hair, and make you all famous."

The white one grunted and looked away as Sam regaled us with his fool-proof scheme for building an international camel-racing track.

I cut my eyes at Sid. "Come on, Sam," he said. "Let's go have a bite to eat."

We managed to lure him away from the corral and back to town, only overcoming his entrepreneurial dreams with promises of a home-cooked dinner. So easily, in fact, I began to suspect he'd been pulling our legs again.

Gage and I had a different fright the next afternoon, though. I was in the kitchen scrubbing a pan when I heard him shout. I came running into the parlor just in time to see a painted mask of a face pressed against the window.

"Indians, Indians!" screamed my son. He darted past me and grabbed Huck's gun from the chest in the bedroom.

"Gage, no!" I cried, lunging for his arm. How had he known it was there?

He swung the Colt up at the window and the apparition vanished. Just then I heard Margaret O'Shaunessy calling, banging at our back door.

"Put that down now, son," I said slowly and carefully. "You might shoot the neighbors."

"But, Mama! Didn't you see—?"

Margaret barged in, hallooing as she went. An Indian woman was walking close behind. "Becky, this is Annie Marsh. She's Paiute." Margaret pulled the squaw out where I could see her.

"Lord God," I whispered. The girl, for I saw now she was very young, still gangly and slight, had painted her face all over red, then applied bold white and blue lines to chin and cheeks. She wore heavy ropes of robin's-egg beads and gleaming chunks of silvery shell draped over a loose calico print dress with three flounces from knees to ankles. A scarf partly covered black hair shiny and recently oiled, for it smelled strong of bear musk.

"She's a mighty hard worker, sure," said Margaret. "Can do your washing or any common housework. She'll want to be getting home afore dark, though. Paiutes don't mix with whites verra much."

It was impossible to say no to Margaret. And Annie was a hard worker, so quiet, she would've seemed a ghost, except her beads and shells clanked and rattled so you could hear her coming two rooms away. A blessing, since

I'd forget about the face paint from one day to the next. Coming around a corner, it did indeed give a soul the heebies.

Annie had been taught at the Sisters' school, and spoke better English than our Dutch neighbors. As we worked side by side, I discovered that, aside from the paint, she was like any other young woman. She had a suitor who worked in one of the mines. They planned to marry the following year. "We want five children altogether," she told me one day. "But no more than that." She liked peppermint sweets and satin hair ribbons and to sit at the kitchen table and look at the pictures in my books.

We soon had the house in order, but Sid's practice failed to thrive. Then he began to talk about mining. "It seems a good way to make a deal of money," he pointed out.

"Well, yes," I agreed. "Sam said every man in town was rich—but only on paper."

The few that had sold out for great sums usually left town shortly afterward. It seemed to me there were even more mines than miners, and every man and some women owned shares of feet. Yet most hadn't yielded a rock worth displaying in a front garden, much less one carrying good ore. Still everyone merely shrugged and said, *Ah, just wait till we reach the solid ledge!* And kept on prairie-dogging. Any hole in the ground carried fancy engraved stock certificates, and people clamored to buy and trade them all day long.

Sid agreed at first, but the lure of El Dorado finally proved too strong. Six months to the day after we'd arrived, he came home owning feet in three different mines: the Wildcat, the Silver Star, and the California. His good sense had been overruled by a need to jump in the fray. One mine was way out in the desert; the second near the main Comstock operation; the last in the cellar of a shack on C Street.

I think, looking back, no one living in such a place could have resisted the dream of easy wealth for long. As soon as a new claim came up, the owners rushed to one of the news offices, gave a reporter forty feet as a gift, and got him to write the mine up. The articles always praised the new enterprise in lofty terms, although if you read carefully, they only really promised the thing was six feet wide, or looked like a well-dug shaft, or that the ore therein *resembled* the Comstock's. As if all the local rock didn't! But if reporters went into rhapsodies over square new beams or shiny wire ropes or smooth-cranking windlasses, the owners were satisfied. And the stock sold.

Another month passed, and we were getting low on funds. Sid sold his holdings in the Sliver Star for a couple hundred dollars. That helped the money problem. Then suddenly Sam Clemens got into a great deal of trouble, and presented an even trickier one. His camel racing scheme had come to nothing. But even without Sam's editorial help, dueling had come into fashion so hard, every man in town was eager to play. Any excuse would do. Over dinner one night I had told Sam and Sid I didn't understand the attraction.

"You men," I scoffed, throwing down my napkin. "What is this great Void inside that always drives your species to cards, to rum, or to war? Why must one of you always get the upper hand? To fight over a facial tic, or take umbrage at a sneeze?"

"I'm not rightly sure," Sam had mused, carving his beef into neat cubes. "I myself have no desire to fight a duel, nor to provoke one. It's a dreadful failing, and my friends and colleagues are all ashamed of me. But I somehow bear the disgrace."

Yet here he was a few days later, sitting in the armchair in our front room. I sat across and Sid stood behind me, since he hated the prickly feel of the horsehair sofa. Sam held his hat in his lap, stroking it so sadly, it might've been a sick cat. "Sid, I am called out on a matter of honor. Will you be my second?"

Sid's hand tightened on my shoulder. When I looked up, he was staring in disbelief, even horror. He seemed speechless.

"But what in the world happened?" I asked at last, since no one else seemed able.

"Joe Goodman went off on holiday," Sam replied.

"Hardly a dueling matter, is it?"

But when Goodman, the chief editor of the *Enterprise*, had gone to San Francisco, he left Sam in charge of the office. Sam was pleased at first, thinking editing would be easier work than reporting. But he'd soon run out of new ideas for columns, and finally resorted to insulting the rival paper, the *Union*, whose editor had also gone on holiday. When their acting editor, a man named Laird, came back at Sam in print in a fury, every man at the *Enterprise* rejoiced. They looked forward to the coming challenge—the saving of Samuel Clemens's honor.

But the challenge didn't come, and didn't come. Finally the staff, with much liquid encouragement, got Sam to agree to throw down the gauntlet himself. Unfortunately he let another reporter write out the note. His friend had outdone himself in vile epithets and abuse. He kept issuing challenge after challenge until Laird at the *Union* had no choice but to accept, or else crawl on all fours down C Street like a whipped dog.

"So now what will you do?" asked Sid. He knew as well as I that Sam was no fighter; he'd been sickly as a boy and had never even wrestled, much less dueled.

"Well, I've made out my will," Sam said miserably. "Now I'm supposed to go home and sleep, then get up and go kill poor old Laird tomorrow."

"But if you do, you'll be arrested," I pointed out. "Or if you don't, you'll both get two years in the penitentiary. If—if you live."

"What?" said Sam. "Oh, of course. The new law."

Then, as if called to the bar, Sid came from behind my chair to stand in the middle of the room, becoming before our eyes a lawyer. "Yes, because Governor North has got so fed up with the new dueling craze, he's aching to try out his new ordinance, which makes it a crime to even call out another man. Didn't you print that up in your paper?"

"I seem to recall it," said Sam indifferently. "But that won't deter Laird. The man's hot. And you know I can't hit the side of a barn door with a cannon."

Sid looked thoughtful. "What time's your appointment tomorrow?"

"Six."

"Well, come with me."

They rose and went out back. When I came out a few minutes later, they were cursing and sweating, taking the warped door of the big shed behind the house off its hinges. When I asked what they were doing, Sid paused to wipe his brow. "We have tonight, then another hour of light in the morning to practice."

He set a fence rail up against the door and handed Sam my revolver, which Sid by then had taken to wearing every day slung on his belt.

Sam began by aiming at the upright rail, which was supposed to represent

Mr. Laird. Of course he couldn't hit him. Out of six shots fired, only one even nicked the corner post of the shed. "It's no good," he said at last, hanging his head. "Laird's even taller and thinner than that rail."

"Then aim at the door," suggested Sid. "You can't give up now."

Sam reloaded and tried again. This time he hit the tin roof, then a mesquite bush I was standing next to. Anyone directly in front of him would've been perfectly safe.

"We'll work on it again in the morning," said Sid, throwing an arm over Sam's shoulders and walking him back to the house. Our friend nodded, but doom felt palpable as a rain cloud.

After he left, I turned to Sid. "Well, what about this Laird?"

He shook his head. "A crack shot, so I've heard. Don't tell anyone about this-here practice, for God's sake."

I could see he was trying to make the best of it. Sid must know what it was like to shoot other men; certainly he himself had been shot. I thought he dreamed of it again sometimes in the night, for he'd wake and sit up with a shout, but never tell what was the matter. So I'd never worried my husband might provoke a duel, though he'd surely fight if challenged. He was proud, nearly as proud as his cousin. As Tom *used* to be, I reminded myself. And since childhood, Sam Clemens had always modeled himself on his hero.

THE NEXT MORNING, after Sid left for the dueling ground, I asked Margaret to sit in the house so it wouldn't be empty when Gage woke. I didn't tell her why, for if my friend had a flaw, it was a helpless love of gossip. I packed a bag with bandages, whiskey, boric acid, and the laudanum we kept for headaches. I knew where the men must be going—to an infamous gorge a mile from town. Several had died or been maimed there already.

I reached the spot but hung back behind a boulder at the entrance. I stood trying to catch my breath, taking in the spiced perfume of sun-baked sage. I already regretted my second cup of coffee, and hoped the duelists would arrive before any urge of nature. Maybe they wouldn't even go through with a duel before a pregnant woman, not if I came boldly out in view.

No, they would. This wasn't Hannibal, but the West, after all.

I leaned against the sun-warmed boulder, hugged my bag to my swollen belly, and waited. At least I might be able to staunch any blood they shed, and perhaps prevent a death. The baby kicked hard, unable to resist putting in an opinion.

The sun soon burned off the haze, and it got very hot. Sid and *Enterprise* reporter Steve Gillis—the chief instigator and purveyor of vile epithets—finally arrived with Sam. They soon had him banging away at rocks and empty bottles with the same results as the night before. At last Sam slumped against a boulder in despair. Sid talked to him long and earnestly, with broad gestures, but Sam kept shaking his head. I supposed my husband was trying to get him to back out, or apologize, or whatever gentlemen did when they had a rare stroke of common sense.

Gillis looked guilt-ridden and distraught. He threw his hat down, clutched at his hair, and paced up and down. A brown bird lit in a sage bush and began to pipe a few monotonous notes over and over. Sid argued; Sam despaired; Steve Gillis paced. And the bird chirped on and on, drawing my nerves tight. Suddenly, with a cry of rage, Gillis whirled, whipped out his revolver from his belt, and at twenty yards shot the damned sparrow's head off.

Just then a group came over the ridge: Laird and his second and friends. As I looked down at the dead bird an idea came to me. I stepped out from behind the rock, in plain view of all the men.

"Becky!" cried Sam, as if I were a guardian angel come down to save him. Sid looked only a little surprised; perhaps by now he expected me to turn up anywhere, eventually. I ignored them both and rushed over to the sage bush, then bent and scooped up the bird.

"Oh my, what shooting!" I said loudly as the three strangers approached. "Why, I've never been so amazed."

A man stepped forward and peered down at the bundle of feathers in my hand, which was leaking fluids abominably. He lifted it by one wing. "Huh. Who did that?"

Before I could utter another word, Gillis cleared his throat. "Why, Clemens," he said offhandedly. "To warm up his barrel before the event."

"Looky at this, Laird," said the man. He turned back to Gillis. "Say, how far off was this-here bird?"

Steve shrugged. "Not that far. Mebbe thirty yards or so."

The man handed the poor stiffening thing back to me. "Huh. But surely he can't do that very often."

"Just four times out of five," I blurted. "Sam was with the Hannibal Mounted Rifles during the Unpleasantness. He was at it again in my backyard just last night. I swear, we haven't got a songbird left for blocks."

Laird and his men exchanged looks.

I pressed on, feeling encouraged. "Why, he even killed two with one shot. Left-handed!"

Steve Gillis frowned at me, and for a dreadful moment I thought I'd overdone it. Sid stepped closer and took hold of my upper arm more firmly than necessary. "Think of your condition, my dear," he murmured. "This is no place for ladies."

"I'll warn any wandering ones off," I said, jerking the arm back.

The other three were conferring. "Well, it's damned impressive," said one loudly.

One of them looked as pale and sick as Sam. "And here I supposed he couldn't hit the side of a church," he muttered.

Of course, that was the truth. But we four kept silent, staring off at the horizon, or at our shoes, or up at a cloud. Sam started to whistle, although the tune started off shaky.

Laird's second turned to us again. "I believe we are all reasonable men here," he began. "And a lady, of course." He bowed to me, and I made my smile as modest as I could.

Sam and Laird, who'd both been looking white around the eyes, perked up a bit.

"I propose this," the second continued. "Enough blood's been shed in this infamous spot. We ought to larn to disagree more like rational folks."

Sam rose from his slump. "Now, see here. I came for satisfaction, and—"

Sid and Gillis hauled him off to shake sense into him. Laird produced a flask of whiskey, brought either for medicinal purposes or an anticipated celebration. He passed it around. He and Sam were dragged together and forced to shake hands. All parties bowed to me and wished us a good morning. Gillis took a firmer grip on Sam lest he get carried away with words again. Then Laird's second braced him up and escorted him back over the ridge.

By lunchtime the news of the meeting, and of the notes Gillis had carried to the *Union* office, was all over town. The culprits waited anxiously, but Governor North sent no marshal to arrest them. However, two days later a formal message did come, signed by the lieutenant governor, suggesting Sam should leave the territory on the next stagecoach. The letter implied he would be searched for, but not hard, if he took this good advice immediately. Because, it explained, North was indeed most eager to try out his new law, and the governor was no man to hand out pardons to loose cannons. Or words to that effect.

We went to see Sam off early the next morning, on a stagecoach bound for San Francisco. He promised to stay out of trouble in California as long as possible, since we wouldn't be around to help. And never again, he vowed, would he dare anyone to duel. "It's sinful and unwise," he said soberly.

"Hmm," said Sid. "But what if someone should call you out?"

"If any Christian should ever challenge me again," Sam blurted, "I'd take him kindly and forgivingly by the hand, lead him to a quiet corner, and kill him first."

On that note of reform, we said good-bye. The stage lurched off with Sam hanging so far out the window and waving so vigorously, I feared he'd fall out. When he was gone from sight we turned away and headed for home. Sid tucked some papers into his coat pocket. When he saw I'd noticed, his face reddened, so then it interested me all the more.

"It's nothing," he said, trying to fend my hands off.

But I'd already seen the fancy engraving and gold borders. "Oh Sid! What've you bought now?"

"Only one of Sam's lode claims. He needed traveling money."

"Lord God. Which mine?"

"The Missouri Rose." The very one Sam had always said he was sorry he'd bought himself. As if we could afford it!

"Couldn't you have just loaned him a few dollars? Or taken up a collection at the newspaper?"

"Becky. Do you really think the governor noticed that little altercation in the gorge?"

"What do you mean? He sent Sam a letter."

Sid pulled me into an alley, looked around, then muttered, "Swear you'll never tell a soul."

"What? But I don't . . . Oh, all right. I swear."

"There is no lieutenant governor. I went back to my office and found a sheet of stationery from a job I'd done for a swell in Gold Hill. I scratched out the letterhead, and wrote it up."

"So *you* were Governor North!"

"No, no—only his deputy. Don't you see? If Sam had stayed, it would happen again. Some young fool dreaming glory would hear the headless bird story, and call him out."

I hadn't thought of that. We turned back onto the sidewalk and went on, and I was speechless for at least three blocks. I had been dead wrong. Sid was obviously well-suited to the law, after all.

Twenty-one

ANY UNION VICTORY BACK EAST sent excitement blowing through Virginia City like a dust storm. Someone had fastened two small cannons to timber platforms and set them up on a rocky point east of Gold Hill, overlooking town. Whenever telegraphers posted news of a victory, the miners climbed up and fired these off. We felt the concussion the length of the canyon; I'd lost one windowpane already.

One cool May morning, after the cannons had made our sugar bowl do a spirited jig, we sat back down to our breakfasts. But as we lifted our forks, there echoed back, as if spawned by the big guns, the sound of small-arms fire all over town.

"What in the world?" Sid rose from the table, forgetting the napkin still tucked in his collar. I followed him, Gage close behind. As we stepped out, mounted men galloped past, firing rifles in the air. I shoved my son back inside quickly, over his protests.

"Have they gone mad? What's that they're shouting?" I cried to Sid.

He came in again and shut the door, a peculiar look on his face. "That Mobile is taken, yesterday. And that—" He paused, passing a hand over his face. "Rob Lee's surrendered at a town called Appomattox Courthouse. So it's over."

I grabbed him and spun him. "Oh, that's wonderful!"

But his face looked as sick and pale as when I'd stood in Reeves's camp dressed in men's clothing and told him our baby son had died. "It's not our celebration," he muttered. "You can no more win a war than you can raise the dead."

I laid a hand on his arm. "Sid? I am sorry. I didn't—"

"Gone with a crash," he said slowly, removing my hand as if he didn't know it. "Four long years. Tell me again, what was it all for?"

I had no answer, for the ones that came to mind seemed worse than nothing: To line the pockets of the men who made cannon and shot? To tear apart families and friends? To prove to the world who's the bigger fool? For the Union to show the South it would not be allowed to withhold the money which ever flowed northward?

I was glad the slaves had been freed, for that Peculiar Institution was a trap, a soul-killing burden for black and white alike. But the plight of men like Jim had not been the first reason given for this war to begin; only the most palatable and high-sounding one handed out later. A splash of cologne on the gory jaws of a death-dealing machine.

He stayed home that day, and it was the only time I ever saw Sid take whiskey so slowly and methodically, or at such length. And without any sign of enjoyment, merely the clear intent of becoming sodden. He pulled a chair into the open doorway and sat and watched the men who ran or galloped past whooping and shouting. Cheering rose from the lower streets, and loud off-key music. The saloons threw their doors wide open; some dragged pianos onto the sidewalks. Many small high explosions came as well; fireworks from the Chinese neighborhoods. Between loud reports and shotgun blasts we heard screams; cries which could've signified either great joy or a murder in progress.

More people straggled by on foot, laughing, dancing jigs, waltzing with each other. Women stumbling and singing, just as drunk as the men. The sounds of breaking glass, of song and revelry rose to us as countless barroom Gettysburgs played out below.

Around noon Margaret O'Shaunessy appeared at the back door beaming, bearing a pound cake. "It's happy days now, dearie," she said.

I took it and quietly thanked her. "I'm afraid Sid is unwell, or I'd ask you in."

She was indeed my friend, for she asked no awkward questions. Only hugged me quickly, then left.

I worked a puzzle with Gage, then sent him to bed early, saying it was too dangerous to go outside with bullets flying. What else was left to do? Sid was right; it wasn't our party, after all. Even though we, like those grizzled, saddened veterans of Lee's, had survived.

BY JUNE THE LAWYERING BUSINESS trickled away to nothing. That, combined with the end of the war, gave Sid a case of mining fever. At first he still dressed for work in the mornings as if reporting to his dusty little office below the *Enterprise*. But I noticed he also bought shovels, a pick, and rockers. Then, other objects close to a prospector's heart: an axe, a new Henry carbine, a set of scales. He already owned the playing cards and segars. He took to leaving his boiled white shirt at home, saying the other miners hated nothing worse and kept trying to pick fights. He went around in blue wool and worn boots and a brimless felt bowler. I didn't mind so much about the clothes, even the ugly hat, if he was happy in his new work.

But over coffee and biscuits one morning, Margaret O'Shaunessy warned that a miner's wife often had more than eccentric style to worry about. "If he's associating with that bunch, ye'd best watch out. Lice and bedbugs are bad enough. But the clap, that's another thing altogether."

"Oh really, Margaret. Sid's not that sort." I couldn't picture him seeking out a fancy woman from one of the saloons on C Street. When we encountered such women on the street, he always reddened and looked away, as if embarrassed for Virginia City's plentiful soiled doves.

She snorted and set her cup clattering into the saucer. "A man is a man. Still and all, he's a good provider. I'll give him that." She glanced around the kitchen approvingly.

Most Comstockers lived in plank-partitioned boardinghouses or unpainted shacks. Our lodging was much better. A woman had been there before me, for someone had pasted up sheets of magazines on the canvas-covered walls, and hung flour-sack curtains in the kitchen. Still, the first winter we'd nearly frozen between its thin walls, or when huddled out in the privy.

Some miners did freeze, or collapse of heat exhaustion in the deeper mines. Most got pneumonia and rheumatism, and were ground down by hard toil, boredom, and terrible weather. A quarter of the citizens were in jail much of the time for fighting, disturbing the peace, drunkenness, or sleeping on the sidewalk. They regularly sought comfort in strong drink. Our neighbor across the street put away a quart of whiskey a day, judging by the heap of bottles pitched down the gully behind his house. I began to wonder if I wanted to be a miner's wife.

I was curious about the work, but Sid refused to let me climb down into the pit or the branching tunnel he'd carved in Sam's old mine. "Certainly not, in your condition," he said. "But I'll take you to visit one of the bigger works."

Mines had even been sunk in the middle of downtown. A body got used to stepping around pits and piles of dirt and tools in the road. The Savage Mine was well named. Surrounded by shops and homes, it resembled a factory above ground. The main building sat over the shaft head and hoisting works. In the wings, carpenters and blacksmiths and machinists raced about. The huge main room had a pine-plank floor so fine, I wished it graced my house. Even the steam that rushed up through openings, as if we were situated over a Turkish bath, would be handy and warm.

The pit itself was less cozy: five feet wide and twenty feet long. Men swarmed around it dressed only in long john bottoms cut off at the thigh, or even breechcloths. Their bodies glistened in the light of a hundred candles. They resembled ancient, mythic Kobolds risen from the depths of a mysterious subterranean lair, skin white as milk except for the soot smeared on their faces, and the dirt that stiffened their hair. And the unlit chewed cigars in their teeth.

They kept climbing into or out of iron cages, ascending or descending into the steam and mist, blinking in the gloom like pale, dirty moles. Tense, frowning engineers ran the hoisting engines with an eye on the dial, raising and lowering the cages on their thick wires. Everything moved so fast, it terrified me.

Sid drew me over. "Becky, look at the works of this elevator," he marveled.

Just then a car roared up next to us. I heard a thud, then agonized screaming. A man had stuck his hand outside the cage as it hurtled upward, and lost it instantly in a dreadful explosion of flesh and bone. Other miners dragged him off and tied a dirty bandanna around the spurting stump. They carried him away as he writhed and sobbed. Then, others stepped aboard and the cage dropped out of sight once more.

When I leaned against a timber to steady myself, I saw my dress had been showered with blood and bits of flesh, my hand smeared where I'd gripped the timber. It was Iron Mountain all over again. The candles swayed, melted into dark. The next thing I recall is Sid lifting me off the floor. And a somber, staring circle of dirty half-naked men stooped over, fanning me with their hats.

"Ah, that ain't nothing, ma'am," one said kindly. "Why, last week a stray dog tried to jump acrost the shaft and missed. He dropped a hunnerd feet, yelping all the while, and fell on two poor bastards down below. Killed 'em dead. The dog, too. Shame, it were a good pup. We called him Pete."

I closed my eyes again.

Sid held my hand, and four of them picked me up as if I had delicate corners and were made of glass. Their hands were dirty and rough, and the place smelled nothing like a church. Yet as I relaxed into their supporting arms, the little procession felt like a silent sacrament conducted for the spiritual benefit of us all. They carried me to the main office, where I lay on a broken-backed sofa until I felt well enough to walk on my own.

After that the Savage Mine seemed to me less benign than a bathhouse, and more akin to the first level of Hell. On our way out, the foreman completed the tour by telling us, "At fifteen hundred feet, underground waters heat the rock face so hot, it'll burn the skin off a man's palms like a pan just off the stove."

I leaned hard on Sid's arm. "Do you think the shock might've injured or marked the baby?" I whispered.

He shook his head. "No, no. Not at all."

"You cannot do this, Sid," I told him as we left. "It's impossible."

"I won't be working *here*, Becky. I'm digging safely in my own small shaft with nothing but hand tools."

This cheered me a bit, until I learned more about shaft mining. On a lode claim on the Comstock, placer law granted a man three hundred feet along the north-south lode, plus all the ground east and west of his claim the various offshoots might occupy. Most excavations began as open pits. The ore was so crumbly, a miner could hack it out of the tunnel face with a pick, lighted by a stub of candle stuck to a ledge. But Sid failed to mention that as the soft, sandy sides of a shaft slumped inward, you had to dig in timbers for support. Miners who didn't bother often got buried alive. As you went deeper, things got more dangerous. Yet they all dug on like crazed hounds after a golden bone.

Miners first used post-and-cap timbering: three beams set up like a post and lintel doorframe. But in a deep pit, these collapsed and miners died. Then a man named Deidesheimer, an engineer from Germany, came up with square sets. He took short, massive timbers, mortised and tenoned both ends, and fitted them into hollow cubes, like a honeycomb. Men could safely work inside these frames, he said. They required lots of timber, though, so the slopes all around were soon stripped of pine, the wood hauled in on huge wagons along a new road.

As Sid began to dig and chip out mounds of ore and wash it, looking for traces of gold, piles of heavy blue sand clogged the rockers. He cursed the stuff, for it made his arms ache all night after he'd spent the day scooping it out, then throwing it away. One afternoon a grizzled old prospector came along and, stroking his dishrag beard, silently watched Sid work for a while. "What you gone to do with this pile here," he said at last, pointing at the hill of blue-gray muck by the shaft.

"Not a blessed thing," said Sid, wiping his brow. "Hope it all blows away."

"That so?"

Sid began to wonder at his interest. "Yes. Why?"

For the price of two segars, the old man finally told him, cackling like an egg-laying hen. "Son, that there's silver ore. Iffen you don't want it, I'll get a barrow and truck it off."

Sid burst into the house in his grubby getup, leaving footprints of blue mud all over the damp parlor floor Annie had just scrubbed. He rushed up to where I sat resting, my swollen ankles propped on a chair, and grabbed both my hands.

"We'll be kings," he said breathlessly, squeezing my hands and kissing them. He nearly ran one of the knitting needles, which I'd reluctantly taken up to make a baby blanket, right through his eye. "And Gage will be the prince of the Sierras!"

I feared he'd gone mad from breathing in thick blue dust all day. He ran out again before I could even haul up from the chair under the weight of my happy expectations. "Sid, wait!" I cried, clinging to the doorframe. "Is this something to do with gold? Have you found a nugget?"

It turned out he'd taken a sample of ore to flux and fire. Since he didn't have a furnace, he'd gone into the hills, cut a cottonwood branch, and made a hole in it. He poked powdered ore into the hole, put it in a roaring fire, then he raked through the ashes. A bead of silver remained.

Sam Clemens had been looking for gold and found none. But his Missouri Rose held a world of silver: a vein over a hundred feet wide.

The next day Sid went and got a true and proper certificate from a reputable assayer. This was important, since some were either scientifically incapable, or crooked, or both—notorious for getting rich results of any and all specimens brought in. The assay was so good, he hired laborers off the street and bought as many square sets as he could lay hands on. They set to digging and shoring, taking out barrows full of the once-scorned blue rock.

They wagonned it to a quartz mill, an iron monster with six tall rods big around as both my ankles and a flat head of steel, all lined together like slats in a gate. These rose and fell in ponderous order, slamming into an iron battery box. One man broke up masses of rock with a sledge while another shoveled it in. An operator mixed the resulting powder with water into a creamy blue paste, drove it through a fine screen, then washed it into huge steam-heated amalgamating pans.

They put quicksilver in the battery, and it snatched up any gold or silver particles. The whole mess was run through a buckskin sack every half hour, with coarse salt and copper sulfate to destroy base metals. A long, tiresome process, but the silver eventually floated down run-off troughs, and the men trapped it in blankets. These were washed out, and the process started again.

Only when I saw a batch of refined silver did I believe at last in our new-found wealth. The shining chunk Sid placed in my hands was smooth and warm. "It feels . . . alive," I whispered, stroking it reverently. He smiled as if at last satisfied that I understood.

But I saw the producing of it was like housework—always something to do, over and over, in a silver mill. Men stood sweating over the battery, scooping out pulp and washing it in horn spoons to see if the globules of quicksilver were soft and needed more salt or sulfate, or hard and filled to capacity with silver. You'd have been hard-pressed to get any man in Virginia City to swing a broom or lift a dish to wash, for *that* was woman-work. But nothing discouraged them from gold and silver fever.

THE FIRST LOAD YIELDED a lot of silver at sixteen hundred dollars to the ton. Not the four thousand dollars in silver and gold combined the first Comstock claims had brought to their owners, but quite respectable. If not precisely rich, we were suddenly well-off. We picked out a lot in Gold Hill on a high slope and commenced building a new house with five bedrooms and a real water closet. I paged through furniture catalogs from San Francisco. Gage got new school clothes. And Sid seemed happy, as if at last he believed us right to have left Missouri behind.

As he warmed to Nevada's riches, I'd fallen in love with its freedom. Back East, no lady could appear in public without squeezing herself into a corset. Once past girlhood, no one went out unlaced, even when expecting. But a few weeks of walking uphill in Nevada's heat and dust made me shed my stays for good. By the time I was eight months along, we were experiencing the dry, parching heat of a Nevada summer. A body would need reviving every ten minutes to restrict her lungs as tightly as women did back East.

Out West, a woman couldn't sink back on the divan in a faint twice a day. Too much to be done. Some of it men's work, but no help for that if your husband was off in the grip of gold fever, or dead of a duel or a cave-in. Between the dust, heat, and chores, a lady undid a few buttons. When that didn't result in ruination, or the end of society, she loosened her stays. Generally she soon shed more clothes, and deportment. Survival trumped tradition and fashion.

I liked this new life. I'd never been an indoors sort, and now I had to be outside much of the time. I longed to wear trousers again, though. I'd gotten used to the feel of the loose cloth encasing both limbs, the whisking sound when I walked. The way I could stride as long as any man. Trousers on women weren't accepted here either, and thus felt more attractive for being forbidden. I purloined a pair of Sid's and wore them indoors, when Gage was at school.

At last my expectant belly grew so round, I could no longer button these. Then it was back to a loose-waisted dress. But Margaret O'Shaunessy continued to slip over to my house most afternoons to put on a pair of bloomers. Then we'd break out the tobacco and sip tea with whiskey. I resolved to get back into trousers as soon as I was delivered and back on my feet.

On a hot July morning I was helping Annie Marsh with the laundry, when a pain flashed like a knife-thrust from my belly to my lower back. It didn't go away but expanded, clawing its way over my hips, weakening my knees. "Help me to a chair," I gasped.

She did so, then ran to fetch Margaret, who arrived puffing with excitement. "Who's your midwife? You don't see the China Doctor, do you?"

"No, no. Get—get Doctress Hoffmann. She's on C Street."

I staggered to the back room, stopping often to accommodate a new surge of pain, pulling myself along on tables and chair backs. Margaret returned as Gage burst through the door from school. She shooed him over to her house for biscuits and milk.

Doctress Hoffmann arrived in a neat little gig. As the stout, gray-haired lady began setting up for business, it reminded me of Mrs. McGill from the Ozarks. That made me recall Sid's pillow-padded belly and lace nightcap, and I laughed. The doctor, rinsing her hands at the washstand, glanced over with concern. She laid the back of one hand on my forehead, as if she thought I was delirious.

"It's just, I remembered something funny," I gasped, clutching at my belly as another pain shot around from my lower back.

"Oh, *ja*? Well, tell me of it," she said, sitting at the foot of the bed.

I hesitated, wondering if she was Union or Confederate. Then I remembered: The War was over. So between pains I told that story, then the rest of our journey. Hers was a clever question, for with my mind on old times, the hours passed quickly and I barely noticed the pains coming faster and harder. At least not until the urge to push got too strong to ignore.

She rolled her sleeves, lifted the sheet, and looked under my nightdress. Then pulled a brown bottle out of her bag, rubbed oily fluid into her palms, and reached under again. I flinched when her fingers circled between my thighs, pressing here and there. If this was German school medicine, I didn't like it.

She glanced at me over my raised knees. "No worries, Missus. I shall massage with sweet oil. If muscles relax, less tearing when baby comes. And you heal faster."

By then I was too gripped by pain to answer. Gage and Tyler, both large babies, had torn me so badly, it hurt to sit for weeks. Old Dr. Bonniwell had sewn me back up, and the stitches had first chafed, then itched terribly.

Doctress Hoffmann looked up again over steel spectacles. "You are doing well. But we must get you up. Gravity helps the work."

She grabbed me under the arms and hauled. Not a dignified posture, to crouch on the bed like a panting savage, twisting the sheets in my fists and gasping. But she was right; things seemed to speed up.

Before sundown we had a good-sized daughter. Sid arrived home from the mine as I was checking her fingers, toes, face, and hands, relieved to find no mark or lack or blemish to remember our awful trip to the Savage Mine by. We named her Paulina Sierra Hopkins. Sid wanted to honor his mother, and Gage contributed her middle name.

"Because she's not a Missouri girl," he said. "She's our Nevada sister."

Mostly we just called her Polly. She looked so much like a tiny Aunt Polly, especially when she was hungry or needed changing. Then she put on the same reproachful expression Sid's mother had used when he or Tom had misbehaved.

Three days later, with Polly in my arms, I got up to cook breakfast, and didn't lie down again. I took Gage to see his father's mine. I ordered a new cradle, and a set of storybooks for the children. I replaced our rustic crate and box furniture with an oak china cabinet, a round pine table, and four press-back chairs.

Gage and I took to visiting the mine at least once a week. But we weren't there the hot, cloudless day in August Sid and his men followed the silver vein deeper. As they excavated, two workmen gouged at the face of the new tunnel, and the ore crumbled easily and rapidly. The third man was Norval

Bass, the old prospector who'd pointed out the silver ore to Sid. He hauled the stuff up with the bucket and windlass, to a waiting barrow.

Sid told me later he'd heard a rumble, as if an overloaded draywagon was passing. Then sand and rock rained on their heads. All of them lunged for the main shaft, but before they reached it, the new tunnel collapsed, pulling part of the old one down with it. Sid was thrown forward, slammed in the back by a giant fist. He heard the young laborer, Albertus, cry out. Then he heard nothing at all.

When he woke, it was dark in the shaft. He felt around with his free hand and discovered both legs and the other arm pinned by fallen ore and sand. He found it hard to breathe, lying facedown under so much weight. He called for Albertus, who'd been behind him as they'd rushed out. No answer. He hoped Norval Bass had raced to town for help.

Bass returned with a group of men who climbed down and began to dig. I arrived soon after, on a horse Margaret had lent me, just as they were cranking the windlass to pull up first Sid, then his young helper, with ropes under their arms. Sid was blue gray all over, as if he'd already died. Albertus looked even worse, with blood darkening his trousers. The rescuers carried the two of them to a saloon in Gold Hill, and laid them on plank tables.

I leaned over Sid, wiping away the blood seeping from cuts on his face and hands. When I pressed on his chest and sides, he gasped. So, broken ribs. But Albertus was in dire shape, a jagged bone protruding from one thigh. I feared both legs had been crushed. His face was contorted in pain; he whipped his head from side to side, babbling. When the bartender tried to pour whiskey down his throat, he choked and it dribbled out again. Then he fainted.

I took Sid's hand. "How do you feel? Are you in pain?"

"Where's Albertus?" he mumbled. "How is he?"

"Out cold," I said. "It's probably for the best."

A townsman nodded. "Be one sorry fella when he come to. There's a Paiute medicine man up the hill. And the China Doctor at the edge of town. It's too far to get a white doctor here anytime soon, so—"

"Go get Doctress Hoffmann," I said. "Right now."

The men all turned to stare. "The Dutch lady doctor?" said Norval Bass, squinting and chewing on one side of his cheek. "Don't she tend to wimmin's gripes?"

Yes, she advertised for children and women's complaints. But she'd been calm, competent, and clean. I'd seen the handiwork of some of her male colleagues, such as the legless miner who rolled about the sidewalks on a wheeled cart, his four-inch stumps stretched out before him. He sold shriveled apples and cheap ribbons, or begged with a dented tin mug. Judging by the cloudy sliver just showing under his half-closed lids, he spent his pittance with the Chinese, in a den of bitter smoke.

Most who called themselves Doctor in Virginia City had trained on the battlefields of the War. They were quite at home cutting parts off. Some also liked to bleed and purge, which did little good far as I could see. Lucky patients were dosed with opium first, and died in a fog of drugs. At least they escaped their so-called treatment, only to lie under a wooden cross next to all the Killed Men. Doctress Hoffmann was concerned with bringing life into the world, not torturing and then hastening it out.

"Get her now, Mr. Bass," I said firmly. "Remember, I'll be the one paying you today."

Still grumbling, Bass stumped out to the wagon, hoisted himself up, and whipped the horses into a trot.

Half an hour later Doctress Hoffmann walked in with her bag. She ignored the stares of the assembled miners and sent them out to find two straight planks. She gave laudanum to Albertus, then washed the dirt and dust off him, further astonishing the men in the room. When the others returned with planks, she cut away his trousers while they slid a board under each leg.

"Grip him here, so," she directed. Two of the strongest held Albertus down while she pulled his right limb straight again. He roused to scream and arch his back, then passed out again. She calmly tied the set leg to the board splint with strips of canvas, then probed all around the thigh wound, checking for bone splinters.

I had no time to feel squeamish when she turned to me and ordered, "Ready a needle, please." I took a deep breath, rummaged in her bag, and found a spool. I pulled a length of coarse black cotton, threaded a curved needle, then handed it over. She hummed a waltz, stitching the torn meat as matter-of-factly as I would've mended a shirt. Then, the same procedure with the other leg. Fortunately, through it all Albertus remained unconscious.

"My dear, that is all I can do *mit* him," she murmured. "Someone must give the poor fellow this, two times a day." She handed me a bag filled with spiky dried stems. "He shall chew it *gut*, never mind how bitter. When of its taste he complains too much, he no longer needs it."

I pinched up one shoot and sniffed. "What is this?"

"The desert bush *Eplieda nevandensis.* Mormon tea, some call it. Helps the bones to knit fast. There is no guarantee, though, that this man he will walk."

She wrapped Sid's ribs while I cleaned and bandaged his cuts, shamefully happy he hadn't broken his legs like Albertus, that the limb injured in the War had been spared this time.

Poor Albertus healed without much infection, but never did walk again. More than his legs had been crushed, for they hung limp and useless, without feeling, and collapsed if he tried to stand. We sent his family four hundred dollars, nearly all our profit from the mine. "We can get more money," said Sid. "But that poor fellow won't be earning a living of any kind now."

After his ribs mended, Sid went back to work in the Missouri Rose. Then in a way I was sorry, for if he'd been hurt a little worse, I could've insisted he lay up longer. He hired a new man, and each week I expected him to be crushed by falling rock or smothered in sand. I thanked God when my husband appeared each evening, dirty and tired, but in one piece and alive. He always took pleasure, at the dinner table, in detailing his day underground. And in putting into my hand the lump of silver they'd refined that day.

DISASTER, WHEN IT FINALLY CAME, arrived from a very different source.

Virginia City's seventeen brothels, twenty gambling houses, and fifty saloons were open every day of the week. A body would never know it was Sunday unless they marked the days off on a calendar. We had an elected sheriff, and deputies. Unfortunately some of these were robbers and desperadoes to match any they'd sworn to fight. We were also plagued with bunco artists who swindled newcomers with phony mine certificates and faulty gear.

There were frequent brawls, shootings, stabbings, and fistfights. Sam Clemens had overstated the murder rate, but only a little. Gambling, drinking, and fighting went on all night. Several times a week someone was wounded or died in a gunfight, or of a knife in the back. Mostly over trivial things: a loss at faro, the disputed affections of a D Street nymph.

The jury system was no better. Few jurors could read, and most were drunk. No matter how conclusive the proof of guilt, nor how hard prosecutor and judge worked, if a criminal was popular, the verdict was bound to be Not Guilty. No man willing to hand out ready cash ever saw a gallows. The papers lavished long columns on crimes and trials, describing victims, perpetrators, the wounds received, the goods stolen, all in loving detail. But anyone who checked up after the latest nine-days wonder would see few were actually punished in the end.

Sid was too busy working to get into trouble. His leg was bothering him, though. The old wound had been aggravated by the cave-in. Standing long hours became a strain. He still went out each morning, though, even when pain kept him up at night.

He'd always been a patient father before, but he became short with the children. Unlike some men in the neighborhood, he never struck them or me. He simply began to ignore us when he came home, to sit alone with a bottle and glass. I knew he drank to dull the pain, but couldn't forgive the way he snapped some nights when Gage rushed up with an eager, innocent question. I hated to see the joy of curiosity doused in the boy's eyes when his father ordered, "Be quiet, can't you? Go and leave me in peace."

Some days I disliked my husband. But then my own considerable flaws came back to haunt me. Sid was no saint, and perhaps he was harder to live with each day. But I, above all, had no right to accuse him of human failings.

Twenty-two

ID KEPT SUPPORTING CRIPPLED Albertus's family, though he never mentioned it. He came home in pain most nights, ate dinner, then drank till he went to bed. Gradually he came later and later, and I began to wonder where he might be going. Plenty of opportunity in Virginia City for a man to hide out and toss back whiskey, or lose money, or find female companionship.

I wasn't the only one who noticed his absences. "Is your man after the opium dens, then," said Margaret one afternoon, as she helped me hang out wet clothes on the line. In the parched desert air they stiffened and dried almost as soon as we pegged them up. "Ah, well," she sighed. "He wouldna be the first."

"Of course not," I said. "He's just working very hard." What if he did have a drink, or toss some dice on those nights—hadn't he earned a small respite from drudging all day? It never occurred to me he might be at bars or gambling dens for a different reason altogether.

The year before, certain merchants, miners, mechanics, doctors, and lawyers had banded together in a pledge to bring justice to Virginia City. I heard whispers that these citizens took days off from their own work to track down criminals the local lawmen were too friendly with. The Vigilance Committee returned stolen property to rightful owners or grieving heirs. Its members carried revolvers, a rifle or a shotgun, a blanket and some rope, and always left a note on the body as a warning to other criminals. The use of spirits was strictly forbidden among them. I suppose that was one reason it never occurred to me Sid might be involved.

A week or so after I'd talked to Margaret, Sid came in so late, it was nearly dawn. When I sat up in bed and turned up the oil lamp I'd left burning, I saw he had blood on his face and was gripping his shoulder as if he'd injured it. I slipped from the covers and rushed to him. "Sid, what happened? Where've you been?"

"An accident," was all he would say. "Nothing important."

I picked up the lamp and made him follow me to the kitchen. As I tended to his injuries, he finally confessed. "A few weeks ago, on my way back from the mine, I came upon a group of rough-looking men outside town. Some with their hat brims pulled low, a few even wearing bandannas like that Jesse character of yours."

I nodded. "I remember, but—"

He smiled and shook his head. "Yet these were dressed in suits like businessmen."

He said they were prodding a fellow with hands bound behind him over to a mine pit. As Sid approached, two men were tossing a rope over one beam. Sid asked the nearest vigilante what was happening. "They told me the condemned man had murdered three miners for the coins in their pockets. So I asked, if it was to be a hanging, where the sheriff was, or the judge and jury. And they laughed."

When he said he was a lawyer, and recommended turning the killer over to the sheriff, the vigilante he was speaking to snorted. "Haw. His best friend is Deputy Jack Williams."

Even I knew of Williams, a legendary local bully happy to empty the pockets of innocent men himself. "Ah. Well, in that case," Sid had said, and stepped aside.

"Not so fast," said the other. "Now you're here, you better come along, too." He produced a revolver and prodded Sid ahead of him to the pit mouth. "So of course I wondered if they meant to kill me, too. What happened next was strange," Sid told me. "The criminal fell silent, regarding the rope. They stood him on the broad beam, and looped the noose about his neck. And when they asked if he had anything to say, he wanted to hear the names of all the men they'd hanged before him."

One vigilante, a banker, stepped forward and recited the list—quite a long one. As he finished, the condemned man nodded sadly. "Not one innocent among them. Good-bye, boys, and bless you. You're on a good undertaking."

"They pushed him in and his neck snapped clean," said Sid. "When he stopped kicking, they pulled him back up, laid the body by the side of the road, and tucked the usual note in his hand." He looked up at me again.

"But your face. What happened tonight?"

"I told you," he snapped. "An accident. But you're a judge's daughter— what do you *think*?"

I threw up my hands. "I don't know. I'm used to having the law handed out by lawyers and sheriffs and judges. Back in Hannibal, we always—"

"But we aren't back in Hannibal," he pointed out. "In a place like this, with gold and silver and guns everywhere, nothing but severe, quick punishment will prevent crime."

"I suppose that's true," I admitted. "But then who'll keep an eye on the vigilantes?"

He looked at me intently, as if there was more he wanted to confide. He seemed to decide against it, for all he said was, "Even your father agreed folks have to take control when their government fails. Or the savage element will dominate."

I felt a prickling on my spine, thinking of his time riding with Reeves's Fifteenth. But he'd come away disheartened by both sides during the War. "You don't mean to join them?"

He struck his lamed leg with the flat of a hand and laughed. "Some good I would be!"

"I'm glad you see that." Then, realizing what I'd said, I touched his arm. "I only meant, I don't want anything else to happen. You've done your part already, and suffered enough for it."

Probably it should've occurred to me that, since the vigilantes had a strict policy of secrecy, and Sid had seen their faces, he might've been pressured to join and swear allegiance on the spot. And then of course be unable to tell me. Their alternative would've been to kill him, and that was the sort of crime they were supposed to be preventing.

The next week Jack Williams, the crooked deputy, went into a billiard saloon on C Street looking for Billy Brown. Brown was a drifter who talked loud and bragged hard, especially after a few drinks. He'd never Killed His Man, but managed to gravely insult many. Williams was apparently one, because he came in and threatened Brown until another deputy pulled him off to the side.

Brown walked up to the bar past Williams, and ordered a whiskey. "You see? I'm good as any man," he told the bartender. Then he staggered back to the billiard table, set the whiskey glass on it, and drew his revolver. A friend grabbed at his arm when he aimed at Deputy Williams. The bullet went wild, right through the ceiling.

"I have his pistol, I have it!" Brown's companion shouted, keeping his arms and Brown's raised to prove it. "No need to shoot, Deputy. My friend here's just had too much to drink."

Williams only grinned and fired twice. Brown fell across the billiard table, bleeding from the stomach and chest. Then the deputy ambled over. "I'll take care of this affair, gentlemen," he said, pulling Brown's wallet and a sack of gold dust from his pocket. "For the funeral," he added, then walked out.

Once blood's been shed, more shooting and cutting and fighting follow. The next week Williams was sitting in a saloon, at a card table with friends. Someone thrust a gun through the cracked front door and fired twice. Williams fell, already dying. A *Union* editorial opined that some of Brown's seedier friends held a grudge, and had caught up with him.

But two days later a woman, unnamed by the newspaper, was killed. From the red light district, and said to be Williams's girl, she was shot in the head and dragged into an alleyway. The next day the deputy friend who'd pulled Williams aside before he shot Brown was hit over the head with a sack of ore, his skull cracked so badly, he lay unconscious for days.

Sid went out that night and didn't come back before I went to bed. I woke an hour or so before dawn to again see him standing in our bedroom. This time he was turned away, gazing out the window.

I sat up. "What's happened, Sid?"

Even in the dimness, I saw he jumped when I spoke. But he didn't look at me. "I couldn't sleep. That's all."

"I was worried. Have you eaten?"

"Yes. I mean, no. I'm not hungry."

He came to bed then, but I don't believe he slept.

The next day we walked into town to do some shopping. As I was about to enter the butcher shop, Sid took hold of my arm. "Go ahead. I'll be back here in a minute." He turned and walked across the street, so I went inside. It was the cleanest shop in town, but the bitter-copper stink of blood still gave me a turn. Because of the battlefield at Iron Mountain, perhaps it always would. The butcher, a large, genial man named Bender, greeted us from behind the counter. I shifted Polly Sierra to one hip, and began pointing out the cuts of loin and the chops I wanted. Then there Sid was, back beside us again. "Almost finished," I said. "Where'd you go?"

He glanced around, then said in a low voice, "To see the sheriff."

"Oh." I looked up at him. "But why?"

"Nothing much. Never mind, Becky. I've taken care of it."

The bell jangled as someone came in behind us. My husband glanced over his shoulder, then stepped away from us, I assumed to speak to an acquaintance. Polly squirmed in my arms, smiling over the counter at the butcher, already a shameless coquette.

Behind us a fellow spoke to Sid in such a low mumble, I couldn't make out words. The butcher was wrapping my purchases, so I turned to see who it might be. A stranger to me, tall and heavyset, wearing a blue woolen shirt and high boots like every other miner in the Nevadas. His face was vaguely familiar, but I didn't know a name.

I did hear Sid's next words, though. "Perhaps. But it's a cowardly thing to kill a man in such a way."

"He got as good a chance as he gave Bill Brown," said the other. "And you ain't God, anyhow."

"No. Nor are you." Sid sounded so calm, nearly amused, that I wouldn't have thought anything was amiss. Except his face was chalk.

I took a step forward and touched his arm. "Who's your intimidating friend, dear?"

"This must be the wife," said the man, turning with an ugly smile toward me. "Oh, and a baby, too. Coochie-coo!" When he put out one grubby-nailed hand, I pulled Polly out of reach.

"Stay away," said Sid. "The Committee has nothing to do with them."

The miner stopped smiling. "A fellow turns on his friends, his whole family mought expect trouble."

He seemed about to reach down for a revolver strapped to his leg, but Sid lunged first. He punched the miner in the face, then jerked the man's gun from its holster. He set it behind him on the meat counter. The butcher, more quick-witted than I'd suspected, wrapped the revolver in brown paper and laid it behind him on a shelf. "That's enough of such talk," he said.

"Justice and Vigilance ought to go together, don't you think?" Sid asked the scowling miner. "But we'll all have our say about it, in court. Now get out."

Wiping his bloody nose on one sleeve, the man backed up a step. "Sure, sure."

He turned for the door, and I rushed to Sid to see if he was all right, to beg him to leave now. Just as I reached him, the stranger turned back. I never knew or saw where the knife came from; maybe the sleeve he'd wiped his nose on. He slid it right under my arm, and I heard the blade scrape past my husband's just-healed ribs, deep into his chest. I hear it still, sometimes, the terrible rasp and scrape of steel on bone, and Sid's startled gasp.

Clutching Polly like a sack, I tried to hold my husband up as he sagged over onto the counter. But his weight was too much; I lost my grip and he slid slowly to the plank floor, smearing the glass front of the meat cabinet with his blood. Mr. Bender rushed from behind the display case with a club, shouting, "Here, you!" at the assailant. From what seemed a great distance I heard running steps, a scuffle, a door slamming, and the tinny jingle of the bell above it.

"Sid? *Sid!*" As I knelt over him one part of my mind was aware of others crowding in, of men roughly pulling away the coward who'd stabbed him. But I was busy pressing on Sid's chest with my free hand, balancing our baby in the other arm. Hot blood leaked through my fingers, I did not have enough hands to stop the horrible pulse of red as it left his heart, leeching the color from his face. "Help us," I cried out to the room. "Someone help!"

"Sorry," Sid muttered. "Knew better."

"Hush, hush," I said, and shouted at the butcher, "Get the doctor!"

Sid smiled. "No—no third chance. Ah, Becky—Polly."

"Sid, no." I cupped his face. "Why ever did he do this?"

"For the—Vigilance." His voice caught on each labored breath. "Had to—join. Wanted to. But—bad as Missouri Militia."

"The vigilantes? But I thought they—"

"No." A spasm contorted his face. His breath smelled metallic, like the blood soaking his shirt, pooling on the gritty planks. "No better than Reeves."

"But you are," I insisted, choking on hot tears that burned my cheeks and scoured my throat. "A better man than him, or—or Tom Sawyer, or anyone. You won't leave us."

I don't know if he heard, for just as I said it, his last breath brushed my face, stirred the damp strands escaping my tortoiseshell combs, like a soul rushing home. Polly was squirming again, slowly slipping from my one-armed grasp. I raised the other hand to steady her, and saw it was clotted with gore. So was the baby's quilt, and Polly, not understanding, took one whip-stitched corner and lifted the cloth splotched with her father's blood to her mouth. I cried out, and suddenly Mrs. Bender, the butcher's plump wife, was kneeling at my side. She gently pulled the baby away, soothing her while Mr. Bender helped me up and over to a bench against the wall.

"Where is the doctor?" I demanded. The butcher and his wife exchanged a glance, and she took Polly away into the back.

"Now, Missus," he began, but one look at my face silenced him.

Mrs. Bender had dropped Polly's soiled quilt on the floor beside Sid. I slid from the bench and began to mop up his blood with it. I would take back every drop, even if I had to chase it down the cracks between the planks. When that task was done, and the doctor still hadn't come, I sat back on the hard bench, gripping the sodden cloth in my lap. "For God's sake, where is the doctor?" I asked, but no one would answer.

A deputy arrived, an overgrown boy barely old enough for the sparse blond whiskers he'd tried to grow. By then I could see that Sid looked empty as a shell, but I would not believe it so.

"You took your time," I told the lawman. "Where were you an hour ago?" He wore a flat tin star pinned crookedly on his flannel shirt, as if such a symbol were of any use in this place. Two others came and lifted Sid onto an army blanket, saying they'd carry him to the undertaker.

"No, you will not," I said, and struck the nearest one with my fist. I crouched there gripping Sid's hand so they could not steal him from me. But then the doctor arrived—a stranger in top hat, not Doctress Hoffmann—and I have no recollection of anything more, until I woke at home in bed. Margaret O'Shaunessy sat in a chair beside it.

That night, after Margaret left and the children were in bed, I sat at the kitchen table in the dark, Huck's gun and Sid's bottle before me. By then I understood this much: certain men in Virginia City hadn't liked Sid's insistence on regular justice, even among vigilantes. That was why he'd gone to see the sheriff, and that was why they'd killed him. I poured a glassful of whiskey and gulped it down, though it scorched my throat and burned my eyes. It made me imaginative; I stroked the Colt's barrel as if cold metal could feel. Thinking, over and over: *I will show them Justice. I will be Death and Destruction.*

Death and destruction were all I'd brought Sid to in the end, when I'd meant only to save us. He was a good man, a good husband and father. His flaws were as nothing compared with my own, and he'd loved me far more truly than I'd loved him. Had he heard my last words to him? Now I would never know. I had much to answer for, and even more to regret. But first, I would get justice for Sid.

But no . . . a gun was all wrong. I wanted an eye for an eye, a man for a man, but not with the impersonal twitch of a finger on a trigger. And our friend Sam had already given me the answer to that problem, when we'd first come to the Sierras.

The next day, after I made the funeral arrangements, I took the children to Margaret's. Then I went home and slipped a carving knife between my basque and the stays of my seldom-used corset. I pulled a shawl around my shoulders and walked to the sheriff's office, pushed through the swinging door, and fetched up at his desk. "I'm here to see the coward who killed my husband."

Sheriff Gatlin was tall and balding, with a curved scar beneath one eye. He got up slowly, as if he had no call to hurry, ever. "Sorry about your loss, ma'am."

"Just tell me his name," I said. "The murderer."

He drummed his fingers on the desktop, frowning. At last he said, "It's Thibadeaux. Jacob Thibadeaux. Folks call him Tibby."

Tibby. What one might name a pet cat. This low creature with a foolish name had killed the man I'd grown to respect and love more than I'd thought possible, back on my strange wedding day. I squeezed my eyes shut, then headed for the back. "I can get to the cell on my own," I tossed over my shoulder.

The sheriff cleared his throat. "Well, but he ain't there, y'see."

I turned back, staring. "What do you mean?"

He hooked thumbs in leather galluses. "It's just that, after old Tibby give himself up, we went—"

"But he did no such thing!"

The sheriff acted as if I hadn't spoken. "—we went and took him before Justice Atwater. The judge, he discharged him, so's Tibby could appear on his own recognizance for trial. Next Monday at six in the evening." He sat and began mining dirt from under his fingernails with the tip of a barlow knife.

"You know damn well he won't appear." My voice sounded low as a bitch dog's growl.

He glanced up, frowning again. "A *lady* don't have no business in here. Or talking like that in public. Now take yourself out, afore you're the one in the cell."

The concealed metal of the blade was heating up against my breast, burning my skin all the way through the bone and fabric of my corset. I raised a hand to the first button at my throat. Then I recalled Gage and little Polly back home, with Margaret O'Shaunessy. If I was jailed, maybe even hanged, the children would be sent to the Sisters' orphanage. Mary might not be able to come get them, to take them home to Hannibal.

Despite the laxity of law in Virginia City, it seemed a woman could not Kill Her Man. A mother could not afford the luxury, the satisfaction of revenge. I turned abruptly and walked out.

IT WAS BRIGHT AND SUNNY the day of the funeral, the sky glowing fit for a picnic. My blood felt so sluggish, my body so heavy, it was an effort to hold up my head. Finally Margaret took Polly and carried her while I stood clutching Gage's hand. It appeared that half of Virginia City had turned out for Sid. I narrowed my eyes and looked them over through my black veil. Hypocrites. They'd come only to make sure he was dead and buried. How many of them were in on the plot? Surely not Mrs. Bender, the butcher's wife. She'd taken my arm and told me to lean on her as we came out of the church. But what about her husband, who was peering surreptitiously at his silver half-hunter, checking the time?

When I leaned away from her, Mrs. Bender glanced at me, concern in her eyes. "Are you holding up, dear?"

I shook my head and closed my eyes against them all.

The grave was half-full of water from the previous day's rain; it looked like the battery pan of the silver mill, creamy blue-gray pulp swirling in the bottom. First Nevada had refined my husband, rendering him into someone I barely recognized. It had pounded and molded and strained off pieces of the old Sid, then taken the new one away from us for good.

But I was the one who'd insisted we come West. I was as heartless and selfish, as much to blame as anyone. If we'd stayed in Missouri, or gone south to Tennessee, or to Virginia with my parents, Sid might still be alive.

The service passed in a blur of white faces, black clothes, shoveled clods of gray dirt. Then I seemed to have been magically transported to a seat on a horsehair sofa in the Bender house, fending off cups of lukewarm tea, sympathetic pats, and heaped plates of funeral food.

One long week later, I sat just as stiffly in the first row of the courtroom on Back Street, staring ahead as all around me the players in this farce assembled. Judge, sheriff, prosecutor. A rubbernecking gallery who behaved as if there'd actually be a trial to watch. By five minutes to six, everyone was in place. Everyone except Tibby, of course. I pulled Sid's gold watch from my reticule and looked down at it. The ticking sounded very loud. I hoped everyone could hear.

At ten to seven I got up and walked down the aisle. As I passed each row, faces turned up to me with open mouths, then turned back to whisper behind their hands. Up front, the judge was dismissing the court, banging his toy hammer like a peeved child. I pushed past Bender, the butcher who'd threatened Tibby with a club to make him drop the knife after he'd killed Sid. Unless the man was a vigilante, too, and that had been all for show.

Mr. Bender said something but I shook my head without looking up. I kept my gaze on the ground all the way down the steps, all the way home.

The next day I went down to the *Territorial Enterprise* and took out an advertisement to sell the building lot with our unfinished house. Then I posted a notice in the assayer's office, and the next afternoon sold the Missouri Rose to the Ophir Mining Company for fifty thousand dollars. The money, along with a gold pocket watch, a tinted wedding photo, and a few pieces of clothing, was little enough to have left of a man's life.

I could buy tickets for me and the children on a stagecoach headed East, then board a steamer to St. Joseph. I could go home to Hannibal and still have plenty left to live on. I was as wealthy as the Widow Douglas now. I wondered if she'd felt half so bitter about her good fortune as I did about mine.

I went off to the telegraph office to send word of Sid's death home, but the lines were down due to the earlier storm. It'd be some time before Mary got the letter I mailed instead.

My Dearest Sister,

> *I take up my pen with a heavy Heart and terrible News to relate. God in His wisdom has seen fit to call Sid . . .*

As if God Almighty had anything to do with it. Maybe a stagecoach would even beat the mail back East. Then I'd have to face gentle, loving Mary and tell her to her face how her beloved brother had died, to see the horror in her eyes as I related all the bloody details.

Oh God, I wished I were a man. If I couldn't shoot every damned vigilante in Virginia City, I'd stand for the legislature and make hard laws against them. But I was a woman; I couldn't even vote for such reforms. We were too delicate, too limited in our minds, and in need of too much protection. That was what everyone said, though none had ever bothered to explain what a woman in a situation like this might do. When you were suddenly, truly without protection and almost on the streets, they all looked the other way. Whether you went back East, or on to the altar with the next man to ask, or down to the cribs on D Street, it was all the same to them. As long as you didn't become inconvenient, an embarrassment in their neighborhood.

Going back East would be giving in, admitting defeat. And silently agreeing to live among the shadows of what was lost forever: Baby Tyler and Sid. And yes, Tom. How I wished *he* were alive again and here in Virginia City. Tom Sawyer would make his cousin's murderers pay their bill double. For Sid was family, no matter how they'd fought and disagreed in the past.

The vigilantes who'd sought to clean up Nevada had turned into the thing they'd taken up arms against. Not one would ever tell where their hired murderer had disappeared to, or who might be concealing him in town. Or who had paid him to kill Sid. If only my husband had trusted me enough to whisper names in my ear, one night as we lay in bed. He'd been too loyal to men who'd dragooned him at gunpoint. Now he would keep their dirty secrets forever.

But I would not let it rest at that. If I stayed, I'd find them out and do something about it. Something, except . . . I looked across the table at Gage pushing Margaret's overcooked peas and dumplings around on his plate, at baby Polly tied into her chair with a length of soft flannel, banging a wooden spoon on the table. Even if I could find him, even if I pulled on trousers and strode out with Huck's gun and shot this Tibby, how could I escape with two little children clinging to me? And if I went to jail and was hanged like a man, who would take care of them?

There was always back East. The Judge's house in Hannibal. I could make a home among the things of my childhood, back in my parents' house.

I looked down at my plain, loose calico dress. At the heavy boots on my feet. No one in Hannibal dressed this way unless they were unspeakably disreputable, or so poor, they had no choice. Proper women back home wore useless little bonnets and toe-pinching buttoned shoes and gloves that soiled in five minutes. They never made a fuss, and kept quiet in public. And if they ever dared climb onto a horse, they hooked one knee around the pommel of a sidesaddle, and clung for dear life . . . even though they were delicate creatures, and it was a damn sight easier and safer to straddle the animal like any man would.

I hated Nevada with a passion now. And yet . . . and yet, having tasted and enjoyed its small freedoms, how could I ever go back East?

Gage stuck out his lip and dropped his fork on his plate with a clatter. "I hate it here. There's sand in my potatoes. We had a river back home, and grass, and nice big trees."

I pushed my plate aside, too, for I wasn't hungry. Gradually a plan was creeping into my mind. "Did you know there's a whole ocean just across the mountains?" I asked. "They say it's the Garden of Eden out there."

He frowned, looking both angry and close to tears. "But ain't we ever going home again?"

"*Aren't* we ever going. Don't say ain't." He lowered his head and I patted his shoulder. "Oh, never mind, darling. Say it however you like." What did such things matter now?

I stalled on making a decision by clearing the plates slowly and putting them in the pan to soak. Hannibal was a lost world. I'd tasted freedom first in Missouri, then here. In small ways, yes, but large in comparison to the petty restrictions of proper Eastern towns. Out here we had to work like dogs, but with this new, increased responsibility no one could argue women weren't essential to the making of some kind of civilization. Our very scarcity past the plains of Kansas made men value us more, even as they were less able to "protect" us.

I gripped the edge of the table, leaning on it heavily. Looking down at the rough grain of the pine, I saw this much plain: I would not willingly give up the chance to go on living in a more practical, unrestricted way, enjoying a freedom men took for granted. No, I would not go back.

I moved to the sink and pumped water over the dirty plates. "Your uncle Sam wrote us another letter from California," I said to Gage over my shoulder as I washed and stacked plates. "He's writing for a newspaper there, the *Morning Call*, under the name of Mark Twain. He says California really is a Paradise. Exotic flowers grow in the sand, within sight of the ocean, and it never gets too hot or too cold. And when there's an earthquake, everyone rushes out into the streets in any old getup, even their nightclothes. And they have a big party."

Polly teethed on her spoon, smiling around it, then banged it again. Gage laughed at the idea of a nightgown party outdoors. Then he looked concerned. "But—what's an earthquake?"

"I'm not sure. Some accident of the weather. But it doesn't sound very bad."

"Then we should go live with Uncle Sam," he suggested. "Daddy wouldn't mind."

I wanted to laugh and cry both. "I'm sure Sam isn't ready to share his bachelor rooms with the three of us. But we could go to San Francisco, and see if we like it there."

"Hooray!" Gage pulled me away from the sink and we danced around the room. It felt for a moment like spring after the tail end of a dreary, snowbound winter. I'd have gone far, much farther than San Francisco, to hold that rare feeling a few moments longer.

By the end of that week I'd sold all the furniture. A German family bought the lot with the foundations of a big lovely house we'd never live in. I got stage tickets and said a tearful good-bye to my friends Margaret O'Shaunessy, Annie Marsh, and the Doctress. Then the children and I boarded a stagecoach bound west once more. We bounced along through heat and dust, our wheels rumbling over far western plains and through green valleys. We climbed the Sierras up to the very clouds. And there, for just a moment, we gazed down like little gods on a vast redwood forest. On our new home, the seaside garden they called California.

1867

SAN FRANCISCO

Twenty-three

LIKE ROME, SAN FRANCISCO was built on hills. Not just seven, though, but a hundred or more, some vertical as chimneys. When we first left the station and walked up and down looking for a room and a bite to eat, it felt like trudging the terraced streets of Virginia City. You could see where you wanted to go, but it was always farther away and more of a climb than it first seemed.

I finally chose the California Hotel. Our suite was furnished in varnished mahogany and flocked hand-tinted wallpaper and thick velvet drapes. It felt like a cathedral, frighteningly overcivilized after Nevada. The whole place was so gilded and fashionable, it made me anxious. I rushed out to buy a new gown for Polly and a black mourning outfit for me, and new shoes and a suit with short pants for Gage. Anything to take my mind off what we were actually doing—starting over, yet again.

The next day Sam came calling. When we met in the lobby, I saw him bite his lip at my mourning attire: the crow-black dress, onyx brooch, soot-colored gloves. He choked out condolences while wringing my hand. "Sorry for your terrible loss, Becky. He was a good man, poor fellow, we shall miss him."

I couldn't bear to speak of Sid yet, especially in platitudes. Nor of the way he'd died, nor the damned cowards who'd killed him. I bent my head and fiddled with the tiny buttons on Polly's sprigged gown. I blew my nose on a black-edged hankie before I turned back. Sam seemed to understand. He squeezed my hand and didn't mention it again.

As we came down the hotel's front steps, a huge bearded man wearing a blue shirt and denim Levi's like a Comstock miner walked right into me. He backed up to apologize, then stared as dumbstruck as if I'd slapped him. Polly was in my arms, wearing a green ruffled day gown that made her curls look red as copper shavings. The man gawped openmouthed, as if he'd never seen a baby before. "Excuse us," I said stiffly, waiting for him to let us pass, fearing he was not right in the head.

"By God," he boomed. "Why, is it—? If it ain't a little girl-child!"

He dug in his pockets and dragged out a deerskin poke. "I come in from the Sitka digs, ma'am, up in Russian territory. A hunnerd in gold dust right here. I'll hand over all of it iffen you let me give the child a kiss!"

My turn to gape. "Why—certainly not! Sam, tell this—this gentleman— to let us pass."

Instead Clemens cocked his head. "Did you say a hundred, in gold?"

"Lord *God*, Sam!" I caught Gage's arm, and we went back into the lobby. I waited five minutes, then ventured back out.

Sam lingered at the foot of the stairs, turning his hat in his hands, abashed. "Sorry, Becky. It's only, I've been so broke, for a wild moment it seemed like a good idea."

"Never mind," I said, but resolved not to let him take either child on a jaunt without me. He might sell them outright.

We looked over five houses, each recommended by either his editor or his landlady, mostly in the Rincon Hill area. At last I decided on a clapboard Italianate cottage with a deep piazza, situated on an amazingly steep, snakily crooked street called Lombard. The house was painted deep yellow, with green and eggplant-purple trim. It sat only a few blocks from the Fisherman's Wharf, which felt reassuringly like the waterfront in St. Louis.

"Oh, very fashionable," Sam assured me. "Just the thing. And a good neighborhood, too."

It felt strange to write a check for the full amount; to buy a whole, finished house all at once. How dearly Sid had paid for those figures in my accounts! How dearly we all had. Perhaps now we were entitled to a bit of peace and security, Gage and Polly and I.

SAN FRANCISCO HAD BEEN LAID OUT like a string of beads along the Bay, the land made flat by shoving a bunch of sand hills down into the water. On Market Street, the broad main boulevard, shops and professional offices loomed overhead, hung with fancy signs. Still, they hadn't quite as many posted advertisements or as much noise here as in Virginia City. Standing on a busy city street that first week, for a moment I felt panic. I missed the raw, rude clutter of the Sierra Nevada. How would we know where to go, what to do, how to find things we needed?

"If you stick pretty much to Jackson Square at first, you can't go wrong," Sam instructed. "There are your theaters, your cafés and shops, and a dozen banks full of Comstock gold and silver. That's Montgomery Street between Washington and Jackson, and Jackson Street from Montgomery to San-some. But if you ever decide to go see the Elephant, by all means avoid the Poodle Dog Café. It's much too fast a place for a nice girl like you."

I stared at him in confusion. "Elephant? Poodles? Well, I suppose Polly and Gage would enjoy a circus—"

He guffawed at that. "I meant, to visit Frisco's night spots. Some are very wild, so—"

"Oh, please, Sam. You're talking to a lady from Virginia City," I said dryly.

"Nonetheless, you must especially take care to avoid Pacific Avenue and Broadway. Those are the borders of the Barbary Coast."

"The what? First elephants, now we're playing pirates. Or is it Free-booters?"

Sam grimaced. "Indeed, it's even more perverse. The Barbary crimpers shanghai sailors every night of the week. The love shops are full of madams and girls. And there's a woman at the Boar's Head Tavern who gets up on the stage every night with a large boar hog, and—well, but I can't speak fur-ther of that to a lady."

So I saw there was variety here to spare, in every line of work. And the shops were stocked with every product imaginable, not only from back East and Europe, but the Orient as well. It felt overwhelming, after the plain fare back in Nevada.

I'd thought men had rushed about back there. But in San Fran, the streets were crowded morning and night with carriages and rumbling dray wagons; the sidewalks with dark-suited, top-hatted men in such a mortal hurry, they trod on each others' heels and jostled everyone rudely. I kept expecting a fight to break out, but they were all in too big a rush to stop for one.

Every two weeks, when the big Panama liners docked, the City merchants turned out to settle up accounts. Hundreds poured out of their shops with sacks of gold slung over their shoulders. Downtown on a steamer day, the music of twenty-dollar coins rang out like brass bells through the open doorways, as they were stacked and counted and stacked again.

The people were a cross section of the world. Many were bog Irish, though pigtailed Celestials were plentiful, too. Each group had its own banks, groceries, and restaurants, and its own odd temples of worship. I stepped into one by mistake once, while looking for a laundry. A dismal brick cube set back behind the shops, dusty and dim as a bread box, lit by one guttering candle stuck on a table. Behind it sat a glowering carven god, striped red and yellow, surrounded by thin smoking sticks that gave off a musky perfume.

Coughing, trying to back out gracefully, I fell over a slight, elderly man bowing from his knees, face hidden in his hands. I stumbled back. "Oh dear! I'm so sorry."

He didn't respond. I fled in a hurry and found the laundry in the next street. A steaming, churning cauldron of sweating Asiatics in dark shirts and baggy trousers, laboring amid mountains of sheets and soiled linens. One thing there I noticed right away: The women wore wide-legged cotton trousers while they did their hot, sweaty work.

A week after we moved in, Sam turned up again, looking exhausted and miserable. I sat him down and poured cups of tea, and coaxed him to tell me what was wrong.

"Oh, it's the work," he said, dragging a hand down his weary face.

"Journalism didn't exhaust you so much in Virginia City."

"But San Francisco's enormous!" he cried. "And, anyhow . . ." Then he reluctantly confessed. "I am the one and only reporter on the *Morning Call.*"

Ah. Well that was a comedown he was clearly touchy about, on top of being exhausted. Early every morning he had to be in police court to record
the lawbreakings and arrests of the evening before. Then each night he had
to visit at least six theaters, stay a few minutes in each, then use that glimpse
of play or opera to write up a convincing full-length review.

"Nothing but fearful, soulless drudgery," he groaned. "It's worse than
slavery."

"I sincerely doubt that," I said. "And it sounds a cut above prospecting,
mining, or dueling. Safer, anyhow."

Still, I supposed this schedule might feel like bodily servitude to a man
who was always first to admit he never looked for more work when he could
get by with less. So a little later, when he put on his hat to leave, I murmured,
"Gage will begin at school soon. I've hired a Galway girl to clean and look
after Polly. I could even bring the baby along if I had to, to write up some of
the simpler bits. Perhaps I'll take in a matinee this afternoon. Did I tell you
I was once asked to write a column for the newspaper, back in Hannibal?
When I was still teaching."

He seized my hand and wrung it till the bones popped. "Becky! That
would be grand."

I smiled at his sudden energy. He kept hold of my hand and, still gripping it, leaned forward. I feared then he would attempt to kiss me. Fortunately the baby shrieked from the next room and the awkward moment
passed. But Sam seemed cheered by the prestige of having an assistant, especially a free one. In any case, I did not need more money. At first the figures in my bankbook had seemed to multiply mysteriously each month,
until I recalled why: I was still receiving, as agreed at the sale, one-eighth of
the profit from our old mine.

Sam took me down to the paper the next day. On our way upstairs we
passed a slight fellow with a prim mouth and well-cut suit, his floppy, fop-
pish tie a riot of turquoise and yellow.

Sam paused on the landing. "Mrs. Hopkins, may I present Mr. Bret
Harte."

Harte bowed to me, then Sam, twisting up his red lips.

"Bret used to be a type compositor upstairs," said Sam in an oddly subdued voice. "But now he's a Writer. Lifted from the fray and taken up by a
rich patron."

They both smiled, but it was clear they despised each other. Harte extended cool, thin fingers that barely brushed my own, then continued
down, crossing the lobby with a mincing gait that so suited him, it didn't
look affected or odd.

"His heart is merely a pump," whispered Sam as we resumed our climb.
"It has no other function."

I covered my smile with one hand. "And what does Mr. Harte write?"

"Oh! Nothing to speak of. Mere fictions about gold-grubbing." Sam
flapped a hand airily, the envy in his voice barely suppressed. "But *he* has
never soiled his hands with western dirt, of course."

"I see. Unlike you." And I wondered then if, beneath his affectation of
laziness, Samuel Clemens might not harbor some bigger ambitions than
regular newspaper work, after all.

THE FOLLOWING SATURDAY I was on my way again to meet Sam, wheeling
Polly in a perambulator. A pack of Irish hoodlums burst from an alley,
chasing a lone Chinaman too weighted down with packages of laundry to
run. One hefted a stone and struck the poor man between the shoulders.
Two city policemen standing on the corner laughed. Sam came up then, late
and breathless. "Why, what's the trouble?" he asked.

I told him, and he started after the Irish thugs. "Stop, you cowards!"

I grabbed his coat and reeled him back. "Sam, don't! They'd beat you
bloody, or worse."

"Yes, but . . . Oh, look! The poor fellow's gotten away."

The Chinaman had ducked into a nearby laundry. The toughs stood
outside, making faces through the glass, pulling their eyes into exaggerated
slits, sticking out their teeth like demented rabbits. At last they sauntered
off, slapping each other's backs. The policemen resumed staring into space.

That evening I was still livid. I wrote the scene up vividly, with great in-
dignation and many colorful, musical adjectives. Sam picked up the copy in
the morning, glanced through, and pronounced it powerful and moving.

" 'Bigoted Brutes!' 'Bullies of the Boulevard!' Splendid, Becky! You have a knack for the descriptive phrase."

"Do you really think so?" I was afraid I'd gone overboard, but he scoffed at any notion of toning my prose down. He scooped up the work I'd completed and stuffed it haphazardly into his bag, then dashed off to the office.

I looked for the column the next day, and then the next. When it didn't appear after a week, I asked Sam if anything was wrong.

"Hmm, I don't know. Been so busy, I forgot about it. Perhaps the pages fell off the compositor's desk, or drifted under a table."

He searched his desk, then all over the copy room, crawling on hands and knees around the presses and digging through baskets of articles and editorials, as well as the overflowing wastebaskets. Finally he asked the typesetter, and then the printer's apprentice. "Oh yeah, that," the ink-smeared boy said. "Mr. Barnes done pulled the galley proof and kilt the story."

"What! But why?" Sam cried.

They both shrugged and turned back to their inky labors. Sam hurried to Barnes's office. The owner was sitting at his desk reading rival newspapers, as he did every morning. Sam explained why he'd come, and demanded an explanation.

The owner tilted back in his chair and regarded him coolly. "Our *Morning Call* is the washerwoman's paper. The only one cheap enough for them to afford."

"Well, but aren't washerwomen poor and oppressed, too?"

"No doubt. But they are also Irish," said Barnes. "Like the hoodlums and police. More to the point, they are our bread and butter. And they hate Chinamen, their biggest competitors."

Sam told me he drew himself up tall and fixed Barnes with a withering stare. I feared next he would tell me he'd challenged him to a pistoling. "So you mean to tell me, sir, we won't publish anything which offends our readers?" Sam shot back. "Even if their rougher members break the law. Even if they molest or kill each other?"

Barnes stood and braced his hands on his desk. "I'm telling you we won't set out to rouse the whole bog-trotting hive. They'd pay us a visit and seriously damage this newspaper operation. To say nothing of our persons."

Sam paced my living room, muttering. "I'd have resigned on the spot, except I have an assistant to support. Lord knows, I can't leave you in the lurch. I'm a responsible fellow, really."

I stifled an incredulous laugh. "But Sam, you don't pay me. In any case, I have quite enough to live on. I'm not fabulously rich, but I've made some new investments. No, not in mines! I've bought land south of town."

He kept raking his fingers through his hair, making orange peaks and crests. I sank into a chair and watched him stride about, nodding and flapping his arms like an angry woodpecker. He didn't seem to be listening to me at all. "I told Barnes there's far too much work. Told him the same a year ago, but it always has to be his idea, doesn't it? He said, get an assistant on half wages. My wages, that is."

"Ah. And you have. So now you don't need me," I said, feeling suddenly crushed.

He whirled to face me again. "Oh, Becky, your work's too good for a Philistine like Barnes! You can write up anything and make it sound interesting. Even that damned frippery, that women's stuff. You ought to get a job where they would appreciate you as much as I do."

I thought about that. "Hmm. And even pay me?"

He flapped a hand impatiently, as if money were too inconsequential to mention in the same breath with writing. The one moneymaker he'd ever owned was the Missouri Rose mine, and he'd sold it to Sid. But he'd never thrown *that* in my face, and in that respect Samuel Langhorne Clemens was a true gentleman, despite all his protests to the contrary. Even though his Nevada stocks had gone bust, and he owed huge sums to every saloon, haberdasher, and café in town.

"Pay?" he said at last. "Well, yes. Yes, of course. But it's a dirty, foul, heartbreaking business, I warn you!"

By the next week he had an official assistant writing under him: Smiggy McGlural, a hulking boy he'd plucked from the counting room. McGlural's prose was terrible, his spelling and grammar enough to make a feral child weep. No one at the paper seemed to notice, though.

"Lord God, he's an idiot!" I complained to Sam after reading one issue in which Smiggy's ghost-work figured prominently. "Look at this. He can't compose a sentence more than three words long without destroying all the sense in it."

Sam nodded. "Exactly. He conducts my assigned work to perfection. Accomplishes the whole of it, in fact, with no need for me at all. My Emancipation has arrived!"

Barnes must have decided the same, because the following month he fired Sam. Word of the killed story about the Chinaman had somehow leaked out. The police heard of it and complained. Sam was mortified, for in all his misadventures up and down the Mississippi and across the West, he'd never actually been fired—he'd always resigned first. This new shame tore at him.

"Barnes was the guilty one!" he raged, pacing my carpet again. There should've been a smooth path worn through the cabbage roses by then, like a dogtrot. "Ah, but calumny always falls on the innocent."

I felt little inclination to argue that. "Yes, it does seem so at times. But you mustn't give up, Sam."

"All that keeps me going on is knowing that someday the guilty in this backward, ruffian town will be punished. With fire and brimstone, if there is any justice!"

I poured a glass of whiskey to calm him. He drank it off and asked meekly for another. I handed a second serving over as well. But by the end of that week I realized offering liquid sympathy had been a mistake, for each evening he arrived expecting more kind words and the same medicinal dose. "Sam, you're drinking too much," I said at last. "It won't help a bit."

"True," he mused. "But it's easy enough to stop. I've done it a hundred times."

After that I locked up the bottle, though it was a hard thing to do to an old friend. His credit was so bad by then, he couldn't show his face in any saloon in San Francisco. But I didn't want to assist in the ruin of another man, when this time it would be so very easy to avoid it. Sam took the loss of his medicine well, perhaps because he knew his own weakness. Or perhaps because I still fed him.

POLLY AND GAGE and I experienced our first earthquake the following year, in 1868. A notable shake, it tore the pediments from downtown buildings and sent folks scurrying into the streets. The newspapers covered the whole thing with detailed engravings. The most memorable was in the *California Police Gazette*, which Sam brought round a week afterward. It featured the fat backside of a well-known politician as he raced from a Portsmouth Square brothel. He was accompanied by two Soiled Doves, and dressed only in his nether garments. We laughed over the rough, apt engraving, so different from the refined illustrations in *Harper's Weekly*.

But in general, Sam's spirits failed to lift, and his creditors grew more threatening. He decided to move north to Tuolumne with an old friend, to prospect. Three months later he turned up again at my door, hair snarled, coat dusty, clothes reeking and ready for the ragbag. Until he removed his drooping hat, I thought he was a bummer, and had been about to send him around to the kitchen door for a hot meal.

Of course, he was broke. I heated the beef and cabbage and potatoes that Kate Rooney, the girl I'd hired, had made the day before, and set a heaped plate before him. "Fling a lip over that, Sam," I urged, trying to sound offhand and cheerful.

He dug in, wolfing the first bites. His face reddened when he glanced up and saw me watching. So I got up and put dishes in the cupboard, until he'd finished and paused to drink some buttermilk. "All right, now tell me," I said.

He leaned back. "It was a lovely cabin on a verdant hillside, overlooking God's own hills and forest. The grassy solitude of this paradise—"

I sighed. "Sam, for Heaven's sake."

"All right. It was an empty hive, a town in decay. A handful of old miners scratching at the dirt like a decimated flock of aged, demented chickens. They forgot the world, and it returned the favor. I've spent a melancholy exile in a ghost town."

He was completely busted, with no lodgings, so I took him in. He slept on a cot in Gage's room. After searching for weeks, he landed a position with the San Francisco edition of the *Territorial Enterprise*. But he seemed to have lost his taste for the news business. He stuck the job out for five months, though, and paid off his bills. I thought he'd be happy just to be out of debt. Yet he moped around, depending more and more on me and the children to cheer him up. It got quite tiring for us.

Finally he heard of a great opportunity: The *Sacramento Union* wanted a correspondent to sail to the Sandwich Islands and write back a column of letters. "It's an excellent journal," he exulted. "And liberal with its employees."

"I certainly hope so," I said, wondering if he'd ever settle down or be happy with what he had. But it was just as well he was leaving. Any guest is pretty much at the end of his host's good will after five days, never mind after five months. By then my neighbor next door, a busybody cinched in whalebone and yards of black bombazine, stood in her front window morning and night with opera glasses. On the street she'd asked me outright which of my children was Sam's.

"Oh, *those*," I'd replied, after a moment of consternation. "I'm afraid I had to leave them back in Nevada. The five of them simply don't get along with these two."

The day of Sam's departure we trailed down to the wharf to see him off. The Pacific wind whipped our hair and skirts and coats. Gage wore a new blue sailor suit he hated to take off, even for bed. I carried Polly, who clutched in one plump, grubby fist a tiny paper flag, which she tasted from time to time. She batted her coppery lashes at anyone who paused to admire her curls, a heartbreaker at age two.

At the foot of the gangway, Sam turned to me. I was touched and alarmed to see tears in his eyes. "I'll never be able to repay all your kindnesses, Becky—here, and back in Nevada. Nor will I ever forget Sid or Mary or Huck or Laura . . . or—or poor dead Tom, or any of the old gang. But I'll make it all up to you someday. I'll tell the whole world about the people who made me what I am. Mark my words, I will!"

My eyes watered then, too, especially at the mention of Sid and Tom. Just the month before, I'd had Sid's coffin exhumed and forwarded from Virginia City. I'd put up a marble marker in the local cemetery for him, and one for Tom as well. But even with two headstones to visit, it seemed impossible they could both be gone.

I bit my lip and nodded, then patted Sam's cheek. He caught my glove and, turning it over, planted a kiss in the palm. Then bounded up the gangway, carpet satchel swinging. And with a jet of pale smoke and a piercing blast of the whistle that made Gage hold his ears and Polly shriek, Sam and the *Ajax* cast off for the Sandwich Islands.

We stood for a long time, waving. Gage claimed he could see his uncle Sam clear as anything standing right on the forward deck, but I couldn't make him out. Not to be able to catch one last glimpse of our old friend felt wrong. I feared it was an omen.

I CONTEMPLATED SAM'S ADVICE about a career in journalism. Perhaps it was time to do more than mourn the men I'd lost, and care for my remaining children. I wanted to write stories, yes. Though not, as Sam had put it, "That women's stuff."

We lived well in San Francisco; I didn't need to earn our bread. Yet I'd already begun to feel stifled by the respectability of the place, the strictures and prohibitions that always grew along with a civilized city. I was certainly not contemplating another move, for we were fetched up against the farthest shore already. But the farther West I'd come, the more advanced I'd expected things to be. Alas, this was not the case. True, Chinese women walked about in loose black trousers, but there seemed an official ban on White or Colored females wearing pants on the street, or even for riding. I began to dream of flouting this insane rule, though in my nighttime fantasies more often I ended up strolling Sutter Street with nothing on at all.

On a cool fall morning after Sam's departure, I rose and pulled on a beloved, tattered pair of Sid's old denim trousers to wear while transplanting lilies. I walked out into my backyard and began to dig in the beds. Through the fence, my snooping neighbor and her Monday whist party spotted me. From the stifled shrieks and catty whispers, I might've been posing in a nude tableau of After the Fall. I turned my back, digging furiously, hoping I sprayed their cucumber sandwiches with good black California soil. It appeared I could not find a satisfactory outlet for my peculiar ambitions, even at home.

That was the push I needed. The next day I collected all my unpublished work into a portfolio and took it downtown, past the newsboys scrambling and hooting around delivery wagons. First I called on the editor of Jim Fair's bedsheet-sized *Alta California*.

No sale. I was first mistaken for a Temperance lady, and then—when I cleared up that ridiculous idea—escorted firmly to the front door by the assistant editor, having failed even to reach the rarefied empyrean of the publisher's office.

At the understaffed *Morning Call*, I wandered the empty corridors until I reached the pressroom, where I tripped over a grubby lad delivering a sloshing growler of beer to the pressmen. Sam's old boss, Barnes, refused to see me. He was obviously still in thrall to that word-butcher Smiggy McGlural. "Philistine," I shouted, and left.

Next I called at the *Chronicle*, which kept offices at the corner of Kearny and Bush. Sam had told me the staff there styled themselves after the whiskey-drinking, gun-toting editors of the Comstock. I felt I could deal handily with such fellows now. I knew its founder, Charles DeYoung, had died of lead poisoning with his own revolver only halfway out of his pocket. His son at least listened politely before turning me out.

At the *Territorial Enterprise*, editor John MacKay did listen to my proposal quite attentively. When I finished, he rose, telling me to wait there in his office. I felt encouraged, thinking he'd gone to find a contract form. He came back with a horse whip. "This is my answer to suffrage-obsessed females," he said. Then drew his arm back and cracked the thing so near, it caught in the hem of my skirt. A crowd of men gathered in the doorway to gape.

I'd seen his ilk and worse in Nevada. So I leaned down and took my time disentangling the whip from the shredded cloth. Then I straightened and looked him in the eye. "You, sir, are as foolish and blind as you are melodramatic. I pity your wife her lifetime indenture."

"I have no wife," he said through clenched teeth.

"I'm not surprised," I snapped back. "Regarding your insinuations about my political views, I am a Missouri native. We care nothing for the buncombe of politics. As for your pitiful display, I've endured a battlefield, a stagecoach robbery, and the lethal dangers of a mining boomtown. Experiences I doubt you, or any of your sniveling associates here, would hold up under."

He stared a moment, then whipped around to glare at the men behind him. Was it laughter I heard? In any case, the audience soundlessly melted away.

I rose with as much dignity as I could muster and swept past the panting, red-faced MacKay. His lackeys huddled down the hall, whispering and staring. I pushed through, knocking one fellow's green eyeshade askew. I'd just reached the front door when someone touched my elbow. I spun to face him with my portfolio upraised, prepared to flog the next idiot who tried to impugn my character or intellect.

The slight young fellow who stood there flinched when he saw my upraised arm. "M-Mr. MacKay would like to see you again, ma'am," he quavered. "I believe he was f-favorably impressed with your—your work."

Back in MacKay's office I sat again, smoothing my skirts and trying to look uninterested. He cleared his throat and gazed at me. "I've run off quite a few fellas with that whip," he said at last. "But even the ones who didn't bolt weren't as cool as you."

"A whip is a terrible instrument," I said, swallowing back nausea as I recalled the blacksnake my grandparents' overseer had wielded so many years ago. "Yet it's a paltry threat when you've faced cannons and rifles, and dragged bleeding men off a field."

"Hmm, I see. Well, then. Only seems fair I look over what all you brought in. As a courtesy."

I handed over the portfolio. He opened it and began scanning pages. "Hmm," he said once. And then, "Ha! That's a good one."

He finally closed it and looked up. "You have a certain way with prose, Mrs. . . ." He glanced down at the portfolio again. "Hopkins. Yet you are a woman. And I don't approve of women in a man's job—"

I braced my hands on the chair and began to rise again.

He held up a staying hand. "—but I'm also a businessman with competitors. As far as I know, none has a woman writing for them at the moment."

"I'm not a dancing pony, Mr. MacKay."

"If I could find one that could hold a pen, I'd hire it, ma'am. To survive, a newspaper must beat out the competition, Mrs. Hopkins. And I aim to do that."

So a few moments later I found myself shaking hands with a whip-wielding oaf I didn't much care for. Now that I had the job, my knees suddenly felt like India rubber. What did I know about journalism, anyhow? I glanced at my new colleagues as I promenaded back through the pressroom. One was paring his dirty nails with a penknife; another had his head down on his desk, openly snoring, a bottle half gone at his elbow. The place reeked of segar smoke so strong, my throat closed up. What a sty men alone made of their lives!

Well, I thought, *how difficult can it be?* Sam had claimed I had a talent for prose, and so did MacKay. In the event, I'd most likely be assigned to dole out pickle recipes and quaint proverbs, or patronizing columns on feminine hobbies, paired with engravings of suitable arts and crafts. What I wanted was to write more Chinaman stories. To expose injustice: the corrupt workings of criminals, vigilantes, and the shadowy powers above them guilty of even worse crimes. What else could I do, now, to avenge Sid?

When I received my first assignment, my spirits sank. I was to cover a flower show at the Exhibition Hall downtown. I took the streetcar down. The echoing hall held a surging tide of chattering women in fancy afternoon dress; twice I was nearly impaled on the business ends of parasols. The sweet miasma emanating from the thousands of blooms made my eyes water and my nose run. After a half hour I grew bored with the comparative virtues of pyramid-style arrangements versus fountain shapes.

In the middle of a talk on the proper way to dry hydrangea blooms, a scream echoed through the hall. Then another. Welcoming any diversion, even murder, I rose from my chair and pushed down the aisle, treading on feet but not stopping. I pushed through the thickest part of the crowd and saw, before a lush display of hothouse orchids, two women rolling on the floor in a tangle of skirts, shrieking and pulling each other's hair. After a moment's hesitation, I waded into the fray. With help from other brave souls I pulled the two scufflers apart. "I'll go find a policeman," I said.

Both women burst into tears. The older one begged, "Please don't, Mrs. Hopkins."

She looked familiar. "Do I know you?"

"I live on the next block," she whispered. I recognized, through her dishevelment, a handsome older neighbor I'd bowed to several times on the street. "My husband's the chief of police. And this—this is his—" She gestured at the younger woman, who flushed but stared at me defiantly. I understood immediately.

I rose and shouted, "Everyone move on now. Give the poor woman some air. Her—her friend and I will see to her if she falls into a fit again." The crowd of women drew back, shaking heads and whispering behind their hands, and gradually drifted away.

"Now tell me what happened," I said.

The police chief's wife gave details while the young woman sullenly pinned up her hair again. Each had been admiring one side of an orchid arrangement shaped like the Liberty Bell, then recognized her rival through the blooms. Whispered insults had led to blows.

My mind raced as I left the hall. What sort of story could I make of this? Yes—something about how the mighty are fallen. If I wrote it up, a scandal would ensue. Though I doubted a lawman would lose his job over this, in a city that hosted the Barbary Coast. Perhaps a poor marriage would be ruined. If this sort of man was in charge of the law in Frisco, no wonder the police stood on street corners and laughed to see Chinamen abused by gangs of toughs.

Then I realized that in all the excitement I had not told them I was a reporter.

At the office the next morning MacKay listened to my story. "Well, we can't print that."

"Yet you don't look disappointed," I said.

"I refused once to pay 'protection' to a couple of Chief Miner's boyos. Since then we've had two burglaries and a smashed press. Now, what did I say when I hired you?"

"That you must always beat the competition."

He winked. "This is how things are done in San Francisco. We won't print it—but I'll personally call on the Chief and tell him I fear we are bound to." He leaned forward and pumped my hand over the desk. "Good for you, Mrs. Hopkins," he said. "Good for you!"

I left the offices on a cloud of mingled confusion and high spirits. It seemed I would not after all embarrass two abused, misguided women, and yet the adulterer toying with them would still feel the shoe pinch. MacKay's approval, though it was not for any high reason, felt like stepping into a warm bath after a long, exhausting day. As if the choking dust, the sticky sweat of banging my head against unthinking rules from childhood on, was falling away. I might not be able to beat men at their own game. But I saw now that with a few modifications I could, by God, play it just as well.

Twenty-four

GATHERING NEWS AND WRITING ARTICLES, and caring for two growing youngsters made the days and nights very full. I still missed Sid and Tom, but not in that sharp, unbearable way, as before. Now I could turn over memories like cherished daguerreotypes, remembering and admiring each scene without grieving. I even missed Sam from time to time.

At three and a half, Polly was learning to read. She watched my finger as I ran it along under the words, and devoured books as I had, falling on each new one like a starving person onto bread. She loved to page through, chortling over the illustrations. Gage was quieter, more serious. At eleven he'd already decided to be a lawyer. "Like my father," he said.

When I looked at my children, I sometimes felt confused. How could Gage be so much like Sid, and Polly so much like Tom, when everything I knew about their beginnings and heredity said it should be the opposite?

In the afternoons our house was happily noisy, with me the eye of the storm, as I doled out biscuits and milk and apples to small outstretched hands. I did this quickly so I could rush off and close the door to my study. And then, write like mad and hope the children didn't set fire to the curtains, or tie up the patient, forbearing Kate Rooney before I'd finished scratching out my next article or review.

Fortunately, it was not at that noisy time of day when a knock came on the front door that changed our world again. Otherwise I might not have heard and answered. I was at my desk, beginning a measured but witty response to a letter written to the editor of the *St. Louis Democrat.* Mary had clipped the page and sent it to me the week before. Each time I read the text, I ground my teeth. One paragraph in particular drew my eye, and my ire.

> Women, go your ways! Seek not to beguile us of our imperial privileges. Content yourself with your little feminine trifles—your babies, your benevolent societies and your knitting—and let your natural bosses do the voting. Stand back—you will be wanting to go to war next. We will let you teach school as much as you want to, and we will pay you half wages for it, too, but beware! We don't want you to crowd us too much.

It was signed Mark Twain.

"Knitting!" I cried when I'd first read it that morning over breakfast. "Half wages! Lord God, I'll kill Sam Clemens!"

"Mama, calm down," said Gage, who was preparing to leave for school. "Maybe Uncle Sam was joking. Stop talking to yourself so much, or we might have to lock you in the attic."

"Why shouldn't I talk to myself? I have a perfect right to my own opinion."

"I didn't say . . . Oh, never mind. I'm late," said Gage. He downed his milk and coffee, and rushed off to class, while I muttered and slathered orange marmalade on Polly's toast.

Later that morning I was organizing my response in a letter. Just as I lifted my pen again, I heard two sharp raps at the front door. Of course, some inconsiderate fool would choose this moment to pay an unannounced visit, I thought. "Kate?" I called hopefully over my shoulder. "Oh, Katie! Get the front door."

Silence. Then I remembered I'd asked her to go out and pick up a beefsteak and some turnips at the market, for dinner. "Damnation," I muttered. How did they always know when I was writing? I threw down the pen and stalked to the foyer. If it was a bummer, I'd give him a nickel to go eat elsewhere. If it was my black-clad neighbor on some busybody sortie, I'd boot her backside all the way down our crooked street.

I wrenched open the door. A boy younger than Gage, wearing the red uniform of Western Union, stood on my stoop.

"Oh," I said, backing up a step, my anger draining away. "Is that—for me?"

He held out an envelope. "Yes'm. If you be Mrs. Hopkins."

I stared at the yellow envelope, then grabbed it and tore it open, hands by then shaking with fear. No one in our family sent telegrams unless the news was very bad indeed.

The boy wiped his nose on his sleeve and cleared his throat. I groped behind me for the dish on the hall tree, then thrust a fistful of coins into his hand. Without waiting to be sure he was out of the way, I slammed the door.

It was from Mary. I closed my eyes, silently uttering a prayer. I hadn't that many relatives left, and didn't want to lose any of them. Was her consumption back, and so bad, she wanted to prepare us? Were the children all right? Lord God, was O'Brien—? I opened my eyes and read the thing at last. As it turned out, nothing could have prepared me for it.

BECKY

HAVE LETTER FROM FINN AT CHAGRES RIVER GATUN PANAMA STOP TOM ALIVE BUT VERY ILL STOP URGENT WE GET HIM HOME STOP CAN YOU SEND SOMEONE FROM THERE STOP

MARY

It couldn't be—this flimsy bit of paper promised the impossible. Tom was long dead, drowned in the Mississippi after the steamboat explosion, back during the War. I'd watched it happen, had seen the big wheel walk over him, had even been partly to blame. And yet . . . who would bother with such a hoax, pretend to be Huck Finn, and wire such news?

The writing wavered and merged. I blinked and read it again and then, with a supporting hand on the wainscoting, backed into the parlor and sat abruptly on a hassock.

Tom, not dead. But where had he been all this time? I wasn't certain about the location of the Chagres River. But Panama, on the Pacific coast, was where California-bound gold-seekers had embarked ever since the Forty-niners. They crossed the isthmus via railroad and mule, then picked up steamer passage north for the Pacific leg of the long trek to the California fields, or the frozen northern wilds of the Yukon.

So he was a prospector? If not, he'd be one of the few males around who wasn't, or hadn't at least dreamed of it. Men sought gold all the way from Baja California to Sitka in the Russian-owned north. Some wandered the wilderness for decades like biblical prophets. When their clothes fell to pieces, they wrapped themselves in stinking furs. Forgot wives, children, parents, country, and finally their own names. Forgot everything but the lust to keep digging and panning. Had Tom come to this, too?

But none of that mattered. This flimsy scrap handed back years of a lost life, a passage to a country where Tom and Sid and even little Tyler still moved and breathed. Where the dead could be seen and touched and spoken to.

I decided then not to send some hired male hand. If he was still alive, if it was truly him, then I'd do it. I'd rescue Tom Sawyer myself.

I RUSHED TO BUY MY TICKET that afternoon. The agent looked at me dolorously over rimless spectacles clouded with overlapping fingerprints. "'At's a hunnerd twenty fer a first-class berth."

I pushed a check across the counter. He licked his thumb, picked the slip up, and examined it, then squinted hard at me. "Miz Hopkins, is it? The one what writes stuff for the *Enterprise*?"

I braced myself. "Yes. Yes, I am that lady. Now may I have my ticket?"

"Hold your horses. I got to tell you, it were a good job on that write-up about the Temperance ladies. I don't hold with spirits myself."

"Oh," I said, relaxing. "Did you really think—?"

"Now, when you dock in Panama, there'll be a mad rush to the steamship office, see. As all the folks waiting to go back north tries to buy passage and board."

"I've ridden steamers before."

"Not such as this. They'll knock you down easy as look at ya. Back in '55, folk hadda wait a month to get a berth. And that was doubled and tripled up in the staterooms. Not s' bad now. Still, better get you a prepaid return."

So I bought two return passages: one for me and one for Tom. I would not acknowledge that he might die before I got there. That he might already be dead. For that way lay sleepless nights, and I'd need to be strong and healthy to find Tom Sawyer and get him back safe to the States.

Two days later, Gage and Polly and Kate Rooney went down with me to the docks. My eleven-year-old son was tight-lipped and silent. He disapproved of my going off alone on this mission. Gage was a homebody—I suppose he'd had enough travel on our journeys from Hannibal to Virginia City to California. Polly, on the other hand, cried and clung to me and begged to go, as if she knew exactly how far away I'd be in Panama.

At the ticket office, Gage dropped the larger of my bags with a thump. "I don't even remember this man, this *Sawyer*," he said, kicking the bag testily. "Who is he to us?"

Your father, I wanted to say. But Gage had only known Sid. I had no right at such a late date to take that cherished image away, and replace it with that of a stranger. Even if he was a man I'd loved since I was twelve, and the reason Gage was here on Earth.

I patted his shoulder. "He's family, that's all. We look after our own. You know that."

"Well, I don't like it." But he didn't pull away.

I checked to make sure I had tickets, money, and quinine. I kept whispering to myself a saying our Kate was fond of. "All will be well, and all manner of things will be well."

"Mama," said Gage. "You're talking to yourself again." He blinked and bit his lip. Polly burst into renewed wails, and Kate hugged me so tight, I could not breathe.

The SS *Uncle Sam* was at the pier, already boarding. A side-wheeler with a hurricane deck and three masts, a boat Tom would no doubt approve of. She looked tired, but this was no time to be choosy. I supposed making the run between San Francisco and Panama for twenty-three years would wear out anybody, human or machine.

The warning whistle blew. "My dears, I must go now," I said. "You'll deliver my pages to the *Enterprise,* won't you, Kate? I can't let Mr. Twain off the hook, even if I am leaving the country."

The children hugged me as if they'd connived not to turn me loose at all. I kissed them and tried to look sad for their sakes, but the truth was by then I couldn't wait to be off. I gently broke away, gave each one last squeeze, and flew up the gangway. I rushed to the upper deck, clung to the rail, and waved down at them. I kept at it hard as we pulled away, even after I was sure we must be out of sight. If anything went wrong on this trip, I did not want their last recollection of me to be like the one I still carried of Sam Clemens. I didn't want them to think that, once out of their hands, I hadn't bothered to turn to look back, and perhaps not miss them at all.

The steamer held berths for five hundred passengers, and every one was filled. Folks were stacked in the hold, some even sitting on deck, since every bench and deck chair was taken. But I'd paid top dollar for privacy, so the extra berth crammed into my first-class cabin was unoccupied. I tossed my valise on it, but didn't unpack. The cabin steward had set up my steamer trunk in one corner.

Uncle Sam carried livestock as well. Chickens, turkeys, geese, ducks, lamb, pigs, and cows; those last for milk, I supposed. The others were to be butchered. The smells wafting from that area of the deck were overpowering, especially after a few days out. But the food was certainly plentiful. The dining parlors hadn't been designed to hold large numbers, so meals were served continuously, day and night, to be sure everyone got fed.

I awakened the first morning from a dream of being rocked by my mother in the old chair that sat in my first bedroom. The sea was lifting and lowering me in my berth as the boat rolled and wallowed. I pulled back the little curtain over the round glass port and gasped. Overnight, the ocean had taken over the view. Whitecaps flashed. Waves tumbled over each other out on the deep blue. My first time at sea, and I felt sudden happiness. This lovely, wild water was carrying me to Tom.

A sea voyage can be relaxing if you're taking things slow. However, I was not. After a few days, the sight of water became monotonous; the time dragged. I looked forward to any diversion then, even a stomach-turning squall. I read all my books, some twice.

When we docked in Panama City, I rushed down the gangway. "Send my trunk on to French's Hotel," I called back to the purser.

A room was reserved for me at French's, which was supposed to have a lovely café. But when my grilled snapper with red peppers and saffron rice arrived, I felt too unsettled to eat. The din of voices all around was annoying. I didn't want to sit still and dine and wait. I felt like a prisoner, despite the luxurious accommodations. I wanted only to be on my way, but no help for that until morning, when a Panama Railway train would depart for Gatun, and beyond.

I left my dessert untouched and went to the front desk for my key. The clerk, a pleasant young Negro man in a white vested suit, smiled at me. "Good evening, *señora*. Have you a request, or a question?"

"Yes. Do you get as many people as this always?"

He shrugged, pale palms upturned. "About six hundred a day come through Panama, *señora*. I never count."

"Have you ever gone to Gatun?"

He looked puzzled. "Why would I want to?"

My turn to shrug. "I suppose you don't know where the hospital there is located, then."

"Hospital?" He hesitated, biting his lip, as if trying to decide how best to break bad news. "Well, there really isn't one, *señora*. They do get much fever there, so I advise quinine, and plenty of it."

"Thank you. But what do white folks . . . I mean, travelers . . . do if they get sick?"

"Mostly they stay away from Gatun. The locals bring their sick here, sometimes. We have a good hospital in Panama City. But any soul sick in Gatun is most likely nursed at home."

Then how would I find Tom? I thanked him and went up to my room. I rang the bell to order a bath, then wrestled with the mosquito netting that hung from a ceiling hook over my bed. What an infernal contraption it was! Later I was glad, though, for I heard the little demons buzzing outside it every time I woke.

When the locomotive pulled into the station the next morning, I was on the platform. This train looked larger, or at least wider, than those I was used to back home. Perhaps because Panama was smaller, and the buildings not so tall. I chose the second passenger car and boarded.

Up to then I'd fancied myself broad-minded about such things, but to be honest it felt strange to sit in a car with so many dark-skinned people. For one thing, they all seemed to know each other. All were speaking rapid Spanish around me and over my head—a language I'd picked up only a few words of since we'd come to California. Finally I decided it was a blessing I couldn't understand them, nor they me. Instead of trying to make dull travel conversation with a stranger, I could daydream of what it would be like to see Tom again after so long.

We chugged slowly through thick green jungle, then over a swamp, then through jungle again, stopping at villages to unload locals and mail and crates and barrels. The air was hot, damp, and heavy, too thick to pull all the way down into my lungs. Just breathing was a job of work. No wonder they had so many fevers, with poisonous miasmas rising from all the stagnant swamp water and decaying plants. I was glad I'd secured plenty of quinine in San Francisco. I'd hesitated at first to take much, thinking to save it all for Tom. But it would be foolish for me to get sick. Then who would get us home?

The tracks ran along the Chagres for many miles. We finally crossed the river on a large echoing wooden bridge. Gatun sat on the west bank, the shadowy, ruined walls of an old Spanish fort brooding over it. I hiked uphill past a wooden church with a modest priest's cottage behind it. Then, a one-room school where giggling children of brown and white and yellow ran and played together. The nuns there must've decided that the Radical Experiment had worked. They ought to send word of it to the Sisters of Charity in Virginia City.

A dozen shops lined an unpaved street made of holes covered with a velvety layer of cocoa-colored dust. With my poor bits of California Spanish, I could decipher that marketplace eggs were going four for a dollar, an outrageous sum even back in San Francisco. One homeowner came out and offered charmingly, in mixed English and Spanish, to rent me a hammock in his garden for two dollars a night.

"*Gracias,*" I said, smiling and backing away. "I shall seriously think about it."

Beyond the market lay bamboo huts topped with pyramids of palm thatch, and wooden shanties that might've been transplanted from a mining town in the States. The clerk was right; I saw nothing resembling a hospital. Those I passed on the street were white and black, a few Chinese, perhaps former railroad workers. This, too, seemed reminiscent of Virginia City. But the constant, humid heat did not.

I was still walking, blotting face and neck with a hankie and wondering how to ask where to find Tom, when a tall bearded white man stepped out of a tin-roofed shack. I stared as he hiked away, for I knew those broad yet hunched shoulders, and that long, loping gait.

"Huck!" I cried. "Wait!"

He flinched, then turned and grinned when he saw it was me running toward him. "Why, Becky Thatcher! Had a feeling they might send you."

At first glance he looked just the same. Then I noticed silver threading his tawny hair. "How are you, how's Tom doing, where in the world is he?"

He stepped back, as if so many questions staggered him. "Well, I'm good, thanks," he drawled. "And he seems a mite better than yesterday. Chagres fever's bad, all right. But he got the worst case I seen yet."

"Huck!" I grabbed his arm. "Tell me—where *is* he?"

"Oh, yeah. Sorry." He jerked a thumb at the shack. "Right in there."

I'd imagined so often, during my journey, rushing into a big clean hospital to get to Tom. Knocking down nurses and doctors if I had to. Yet now I stood in the dust with my arms hanging limp. I was afraid. Not that Tom was about to die, since Huck had just said he was better. It was more that I'd rushed so hard to get here, I hadn't had time to think what it might actually feel like to see Tom again. Our last meeting had been more than five years back. I'd got used to thinking of him as gone from this earth. To see him now would be like raising someone from the dead.

"Wait," I whispered. But Finn already had a grip on my arm, hauling me up the steps and into the dark little house. It was hard to see anything at first, for the day was so bright and the interior so dim. "Back this way," said Huck, leading me into the gloom. A smaller shuttered closet in back stank of stale sweat and sour, dirty clothes, and the ammonia reek of an unemptied chamber pot. As my eyes adjusted, I made out a crude table, a bed, a dark form reclining on it. "Tom, look who's here," said Huck in a jovial tone.

"Open these shutters, Huck," I said. "It stinks in here. We need fresh air."

He shrugged. Now, at this late date, he seemed annoyingly unflappable. "Tom was shivering with the ague. But then he gets the fever again. It's hard to keep up."

He unlatched the hanging shutters and pushed. They swung up with a screech of rusted iron, and he propped each open with a stick. Sunlight oozed across the floor, toward the bed where Tom lay turned away from us. His hair was much longer, but the same red-gold color. When the light reached the bed, he stirred and flung an arm over his eyes.

I sat carefully on one corner of the mattress. "It's Becky, Tom. How are you?"

I'd imagined in my daydreams that he'd look the same. He dragged the arm slowly away from his face, which the last time I saw him had been full of life—the skin tanned, his boyhood freckles faded but still visible. I recognized the snub nose, the strong jawline. But now his freckles stood out like walnut stain on yellowed linen. The forehead and cheekbones were definitely Tom's. But the skin stretched over them seemed too thin, too taut, tailored for another, smaller person. His cheeks were hollow. But his eyes were the worst: the bright blue faded like wilted, sun-bleached violets.

"Becky?" he murmured, like a sigh of wind through dry branches. "Is it really you?"

I looked away and took a deep breath, just in time to see Huck quietly steal out. I turned back to Tom, laying a hand on his forehead. It was clammy, and he was shivering again.

Suddenly his eyes widened. "The Injun," he gasped. "He followed you here!"

I glanced over my shoulder involuntarily. Of course, no one was there. Tom was out of his head with fever still. "That was just Huck," I said, trying to make my voice as soothing as possible. "Now, tell me—how can Tom Sawyer still be in bed at this time of day? Here—can you sit?"

Oh, he felt so light! It was far too easy to help him up. Heat rose from his body in waves. I wedged a flat, grimy pillow behind him. Leaning close, I saw some of the spots on his chest were eruptions, stains of blood under jaundiced skin. I understood then my carefully transported quinine might do no good. How I wished I had Doctress Hoffmann with me! What did I know about treating exotic airborne miasmas?

"Huck!" I called, and he came running back. "It's not malaria, I think, but some eruptive fever."

"We c'n take him to the hospital in Panama City, then."

I thought of the treatment Tom would receive there. They'd purge him with calomel and salt water. Lance and bleed him until he passed out. Sweat him. Leech him. Blister his back with hot glass cups. Who knew what other exotic, diabolical tortures the doctors of this foreign place might add as well? One look at Tom told me he'd never survive medical attention. If this was the yellow jack, it was a miracle he was still alive at all.

"No. No hospital, Huck. I'll care for him here. When he's stronger, I'll take him back to California."

Finn hesitated, then nodded. He didn't argue just to be contrary, as he would've done years ago. That was as big a change as Tom's appearance.

Over the next weeks Huck and I took turns sitting up at night, first dribbling water down Tom's throat, then a thin broth made from scrawny roosters haggled down at the open-air marketplace. Huck had a job of sorts guiding wealthy English hunters up the rivers, but he took over the watch from me some days. When he did, I slept on a cot in the front room, while Huck made a pallet on the floor by Tom. It was as if our youthful games, the playing at being warriors or knights or explorers, of making campfires and sitting up all night had been in specific preparation for this.

But one of the most surprising things was that Huck and I could talk of days past, and of what best to do, without the old animosity getting in the way. Without bringing forth that stubborn unwillingness that I saw now had really been both our selfish natures. Because each of us wanted Tom for ourselves alone.

"For years we thought he was dead, you know," I told Huck that first day. "The papers said he'd been killed in that explosion on the *Madison*."

All those years thinking I was the one who'd caused it, only meaning to save him. When I closed my eyes, I could still see that poor doomed figure struggling down in the water. And the horrible, relentless way the huge paddle wheel had swung right over him.

"He near about was," said Huck. "He almost got drowned. But he made it to a mudflat downriver. He thought back then it might be a blessing if you'uns thought him dead. Him being connected with Reeves, a wanted man and all."

And I remembered a time even further back when the two of them had disappeared on the river, having run away to an island to be pirates. Thereby grieving Aunt Polly and Joe Harper's mother terribly. And then reappearing like the Second Coming, in the church, at their own funeral.

"He give the federals the name of a dead man when he got captured later at Nashville," said Huck. "They sent him up the river to Alton. He got early release by agreeing to pilot steamships again. But then we bolted for Cuba."

"Cuba? My, you've been around. Even farther than I'd imagined."

Huck ducked his head and kept whittling on a stick of some soft reddish wood. "We never settled long in one spot. After Cuba, it was back to New York, where the steamships carry Yankees with gold fever down to Colón."

"That's where he fell ill?"

"No, it was in Cruces. Malaria then, I expect. He got up and went back to work. But this new thing has near about killed him."

In this way, we shared Tom equally at last, through steaming days and nights when the air smarted with mosquitoes, and our music was the shouts and drunken singing from a little cantina down the way. Sometimes I feared we would not be able to hold on to him. But gradually he began to improve. Soon he could sip broth himself, then sit up. The red spots on his skin started to fade. When he finally began to make jokes, it was like old times. He asked a million questions about Hannibal, about Mary and her new family. I finally told him of Sid's death, and he lay back down, looking peaked again.

"I'd of made them pay for it," he whispered. He tried to push himself off the pillow, to get up, but his body fell back. "But just yet I'm none too strong."

"I know. That's what I told myself then, too." I blinked back tears. "But you'll be better soon. Isn't it odd how we've all changed? Do you know, I've got a son nearly twelve, and a little girl, too. And back East—I mean Missouri, it's all East to me now—that seems like a lifetime come and gone. I recall the War as more of an adventure, instead of the bloody horror it was. Isn't that strange?"

Tom nodded. "And yet you ain't changed one bit." He called over to Huck, "She looks just the same, don't she?"

Huck cleared his throat. I could feel him behind me, twisting his mouth and rolling his eyes. "That's right. Purty as a gold piece. Say, I'm going to see about some supper. Scrambled eggs all right with you two?"

I felt as embarrassed as a girl with braids and skinned knees pointed out for comment in a school yard. Because I knew well enough my hair was beginning to gray, and that I was not quite so slim as I'd once been. There were lines around my eyes and mouth now that stayed even when I wasn't squinting against the sun.

"You needn't flatter me," I said, more sharply than I meant to. "I'll take care of you anyhow, Tom."

He looked surprised. Then nodded to himself, as if confirming some detail he'd long suspected. "You don't take a compliment no better now than you did twenty years ago."

Maybe he was right. About that part, at least. So we let it go.

TOM'S ATTACKS OF AGUE and fever abated. He started pottering about the tiny house, then slowly walking around the village. He accompanied me to the open-air market in the square. Its stalls held fruits and vegetables I often didn't recognize, strange-looking fish, and stacked baskets crammed with cackling hens and turkeys. Standing amongst strings of dried red and green peppers, inhaling the smoke of grilling meat, I could not believe I was actually shopping for groceries with Tom Sawyer. And what's more, he took a keen interest in the color of the melons, in the freshness of the silvery fish laid out for our perusal on plaited palm mats. One morning I stared openmouthed as he haggled like a penny-pinching housewife with a pipe-smoking Choco Indian woman over a bunch of bananas. That alone was worth the price of a ticket to Panama.

Four weeks after my arrival, we bade Huck good-bye and boarded the train back to Panama City. There we took the steamer north. Once on the boat, I had plenty of time to worry less about Tom, and more about what would happen once we reached San Fran. What would Polly and Gage think when they saw him? Should I tell Tom about Gage now, and vice versa? Perhaps he'd rather go back to Hannibal. Though I'd heard from Mary steamboating was dead there and had been ever since the War. Most everyone shipped by rail these days, back East and out West as well.

There was something else, too. Of course there was. But I did not let my thoughts venture in that direction. It might hurt too much; it might hurt more folks than just me. And who knew anymore whether or not such a thing was even possible?

Twenty-five

BEFORE WE LEFT PANAMA, I'd wired to Hannibal about Tom's recovery, and also a message to Kate Rooney and the children so they could meet our steamer at the Embarcadero. The trip up the coast was much the same: lots of water all around and plenty of time on my hands. Tom was still weak; he slept in his cabin a good deal and came out mostly for meals. The SS *Uncle Sam* finally crossed San Francisco Bay, belching enveloping clouds as it approached its slip at the Davis Street landing.

We waited until last to debark, skirting a herd of pigs noisily rooting the grass and dirt around the waterfront. Kate and the children were waiting. Polly squealed and rushed up to throw her arms around my knees. Gage hung back, looking much taller somehow, and very dignified. He kept shooting suspicious glances at my traveling companion.

"This is your uncle Tom Sawyer," I said. "He'll be staying at our house while he recovers from his illness."

Kate shook his hand and welcomed him warmly. She'd told me the day I hired her that she had thirteen brothers and sisters back in Galway, so a crowded house was nothing to her. Polly took to Tom right away, staring shyly as if a romantic figure from a fairy-tale book had stepped out of the pages to greet her.

Her brother was much warier. Gage spoke politely, but his stiff back and disapproving expression made it clear he didn't like Tom at all. Over the next few days, as I got back into my home and working routine, Gage scowled, made comments under his breath, and once or twice was outright rude. He seemed to resent any time I spent making Tom meals, or taking him outside, or speaking to him at all.

After a week I drew my son aside. "Lord God, Gage," I said. "This is still my house. When I'm dead and it belongs to you, you may entertain only the people you like. But until then you must accommodate my annoying whims."

"But, Ma, the man's not respectable," he insisted. "You can tell by looking at him. His clothes, for instance."

I stared at my son. If only he knew who he was rejecting so out of hand! But perhaps it wouldn't have mattered. For who was this lean, tanned stranger to Gage Hopkins?

I felt like crying, but that would do no good. I laid a hand on his arm. "Gage, Tom and another friend hid your grandfather when he was in trouble. They helped me find your father during the War, and bring him home. It's true Tom Sawyer doesn't dress and talk like a Montgomery Street banker. But I've known him all my life. He's your own . . . your own relative, after all. And he means a great deal to me."

A stony look was the only response I got. Very well, then; I decided I must finally tell the whole truth. "Gage, you *must* be kind to him. For you see, he's your—"

"My what?" he interrupted belligerently. Yet he looked more curious, and less angry.

But again my nerve failed me. How could I just blurt out such a thing? What if this was the worst possible time to speak, and that long-concealed truth only made him hate Tom even more—for Sid's sake? And hate me as well.

"He's actually . . . your uncle, blood kin. As I just said. And we have more than enough of everything to go around here: Food. Beds. A house. Even love. There were times when we had little of these things. Will you try to remember that? Then maybe you can gladly share with him."

Gage pressed his lips together as if he had a good deal more to say, but had thought better of it. At last he nodded, and went off to study for an examination.

Tom spent those first weeks resting and eating, for he'd lost a deal of weight. Presently he began walking. First down the block, then all the way to the Embarcadero. He went with me, then finally on his own, to watch the ships come in and the draymen working. He said it reminded him of Hannibal. Some days he brought back fresh-caught fish for dinner, or something odd he wanted to try, like abalone. After the first week, I didn't tag along much, for I still had work to do for the newspaper.

I took Tom downtown the third week to show him the offices of the *Enterprise,* and introduce him to Mr. MacKay. Tom seemed impressed with the operation. "If only Sammy Clemens could see all this! Why, he'd be green."

"If only," I agreed, all but biting my tongue. We'd had no letters from Sam since he'd boarded that steamer for the Islands. I knew, however, that he'd moved Back East, to New York, and that he wrote letters and columns in the eastern newspapers. And that he'd visited the Holy Land, for he'd recently published a book about that trip with the amusing title *Innocents Abroad.* I kept meaning to get a copy.

Mostly I stayed out of the way, intent on not crowding Tom. It was hard at first. I wanted to mother him as if he were one of the children. He didn't look delicate on the outside, but by then I'd come to understand life was more fragile than bone china. Against all my hopes and expectations and desires, I'd had to let go of Tyler, then Sid. Tom, too, had been lost, then found, then nearly lost again.

We are often called on to stand such tragedies, before we leave this earth for a higher plane. Two months after we returned from Panama, I received a letter from Mary. She was so very sorry to tell me, but my parents were dead. The Judge had driven their carriage into the path of an oncoming train. He'd apparently gotten too deaf to hear the warning whistle.

I sagged against the hall table. It was all too easy to visualize: my father impatiently flicking the buggy whip; the train shrieking a warning; my mother too polite and well-bred to speak up and point out his last, fatal error.

I was leaning there still when Tom returned for lunch. He took one look at my face, then stooped to pick up the letter that had slipped through my fingers to the floor. He glanced at it, then put an arm around my shoulder and led me to the divan in the drawing room.

"Lie down a spell," he said, but I shook my head.

"I'm not going to faint. It's just that, the last time I saw them in person, each of them, I wasn't—I didn't—" I had to stop there. How could I explain it? That I'd disappointed them and failed to understand them, as they no doubt had never understood me. And now there would be no more chances.

"You did the best you could," he said. "And it may be, so did they. That's all a body can ask."

I wasn't convinced. Somehow I'd thought one day there'd be a reunion, a reconciliation. That I'd return as a grown woman who embodied all that each of them admired. Or they'd come here and see for themselves. Though each time I'd extended an invitation, my parents had politely refused to make such a long journey. "I should've gone back," I said.

He nodded. "But you didn't, and they didn't, and now all you can do is raise up two young'uns, and do a little more good in the world. Like—like you done for me."

Words are no balm when you feel guilt over things you can never put right. I went up to my room and lay on the bed and stared at nothing in particular. I heard the children come home, and Kate making dinner. And I finally fell asleep.

I woke later, in the dark, to see Tom standing by my bed. I sat up quickly and began to struggle from under the covers, groping for my wrapper. He'd never set foot in my room before, and I assumed the worst. "Tom, what's wrong? Are you ill?"

"Not a bit," he said. "I was watching you sleep."

This rattled me. I was apparently capable of vanity, or at least humiliation, even in the midst of grief. That proved beyond a doubt my bad character. I felt how swollen and red my eyes must be, and the tangled rat's nest of unbraided hair slipping over my shoulders and down into my collar.

The springs squeaked as he perched at the foot of the bed. "Becky, I can't recall if I ever thanked you, back in Gatun. For saving my life."

He was changing the subject to spare me, to take my mind off my loss. "No need of that, Tom." I shook my head. "A family takes care of its own."

"Is that what we are, a family? I only mean, I'd like to know how we stand. I ain't so full of myself as to think I could make up for what all you lost. But I wondered, how do you see me—as a brother? Gage and Polly call me Uncle."

"Well, I had to explain you somehow. And at very short notice."

"Guess that's true." He grinned, and for a moment in that dim room he was again the twelve-year-old miscreant who'd wooed me by walking down our street on his hands. Of course I didn't see him as a brother! Or even just a friend. I never had.

When I didn't say anything else, he stopped smiling and looked downcast, perhaps at his change of identity. Or his change of place, the way he'd been absorbed into our already organized and settled lives. He could not be expected to know that, inside me, neither his place nor his identity had ever really changed at all.

It seemed only natural then to throw back the quilt, to get up and go to the chest of drawers across the room. I fished around in a mess of gloves and stockings and scarves until my fingers touched cool, rounded brass. I carried the old andiron knob over and slipped it into his hand. "I wonder if you recall this?"

He looked down at it. When he raised his head again, I thought I saw the glint of a tear. "Don't worry. I took good care of it all those years," I added.

"It came from my folks' cabin," he said, voice so thick, I could barely understand. He cleared his throat and began again. "Becky?"

"What, Tom?"

"I guess you wonder why I stayed away so long and never let you know I was still living."

"We all thought you were dead. But then, when I got the telegram . . . of course I wondered."

"I don't know that I can explain it right," he went on. "It's just, after we met again at the camp, I knew I still wanted you with me. But I was no good for anyone, not then. And you had Sid." He paused and took a shuddering breath. "He was the better man. He always was."

"He was a *different* man—," I began, but Tom laid a finger across my lips to stop me.

"Don't try to slap a coat of whitewash on me now," he said, smiling at his own joke. "When I got out of Yankee prison, I figured to disappear before they discovered the name I'd given wasn't mine. Then it seemed best to stay lost, since I never settled in one place long before itching to move on. And if ever I saw you again, I knew I'd try to make you come along. That's no life for a woman."

"Perhaps not," I said, determined not to take offense at what no longer mattered to me. "But events have thrown us together again."

"Becky—"

I pressed my fingers over his lips then, to hush him. I was afraid he was going to ruin things again. To go on apologizing for everything: for our youthful quarrels; for leaving me on my wedding day; for simply being Tom Sawyer. I could not have stood that. So I drew him down onto the quilt. And then no more words were needed.

At last I was not sneaking him into my bed as if my parents and Trenny were in the next room. Nor was this the cold, rocky ground of a secret camp in the Ozarks, where a hundred men might wake and hear us. Poor, dear Sid no longer stood innocently between us. My bed was my own, wide and long, the feather tick made up with clean, fresh-ironed linens. It hadn't been bought by my parents, or used by some other couple before us. And we would not have to part in the morning, or even earlier—if we didn't wish it to be so.

Imagine my surprise then when Tom shook me awake later and insisted we get married right away. "I don't intend to go slinking around like alley cats, or have nobody be shocked."

I laughed. "By what? That a man and woman of nearly forty live in the same house?"

"You know what I mean," he said. "The children got to know where we stand. Otherwise they might try to evict me, and they'd be in the right. I'm not after your money, neither. I'll sign a paper saying it all goes to them."

I did know what he meant, of course, and he'd made some good points. So I agreed.

The wedding was small and quiet. We invited only Polly and Gage, and a couple of friends. Of course, we sent word to all the relations left back in Hannibal. None felt up to that long a journey, but Mary and family sent their fondest regards.

We took our honeymoon in Honolulu, because Tom wanted to see the Sandwich Islands. He said he'd read an article about them once, and yearned to get there ever since. I agreed it sounded lovely. I didn't tell him, until we arrived in Honolulu, just who this travel writer named Mark Twain really was.

TOM WAS STILL PLAGUED occasionally with bouts of tropical fever. But he was well most of the time, and for recreation rebuilt an old rowboat to keep at the wharf. He sometimes took tourists out fishing, or to look at the harbor. I begged him to avoid the dangerous bar there, but he only laughed. "If you ever get bored with charter, you can start a fence-painting business," I joked, though I was half-serious.

But sometimes he'd get a distant look, at which I worried. Was it past journeys he was thinking of so longingly, or fresh ones? He never said, and I forbore to ask. I might not like the answer. After two marriages and moving thousands of miles, I'd come to understand that though I might *want* a man, I did not, strictly speaking, require one. If Tom left me again, I'd be sad and very sorry. But I told myself I would not die of it.

I searched out things to interest him. Such as getting up at six o'clock of a morning for breakfast at the Cliff House, where we could view the beach early, while it was still warm. Afternoons, the cold wind off the Pacific could be bitter. The old mansion was reputed to host wild parties. I'd seen shocking engravings in the *Police Gazette,* and the recollection of those scenes gave the place a pleasantly wicked air.

By the time we finished our coffee, and a beefsteak scantily garnished with potatoes, the mist that hangs low and heavy for an hour or so after sunrise had lifted. The broad veranda was packed with eastern tourists. We leaned out to look down on the sleek, glistening sea lions heaving themselves to and fro on the slick gray rocks, barking and trumpeting whatever news marine mammals find of great import.

"Here we are," said Tom, putting an arm around my shoulders. "Taking in the view of some mighty strange creatures, even stranger than ourselves. And there across the water, all of China and Japan, maybe even the Pirate Queen of the Cannibals are looking right back at us."

"I wonder what they see?" *No doubt of it,* I thought. *He has got the urge to wander.* Well, I'd not try to hinder him, though it'd be the devil of a problem to keep silent. And hard—oh, very hard—to lose him again. You may believe this or not, but Tom made a good father. He was much more patient at nearly forty than he'd been at fourteen. Yet he was in some ways still the same boy who'd played Pirate King and Cowboys, and buried prized marbles under a spell to lure all his lost ones home. One thing you may be certain of—he had no trouble entertaining youngsters.

THE AFTERNOON OF OUR THIRD WEDDING anniversary, in 1876, I pulled out the heavy silver candlesticks, and the good linen napkins I'd bought but not yet used. Then Kate set the table for our celebratory dinner. We'd have rack of lamb with mint jelly, and tiny new potatoes, and a lemon sponge cake for dessert. All Tom's favorite dishes, prepared by the new cook I'd engaged. The smells wafting from the kitchen were so heavenly, my stomach was growling by four thirty. Tom came in at a quarter to six and rushed up the stairs hiding a parcel behind his back. I hoped he hadn't bought some expensive geegaw—gold jewelry or a lace mantilla. The week before, I'd spotted a heavy silver segar case in the window of a shop on Sutter Street. The silversmith had engraved our initials on it, entwined. A reminder, I thought, in case he ever strayed from home again. It was extravagant, too, but at least a useful object. I would in any case be overcome with delight at whatever Tom had picked out.

After the main course, Kate took our plates away and then poured coffee. I produced my tissue-wrapped parcel for Tom and set it on the table.

"Oh, presents!" cried Polly, clapping. She loved gifts and enjoyed watching others unwrap theirs almost as much as getting her own.

Gage stood, scraping his chair back noisily. "I've got reading to do for school."

"But you haven't asked to be excused," I pointed out. *And must you be so sullen, even tonight?* I nearly blurted out. But I supposed he did—especially on this night.

"Ah, let the boy go, Becky," said Tom. "Such grown-up stuff as this, well, it can't be interesting for him."

At that, Gage sat down again and folded his hands on the table, as if he'd suddenly changed his mind.

Tom winked at me and got up. He came around to my side with a squarish object wrapped in brown paper, tied clumsily with string. "It ain't much compared to all the trouble you've gone through for me. But it seemed to me a thing you'd want to own."

By then Polly was bouncing on her chair. "Open it, open it!"

I took it from his hands. "Oh," I said faintly. "Oh, my." For the rectangular parcel, with its hard, definite corners, felt so familiar. So much like the moment on my front porch, fifteen years past, when Sid had asked me to marry him. His gift had been a book, too. That well-thumbed volume had traveled far, and sat on my desk still.

"Mama," begged Polly. *"Please."*

I looked up. Tom was regarding me anxiously, as if he feared he'd made a mistake. "Feels like a book," I said, smiling. "The best gift of all."

He relaxed and sat back. "Go on, then."

I blinked back tears as I undid the string, struggling with the knot longer than necessary so I could hide whatever might be in my face just then. At last I could slide the book from its wrapper. I turned it over and gasped.

The volume itself was unremarkable: clothbound, without fancy leather trim or gold embossing. But first the title, then the author's name jumped out and jerked away my breath.

The Adventures of Tom Sawyer, it said. And underneath that: *by Mark Twain.*

"Now, ain't that something?" said Tom. "Soon's I saw it in the store, I had to get it. What d'you think that fool Sam Clemens is up to now?"

"Goodness. I have no idea," I whispered. "How intriguing." I forced a smile, and set the book carefully aside, like some clockwork armament that might go off in my hands. Then I leaned across and handed him my carefully wrapped package. That fine engraved chunk of silver seemed a remarkably mundane gift next to his. As Tom began to work impatiently at the gilded paper, I politely passed the book around the table for everyone to admire.

"Please, may I read it?" Polly begged.

"Perhaps after I have," I said. Lord God, what all might lie between those covers? Just as in life.

Gage eyed the volume with suspicion, then opened to the title page. "This is a book about—about *our* Tom Sawyer?" For once he didn't act as if he were choking on the words.

"Yes, yes," cried Polly, cheeks crimson with excitement. "Like those tales you read to me about Kit Carson, and Colonel Fremont, and Buffalo Bill. Only this book looks much fatter, and fancier, and—"

"Gage!" I'd forbidden him to read such trashy dime novels to his little sister anymore. All the scalpings and shootings and ambushes gave her nightmares.

"Sorry, Ma," he said, though he didn't sound repentant. He cast a quick, speculative glance at Tom. I could hear the thoughts churning in his head: *A whole book, about him?* But would this fictional portrayal raise Tom in his estimation, or lower him?

When it finally came back to me, I turned the thing over and over. I had no earthly idea what Sam was up to, but aimed to read the thing right away and find out.

I took *Tom Sawyer* upstairs when we turned in that night, and kept the candle by my side of the bed burning so long, Tom complained. So I got up and went downstairs, lit the lamp, curled up in a chair, and kept reading. I only paused every now and then to say, "Lord God!" or grit my teeth or clamp my hands over my eyes in horror. For in his story, Sam had used the town, and all of us—but he'd told everything slantwise.

". . . AND LISTEN TO THIS," I demanded as Tom forked up the last of his breakfast eggs. "He's got you chasing me around the schoolhouse for a kiss. '. . . *By and by she gave up and let her hands drop; her face, all glowing with the struggle, came up and submitted.*' He says here that I cried and cried, merely over you liking Amy Lawrence." I slapped the thing down on the kitchen table. "I never stood in a corner and hid my face in a little white apron. I never *wore* a damned apron! That's not at all how it happened."

"That's true," Tom agreed, washing Kate's cinnamon-sprinkled toast down with coffee. He pulled a face; my diatribe had made him forget to add sugar. "But would it be so bad if—?"

I refused to listen if he was only going to defend Sam. *Submitted.* For

Heaven's sake! "No, you be quiet, Tom Sawyer! Listen to this one." I flipped forward to another page I'd dog-eared. "Here it says I planned a Sunday school picnic and didn't invite you, out of spite. And when that didn't make you jealous, he writes that I had *'what her sex call "a good cry."'* Then it seems I threw you over for some fancy boy from St. Louis named *Alfred.*" I ground my molars in rage.

"Oh, Becky. You're jumping around like Aunt Polly's cat, the time I give her the painkiller—"

"Well, that's in here, too. He's told everything. But it's all wrong!"

Then Tom frowned. "Did you say a picnic? He don't mean the one . . ." He trailed off, no doubt thinking of that terrible time in the cave, and how it had broken us to pieces, afterward.

I snapped the book shut. "You chickens scurry off to school. And Gage, be sure to walk your sister to the door. The headmistress tells me Polly's coming in late with dirty knees and grass stains on her skirt. They had to send one of the older girls out to find her last week."

Polly giggled. "I was only picking flowers. We should have our lessons outdoors."

Gage huffed. "Come on, Poll. You'll make me late again."

"Don't slam the front door!" I shouted, just as it banged behind them.

Tom pushed his plate away and scrubbed both palms over his face. "Does Sam say anything about . . . that night in the graveyard? Or the one in the cave?"

"He says Injun Joe stabbed the doctor. That you testified and saved Muff Potter. And that Joe escaped and hid in the cave meaning to kill us. That I cried a lot. And that you saved me in the end."

He bit his lip and grimaced. "Well . . . I s'pose it somehow might read better that way."

I jumped up and began clearing the table, though it was really Kate's job, clanging silverware and stacking plates. I had to move around, to do something. "Oh, Tom. Sam knew the truth. He was there!"

But when I returned from carrying the dirty dishes to the sink, Tom's chair was empty.

It would be no use going after him. I put Clemens's "novel" aside and went to the front hallway. Though the mirror said otherwise, I still felt like that same Becky Thatcher who'd climbed trees and raced up Holliday's Hill. The one who'd waited at my bedroom window late at night for a cat's meow, in order to climb out and follow two rascals around Hannibal after dark. Tom and Huck and I were still those people, only older. We knew things about each other no one else did. Yet now any person who knew his letters, who had a few dollars in his pocket or a card for a lending library could read about us. Everyone would believe they knew all our secrets, when in fact they knew nothing at all.

Maybe I was worrying for nothing, though. Perhaps only a few copies would sell, and then the book would disappear into quiet obscurity. After all, who could possibly care about the silly doings of children in such a small Missouri town? Still, I found it hard to understand Sam's feeding off our lives as if they belonged to him. And yet not even telling the truth, as if we were simply grist for some money mill. I decided then and there I would not speak to him again. If ever I saw him on the street and he approached, I'd cut him dead. Assuming he even cared enough to try.

Tom came in very late, and crawled into bed smelling strong of whiskey. That was unusual. But it had been an unusual sort of anniversary. He scooted close, and I pressed myself against the length of him. He felt too warm, but he often did, thanks to his time in Gatun. I didn't ask where he'd been.

"I love you, Becky," he said. "But you deserve better than an old bummer like me."

"I shall be the judge of that, Mr. Sawyer," I said, in such a good imitation of my mother's voice, we shook the bed frame laughing. "I wouldn't trade you for all the dime-novel heroes in the West."

"You might want to sleep on that," he said. "My knees ache something awful tonight. It's the damned San Fran fog."

And I thought then, with some relief: *A man with incipient rheumatism is not likely to go looking for far-off adventures.*

Oh, how wrong I was.

AS EVERYONE KNOWS, Sam's book did not fade away or become obscure—quite the opposite. As Mark Twain, he became celebrated, and Tom closely followed his budding career. Tom read the novel that bore his name over and over, as if it might somehow end differently.

"Why do you keep on?" I asked one day.

"Makes me recall how it was before the War. I think I appreciate those times more, now," he said. "Back then I had no idea we were having so much fun, with so little."

I didn't mind Tom's preoccupation with the novel, because when he wasn't reading it, he brooded. He took to scanning the newspapers like a man searching for something in particular.

"Listen to this," he said one mild April evening as we sat in the parlor after dinner. "Thousands of Injuns've left some of the reservations, around the Black Hills. Guess they'll send the army in after them. Don't seem right, somehow."

I squinted, trying to darn a sock by lamplight, which was proving difficult. "You mean, for the army or the Indians?"

"Well, they was here first. And look at all the room here out West." He laid the paper down. "Why can't we just split up the land and be done with it?"

I snorted. "My guess would be, something to do with gold."

He laughed. "Maybe so. Why don't somebody just speak up and knock heads and make 'em shake hands?"

"Tom." I dropped the wretched, lumpy sock in my lap. He'd been ill all week with a fever. He still looked drawn, his skin yellowish under the light. What was he suggesting with all this talk, now?

"I'm only reading about it, Becky."

Still, day after day he followed the happenings. I asked him once, half-serious and half-teasing, if I'd heard someone practicing with an old pistol in the backyard.

"Sure! They'll be longing to enlist me," he said. "I'm a prime specimen."

He might say such words in jest, but probably didn't believe them. "Why don't you go downtown and find out?" I suggested at last. "Can't hurt to ask."

His laugh turned into a cough. "Ah, I'm past all that."

But I could see the wheels turning behind his eyes, so I insisted he go see the next day about enlisting with the California cavalry. That took only a little persuading. Clearly he'd been thinking about it all along.

He was politely turned down, as I'd hoped. Counting when we were twelve and I'd tossed away the prized andiron knob right in front of him, and a few years later when I'd sat on the ledge of a church window in my wedding finery to taunt him, this was the third time I'd intentionally hurt Tom Sawyer. I had retrieved and kept the andiron knob, though. And now I felt I still had his best interest at heart.

"The enlistment officer there, he's strictly by the book," Tom complained that evening over dinner. "Says he can't help me. Says the officers who decide such cases are all in Idaho, or Nevada, or some such place!"

"Oh, my. That's too bad," I said, thinking the opposite.

He laid his knife down. "So it's good I saw this-here article. They got a need for extra cavalry and infantry at Fort Ellis. In the western Montana Territory."

"Montana? Lord God, Tom. That's so far!"

"I know it. But I can hop a train at least partway, then present myself in person. Maybe I ain't fit for regular army, but they'll still need teamsters and packers."

I stood so abruptly, my plate tipped, spilling fried halibut and peas all over the white cloth.

He rose, came around the table, and kissed my cheek. "And I got you to thank for the idea," he said. "Not many wives would be so liberal. Sit down, and I'll tell you all about it."

I did so reluctantly. I had meddled again, and look at the result.

"I'm not so decrepit as these army boys think. And I got a thing most of 'em don't—years of experience."

I gathered his hands in mine. "But you don't have to go." Lord God, I thought. The very words I'd said to his cousin, my first husband. To Sid, so many years ago.

"I've had a good long run as a homebody, Becky. Soon I'll be too old to stir from the house. And this time, the U.S. Army will pay my way."

I squeezed my eyes shut and forced myself not to speak or shake my head. I'd promised myself when this day came I would not forbid it. I'd vowed to get along with or without Tom. But how bitter it was to keep quiet!

I pulled my hands back, got up, and walked to the window. "Why am I always waving men off to war? Even now, when we should be past such foolhardy doings."

"Ah, Bec. I'll be home before you miss me. Any skirmish won't last more'n a month."

"That's what they said the last time. It's what they always say! You know that."

But when Tom Sawyer got a notion to do something, he up and did it. That much had never changed. The next afternoon I tagged along as he went from shop to shop. I watched dully as he purchased a new revolver, a money-belt, a pair of field glasses, a blanket, a canteen, riding boots, saddlebags.

I stepped over to a rack of canvas dusters. These at least looked practical. "Here, Tom. You ought to have one of these."

I saw how his face shone as he compared and tried on and dickered. Sid had looked the same way when he had outfitted himself in similar fashion for the Missouri Rose mine. I believe it's partly that shiny new gear, all the fancy, special gadgets they covet and treasure, that gets men into such scrapes.

When we went to bed that night, he fell asleep at once, like an exhausted child. I lay awake, staring as wind-tossed tree-shadows moved across the ceiling, alternately thinking of ways to derail his plan, and telling myself I had no right to try. Then I must have drifted off, for I woke in the gray hours to Tom stroking me and kissing my neck. I put my arms around him and for a while forgot about what would happen when the sun came round again.

But afterward, as we lay side by side and quiet again, I began to sob. He raised up on one elbow and rubbed my shoulder. "What is it, Becky? Don't grieve yourself into a fit. I told you, I've had a good long run here."

"No." I shook my head and looked away, out the window across the room, where a gun-smoke gray shroud of fog concealed the sleeping city. *No, not long enough. It will never be long enough for me,* I wanted to say.

He gripped my chin and turned my head so I had to look at him. "What is it, then?"

"Tom," I whispered. "I wanted to tell you, many times, but I was always a coward. And then—"

"Tell me what?"

"About Gage."

The lines around his eyes deepened. "That he's mine, you mean?"

My mouth dropped open. "But—you mean . . . you knew it?"

"Saw him on the street, years ago, in Hannibal. Like looking at myself back in time. Sure, I knew. Just never figured if you did."

I pushed away tears with the flat of one hand so I could see his face. "But I should've *told* you. Both you and Gage. And . . . and Sid."

His turn to look surprised then. "Sid never knew?"

That, I could not swear to. My face burned with shame at my cowardly history. "Maybe, but I never told it. I wanted him to love Gage as a father should. I was afraid that—"

"No, you did right. I was the one in the wrong. Can you forgive me?"

"Of course," I said. "You were no more to blame than I was. We were young then."

After a while we both dozed off again, worn out by love and confessions and impending separation. Just before dawn Tom jerked awake, rousing me as well. He rolled over and squeezed my hand. "It's too late to change my ways," he said so low, I could barely make out the words.

"I know."

"But, Becky—do you think . . . I'll be forgiven the other thing? In the cave, and after."

"You mean Injun Joe. Don't worry over it now. God surely will forgive you anything, Tom."

"Ah, Him," he said. "I meant, I was hoping you might."

"I do, I have! Long ago." It wasn't the unvarnished truth, but I couldn't burden him then with recrimination, when he might not return to be wholly forgiven.

I pulled him close, to keep him near me a little longer. So that, come morning, I might be able to let him go away from us without a fuss. As I had with Sid—and he had been restored to us, in the end. I tried to hold that thought, and sleep.

AFTER A SPARSE, GLOOMY BREAKFAST, all of us—Polly, Gage, Kate, and me—took a hansom cab to the train station with Tom to see him off. I felt as bereft and numb as that day in Hannibal when Sid had read to us from the newspaper, and told us Tom was dead. The rumor of his demise had been exaggerated, then. But out on the plains, Tom would be out of what I considered as his element—water—and face-to-face with his greatest fear. If going out to the Indian wars had to do somehow with Injun Joe, I couldn't figure what actual good it might accomplish.

Perhaps he's on his way to the great and final Adventure, I thought as he hugged each of us in turn. I wondered if we'd both survive it. At last he pulled away and boarded. The whistle screamed, and we waved until the train chuffed out of the station. Then the four of us walked back out onto the street. For the first time I noticed what a lovely warm day it was for early May. But it would not be so mild where Tom was going. Had he packed enough clothing? Undoubtedly not; he was only intent on the chase. On running off like a wild boy.

"Ma?" said Gage, touching my elbow. "Can we stop and get some pie at—"

"Pie!" I cried. "Is that all men ever think of, besides traipsing off to a war? Leaving us at home, frightened witless every moment that you're sick, or hurt, or just plain getting killed!"

I stopped there on the sidewalk, clapped my hands over my face, and sobbed.

"Whist, whist," said Kate, stepping up to pat my arm and calm me. "The good Lord will see him back safe and sound, Missus. You'll see."

Oh, she didn't understand. At that moment I was not a bit free and independent, as I'd promised myself. Instead, I was angry. At Tom, for going on another wrongheaded fool's hunt. At myself, for not stopping him somehow. And yet I knew well enough—indeed, had known for decades—exactly what the man was like. The miracle was I'd been able to keep him at home as long as I had.

IN EARLY JUNE, Tom sent a letter. He'd arrived at Fort Ellis in Montana Territory, and was to leave shortly with the Second Cavalry, marching east as a pack-train driver under Col. John Gibbon. There they were to meet up with several other detachments—and that was all he knew, as yet. He spoke of the pleasure of sitting around a big fire with a bunch of men again, in the outdoors. Of the beauty of the territory. His letter sounded cheerful. And why not? He didn't know, as he wrote to us and got outfitted and acquainted with his string of pack mules, what was to happen next.

Two weeks later, the troops he was attached to met up with Generals Crook and Terry. And then, with Gen. George Custer's Seventh Cavalry. And they all pushed on together, to the banks of the Little Bighorn River.

Twenty-six

I T'S STRANGE HOW WE DIVIDE up our lives into lists: of things to do, of things to buy, of resolutions to transform ourselves into the people we think we most want to be.

I grew used to checking lists back during the War. In July of 1876 I found myself doing it again, anxiously perusing the names of dead and wounded published by the army after Custer's Massacre. The Seventh's dead had been hastily identified and buried on the spot by the troops who arrived later— or so the newspapers said. Tom had not been a soldier but a civilian, a mule-train packer attached to the Second Cavalry. But they'd taken casualties, too. So I read the printed lists, and felt relieved when the name Tom Sawyer did not appear on them.

Days later, as I was reading an updated roster of casualties in the news-paper, I realized my mistake. The lists of the dead I perused were almost en-tirely made up of soldiers, with the exception of one forager and one reporter. Tom was a civilian hired to serve the Seventh Cavalry, a mere teamster. So unless some surviving officer was a great stickler for detail, my husband's name might never appear at all.

I could only wait, and wait some more. In the end, we must bear the very things we fear the most. No need to wonder why. You might as well ask why night must fall, or why fire has to be so damned hot.

When no word came by November, I visited the marked but empty grave in the plot I'd bought at the Old Presidio Cemetery. I'd put a marker there for Tom long before I'd received Mary's telegram saying he was alive but sick in Panama. Should the army find his body now, and send it to me, I'd need only have the stone carver add the true date of his death below the earlier, mistaken one. For if anyone had cheated the Reaper more than once, it was Tom.

Or maybe, I mused, gazing at the carved memorial cross—maybe I should take him back to Hannibal. He could be buried in the Baptist Cemetery near Aunt Polly and Tyler.

Two months passed, and all that time no telegram arrived. You might think that was hard of God, a bitter pill to swallow. But I began to look at it differently, as a gift. A way to let Tom slip away from us without that inevitable decline all we mortals must endure. I could believe, eventually, that he still lived, was still adventuring somewhere. And that every now and then he thought of us with affection and regret: *It's too late to change my ways. But oh, how I loved them. And I stayed as long as I could.*

KATE ANSWERED THE DOOR one day at midmorning, then ran to call me from my office. I'd given her orders to show no one in.

"But you must come, Missus," she panted. "They ain't quite—the usual."

I got up slowly, unwillingly, torn from the midst of another piece for MacKay. Two men stood on my front piazza, though I'd been expecting no one. Both wore starched white shirts and dark suit coats. The taller, light-haired one swept off his hat. "Mrs. Sawyer?"

"Yes?" I glanced at the other. Shorter, darker skinned, slender. He looked so much like a younger, cleaner, less hopeless Injun Joe, I nearly cried out.

"I'm a missionary and lecturer, ma'am. Herbert Hill Wescott." The tall man handed me a visiting card.

Lord God, I thought. *A missionary.*

"While working on a history of the Black Hills, I met John Red Horse, here. Now, ma'am: Do I have the honor of addressing Mrs. *Tom* Sawyer?"

"No," I said quickly, thinking they were tourists who'd read Sam's novel.

In the four years since Tom had vanished, we'd had those turn up before. "What do you want?"

"Do you recognize this case, ma'am?"

I was about to shut the door on them, thinking a sales pitch was coming. But when he held out his palm, in it lay the silver segar case I'd given Tom for our third anniversary.

I snatched it up and looked at it, turning it over. A few dents in the back, the soft silver had been scratched, but our engraved initials were still clear. I opened it, and a folded paper fell out—the letter I'd written to Tom answering the one we'd gotten while he was at Fort Ellis. "Where did you get this? Yes, it is my husband's—it's Tom's."

"Mr. Red Horse met him, I believe, at the Little Bighorn."

My hands were trembling so I almost dropped the case. "Come in, won't you? Please."

In the sitting room, I rang for Kate. "Bring tea," I told her. "For the three of us." She backed out fast, shooting a frightened glance at John Red Horse. I showed him to Tom's favorite old chair by the fireplace.

I discovered he spoke no English, but Mr. Wescott told me he could act as a translator. "Mr. Red Horse insisted he must bring the segar case to you, Mrs. Sawyer. He is now a student of mine, a very promising one, and I agreed to accompany him."

"So he knows of Tom's fate?" I barely had the breath left to ask, "I don't suppose he is . . . alive?"

Wescott frowned. "I take it you have not seen him. Well, then, I suppose . . ."

I tried to steady my voice. "In any case, please tell me what you know."

He turned to the Indian and said a few words, a language like a slow song. And the man who looked so much like a younger Joe began to speak.

Wescott translated rapidly. "At the time of the battle, an encampment of Mr. Red Horse's people was in the path of troops headed to the big encounter at the river," he said. "Apparently some of the Seventh's troops came upon it first."

My Indian guest looked from Wescott to me, as calm and interested as if he were following the conversation. Did he understand us at all? If he'd seen

Tom, I wanted to ask him a million things. Yet it seemed I could not, directly. He spoke again.

"Mr. Red Horse is Oglala Sioux," Wescott told me. "He was twenty-four that summer. He planned to walk under a courting blanket with a young woman at the Cheyenne encampment."

The young man sat silently a moment, perhaps musing on the Cheyenne girl. I was trying to be still and listen, but couldn't. "What does that have to do with my husband?"

Wescott smiled. "It does have a bearing, later. Mr. Red Horse says there was a scalp dance one night to celebrate a victory over General Crook, whom the Oglala called Gray Pox, on the Rosebud River the week before. Many Oglalas were sleeping late. Mr. Red Horse woke hungry, and as she fixed him a meal, his grandmother told him, 'Today attackers are coming.' He asked her how she knew this, but she said nothing more."

I poured out tea as the story continued. Wescott said that Red Horse finished breakfast, caught his pony, and rode over to the Cheyenne camp circle. He found Pretty Sparrow carrying firewood up from the river. After a few words with her, he rode on to visit a friend, a Fox warrior on picket duty. They settled down to smoke and talk. Around noon they saw dust and heard shooting to the south, near the Hunkpapa camp circle. An Oglala rode in at a gallop. "Soldiers are coming!" he shouted in Sioux. "Many white men attacking!" Then other Indians began leading their horses out, all shouting, "*Natskaveho!* White soldiers are coming! Everybody run for your horses!"

The chief, Two Moon, came to lead them into battle. Red Horse said the chief told the warriors not to run away if the soldiers charged, but to stand and fight. He said he himself would stand, even if he was killed.

Wescott paused, shrugged. "Brave-up talk to make them strong in the fight."

So Two Moon's band left to battle Major Reno's troops. Red Horse and his friends were young, but they decided only Earth and the Heavens last. But if they stopped the soldiers, their lives would be well spent. They found a ridge and took cover. Sioux warriors came racing down the coulee ahead of soldiers, dodging bullets. On a bluff beside the ford, Red Horse spotted three Indians who looked Crow, by their hair and dress. Enemies, guiding the soldiers there.

His Fox companion fired his muzzle-loader at them, then squatted behind the ridge to reload. Red Horse had a repeater. He fired, too, until the Sioux were safely on their side of the river. These had only lances and bows, but that made ten of them to defend the ford. By then the soldiers had stopped at the river.

"Mr. Red Horse had never seen white men up close before," Wescott explained. "He says he marveled at how pink and hairy they looked, even having little hairs all over their faces. One soldier carried a flag, one rode a big gray horse, and there was a big man on a roan, leading a string of mules. This one did not wear the blue uniform, like the others."

The Indian sat forward and said something short and insistent. Wescott nodded. "He says the mule man wore a long canvas jacket, and his hair was the color of a fox."

"Mules?" I said. But of course, Tom wouldn't have been the only packer along. I'd bought him a tan duster, but any other packer could've purchased one like it.

"Yes, and the mule man was looking straight at them across the river. The Indians began firing on them. Mr. Red Horse saw two soldiers go down when he shot at them."

My teacup froze halfway back to the saucer. Had this Indian in my drawing room, sipping so delicately from my china, killed my husband? But surely Wescott wouldn't have brought him to me!

"One Oglala rode up the other side," said Wescott. "He raced up to the ridge where the soldiers were standing holding their horses. He charged in close enough to touch some, and rode in circles before them, bullets kicking up dust all around. He came galloping back, and his friends cheered him. Then the Oglala unfastened his belt and opened his robe and shook many spent bullets out on the ground."

"Is that possible?" I asked. John Red Horse must've spoken some English, for he was grinning, I suppose at the memory of such great courage.

"Apparently," said Wescott. "Then he saw a strange thing. The man with the mules kicked his roan horse, broke away from the soldiers, and rode off down the ridge. Before the Sioux could think what this might mean, they heard screaming and gunfire from the encampment behind them. A bigger band of soldiers had gone around behind, while these few kept the warriors occupied.

"Mr. Red Horse and his friends rushed back. At first they could see nothing, for the haze of smoke. And all of his cartridges were gone. As he ran forward, he saw people falling, rolling on the ground. The blue soldiers were firing on the encampment. All he could see through the smoke was brass buttons shining in the afternoon sun. But he grabbed the barrel of a gun and wrenched it from a soldier. He drew his knife and stabbed the man.

"Then he saw another strange thing. The tall white man who'd ridden away was on foot now, running toward a group of women and children. But he did not carry a gun. Two of the blue soldiers were shooting at some young women. One was Pretty Sparrow."

"And Pretty Sparrow was—she was the Cheyenne girl—?"

Wescott nodded. "Yes, his—uh, intended. The white man knocked the guns from the soldiers' hands. He shouted at them until they went away. Then he scooped up two children and carried them off from the fighting, toward a ravine.

"Mr. Red Horse says he ran up and found both Pretty Sparrow and her mother shot dead. He became then like a crazy man. He fought his way to the ravine, following the strange white man, killing two other soldiers along the way. He was shot, too, before he reached the ravine, but he managed to get to his feet again. At the edge he looked down. Other Indians ran past, down into the safety of the rocks and bushes.

"But when he looked down there, he saw a terrible sight: many little children lying dead, lying in pools of their own blood."

The Indian raised a finger to interrupt. He dictated several more sentences in that liquid, exotic speech, telling of more blood and death and horrors.

"'I was feeling weak,' Mr. Red Horse says. So he fell down again. Lying there, he saw more women, girls, and little boys still running down into the ravine, and soldiers shooting them from the edge. He pulled himself up and again spotted the strange white man, who was now shouting up at the other soldiers, holding up his arms as if they could stop the bullets. And as Mr. Red Horse watched, the blue soldiers shot the man down."

I put a hand to my mouth. How often had I envisioned such a terrible scene, except—in my dreams, those killing Tom had been Indians.

"He pulled himself to where the white man lay. He was bleeding from a wound in the chest, and he was crying. Mr. Red Horse says he was amazed. He had not thought a white man could have tears. The man yelled at one of the children who was still unhurt, and the little boy ran off."

Wescott said Red Horse heard death songs rising all around him. He saw the sky turning to night. But before it got black, he saw more Sioux had returned from helping defend the other encampment. They rode up and fired on the soldiers, who retreated.

"He says that when he woke again, the women were going through the dead, stripping their clothes and weapons. Some—beg pardon, ma'am—cut the white men's bodies to pieces, they were so crazed with grief. They'd lost husbands and brothers and babies. But Mr. Red Horse rose and stopped them from killing the white man. He told them how he'd saved children, and had been shot for it by solders. So they carried him to the camp, and cared for him, and—"

"And he lived?" I gasped, earning a frown from John Red Horse, whom I'd interrupted.

"Yes," said Wescott. "But weeks later, soldiers came again and the women and children ran. So he does not know what became of the man. Mr. Red Horse says, 'He gave this silver box to me as I left to fight with the other warriors.' "

Wescott paused and listened to the Indian, his ear cocked. "Oh—he says, 'The man disappeared into the smoke of the guns again. We never saw him after that.' "

I bit my lip and stroked the silver case with the tips of my fingers. "Why is my letter still inside, I wonder?"

Wescott smiled. "Mr. Red Horse tells me it has magical properties. He didn't dare to disturb it. Then I saw Tom Sawyer's name on the envelope . . . Well, I had read Mr. Twain's novel. And there was your return address."

So then I knew what had happened to Tom, and yet still did not know. He'd survived, for a time. He had saved some children, as if the whole point of his journey had been doing penance for Injun Joe at last. And then—he was gone in the smoke of yet another war.

And I sat in my parlor with two strangers, and could no more adequately express my grief to the white missionary across from me, than I could have to the young Indian who regarded me so calmly from Tom's old armchair.

1910

SAN FRANCISCO

Twenty-seven

H IS GRAVE IS EMPTY STILL. And I erected no stone in Hannibal, perhaps proving that, deep down, I am a selfish woman. Having had so little of the grown-up Tom, I wanted to keep his memory nearest to me. The plot between Sid's and Tom's is empty, too, reserved for me. By now I think Sid must understand there's more than one kind of love, each of them more snarled and complicated than we on Earth could ever begin to unravel, before we have to say our good-byes.

At Sam Clemens's farewell on the pier in San Francisco, he had planted a quick kiss in my glove and spoke of paying me back. He promised never to forget us. What he did instead was quite different: He froze us all, forever, in time. You might think we'd be grateful to be handed immortality, even in the pages of a book. Yet his Tom, his Huck, his Becky and Sid are not really us. In life we were more flawed, more complicated, and altogether more human. The tale Sam only seemed to have created, and we, its characters, were always beyond his control. For a true creation, whether book or painting or child, in the end takes over and lives a life of its own making.

But here I am, a crotchety old woman still quibbling about small details.

Despite his faults, Tom Sawyer lived his life better than others of his time. Better than Col. Timothy Reeves and Maj. James Wilson and even the famous Gen. Sterling Price. And worlds above that lost boy, Jesse James, who spent the second half of his misled youth robbing twenty-six banks in ten states. Eleven civilians and three outlaws shot dead, all for a few dollars. And for his sins, Jesse became even more famous than Tom or Sid.

There will always be men like all three. They are what keeps us going. The Jesses are the bad ones we fear and celebrate, for dark reasons deep in our souls. The Sid Hopkinses make their steady, true, and honest mark close to home. While the Tom Sawyers rush out like comets, blazing trails for the rest of us to follow—if we can.

Mary and her O'Brien are yet alive, and their grandchildren write to me still. Of Huck Finn's fate I have no clue. He avoided school back in Hannibal, and never did learn to write. He vanished from the map of our lives after Panama. Perhaps he still wanders the jungles of Central America, guiding seekers toward places shown on no map yet printed.

At the age of seventy-two, after having had two husbands and two sons, I know males are temperamental creatures, a great deal of work to keep around. Yet those I've loved were worth the trouble. I'm too old now to endure any quibbling about who might've loved whom more. For too long I tried to be what I never could: one of them. I envied and spied and followed, thinking that boys—at least, *those* boys—held the magic keys to freedom. And so I grew up believing I must behave like a man, when all along I should've been trying simply to be a person. To carve my own place, and help make more room for other women in this world.

Several times over the years, Mark Twain returned to San Francisco peddling his famous act. I could've turned up then and renewed our acquaintance. But men are not the only ones who think highly of their pride.

So all I have left to relate is the contents of a letter that arrived this morning from Samuel Langhorne Clemens, Esquire—forwarded posthumously from Elmira, New York. Inside the thick cream envelope was a note penned on fine matching paper. Judging by the date, Sam must have written it on his deathbed. He began with an apology, after so many decades, for getting some of it, our lives anyhow, all wrong. Of course, he couldn't let it go at that.

The things that really mattered I did get right, he insists in the last paragraph. *Even if I was never quite as good with adjectives as you, Becky. My darling wife, Olivia, was a faithful editor. But perhaps I could have benefited from having you by my side, as well.*

I had to smile. Maybe Sam lived so long under the spell of his old hero that, in order to become his own man, he had to tame Tom. To make him a puppet he could move around at will, and speak for. After that, I suppose it would've only made sense to drag the rest of us in as well.

The biggest surprise actually came at the moment I slit the letter open. For a number of greenbacks fell out into my lap. Sam had sent me money! And lots of it. I've stacked those bills in a neat pile, and set my favorite paperweight, Tom's brass andiron, right on top. Not that I think they'll take off and fly away.

At first I felt insulted. Did Samuel Clemens picture me as a pathetic, twice-bereft widow lady, hobbling hunched along Market Street in rusty black with cane and ear trumpet, in need of long-distance charity? I guess age has mellowed me, though, for it felt natural to try to see things from his side right away. Back on the docks in San Francisco, he'd insisted he would repay me someday. And a Missouri gentleman always makes good his debts—even if it takes a lifetime.

It would be foolish to take offense. To huff and puff and make a prune face like some elderly busybody in bombazine. So I hope Sam can hear me, lolling about up there in the clouds with Captain Stormfield, when I say, "Thank you, Old Friend. I know just what to do with your gift. It will go straight to a good Cause. A donation to help ensure all women—even the poor, doddering, twice-widowed ones—will one day get the almighty Vote. And then proceed to Go Our Ways, as you once so kindly suggested. So we may change all the things you fellows have botched up these many years."

Now I'm the only one left on earth who knows what Tom Sawyer would say about all that has happened. He'd grin, as he always did when ready to stir up trouble. And say, "Come on, Becky. Drag on some comfortable old pants. Ignore all busybodies and your aching bones, and climb up on any horse you're still longing to ride."

And I believe that is just what I will do, for all the days left to me.